IMMORTAL DARK

IMMO
DA

RTAL

RK

TIGEST GIRMA

LITTLE, BROWN AND COMPANY
New York   Boston

Little, Brown and Company
Hachette Book Group
1290 Avenue of the Americas, New York, NY 10104
Visit us at LBYR.com

Simultaneously published in 2024 by Hachette Children's Group in the UK and Hachette Australia
First Edition: September 2024

Little, Brown and Company is a division of Hachette Book Group, Inc. The Little, Brown name and logo are registered trademarks of Hachette Book Group, Inc.

Library of Congress Cataloging-in-Publication Data
Names: Girma, Tigest, author.
Title: Immortal dark / Tigest Girma.
Description: First edition. | New York : Little, Brown and Company, 2024. | Series: Immortal dark | Audience: Ages 14 and up. | Summary: Nineteen-year-old orphan Kidan Adane, heiress to a fallen House of humans tethered to vampiric creatures called dranaics, navigates her duty to foster human-dranaic relations, but when her sister is kidnapped, Kidan suspects a dranaic and will do anything to find her.
Identifiers: LCCN 2023051680 | ISBN 9780316570381 (hardcover) | ISBN 9780316581448 (hardcover) | ISBN 9780316570404 (ebook)
Subjects: CYAC: Vampires—Fiction. | Sisters—Fiction. | Missing children—Fiction. | Black people—Fiction. | Fantasy. | LCGFT: Fantasy fiction. | Novels.
Classification: LCC PZ7.1.G58365 Im 2024 | DDC [Fic]—dc23
LC record available at https://lccn.loc.gov/2023051680

ISBNs: 978-0-316-57038-1 (deluxe), 978-0-316-58144-8 (standard), 978-0-316-57040-4 (ebook), 978-0-316-58232-2 (OwlCrate)

Printed in Indiana, USA

LSC-C

Printing 1, 2024

FOR THE BLACK GIRLS WHO'VE ALWAYS MARVELED
AT THE DARK BEAUTY OF VAMPIRES.
THE IMMORTALS LOOK LIKE US IN THIS ONE.

&

FOR MY HABESHA GIRLS WHO DARE TO OCCUPY
NEW AND WONDROUS SPACES.
HOLD YOUR HEAD UP, AND LET THEM SEE YOU.

Content warning: Immortal Dark *explores the savage world of vampires and the humans who try to survive it. It features some heavy elements such as parental abuse, blood drinking, death, gore, murder, sexual content, strong language, suicide ideation, and violence. Readers, please take note before you grab your invitation. The gates of Uxlay University are now open.*

UXLAY UNIVERSITY

Seek mind above blood, and if you must bleed, use it as ink.

PIRAN HOUSE

School of Medicine

ROJIT HOUSE

Rojit Hospital

School of Fashion and Textiles

School of History

Grand Andromeda Hall

Maria's Garden

Sweet Fang Bakery

School of Languages and Linguistics

DELARUS HOUSE

Ajtaf Construction and Engineering Departments

Silia's Garden

AJTAF HOUSE

FARIS HOUSE

Azum Buna Cafe

West Corner Tea

Qaros Conservatory of Music

ZAF HAVEN

QAROS HOUSE

GORO HOUSE

School of
Food Science

AHND CEMETERY

MOT ZEBEYA MONASTERY

SICION
TRAINING GROUNDS

HULET PILLARS

AJTAF
CONTEMPORARY
LIBRARY

SECURITY OFFICE

MOT ZEBEYA
COURTS

School of Art

ARAT
TOWERS

Desta Fountain

Hanna's Garden

University Plaza

MAKARY HOUSE

RESAR'S
SQUARE

Makary Law School

School of Philosophy

Student Lodgings

Grand Solomon Library

UMIL HOUSE

Hazen Fountain

ADANE HOUSE

SHEBA
SQUARE

East Corner Coffee

Umil Art Museum

School of
Psychological Sciences

SOUTHERN SOST BUILDINGS

TEMO HOUSE

LUROZ HOUSE

DRASTFORT PRISON

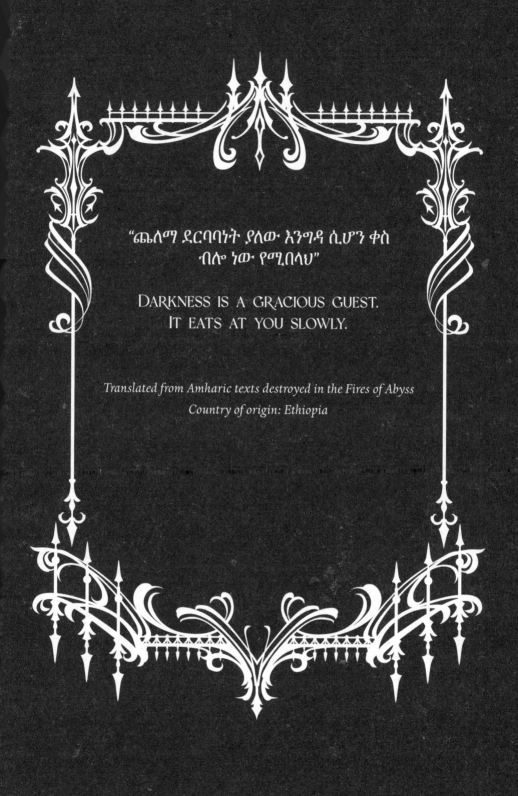

"ጨለማ ደርባባነት ያለው እንግዳ ሲሆን ቀስ
ብሎ ነው የሚበላህ"

DARKNESS IS A GRACIOUS GUEST.
IT EATS AT YOU SLOWLY.

Translated from Amharic texts destroyed in the Fires of Abyss

Country of origin: Ethiopia

PROLOGUE

VISIBLE THROUGH THE CANDLELIT WINDOW OF UXLAY UNIVERSITY, A campus as ancient as the creatures it housed, the dean and her vampire sat in private conversation.

They studied a piece of parchment that detailed the town's layout, and particularly the drop of blood fading near the cathedral. This map was one of the dean's most favorite treasures, handed down her family bloodline before all such tools were destroyed. She never could forgive such a loss.

Before the blood disappeared into the yellowed page, it blossomed into three letters, spelling the word "mot." Death.

"Silia Adane is dead," the dean said, exactly an hour after they'd first sat down.

Her vampire steepled his fingers and responded in Aarac. For a dead language, it possessed an unnatural amount of life, dancing on the tongue like a stirred snake.

"Then it is true. The will of inheritance is in effect."

The dean pushed her chair back and went to the window. Night pressed onward from the forest, wrapping long fingers around the Arat Towers and their mourning spire statues. Golden light poured from the open-mouthed lion statues perched on the stone walls. Each animal came awake to illuminate the entrance halls and corridors.

"There are two more Adanes left," she said.

"You would break your promise to her? I thought she was your dear friend."

The dean's thick brows knitted. Her vampire liked his honesty with an equal measure of cruelty. Even when she was younger, she disliked this most about him.

Of course she did not wish to break her promise. For weeks, Silia's blood had run thin on the map. A rare disease even Uxlay couldn't cure had infected her. The dean had urged Silia to call her two nieces from wherever they hid and entrust one of the girls with the family's legacy before it was too late. But stubbornness was the plague of all the Adanes.

Silia Adane had sought freedom at incredible cost, selfish even if it was not for herself. As such, fourteen years ago, after the death of her sister and her brother-in-law, Silia had disappeared in the middle of the night with her young twin nieces. The dean had forgiven this betrayal of responsibility for one reason only—grief.

Grief had a way of removing duty by its roots. It was why the dean had chosen it as the first enemy to master. Why she was here, planning the next set of events, instead of by her late friend's side. There was no faltering now. It was this very mastery that made her run a campus that kept peace among nature's natural enemies. And peace would not last if the Adanes' will came into effect.

The dean chose not to tell her vampire she regretted the promise. At the time, it had sounded justified. What did it matter if the girls were never to be contacted? The dean had been certain Silia would settle with her lover and birth a child and the great House Adane's bloodline would continue. How wrong she'd been. Death was pursuing House Adane with great intensity, and she had no choice but to bring new life into it.

She studied the growing darkness. "We'll retrieve the girl from Green Heights in a week."

"What of the other one?"

"I'm afraid I don't know where she is. It's said she ran away from their foster home the day she turned eighteen."

She glanced at him. To see if he was aware of this. It used to unsettle her how little their facial muscles moved, how their coal eyes cut into a stare and never blinked.

"Perhaps one is enough." Her vampire remained impassive. "Their presence will cause some unpleasantness."

The dean faced the window. "As all estranged things do."

"True." He considered. "I would enjoy having them in my class. Their mother was one of my brightest students."

The tale of the girls' parents was legend, but legend had a way of bearing tragedy.

"Do you wish me to collect her?" he asked.

"No, I will go."

In the window's reflection, a line marred his mahogany skin.

"You never leave Uxlay."

"I'm afraid it's necessary."

"Why?"

The dean regained her seat, calm as she delivered the next piece of news. "Because Kidan Adane was detained for murder as of twenty-four hours ago."

Pinpricks of light shone in her vampire's black eyes. "Whose life did she take?"

"I don't know yet. It's quite odd, but Kidan Adane believes her sister did not run away. Instead, she's convinced a vampire took June Adane. That they brought her here, to the university, against her will."

Brows lowered, she studied him again. He wasn't frowning. She marveled at how he'd settled into his old skin, handsome and stony as the day she met him. Her, nineteen. Him, five centuries old. She rubbed her wrinkled hand. Time was a frightening thing.

"I would know if June Adane was here," he simply said.

"I thought so too. Surely if such a crime had taken place, you would have dealt with it in the appropriate manner."

"Of course." He showed no sign of offense at her inquiry. She valued this about him. He rarely took things personally. Nor did he ever lie. But these were strange times, and loyalty was the first casualty of change.

"How do you know all this?" he asked. "Surely having the girls followed and watched goes against the promise."

Satisfied he'd passed her questioning, the dean gestured to the pile of letters sitting next to a carving of an animal—a small impala with two magnificent horns.

"Kidan Adane writes quite a lot, always begging Uxlay to return her sister. I have tried to find June, but the girl has disappeared. Unfortunately for Kidan, her aunt Silia made Uxlay the birthplace of all her nightmares."

He moved with the quickness of a shadow caught in light, careful not to touch the glass impala figurine before collecting the letters. The action made the dean's lips curve slightly. Superstition caused most dranaics to avoid the beautiful antelope, in the same way it convinced students that rubbing a lion statue delivered strength. As the vampire read, his brow furrowed, a crease forming.

"You never responded?" he asked curiously.

"I kept my word."

He had stood by her side for nearly forty years and still did not understand her promises, nor how she moved the earth to keep them. Skirting around her vows had made their life very difficult.

"What is different now?" he asked.

She studied one of the letters. Kidan's words slipping into anger and plea in tandem, the sun and moon of a horrible loss.

"Mot sewi yelkal," she responded in Aarac.

Death frees us from our previous selves.

In a very rare moment, her vampire's lips lifted at one corner. It never failed to amuse him when his students quoted his lessons back to him. Especially when they lived long enough to understand their true meanings.

1.

KIDAN ADANE GAVE HERSELF EIGHT MONTHS TO DIE.

The schedule was quite generous, if she was being honest. Two months would have sufficed for the violent act. The extension was a poor attempt at a dream. A dream she wouldn't entertain if she wasn't currently dehydrated and fading in and out of her room.

She wanted to live with her sister again inside that odd little house. Live in a time when innocence didn't need to be proved at every turn. That last thought pulled her out of her haze, made her chuckle. She sounded wronged and, if she dared think it, a victim.

Her laughter rattled again, a clogged chimney inside her chest sounding painful and raw. How long had it been since she'd spoken? The curtains remained closed because of the cameras, so a bulb had become her only source of light. Like any artificial sun, it overheated and burned the air around it, forcing her to work half naked on the apartment floor.

Sweat gathered on her dark forehead now, wetting the file she was reading, her folded leg buried somewhere in the swarm of papers. She couldn't afford to switch off the light. Not when there was so much to do. Not when she was this close. In Kidan's mind, she was trapped in one never-ending night and hell was not dissimilar to this.

Movement—she needed movement. She stood too fast, stumbling, and blood rushed to her folded leg, paralyzing her. She shook off the numbness and walked to the small kitchen.

Murderer.

The word jumped from the newspaper article plastered on her fridge, branded above the image of a Black girl.

Kidan Adane was a murderer. She waited for the prickle of remorse she should have felt at those words. She even pinched her mouth and scrunched her nose, trying to force the emotion out of herself. But just like that fiery night, she failed to cry. She waited for a sliver of humanity to slip through. She was completely dry. A statue carved out of obsidian.

Kidan poured herself a drink. The shutter clicks of a camera snapped, accompanied by tiny flashes of light. She swung sharply to the window, drink nearly slipping from her grasp. The curtains remained drawn, but the reporters clawed at the gaps, like seagulls scratching for bread.

Be patient, she thought.

It would all be clear soon. In eight months, exactly. That was when her trial date was set. Kidan had no plan to attend. Long before any of it, her confession would be found taped to the underside of her bed and the violent workings of her mind unveiled for all.

The camera flashed again, making her wince. It was unlikely they could get her picture, but maybe she should put on clothes. It wasn't her full chest or her wide hips that she wanted to hide. A racy picture of her might actually work in her favor: a gross violation of her privacy making the rounds. It didn't sound bad at all. She shook her head. There she was again, thinking of ways she could manipulate sympathy.

She met her reflection, and a thin, frail voice slipped out of her. "You are not like them. You are *not* like them."

Them.

Aunt Silia called them dranaics. Vampires.

Despite the heat of the apartment walls, Kidan shivered. Dranaics appeared no different from humans. It was the very source of all her disturbance. Evil shouldn't go around in human skin. It was a desecration.

Kidan loathed her aunt. Loathed her inaction. She had waited too long to rescue them from that vile society. Maybe then evil wouldn't have seeped into Kidan as a child. June had fared better, but Kidan had feasted on it. Her morbid curiosity with death, her sick fascination with and collection of films depicting its art, and now committing the final act itself—all this came from vampires. If she could dig into her chest and pull out her twisted heart right now, she would.

Eight months.

Relief punctured through with those two words. All she had to do was wait eight months to die. Make sure June was found. Bear this wretched existence a little longer.

A picture of June beamed at her from her open laptop. They looked nothing alike, despite being born within minutes of each other. June's disappearance received no coverage, not even a whisper in the neighborhood. Where would Kidan be if these reporters had hunted for her lost sister the way they hunted her? No, Black girls had to commit horrifying acts to earn the spotlight.

The papers on her floor were the frenzied tracking of a place called Uxlay University. Kidan had searched for twelve months and twenty days. Her eyes darted to the recording taped under her bed, and the temperature of the room dropped. It held the last, tortured conversation between Kidan and her victim.

Better, she thought, almost smiling. She was assigning blame where it needed to go. *Kidan's* victim.

The recording held the proof, the name of the person—no, animal—responsible for taking June. It was only a matter of finding the fucking place. And him.

Kidan squatted and studied the trail of her search. She reached for a pen, pulled off the cap with her teeth, and started another letter to Aunt Silia, who never wrote back.

If there was even the slimmest chance of finding June again, she'd spend the rest of her life writing.

Her fingers tensed, digging into her palms. Thin arcs of blood irritated her skin. With her forefinger, she traced a continuous square inside her palm. Nerves. She recognized the emotion. So she wasn't completely lost yet. The jagged mirror across the room cut an ugly shape along her dark throat. A cool, unimpressed expression gazed back. If only she could master crying before her trial, the world might forgive her. She might live longer.

Cry, she ordered her image.

Why? it asked. *You would do it again.*

An hour later, once the reporters outside left, Kidan dressed in a large hoodie, grabbed her earbuds, and locked her small apartment. She'd moved here for precisely one reason.

Across the street, at the corner of Longway and St. Albans Streets, waited a single parcel locker. One key belonged to Kidan, the other to Aunt Silia, who resided in Uxlay. After Kidan deposited each of her letters, she'd hide and wait. Sometimes she'd wait for days, sleeping in the café nearby or the alley, but someone would always come and take her letters. Each time, the hooded figure escaped Kidan, either climbing over the park gates with frightening strength or disappearing into traffic.

Every week she played this cat and mouse game. Aunt Silia was reading her letters but, for some messed-up reason, kept ignoring her.

After she put the new letter into the empty locker, Kidan went to wait by the bus stop, a new spot, and hoped blending in with the passengers would give her enough time to identify the messenger.

As she waited, June's sweet voice crackled through her earbuds. Kidan's world jerked into balance.

"Hi," her sister whispered. "I don't really know how to start this, so I'm just going to say a generic intro."

June made fifteen videos before she disappeared. This was the first, and she'd been fourteen. Kidan listened to the videos daily, except for the last one. That one she could only bear listening to once before deleting it so it wouldn't hurt her.

Inside her pockets, her fingers traced the shape of a triangle, enjoying the scratching sound it made. The triangle changed to a square when June mentioned Kidan in the video.

Kidan's attention never strayed from the parcel locker, but there was a shadow in the corner of her eye, unmoving.

A woman under the crooked branch of a tree. Her skin was an aged bronze in the streetlight, and she wore a dark green skirt paired with a slicked bun.

The woman stood remarkably still, no different from a tawny owl perched on a ledge, staring right at her.

The back of Kidan's neck prickled. She had the oddest sensation that this woman, whoever she was, had been waiting for her.

2.

RECORDED VIDEO
May 10, 2017
June, age fourteen, on Kidan's phone
Location: Mama Anoet's private bathroom

"Hi," June whispered, blinking into the camera. Her short braids curled around a scarred, pimpled chin. "I don't really know how to start this, so I'm just going to say a generic intro. My name is June. I go to Green Heights School. I guess I'm making this video because of what happened today. I got in trouble for falling asleep in class again."

A pause.

"I have parasomnia. I know, big word. It means I don't just sleepwalk but scream and kick. My sister takes care of me but . . . I know she gets tired. I'm tired of me." A small laugh. "I try to stay awake as much as I can, but that backfires. Like today. I know what you're thinking—get help. Believe me, I'm trying."

The camera angle shook, capturing the overcrowded shampoos, four different kinds; a butterfly-patterned shower curtain; medicine for anxiety and depression.

"We can't afford a psychologist, really, but our guidance counselor isn't bad. It's actually because of her I'm making this video. Miss Tris said . . . I'm scared of something. Something I don't want to tell anyone about. She told me to write everything down.

"But I hate writing. So she told me to record myself instead—and if I feel brave enough, share it. Good, isn't she?" A small smile that didn't reach her eyes. "So, what am I afraid of?"

June took a hesitating breath, glancing nervously at the door.

"I'm scared of . . . vampires."

The camera went dark, face down on the sink. Water ran, splashing sounds echoed, a minute ticked by. June's brown face came into focus, now slightly damp as she settled in the tub's corner.

"Vampires." Her voice rang stronger. "The good news, if there is any, is that they're no longer dangerous to everyone. So those of you watching this, if you even believe me, can go to bed knowing your blood tastes like poison to them. But they still need to feed, they need blood to survive." The phone shook a little. "Something called the First Bind forces vampires to only feed from specific families. There are around eighty bloodlines trapped in this cycle for generations. Guess who's in one of those families. Yup."

June looked off camera, eyes glazing over.

"My sister and I take having a messed-up family to a whole new meaning. But we escaped. Our aunt took us away from that life, after our parents died, and brought us here, to Mama Anoet's. We're safe here, but I see them every night . . . in my dreams . . . even in the hallways at school sometimes. It's like I know . . . one day they'll come for us."

She inhaled, exhaled. Played with the thin silver bracelet on her wrist.

"Kidan reminds me every night about the Three Binds placed on vampires. It helps a little. Makes me remember they can't get to me so easily. The Second Bind restricts some of their strength, and the Third Bind requires a heavy sacrifice when they turn a human into one of them. Kidan keeps saying the powerful Last Sage didn't know how to use his incredible gift—that he should have killed all vampires off instead of putting restrictions on them. I think she's right. Our lives would have been so different if he had."

Her fingers left her butterfly bracelet, eyes creased.

"So why am I making this video? I guess I do want Miss Tris to know. Maybe even my friends. Maybe everyone. I don't want to be like this for the rest of my life. I don't want to waste every minute of every day thinking about when they'll come and get us. I want to feel safe. I want—"

A loud knocking made her drop the phone.

"June, it's me."

June sagged; the door handle turned.

Kidan scowled at her dripping phone. "Hurry."

Quickly June added her password to make the videos private.

Her password had always been a set of five numbers that added up to thirty-five. That was their biological mother's age when she died, and also the number of vampires, dranaics, assigned to their family. Thirty-five vampires that would have consumed June's and Kidan's blood if they hadn't gotten away.

3.

KIDAN REACHED FOR THE KNIFE SHE CARRIED INSIDE HER JACKET. IT had ridges that pressed into her palm uncomfortably and was curved toward the end. The feel of it triggered a shiver down her spine.

The night appeared stripped of all noise as Kidan approached the woman. Kidan wished she would move. Stillness was found in animals, and animalistic features were found in dranaics.

"Who are you?" Kidan's voice sounded unusually loud in the quiet.

The woman was heavyset, with thickly shaped brows and dark, reflective eyes. A golden pin featuring a black bird with a silver eye was fixed to her chest.

"I'm Dean Faris of Uxlay University. I understand you've been looking for me."

The sidewalk jerked, jostling Kidan's grip on the knife. She was struck speechless by the idea that something she had searched for in blind hope and crushing disappointment could reveal itself by simply dropping from the sky.

"Ux...Uxlay?" she finally said, afraid the place would disappear again.

"Yes."

The answer cleared the fog in Kidan's mind. What was she doing? Her hand left her pocketed knife.

"So, you've come to take me," she rushed. "To exchange me for June?"

Her chest swelled with hope. How many nights did she lie awake in bed imagining every possible variation of this scene? It was a mad manifestation, a goal that kept her heart beating after it should've died the night of the fire.

The dean folded her hands before herself. "Uxlay does not deal with kidnapped humans. Our very laws are against it."

"Laws?" Kidan hurled the word back at her as she stepped closer. "Where were your laws when a dranaic assigned to our family took my sister?"

Her fingers strained with the effort not to strangle the woman. The dean's dark eyes flickered with caution. Good.

"That is a heavy accusation. Do you have any proof?"

Kidan's proof waited in her small apartment, taped under her bed. Her victim's confession named the vampire responsible. But it also proved that Kidan had tortured and killed.

Kidan's voice dipped so low it could wake the dead. "A vampire took my sister."

Dean Faris tilted her head to one side. "I speak to you as a representative of Uxlay, Kidan. Perhaps because you didn't grow up with our education, you don't know what that means. But I am responsible for enforcing peace between humans and dranaics. It's what I hold most important, and I do that through laws and punishment. You believe you have been wronged, yet there is no proof. I ask you to see reason despite your grief. I cannot accuse one of my dranaics without evidence."

Dean Faris spoke like a dignified politician, as if her campus was the setting of all law and order. This clashed against every story Kidan had concocted for the vile place.

She was preparing to argue when a sudden thought struck her. "It was you, wasn't it? You posted my bail."

After Kidan had been detained, a miracle had happened. Her impossible bail was paid in full by a woman with high enough standing that she requested anonymity, and the court granted it.

"You deserve a chance to prove your innocence," the dean said pointedly. "As do all others. You are innocent, yes?"

Kidan stepped back. This woman didn't come here to talk about June. Kindness, especially such as this, always had a price. "Why are you here?"

Dean Faris assessed her for another second. "I'm afraid your aunt Silia has passed. She fell ill, and the disease took her quickly. I'm sorry."

Kidan shot a surprised look at the parcel locker. Dead. Her eyes remained dry, yet the shock knocked her off-balance. Another member of their family gone. Was the same vampire behind this?

Aunt Silia existed mostly in her imagination, in stories, in the world of before, to make sense of the after. To prove that they hadn't appeared out of nowhere on Mama Anoet's doorstep. With this news, Kidan became weightless, another thread snapped from her. Then she thought of June's honeyed eyes and kind smile and felt the ground beneath her feet again.

The dean pulled out a teeth-white envelope with a bloodred crest. "As of now, you are next in line to inherit Adane House. This is your admission letter."

Kidan recoiled from the letter. "I have no interest in being a slave to vampires."

The dean's calm features slipped. "Do not use terms without knowing their consequence. It will be the last time you use that word before me."

Kidan wanted to laugh but only managed a strained scoff. "I'm not interested. I just want June."

"Very well. Believe it or not, convincing students who don't wish to attend my university is not part of my job requirement. Most usually try incredibly hard to land a position at Uxlay." She brought out another letter from her pocket. "Sign this, and I will take my leave."

Kidan eyed it suspiciously. "What is it?"

"A will, signed first by your parents and then your aunt, leaving everything to your last remaining house dranaic."

Her mouth gaped. She snatched the letter. Most of it was blackened over, some sections obviously highlighted. Kidan read, growing more horrified, and crumpled the edges of it.

"Curious, isn't it?" Dean Faris's eyes gleamed. "It's a first in the history of Uxlay, a family choosing to leave their house to their dranaic. The very vampire you accuse of taking your sister is the person your family trusts enough to bestow its legacy upon."

Bile lurched up to her throat. Were they all blind? This was even more proof. Motive. He'd tricked her family out of their inheritance or coerced them. Taken June in secrecy to keep himself hydrated—

"No," the dean said.

"What?"

"You believe he forced them into signing this. That's incorrect. They chose this of their own free will. There are many things you're not aware of in our

14

world. The power of our houses, the power of our laws. It is extraordinary. Knowledge that'll only become available to you if you choose to join us. No soul can enter Uxlay without an invitation."

Kidan eyed the blocked-out sections of the paper. What was the dean hiding?

Dean Faris checked her thin golden watch. From her seemingly endless pocket, she brought out a pen.

"I'm afraid I need to leave. Please sign, indicating you have no interest in contesting the will as potential heiress, and I'll be on my way."

Kidan stared at the pen like it was poison. After some time, Dean Faris withdrew it.

"Perhaps you need time to think. If you are interested, houses at Uxlay are inherited through education. You must attend the university and graduate from a course that studies human and vampire coexistence. I will wait three days for your response."

The woman's countenance disarmed Kidan. When the dean offered her the admission letter again, she took it slowly. The paper was hard and compact, with a seal of two lions with blades in their mouths, positioned at each other's throats.

Why? Kidan stared at the seal, wanting to dissolve. Why had her family done this? When she lifted her head, the woman had vanished.

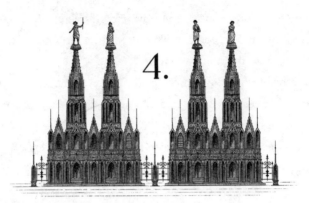

4.

KIDAN THREW THE ADMISSION LETTER ONTO HER CLUTTERED FLOOR and kicked the pyramid of noodle cups she'd made in one corner. There wasn't enough space for them to scatter, so they bounced off the wall and hit her shin. Gently, she sank to the floor and hung her head, braids curtaining her. The room pressed in until she grew uncomfortably aware of her body and its labored efforts to breathe. Paint peeled in the corner of the tight space, the toilet worked only when other renters didn't overuse it, and there was a mysterious stain on the carpet that reeked even after being drowned in bleach. The heat in this place could fry a scorpion. She couldn't take another day of this. Not without her sister. Absentmindedly, she ran her finger along the ridge of her butterfly bracelet. She wanted to go home. Even if it was that cardboard box of a home.

Houses reminded Kidan of a feral pet. They were unclean, often infested, and no matter what decoration was placed in them, they never liked to be owned. Not truly. She found the idea that they rushed to others to feed them when one slacked a horrible disloyalty. Their foster mother, Mama Anoet, had agreed, and so, even when they were young, June and Kidan had gone into the business of making money to pay the rent. By the time she was ten, Kidan was selling the weird bracelets she made, and June baked her addictive, bite-size doughnuts. The memory made her mouth water, then go dry.

With stiff fingers, she reached for her parents' and aunt's will. Fire shot through her veins with each traitorous word. Her family knew vampires were dangerous. Why tear June and Kidan away from everything they knew, erase their identities, and beggar them if that wasn't the case? In her softest moments, Kidan used to wait for her parents to appear at Mama Anoet's door, ready to run away together with them. She had to forgive them for this failure, because they'd died. This inheritance could have been the thing to protect Kidan and her sister, but instead they'd done the unthinkable.

They'd left everything to him.

The vampire's name was signed, the *s* curling itself like a snake.

Susenyos Sagad.

Kidan heard her victim's pleas echoing around the room and inside her chest.

"Susenyos Sagad! That's his name. He...he took her."

She scratched a shape against the carpet, the flesh of her finger burning against the rough fabric. Again, and again and again. A triangle imprinted itself on the carpet. Good. Her mind and body were in sync. There was only pure white fury in regard to Susenyos Sagad.

Sometimes, Kidan's mind hid things from her, and only her fingers could translate them. Triangles for anger. Squares for when the fear became too much, and circles for moments of joy.

Ever since she was a child, she'd used these symbols to unravel her thoughts.

She could barely understand the entirety of the will with the blocked-out sections. Dean Faris had picked the parts of Uxlay she wanted to share. What had she left out?

Laws of Inheriting a House

A vampire inheritor must occupy a Family House for a consecutive set of twenty-eight days in solitude so the will becomes rocis, that is, in effect.

Kidan read it again. Twenty-eight days. How long had it been since her aunt had died? A week? Two weeks? A sickening image of Susenyos Sagad sitting at a dinner table with June spread out as the meal, counting the days until he'd fully occupy the house, turned her stomach.

Rejection of the Will

If a human descendant of a Family House wishes to inherit, they must attend Uxlay University and receive education in human and vampire coexistence.

If the human descendant has not yet graduated but wishes to lay claim to the house, they can take shelter in their Family House during their study of Dranacti.

Dean Faris had highlighted the last line. A loophole: Stay in the house to interrupt the vampire's solitary occupation. Kidan would have to live with him. Acid filled her mouth.

She stood and parted the curtains slightly, glimpsing a reporter and his camera, currently distracted by a smoke break. Out of habit, her eyes slid to the parcel locker.

Someone was there. Opening the locker. Taking out her letter. Kidan jerked to attention.

"Hey!"

The moment the word left her mouth, she was out the door, taking the stairs three at a time. When she burst outside, the figure was already gone.

"Fuck!" Her scream startled an old lady and captured the attention of the reporter.

He ran toward her, and she hurried across the street to the locker. She pulled the key from around her neck, fumbling to unlock it.

A thin man with sour breath, the reporter flashed his camera near her. Her instincts were to shove it down his throat, but remarkably, she restrained herself.

"Kidan, neighbors heard what happened. Did you plan this for a long time?"

She ignored him. Because for the first time in years, something had been left in the locker—a bound book. Her fingers shook as she tucked the heavy book under her arm, secured the locker, and quickly crossed back. The reporter was on her heels. Just when she was about to slam the door, he shouted.

"What does killing a member of your own community feel like?"

Kidan's gaze lifted from the ground and stared straight at the camera. For a moment, she was June, fourteen and hiding in Mama Anoet's bathroom, itching to tell the world all the things that made her afraid.

Evil, she thought. That was what it felt like. *And all evil must die.*

The Dean has sworn not to contact you, but she'll betray that promise if something happens to me. I know her too well. I have had a trusted member in Uxlay leave this for you. They owed me a final favor. And if you're going into the mouth of the lion, you must be prepared.

I truly wish you'd run, but from the persistence of your letters, I see that you've grown stubborn. I pray it gives you some protection.

So, listen carefully, Kidan, and stay alert. It began long before my time, but something has always hunted our family. It took your grandparents, your parents, and now your sister. Uxlay has turned on House Adane.

In this book I've gathered everything I can about the other houses, as well as specific information you must learn. June is somewhere among all this. If you're reading this, it means I've failed to find her. I hope this guides you; use my eyes as yours, my knowledge as yours, and find the truth.

In case you choose to run, ingest the fake poison enclosed in this book. It will not harm you. The poison's effects will be known to your vampire by changing your scent. Uxlay will believe you're dying. A dying heiress is free and of no value. Use it to be free.

Trust only yourself.

Your loving aunt,
Silia

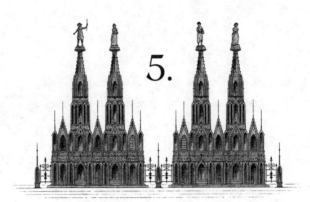

5.

KIDAN DRESSED SLOWLY, PULLING HER TURTLENECK SNUG AROUND HER neck. She liked to cover as much of her skin as possible, particularly her throat. Either a scarf or a tie always fitted around it, a layer of protection she'd taken to.

She positioned her long braids around her shoulders. Their roots had loosened, strands cobwebbing onto themselves. Lack of natural sun had leached the rich brown of her skin to a cool, yellowed tint. Her mouth curved into a frown. She reached for some hairstyling cream and gave herself the appearance of cleanliness.

Kidan had read the first few pages of Aunt Silia's book before throwing it against the wall. There were no answers in there, only more questions.

Aunt Silia had entrusted Kidan and June to a place that hadn't been safe enough, and then she had failed to find June.

All the women who had vowed to protect Kidan abandoned her.

She reached for her butterfly bracelet on instinct. If Kidan peered closely, she could see streaks of blood still stuck to its wings. Its owner's blood added a macabre ruby detail to the silver metal.

"Butterflies," the voice of the owner echoed in her ears. "It reminds us we're in constant transformation."

Tucked inside was a small blue pill. It would only take one swallow to leave this world behind.

Kidan was too young at the time to recall her parents' deaths, but the feeling that came after was haunting. Each moment of her life, she felt like she was alone in a pitch-black room except for an unsettling warm breath tickling her neck. The thing, whatever it was, kept breathing, launching Kidan's heart into a painful frenzy. It never pounced, only waited. Watched.

Mama Anoet had vanquished the beast with tender fingers—parting Kidan's coarse hair, making spiced chicken dinner, slipping on Sunday church dresses.

Safe. She'd tasted safe. A word more unfamiliar than moss growing on skin.

A year ago, during the night of their eighteenth birthday, it'd all been torn to shreds. She shut her eyes against the memory, but it was no use. That visual was stark in Kidan's soul, in her very core.

June slumped in their garden, bathed in soft moonlight, her lips stained red with blood. Kidan struggling against the locked door of the lounge, pounding furiously as a shadow of a man gathered her sister and faded into the night. Kidan had told the police this many times—without mention of vampires. She'd told the fucking world. But June's room had been packed up. Every trace of her gone. She was labeled a runaway girl. A legal runaway girl.

Kidan had tortured and killed to learn the name of that shadowy vampire. This whole time, had he been waiting in her Family House? Had he fed on June that night until she died? Or was he keeping her captive? Kidan's vision swirled, and before she knew it, she was pulling out her phone, calling the number at the top of the admission letter.

Dean Faris answered immediately.

"It's Kidan," Kidan rushed out before she could second-guess herself. "I'll attend Uxlay."

"That's excellent news."

"On one condition," she said slowly, trying to breathe. "I need your best lawyers for my trial. It's in eight months."

A long pause. Kidan needed time to search for June.

"And why would I agree to that?"

Kidan settled backward against her bed, voice steady.

"Because you don't want Susenyos Sagad to inherit House Adane any more than I do."

There was a beat of silence. Her heart drummed.

"Very well. I'll send one of my trusted members to escort you here." The dean hesitated. "But a warning, Kidan Adane. Legacies at Uxlay are not simply inherited. They must be fought for. Are you ready for that?"

Goose bumps climbed along the skin of her back.

"I am."

After she hung up, Kidan sat there in the punishing silence, drawing her shapes.

Uxlay. She was going into their very lair. To live with him. To kill him.

The moonlight seeping in through the window lengthened Kidan's shadow, distorting it to a thin and eerie shape on the carpet barely distinguishable from the figure who'd taken June.

You're not them.

But she was a monster of her own making. And it broke Kidan's heart to know she'd leave her sister behind again at the end of all this, after June was found and kept safe. June wouldn't want to talk to her, let alone touch her, once she learned who Kidan had killed. Even if it was in June's name—*especially* because it was in her name. June wouldn't be able to forgive her, and that was something Kidan couldn't live with. She shivered and played with her blue pill. All that was left to do was hunt and cage all evil inside her so when she did inevitably go, she'd leave the world a little cleaner.

6.

LOCATED NEAR A TOWN STRUGGLING TO KEEP TREES FROM SWALLOW-ing it whole, Uxlay University was an immovable stretch of old stone. Silent as a monastery during prayer, the campus towers caught the sun's first light, glowing against the muted fog. They resembled ancient candles held in the arms of a large entity who woke each day to repent for the sins of its residents.

Of course, Kidan saw a cleaner way of saving their souls. The sun had to burn. Burn with enough fury to engulf those towers with flames and drown this ancient stone in holy fire. That was true absolution.

She hadn't given much thought to the place where she'd die—but here, on this cobbled ground, wreaking as much chaos as she could before facing hell itself? It had a certain poetry to it.

Her smile reflected in the rain-stained window, a rippled slight curve.

Look at me having appreciation for poetry, she thought. *Perhaps I'll make a good student after all.*

The escort who drove her through the night had stopped by the local town, giving Kidan enough time to stretch her legs and grab breakfast. She'd had no appetite, though. The town of Zaf Haven was small, but it had its own rustle of movement, with its humans who flickered with stories and secrets, trapped by the claws of dranaics and calling to her for help. She steadied herself, eyes fixed ahead, listening to June's voice.

As their car wound along asphalt roads, by thick trees, and a sprawling university gate the color of melted gold, Kidan had forced the poor people out of her mind. She couldn't afford to be distracted or lose herself in others.

After receiving an apologetic message explaining that the dean's meeting was running long, Kidan walked alone in the yawning dawn. Despite the early hour, there were sounds of activity, doors opening and closing, the smell of coffee in the air.

She stumbled upon a crisp garden with twittering birds too peaceful for a place like this. A fireplace caged by a grate flickered in the middle of it. She settled on the bench across, facing her palms toward the heat.

A small figure near her feet twitched—a bird, wing broken. Something had cut into its slender neck. Kidan cupped the creature in her hands. The bird's heartbeat fluttered, its feathers struggling in furious swipes as she whispered her intentions.

"Easy, easy. I'll help you."

A place like this must have an infirmary. She looked around and called to the first young man she saw. He walked with his head tilted to the sky, a finger between the pages of a book rested against black pants.

She pulled free her earbuds. "Hey, can you help me?"

He looked older up close, perhaps twenty, dark-skinned like the rest of the people in this place, but with a healthy glow Kidan only found after staying in the sun. His twisted hair was pulled back into a band, two coils free at the front. The look framed his strong jaw well.

"Her wing is broken. Is there an infirmary?"

"Not for animals." His voice was low and secret, as if he didn't speak often.

The book in his hand featured a bleeding sliced grapefruit on its cover.

Kidan studied the bird's soft blue feathers and pearly eyes. They seemed to stare into her soul.

"You will kill it if you continue to hold on so tight." His words came through a tunnel. He stretched out his large palm, waiting. "It's suffering."

Light cut through the remaining fog, illuminating him further. His features were cut like dark glass. An odd urge to trace the morning sun along the ridge of his brows possessed her. A ring of burnished gold had lightened his hair and crowned him like some lost king. The rest of his brown face remained in the shadows. He had the striking beauty of an eclipse, a form to be studied and admired even if it burned the eyes. Kidan didn't want to blink. Or rather, couldn't. She watched him with the horrible, fevered sensation of wanting something that wasn't yours. Even when time turned the act uncomfortable and begged her to avert her attention, she kept watching him.

He let her.

It was as if they both knew he'd slip out of her grasp soon. And he did, slowly, and as gently as the clouds shifting above them and the fallen leaves dancing at their feet. Without the trickery of the rays, his eyes couldn't conceal their truth. They were no longer focused on her face but on her covered neck. Simmering with bone-chilling want. The same hunger remained when he stared at the bird. Pure ice traveled down her spine. He wasn't human.

Her own hands gripped tighter, and tighter still, until the fluttering slowed, stuttered, then stopped. Kidan dropped the bird into his hands. The creature lay curled, neck tucked in.

He lifted his gaze from the dead bird. "Why did you not give it to me?"

"Because you would have killed it as well." Kidan's skin crawled as he regarded her with mild interest. "You're one of them, aren't you? A dranaic?"

His complexion held the earth too close. She should have known. He was beautiful, with eyes that'd lived a thousand years and had found it all rather dull.

His lips almost stretched. "You accuse me of an evil act, yet you committed it—undeniably, you must be human."

Kidan's jaw tightened "I didn't want to kill it."

"What does it matter? Death is death."

"Death with want is cruel. You *wanted* to kill it—would've enjoyed it. I can see it."

He didn't deny her accusation. Kidan rose, brushing her clothes of two feathers. The dranaic watched her, bird still in hand. He waited until they were eye to eye before he flung the creature into the firepit.

She tried to catch it, dropping to her knees and hissing when the hot metal burned her fingers. Kidan watched in horror as the feathers blackened.

A familiar lashing voice echoed from the fire: *"There is evil inside you. It will poison us. Pray, Kidan."*

The vampire crouched next to her, by the warm glow, voice close.

"Death by injury, death by suffocation, death by fire," he pointed out. "Tell me, human, which one would the bird have preferred?"

Kidan's vision colored in black, transfixed by the eating flames. Her vocal cords tightened.

He sighed, mocking. "You meddled in its life and gave it three deaths when it could have had one. If I was you, I would be horrified. An immoral soul such as you shouldn't walk around unchecked."

A moment stretched around them, the fire heating her skin.

"Or," he continued, "you could rise, applaud yourself for quite cleverly extending death beyond its dull limits, and join me for an afternoon of lovely discussion on mortality."

Kidan did rise, slowly, to spit at his feet. His dead eyes danced with amusement, again flicking to her neck. Lingering long enough for her to notice. She wanted to adjust her turtleneck—but more than that, she wanted to hurt him, take her knife from inside her jacket and bury it in his chest, to the audible gasps of strangers. She reined herself in. A knife wouldn't kill him, anyway. Instead, she made herself walk away. There was too much at stake, and it was only her first hour here.

7.

BEFORE YOU MEET YOUR HOUSE DRANAIC, YOU NEED TO UNDERSTAND exactly what you're fighting for." Dean Faris sipped her tea.

They sat in the grand Faris House, inside the belly of a whale. A cool breeze from the open balcony made her shiver.

Kidan's tea had gone cold in her hands. "I'm here to inherit the house."

"Yes, but what exactly is a house?"

Her brows knitted. "What do you mean?"

"Houses are power. Not in the metaphorical sense but in a true sense." The dean paused a moment, letting the words sink in. "For instance, why don't you try to drop that teacup."

Kidan peered down, then back at the woman. Maybe living with these creatures had pushed the dean over the edge.

"Rest the teacup on the table," she instructed.

Kidan did. But when she loosened her grip, the teacup came with her. She tried again, harder, the force making a sharp *clink*. Her fingers remained wrapped around the handle. Kidan shot to her feet and swung her hand wildly. The cup didn't fly into the wall.

"Did you glue this to my hand?" Kidan demanded.

Dean Faris raised a brow. "Please, sit and I'll explain."

Nerves on high alert, Kidan sat slowly.

The dean slid a panel in the middle of the table to reveal written words.

No teacup should be set down in this house.

"Houses abide by a singular law. A law given to them by their owners." The dean's voice was calm, rehearsed. "This is one I thought of specifically for this exercise, of course."

Kidan blinked. And blinked again. She pushed her chair back and marched to the kitchen. First, she tried to peel the cup from her skin by using the counter's edge as leverage. When that didn't work, she found a spoon and tried to screw it between the cup and her palm. That only made her shout a string of curses when the spoon sprang up and struck her eyebrow. She opened the tap and submerged her hand in water, but that only made the porcelain slippery and drenched her sweater.

"When you're quite done, we can continue," the dean's voice called from the dining area.

Kidan shut off the tap and leaned over the sink, breathing unevenly. Impossible. No fucking way.

Kidan walked back, wet and frightened. "Get it off me."

"Certainly." Dean Faris rested her own teacup. At once, Kidan's cup came unstuck and fell. On instinct, Kidan caught it. She stared, jaw slacked, and traced its smooth surface and etchings. Nothing extraordinary about it—and yet it'd shifted the very gravity of her world.

"How?"

"After years of mastery, houses become an extension of their owners. They're very complicated creatures."

The power of houses . . .

Kidan took her seat again, eyeing her cup as if it might break into song.

"Are we calm?" the dean asked.

Kidan managed a nod.

"Good. Now, listen carefully to what I'm about to tell you. For hundreds of years, humans were hunted and tortured by vampires. We were utterly powerless against them. The only ones who could stand against them were the gifted Sages, but they were all brought to extinction." Dean Faris's brows drew together for a moment. "However, before the Last Sage died, he created the Three Binds."

Kidan knew about those powerful binds. She'd recited them enough times to June after her nightmares, holding her sweat-drenched body close. Her favorite was the Third Bind. It ensured that the population of vampires never grew too much.

"The Last Sage also gave us power over our own houses. Each acti, which refers to the members of the Eighty Families, has the potential to become a house owner. In the past, each house could set its own, unique law. As you can imagine, that led to many conflicts between families."

"Laws...like countries," Kidan echoed, her mind still foggy.

"Exactly. Every man and house for himself. When the peace between vampires and humans was forged, vampires were invited to live alongside us, inside our homes as our companions. It changed everything."

Kidan's mouth soured at the words "peace" and "vampire" in the same sentence. They were inherent opposites, and one couldn't exist while the other lived.

Dean Faris continued.

"Uxlay is unique, because we choose to act as one community. Twelve heirs and heiresses came together to practice the same exact universal law in every household. One law that protects us from the outside world."

The fog drained away, leaving red in Kidan's vision. Such power wasted on protection from the outside world? What use was that when the problem was inside these walls?

"Follow me." Dean Faris pushed her chair back and exited out the balcony.

Kidan joined her, bracing against the high winds. The entirety of Uxlay stretched before them. A set of sprawling houses—close to mansions, really—surrounded the campus like a belt.

"If you've noticed, each house's land shares a border with the one next to it, all the way around. Some houses even host a cemetery and a sports field on their expansive land without breaking the circle. The design of it is purposeful, so the universal law continues uninterrupted."

"What exactly is this law?"

"No unauthorized person—human or vampire—can enter or even find Uxlay."

Kidan's hands tightened on the rail. It now made sense why she could never track this university down. The months spent in her apartment, driving herself insane with the reality of knowing a place existed yet being unable to prove it—it'd been cruel. She studied the dean's features, the lines in the corners of her brown eyes that betrayed her age—yet nothing was soft about her stance.

Kidan frowned. "But this house doesn't border the others."

Dean Faris nodded. "As Founders, House Adane and House Faris are the only ones that can set their own law. As such, the roles and responsibilities of being dean of Uxlay have fallen to us."

Kidan nearly swayed. Her ancestors founded Uxlay? They'd been deans? And more importantly, House Adane could set their *own* law. She couldn't imagine the power of such a thing. The shock of this new discovery turned into an exciting possibility. A weapon. Finally, a good weapon against them.

Kidan's eyes shone. "You're telling me I can set any law in Adane House? Just like your tea one?"

Dean Faris's words were careful. "Setting and changing a house law is an incredibly difficult art. One you'll begin to learn next year, if you're still with us. But even then, you won't be ready for some years."

Years...

Kidan's eyes went to the teacup inside. Could it really be that hard?

The dean pointed to a dark shape directly across from them. "Adane House. Only our houses lie inside the boundary, Kidan. It is a great responsibility granted to us, a power we cannot abuse. If Susenyos Sagad inherits Adane House and misuses that power, it will collapse Uxlay."

A bitter smile twisted Kidan's lips. "If you're so worried about him setting his own law, why won't you believe he took my sister?"

Dean Faris spoke slowly, repeating the same frustrating question. "What proof is there that he took your sister?"

Kidan opened her mouth and shut it. Her ears echoed with her victim's confession.

Susenyos Sagad!...He...he took her!

Her tongue soured. Kidan's proof couldn't be used. Not yet.

"House laws can only be changed by their true owners. You can see why the responsibilities of heirs and heiresses at Uxlay are important. You are all key to maintaining Uxlay's community and keeping our people safe."

Kidan was beginning to understand. "And a given law only works inside one house, not outside? Right?"

Dean Faris lifted a fallen petal off the ledge and let the breeze carry it. "Yes. My house law only works on Faris land."

Kidan stared at the boundary circle again with new eyes. Each of those houses shared borders so the law from one house extended to the next, creating a massive protective shield.

"What happens if one of the houses on the border decides to break the universal law?"

Kidan imagined it all as a dam, one good leak and the whole thing could collapse, exposing their existence to the outside world.

Dean Faris regarded her curiously. "Uxlay formed on the basis that it would exist as a safe and hidden community. Anyone that takes issue with that will be removed from our society. We will readjust to account for their loss."

The tone of those words belonged to a general before an army.

Kidan's forehead creased. "But what if the vampires rise against you inside here? Enslave—er, capture and force you to give them blood?"

Dean Faris didn't seem offended by the line of questioning. "It is precisely that lifestyle of death and chaos the Last Sage ended when he proposed this new lifestyle of coexistence. Do you believe vampires are mindless agents of violence? They crave peace just like us. They choose to coexist alongside us, and have for generations. Anyone who doesn't wish to can leave Uxlay, and they have."

They crave peace just like us. Kidan wanted to laugh, but Dean Faris appeared to truly believe her words.

The dean returned inside and poured a stream of cinnamon tea.

"If Susenyos Sagad occupies that house alone for a consecutive set of twenty-eight days, he becomes the sole owner. If you start living with him, the will becomes suspended, giving you time to graduate and claim your house. Please, drink."

Kidan took the warm teacup, a thrumming shooting up her arm. She immediately set it down to see if the law was still changed. It was. How did it all work?

"Or you could just arrest him."

"I admire your bravery, Kidan, but your assumptions and judgments will make life here difficult for you. They are useful, to an extent. Be wary but never cold. Especially when Uxlay's smaller groups and clubs begin to extend their invitations to you."

Kidan crinkled her nose. "I'm not interested in any group."

"But they will be interested in you." The woman's sharp eyes gleamed with warning. "Everyone wants to have a Founding House heiress as their friend. Tread carefully."

"Sure...but do I have to attend class?"

Her features hardened. "Yes, you must attend, and failure is not an option. Any other acti can fail and try again next year with no risk to their inheritance. Not you. The sole reason you're able to take shelter in your house is that you are studying our philosophy. If you fail, Susenyos has the right to force you out until the course resumes next year, and by then it will be too late."

Kidan blew out a breath. Nodded.

"Before classes start, however, there's something important you must do." Dean Faris leaned forward, as if sharing a secret. "I want you to discover the law stated in your household. It will only reveal itself to potential inheritors of the house."

There was already a...law in place.

Kidan's gaze fell to her hands. "I'm guessing it's not about tea."

Dean Faris almost smiled. "No, I'm afraid not."

"So where do I find the law? On a table like yours?"

A line appeared between the dean's brows. Voice hesitant, she said, "The house is an echo of the mind. It presents itself differently to each potential inheritor. The best answer I can give you is, the law will be hidden in the room you least want to visit."

Kidan blinked slowly. "I don't understand."

"You will once you've settled in." She nodded. "Unlike setting or changing a house law, reading an existing law should be simple enough. I have complete faith you can manage it."

The woman's gaze settled on the rippling curtains. They fluttered and swayed with new wind, and she cocked her head as if listening.

"Come in," Dean Faris said, though no one had knocked.

A man with braided hair and unnaturally straight posture entered the room.

"This is Professor Andreyas, my companion and your professor for Introduction to Dranacti," the dean said.

Dranacti—the official name of the philosophy taught at Uxlay. The course she absolutely had to pass. Kidan didn't extend her hand and neither did he. It struck her how well they fit into human skin. His unblinking eyes assessed her, and ice rushed down her back.

"A pleasure." His voice curled like the tail of a scorpion. He leaned to whisper a few words to the dean.

Professor Andreyas's sleeve hosted a golden pin—a black bird with a silver eye, just like Dean Faris had worn. The sigil of House Faris, Kidan had gathered.

"Good," Dean Faris said. "We'll visit Susenyos now. Come, Kidan. I'll explain as we go."

Kidan followed the two out. They made an odd but impressive sight side-by-side. One inhuman, steel skin, eternal. The other a Black woman, soft-fleshed and aging. Yet he walked in her steps, bent to her voice, and fit himself around her movements. A shadow to a sun.

8.

DEAN FARIS AND KIDAN ARRIVED AT A HOUSE THAT BORE THE SAME wealth and rich wood that a haunted manor might. But if other houses reminded Kidan of feral pets, this one had its teeth broken and festered a particular disease inside.

She eyed the windows, trying to glimpse the dranaic who'd conveniently lived through her family's death. If Kidan hadn't struck her deal with the dean, she would have lit this house on fire as well.

"I thought it would be bigger." Kidan frowned, comparing it with the Faris mansion.

"Your parents had quieter taste." Dean Faris's features lightened as she studied the house. "I haven't entered this house in many years."

"Why?"

"I mastered my house when I was twenty years old, at which point I could no longer enter other mastered houses. Adane House belongs to no one at the moment. It is a very rare circumstance, and I'm glad to visit it."

Kidan couldn't begin to understand their customs. She eyed the black chimney and uncleaned gutters.

"I don't remember this house," Kidan said, trying to parse her old memories.

"You wouldn't. Uxlay doesn't permit children to reside here. All children study at our boarding school, where vampires are not allowed. Once they finish, they come here for higher education."

"But if Uxlay is so safe, why do you have to accompany me inside?"

"Because as of a week ago, Susenyos Sagad was expecting to inherit this house. I'm cautious of what we will find inside."

As they drew closer to the lion-shaped knocker, music drifted out. It held an equal measure of a drum and brass instruments with vocals that wrapped around a foreign language. The oak door was heavier than Kidan imagined, swinging inward as if the hinges needed a good oiling. The smell of old carpet and dust settled on her tongue. It appeared both lived in and untouched since its occupants left it. Kidan found she liked this about it. It was an unusual show of loyalty, to keep itself as it was, not erasing history. For a wild second, she imagined she would find her parents upstairs.

"Do vampires not clean?" Kidan asked.

"You do have a house cook, Etete. So you're not entirely alone. She will be very helpful. Unfortunately, her presence doesn't interrupt the will, as she isn't an heiress of Adane House. "

The idea of a house cook wasn't that comforting.

Glass shelves in every corner were filled with antiques and other treasures. Upon closer inspection, they appeared to be East African trinkets, possibly from archaeological digs. Although Kidan was Ethiopian, she barely recognized her culture. Another thing long lost.

The dean lifted her eyes from the picture she was admiring. A woman in a long skirt and coat stood amid ruins next to a shaded man in a wide-brimmed hat. At the bottom it read, AXUM ARCHAEOLOGICAL PROJECT, 1965.

"Your family were passionate about recovering lost things. Just as much, they had a hard time parting with things they recovered. The Axum Archaeological Project investigates the Sage-period site in northern Ethiopia. Many had given up hope that ancient Axum could be found again, but your ancestors were determined to locate it."

They walked into a well-furnished living room. Still no sign of the dranaic. A giant portrait hung above the fireplace. It captured five well-dressed people in exquisite detail. There was a woman who looked like Aunt Silia, in a sleek black dress, hair piled in a messy bun. Kidan couldn't remember if her nose had been that shape. With her were two silver-haired elderly people and, in the middle, a smiling couple, outfitted in a smart suit and red dress. June had their father's eyes, warm and twinkling. Kidan shared her mother's straight nose and high forehead, appearing stern when she didn't mean to. But the loose and curling hair fanning around her was all June. Kidan tugged at the end of her braids, which were coarse and unbending like iron. It was a battle to make her hair submit, with many combs sacrificed to the cause. Her father seemed to understand the pain, instead choosing to wear short, dense hair. Every feature that she and June had came from pieces of these strangers. It felt larger than anything, alive in a way that made her want to weep.

"When was this done?" Her voice betrayed her emotion, wavering. Her parents looked so...young, close to her age now.

"At the Acti Gala, about sixteen years ago."

The dean's eyes slid to the corner signature, and her tone slightly changed. "Omar Umil's work, of course."

Omar Umil...Why was that name familiar? It was a name in Aunt Silia's book. The only person her aunt had spoken fondly of, and who was currently in Uxlay's Drastfort Prison. Yet another mystery.

It took Kidan a great deal of effort to look away, and even as she did, she knew she'd sneak one more glance on her way back.

They followed the swelling music into a common room of sorts, with a study desk and large, towering bookshelf.

Kidan's body was suddenly thrust into a violent, disturbing cold.

Several girls stood in a strict line in the middle of the room. All were blindfolded and blood ran from their bitten shoulders.

"June," Kidan whispered as she burst into the darkened room. She grabbed one of the girls and yanked down her blindfold. Green eyes blinked at her instead of soft brown. Kidan staggered back. She continued along the line, pulling the fabric off the young women one by one. In her lowest moments, Kidan had already imagined this scene, June tortured and used for her blood. Dread tightened around her throat when she reached the last girl.

Please. Please.

Kidan had finally found Uxlay and entered the place Susenyos lived. ...June must be here. She *had* to be. Her fingers shook too much, unable to pull the last blindfold. The girl removed the fabric herself, dark black eyes blown wide. Not honey brown.

"Who are you?" the girl whispered.

Kidan swayed and reached to brace against the wall, trying to force air into her lungs.

Past the girls, three people occupied a table, playing some sort of game. One of them had his back to her, black and thick twisted hair reaching his shoulder.

Dranaics. If Kidan could breathe fire, they'd all be incinerated.

Dean Faris joined her, pity in her eyes hardening to stone once she regarded the vampires. Two of them rose at once—a boy and a girl.

A gold-plated band wrapped around the boy's forehead, his muscled body fitted in a tight shirt. He flashed a shaky grin. "Dean Faris. We didn't expect you here."

Dean Faris's words were barely constrained into formality. "Blood courting is forbidden outside the Southern Sost Buildings. Whose idea was this?"

The dark-skinned girl gave a small bow of her head in apology. She wore a velvet brocade vest and coat, a bloodred flower pinned to her collar at her throat. Her hair was cut at her neck, sleek and curling behind her ear. She looked like a fine lord of the Victorian era.

"I apologize." Her address rang more formal.

Dean Faris frowned. "I expected more from you, Iniko. Report to Andreyas and tell him you're banned from courting for the next three months."

Iniko nodded again, accepting her punishment without question.

The dean eyed the girls. "Iniko and Taj, take your guests with you and wait for me in my office."

Taj, the young man with a golden headband, approached the women. "With me, ladies. Hold hands, yes, this way."

He winked at Kidan as he left. Her nostrils flared in disgust.

Once they were gone, Dean Faris took one of their seats, facing the vampire collecting the cards in swift motion. Kidan remained at the wall.

"Did Iniko tell you about your changed circumstances?"

"Oh yes, delivering news through my closest friends that I'm to be crossed off the will is not something I'd forget."

The vampire's voice sounded familiar, deep, and mocking. Kidan moved forward slowly, heart thundering.

"I figured it was best. She has a talent for reasoning with you," the dean said.

"I suppose she does."

"And the blood courting? Was it really Iniko's idea?"

"She plans to find me a match. I can't deny her wish."

Dean Faris's gaze fell to his sleeves. "You're not wearing your pin. Are you considering joining another house?"

He shifted, retrieved a silver pin from his pocket with two mountains shielding each other, and secured it to his sleeve.

"Always Adane."

He pronounced Kidan's last name with the correct affectation and too much familiarity.

His attention finally flicked to Kidan, striking her still. Eyes deadened with time. Skin that held the earth too close.

"Hello, little bird."

Kidan's vision blackened, her breathing growing heavier.

He cocked his head. "Have you killed any more innocent creatures since I last saw you?"

Dean Faris drew a line between the two. "You have met?"

He gave a thin smile. "I helped her when she was in desperate need, but I fear she sees it differently."

"You were supposed to wait until I introduced you two," Dean Faris said disapprovingly.

His smile deepened his dark brown skin. "There are so few new faces around here. I had to satisfy my curiosity."

The dean touched a hand to her temple. "Kidan Adane, meet your house vampire, Susenyos Sagad."

The smile on his face strained when it returned to her, displeasure breaking through the mask for a moment. Kidan truly felt like the bird they'd killed, already dead, and now thrown into the depths of hellfire.

9.

THEY SAT IN THE CRACKLING ROOM, THE SMELL OF LIQUOR AND BURN-ing wood suffocating Kidan. Susenyos Sagad was at complete ease. Unthreatened in the way arrogant men occupied a space.

No, not a man.

A fine ray of sun from the window reminded her of his immortality. He'd cheated out of rot and decay and tricked one of the mightiest stars to cast him in golden light. When he shifted, the sun did its part in the shadows too. Smoothed his texture like honey and glinted on the edge of his cheek like the horizon, played the part in dressing monster as human.

"Ayzosh, atfri." He spoke in a curving tone.

"What?"

"It's Amharic." His eyes hardened. "You hope to inherit House Adane, and yet you don't know your language?"

He faced Dean Faris with furrowed brows, and they spoke like she wasn't there while Kidan stewed. Susenyos's voice in Amharic was harsh, fast, and cutting. It sounded like a language with teeth of its own.

This language was another thing she and June had abandoned when their biological parents died. It was how they survived. They'd forced themselves to forget Amharic, awkwardly stuffing English in their mouths until it became all they consumed. Mama Anoet made sure. Kidan traced the back of her fingers, remembering the pinch she'd get when she responded in her mother tongue. No one could discover they were the Adane children.

Finally, Dean Faris stood. "It is within your right to speak to her directly, but remember the laws. She isn't your companion yet, but an enrolled student deserves the same extension of courtesy. Kidan, I'll be outside if you need me."

Once they were alone, Susenyos poured her a drink that smelled like gasoline.

"I have served House Adane for generations," he began. "And from the way your back is sitting so stiffly, you appear to loathe this place, which makes me wonder why you're here. I assume you're interested in money. Luxury. There is no reason I can't extend you a small amount of the profits. Things do taste sweeter when shared."

Kidan fought to speak through clenched teeth. "I *assume* in this agreement you receive the house."

He shrugged, reclining in his seat. "Houses are a hassle to maintain."

"I agree." She adopted his relaxed tone. "But I love a good challenge."

His mouth took on an interesting shape. A cross between annoyance and interest. "Are you flirting with me, little bird?"

Breathe. The nerve of this guy. *"No."*

"Not interested in money and not attracted to me. I'm afraid we're running out of things to discuss."

So, he liked to play games. Kidan eased the tension in her shoulders. "Do you always bring blindfolded girls here?"

Vampires couldn't drink from just any human, so those girls were from the Acti Families.

"As Dean Faris said, the rules don't allow it. A shame too, because they provide delicious company."

Her nausea built. "What do you do to them after?"

He tilted his head. "Send them home."

"Did you send June Adane home?"

She delivered it without blinking, careful not to miss any spasm of muscle movement. But there was no reason to look so hard. A person outside the arched window could sense the shift in the room, the playful light of his expression draining into something long dead.

He wouldn't admit it. If the Uxlay laws about humans were this stifling and feared, he wouldn't. But she wanted to speak her sister's name in this house, make it known she wouldn't leave without her.

"I'm afraid you bore me," he concluded with a wave. "Here I am offering you the world, yet you choose to shrink yourself to baseless accusations."

This time, her lips quirked. "My sources are pretty good."

A pinch in his brows. Perhaps concern. He slid a glance at the closed door. Of course. Dean Faris.

"Then why haven't the campus authorities arrested me? Why aren't we in court?"

Kidan could only stare her hatred. If she revealed her source, it had to be timed perfectly, with guarantee of June's safety, or her proof would bury Kidan itself.

Like a child who'd discovered a treasure, Susenyos leaned forward, eyes bright. "You're not the first person to accuse me. I must have the face for it. But I will tell you one thing my enemies fail to realize—I enjoy taking credit for my misdeeds, because they are ingenious by themselves. Taking your sister? What's the challenge in that?"

Kidan reached for her drink, fighting not to smash it across his smug face. Instead, she swallowed the liquid fire. It was hotter than she imagined, but she didn't break her stare.

He watched her set down the empty glass. "So, shall we talk about how much you're going to cost me? A million should be enough."

Kidan rose, examining the luxury of the study. It was old money, furniture rich with expensive wood, cushions velvet and soft to the touch. She ran her fingers over the material.

"That's a Saui Cushion." He spoke near, shadow falling over her. Her spine locked at how soundlessly he traveled. "Do you feel how exquisite the stitching is? The artist made only three of those before he died. I could gift it to you, to commemorate our new agreement."

He treasured things. She could hear it in the cadence of his voice. Objects held more significance than the mention of her sister. Kidan hooked a nail into the stitching.

"Easy," he warned.

Her mouth twisted, knowing he was watching. She pulled at the delicate red thread, unraveling it.

His sharp hiss tickled her neck before he spoke. "Don't."

She faced him slowly, taking in his roiling black eyes and taut posture, the effort to keep his fisted hands by his side instead of around her throat.

She let the thread fall between them, and the red caught in his eyes for a moment, setting them alive. He took a step toward her, stealing all the air from her lungs.

Would he kill her right here?

Dean Faris's low-heeled shoes clicked, announcing her return. Susenyos stepped away at once. Kidan exhaled.

"Well, Kidan, where will you be sleeping tonight?"

Kidan gave Susenyos her first smile, full and sanguine. He was smart enough to be wary of it, his brows drawing together.

"I'll take the main bedroom, I think."

Susenyos Sagad is the last remaining dranaic sworn to our house. He does not speak often, but I believe he has some understanding with your parents. I think he waits for the day I die so he can claim the house for himself. I feel his eyes on me, his shadowy presence never far. I don't know why my sister and your father left their legacy to him, but it is their last wish. They loved their secrets, and I'm afraid it's what finally killed them.

I leave the house to him, but if you want it, you must take it. It will protect you in ways I can't.

Four Houses have turned against House Adane.

Watch for these families: Ajtaf, Makary, Qaros, and Umil. I think Susenyos may be working with them. Guard yourself.

The Laws of Uxlay

Universal Law:
No unauthorized person, human or vampire, shall find or enter Uxlay.

The Ranking of the Houses
(Based on the number of dranaics loyal to each house and current business status)
1. Ajtaf House (234 dranaics)
2. Faris House (124 dranaics)
3. Makary House (100 dranaics)
4. Qaros House (98 dranaics)

5. Temo House (97 dranaics)

6. Delarus House (81 dranaics)

7. Rojit House (65 dranaics)

8. Piran House (55 dranaics)

9. Goro House (33 dranaics)

10. Luroz House (23 dranaics)

11. Umil House (10 dranaics)

12. Adane House (1 dranaic)

—*History of the Acti Houses*
By Yohannes Afera

10.

KIDAN DIDN'T UNPACK. SHE LEFT HER SUITCASE AND BAG IN THE COR-
ner of a spacious bedroom fit for three people. After an hour of loud arguments with the dean, Susenyos left the house in fury. Kidan watched his long
coat sweeping backward as he stormed down the front steps and the dean followed. Kidan didn't waste another second. Quickly, she searched every room,
starting with the floor she was on. Four bedrooms in total, furnished in the
same exact way except for one.

His room.

She couldn't help but compare it with her stifling apartment that was
now thankfully abandoned. Her curtains had always been drawn so the sun
wouldn't interrupt the dark. It had forced her to remain, to revisit the thoughts
that pecked at her flesh in some macabre meditation.

Susenyos Sagad, however, welcomed the sun, an entire wall of glass displaying the distant forest and the approaching dusk. It frustrated her to no end that
he thought himself deserving of any light.

The smell of books and ink was most potent in the middle of the
room. She was familiar with the crinkle and mess of paper, but while her reading
material swallowed the floor, strewn and sliding under drawers, here the papers
were rolled and sealed into scrolls, thousands of them covering the opposite
walls. Annoyance flickered inside her again. How careful and neat and clean it
all was.

She retrieved one scroll, slipped free its ribbon, and skimmed the neat
writing.

Letter to the Immortal,

I feel silly writing to you. My friends think I fantasize too much, believe the cracks of our world conceal wondrous magic beneath them, but what other way is there to live? There must be some other existence for us. Humans can't truly be gifted with a mind to wonder and create and yet be forced to live in an endless cycle of money and work.

I hope I do this right. You ask for name, country, and date.

Please, write back to me. Not because my life is in danger or I request aid but because knowing you exist would save my imagination, and it is all I'd need to change my life.

Rosa Tomás
Luanda, Angola, 1931

Kidan frowned and grabbed a couple more. They were all letters from different countries and years; the oldest she found was 1889. Parchment rolled up into scrolls. Kidan couldn't make sense of it. The best she could guess was he'd run a sort of business and these letters were requests, but what exactly he offered in return was difficult to deduce, as each letter asked for something different. By the fifth letter, Kidan couldn't stand the desperation of the writers. They were begging a monster to save them. Her eyes scanned it all—at least a thousand were here.

His closet held an assortment of expensive coats, loose shirts, and black and brown pants. On his bedside table was the book he'd had when they first met, showing a grapefruit cut and dripping blood.

She rummaged and pulled out everything in his bedside drawers—a set of rings, a box of pens, bound manuscripts, golden flasks.

She'd almost given up and left the room when the unfiltered sunlight twinkled on a silver bracelet, wedged deep in the corner. All sound faded. The tweeting birds outside, the gentle rustle of wind, the creaks and groans of an old house.

Kidan's heart pounded.

Shaking, she reached for the chain, and pulled. A butterfly charm dangled on it.

A sob escaped her, and she covered her mouth. Kidan had made two of these bracelets—one for Mama Anoet, and one for June. This one, the most special one, featured a three-pointed charm, in reference to the Three Binds placed on all vampires. To help keep her sister's nightmares away.

Kidan's voice broke. *"June."*

A cold voice cut through the room. "What the hell are you doing in my room?"

Kidan stiffened. Susenyos stood in the entry, arms crossed, eyes narrowed on the dangling bracelet and the contents of his drawers strewn around the floor.

She needed to get the hell out of here. Get to Dean Faris.

Before Kidan could close her fingers, Susenyos shoved her backward with unnatural speed and reclaimed the bracelet with a piece of napkin.

"Give it back," she snarled, jumping to her feet and attacking him.

He captured her wrists with ease, and her sweater sleeve peeled back, revealing her own, matching bracelet. A line formed between his dark brows.

"Where is she?" She breathed pure fire. "What did you do to her?"

His eyes mirrored the bottom of the ocean. "I'm afraid I don't know who you're talking about."

Spittle gathered in the corners of her mouth as she roared. "Where the fuck is she?"

Susenyos dragged her to the edge of his room with frightening strength. "We're going to need to set certain boundaries. If I find you in my room again, I won't be so gentle."

He threw her out like dirty laundry. Kidan tried to run back, but the door slammed shut. She pounded on it until her fists bruised—and it opened. She rushed inside. The window was open. But Susenyos, along with the bracelet, was gone.

Her one chance. The proof she'd need for Dean Faris to believe her. Gone.

Kidan screamed so loud, the birds nestled in all the trees of Uxlay took flight.

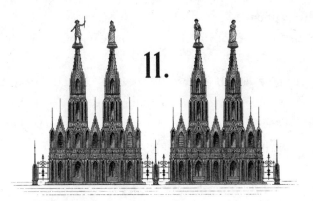

11.

KIDAN RUSHED THROUGH THE OTHER ROOMS, TURNING THEM INSIDE out, venturing downstairs to a creepy wine cellar and a wide empty space containing training mats and equipment that seemed unused, dust flying everywhere when she shifted them.

Back upstairs, she found one door locked. A red tapestry of a lion hung on it, adjacent to the crackling study.

In the kitchen, she found their house cook, an aged woman with gray streaks in her Afro who smelled like sourdough bread.

"Ah, there you are." The woman smiled, flour on her cheek. "I'm Ruth, but everyone calls me Etete. It's so nice to have you here."

Kidan ground her jaw. What was this woman doing in a place like this?

"I'd like to go into the room with the lion decoration on it, but it's locked." Kidan's voice was unfriendly.

"I'm afraid I don't have the key." Etete frowned. "Susenyos has it."

"What's inside?"

"I'm not sure."

"Where does he keep the key?"

"Around his neck."

Kidan swore internally. Even if she shrank into an insect and tried to lift his key, he'd sense her and snap her neck. Kidan returned to those wavy brass handles and could swear she heard June tap-tapping at the wood, calling with fear.

Kidan lasted exactly two minutes.

She hurried to the weed-infested garden shed and brought out an axe, dragging it in front of the red-lion door. She blew out a breath, tied her braids back, and wrapped her hands around the handle.

"Acti Kidan!" Etete came rushing in. "What are you doing?"

"I don't have the key."

"Wait, you can't possibly—"

Kidan swung, gravity pulling her fast and hard until a sharp resistance vibrated in her shoulders. She missed the door handle, and the axe wedged into russet wood.

Kidan glanced back. Etete stared in mild shock, hand on her chest.

"You should leave," Kidan told her as she yanked the axe out of the door.

If Kidan found anything related to June, this axe would find an outlet. She didn't want this woman's blood on her hands.

Etete shook her head, muttering prayers under her breath before returning to the kitchen.

This time, Kidan hit the door handle with a perfect *snap*. The gold metal flew past her ear and landed somewhere in the study. Raw satisfaction pulsed through her. Her arms ached and her breathing picked up, but she had the urge to do it again.

The past few days had been out of her control, as if she'd been swept out to the open sea without a paddle. Well, she had her paddle now.

She kicked the door open and dragged her weapon inside. Cold pinched at her nose instantly, fogging her breath. It was pitch-black. Her thoughts jumped to the worst possible conclusion. A morgue. Why else would this room have the temperature of ice? Would she see June's dead body displayed just like the night she was taken? Brown skin drained of color, delicate lips painted in blood?

Heart drumming, she reached for the light switch, bracing herself. Night gave way to rows of shelves that reached the ceiling and across the floor—filled not with bodies, but with things once used by them.

Kidan passed by a delicate armband with an ancient inscription, a crown crushed as if the owner had been decapitated, a lock of braided hair. The opposite side held the clothes of royalty, embroidered with crosses and diamond shapes. Sandals from another time period, and animal-hide musical instruments she'd never seen before.

Artifacts.

This was his secret? Under any other circumstances, Kidan would've picked up a few to admire their features, working out how to bend them into something else.

But June wasn't here. All interest from her fingers melted into rage. Kidan lifted her axe and smashed an arrangement of pottery with intricate designs. The pieces flew around the vast room like confetti. She swung again. An entire row of trinkets collided into one another and exploded off the shelves. She took down two more shelves, shouting, grunting at the effort.

The crushed crown rolled near her feet, and she lifted it, placing it on her head. It was pure metal, uncomfortable, but the spikes were beautiful, gold crosses with ruby detailing. She caught her reflection in an embellished mirror, a slip of a smile present.

Then she stilled. At the end of the space was a stunning portrait of a goddess. A dark-skinned woman in a cracked mask with twin swords at her back. Light radiated off her, blinding and mighty. The woman's eyes pierced the wooden slit and stirred mutiny in Kidan. It was as if she echoed all the pain and anger bubbling under her skin. In a satisfying slash, Kidan cut into the canvas, ripping it.

It was small, petty even, but she savored the destruction of this room. It was nothing compared with what he'd taken from her, but if any of this meant something to him, it satiated her thirst.

She took the crown with her. It felt personal, a history tied to it, and she'd always enjoyed collecting things that reminded her of life.

Then she called Dean Faris and told her about June's bracelet.

Dean Faris was quiet for a long time before saying, "I will investigate."

Just hours ago, the woman had refused to believe Susenyos had taken June. This was progress.

Kidan took the crown to her vanity and began the tedious work of snapping each metal cross with scissors. It was tough gold and took some sawing back and forth, cutting her soft flesh in the process, but when it broke, a smile touched her lips.

Once she disassembled the crown, she found a necklace chain and looped each cross through it. Kidan would continue to take what Susenyos found precious and gift it to her poor sister once she found her.

She showered, almost relaxing for the first time in a while. She even hummed a little tune as she changed and grabbed her aunt's journal, snacking on a plate of chechebsa. Instead of leaving as instructed, Etete—with a stern expression on her face—had brought a bowl of fried cut-up flatbread glistening with spiced butter. "If you plan to survive here, you'll need your strength. Eat."

Kidan had planned to refuse, but the rich peppery scent had her mouth watering. Her tastebuds were desperate for something other than noodles. So here she was, mouth on fire, feeling an unwanted sense of guilt and gratitude, reading her aunt's words. There were some connections she needed to follow before the university semester started, specifically how the houses had contributed to June's disappearance. How they worked with him.

From the loud string of foreign curse words floating up to her room, Kidan knew Susenyos Sagad had discovered his artifact room had been desecrated.

Her smile grew pure, and she put away her things before going downstairs. She wasn't going to miss the show.

Susenyos had thrown his coat off, loose shirt rolled up at the sleeves as he waded through the mess. Kidan rested on the stair rail, watching every frame of displeasure on his face. The pinched eyebrows, the barely restrained curl of his lips. It was all so lovely.

His eyes swept upward, his hand around a broken chalice, and bore into hers. He stalked toward the stairs, chest rising and falling. She settled on the steps, shaking her head at the room.

"Who would do something like this?" She batted her lashes.

He loomed over her, a vein throbbing along his dark temple. From her low angle, she noticed how effortlessly he dented the chalice with his grip. She wished he'd lay that hand on her, to give her an excuse to throw him out of this house and into prison to rot.

"You don't know what you've destroyed," he breathed out, voice thick. "That portrait was invaluable."

Kidan was careful to look at the room. Let him stew. His breathing became ragged the longer she ignored him, then evened out at once.

"Your family would be ashamed of you."

This made her turn sharply and glare at his taut jaw.

"An Adane daughter that doesn't value history. You're quite a disgrace to your family, aren't you?"

Kidan shot to her feet and spat. "Don't fucking talk to me about my family."

The venom of her words slipped off him without impact. His eyes were bright, cruel. "Truly, I'm glad they all died before they could see what you've become."

Kidan slapped him. The contact snapped something inside her ribs, a sudden awakening of the monster hidden within.

He'd said "all." They'd all died, including June. Was that a confession? Had he killed June?

Susenyos touched his cheek, rolling his tongue. And Kidan's victory drained away. He'd tricked her into harming him first.

"Where is the crown?" he demanded.

How did he notice it was missing so quickly?

"Where is June's bracelet?" She flexed, fisted, and flexed her fingers again, trying to shake out the energy that seeped into them.

His hand shot forward and she flinched, but he restrained himself, forcing himself to grab the rail instead, leaning in to whisper.

"The dean told me the girl ran away, and now I understand. To have you as a sister must be true hell."

Kidan's mouth opened, but no sound came out. Her tongue dried up. He'd pulled free a nightmare she had tucked away and forced her to face the question of why June's bags and clothes had been packed that night.

Her loathing made her entire body shake. The light bulb above them flickered. His eyes slid to a point on her neck, darkening with hunger. She touched it unconsciously, breaking his gaze. He reached into his chest pocket, pulled out a golden flask, and drank. The change in his features was sudden. The ends of his hair bled red, and his pupils caught light, scattering it so it hurt to look directly at him.

Kidan staggered back, voice tight. "What...is that?"

"This is your lifeline. As long as I have this, I won't bite into that lovely neck of yours." He eyed her collarbone, making her shiver.

Kidan's breath gathered speed.

Finally, he stepped back, smiling. "If you want to play the game of ruins, let's play. I've never lost it."

Her forefinger rapidly drew the four corners of a square against her thigh. Fear.

But for whom? It was a startling revelation that Kidan could still feel fear for her body. She balled up her fingers painfully as if to expunge the emotion out of herself. She couldn't fear. Kidan had to eradicate all evil. It was this morality that allowed her to rise from bed at all and function with the weight of what she'd committed. Eradicate all evil—including herself.

Only companions offered their blood to vampires. Did Susenyos have a companion from another house? She wasn't sure and needed to research more into their customs.

Susenyos spent the rest of the night with gloves and a powerful chemical that smelled, restoring what he could of every shattered artifact like a surgeon. The care with which he pieced together each frame boiled Kidan's blood. She was disgusted at how he cared for inanimate objects so intimately. But this was a sign of malice, she realized, touching her victim's butterfly bracelet. Objects gave evil beings more pleasure than those who once wore them. She shook herself free of the thought. She didn't want to draw parallels between him and her, but she also needed to. He'd taken June; she'd taken the life of a human being. Loathing him meant loathing herself, and killing him would mean killing herself. So when the time came, Kidan had to be strong enough. They both had to die.

Her shoulders unwound in her room, and she fell asleep the moment she touched her bed.

Then, at precisely twelve, the house trembled. Her eyes flew open. The phone jittered on her bedstand as if the tectonic plates below the house were shifting. She bolted upright.

A wretched scream came from the slit beneath her door.

Help!

12.

THE HALLWAY'S CARPET RIPPLED LIKE A TONGUE, SALIVATING FOR Kidan to step forward, and were those...eyes staring at her? Her pulse jumped to her throat, and she grabbed her door, ready to shut it, when the cry came again. Someone in agonizing pain.

Kidan gritted her teeth and stepped into the dark, her skin prickling at once. Unsettling warm breath fanned her neck, raising hair along her back. Her body jerked. She knew this monster. After her parents died, it'd visited her night after night until Mama Anoet slayed the beast. How had it found her again? She whirled around, and the foul breath vanished.

"Who's there?" she shouted.

Only her voice echoed down the hall.

"Get a grip," she muttered to herself.

The pained shout came again, and this time it was a man in torture, suppressing grunts. Kidan descended the stairs, following the sound to a room she'd explored and dismissed because it featured nothing but draped furniture pushed aside. What distinguished it was that it branched out from the main house, and it had a domed glass ceiling. Kidan guessed it served as an observatory.

At this hour, the moon was at its highest point, washing the entire space in a deep ocean glow.

A shadowed figure was on its knees. Susenyos, bare chested, mouth agape in a silent scream. He stared at the night stars with fogged pupils. Kidan stepped forward, eyes widening.

What the hell...

"No." Etete appeared out of nowhere, making Kidan flinch. "Don't go in there."

Kidan clutched at her pounding heart. The woman hurried to drape Susenyos with the blanket she'd brought and helped him to the hallway.

"I'll get some water," she said, and disappeared around the corner.

Sweat dotted Susenyos's forehead, and his shoulders shook as he checked his watch. When he realized Kidan was there, he went still. His eyes returned to themselves, burning like night fire.

"Did you come into the room?" he demanded.

She crossed her arms, still confused about what was happening. "What if I did?"

Susenyos moved toward her, the blanket dropping from his muscled shoulders. He placed his hands on either side of her head, trapping her. Kidan's chest rose and fell in sync with Susenyos's labored breathing.

"My bloodlust is uncontrollable in that room. If I find you in there"—he leaned into her neck and inhaled deeply, making her stiffen—"you will die."

His scent was too sharp, summer rain and wet earth. Moonlight rippled across his contracting dark muscles, the power in them vast and threatening. Kidan grew aware of her vulnerability, her body's softness. What chance did June have? June, who cried when a spider was killed. Kidan's fingers danced in a pathetic rhythm. Susenyos glanced down and stepped back, satisfied he'd scared her.

She was just preparing to snap at him when...June materialized, honeyed eyes creased in a smile, standing behind him.

The ground fell away.

"June?" she squeaked.

Her sister's image faded like a candle blown out.

Susenyos's smirk was slow, knowing. "I assume it's beginning."

Kidan shook her head. What was going on with her?

"You can't stay in this house without paying the price."

"What price?" she bit.

His laughter rumbled low in his throat. "You'll see."

Kidan stormed away from him, roaming the hallway, searching for what, exactly, she didn't know until...June's ghost was there again, speaking without sound, ignoring the shadowy figure behind her back.

Kidan squeezed her eyes shut. This was just that same nightmare. Kidan always behind a window, pounding furiously, her warnings fading into inaudibility, a vampire reaching for June's neck, brushing blood on her lips with his thumb, burying his head in her exposed neck.

"*Kidan!*" June screamed.

Kidan whirled around, heart jackhammering against her rib cage, in her throat. She slapped herself in the face, two quick raps to make sure she was awake.

"Kidan? Hurry!" June shouted once again, loud and clear. Kidan nearly faceplanted in the darkness of the hall, running from wall to wall. But it was as if her sister was imprisoned behind the plaster, and if Kidan could just claw through, she'd find her.

"June!" Kidan's yell echoed loudly.

"*Kidan. You never want to do these videos with me.*"

Kidan slowed. She knew this recording, had deleted it from June's videos. She never wanted to hear it again—so how was it playing clearly in this hall?

"*My sister doesn't like cameras. Anyway, where was I? Right. My parasomnia has gotten worse.*

"*I haven't told anyone except my sister, but I think there's someone following me. For the first few weeks I thought I was imagining it, because they kept disappearing whenever I checked. But one of my friends noticed it too, and ever since then, I can't concentrate on anything. I see that shadow everywhere.*"

The fear in her voice broke Kidan apart, and she clamped her hands over her ears.

"Stop!"

"*You have to take your medicine,*" Kidan said.

"*You don't believe me.*"

"*Of course I do. But you've been seeing things all your life, June. How do you know if this is . . .*"

"*Real?*"

Silence.

"*I know what I saw,*" June said, angry.

"*We're safe, June. I promise you that. Just please take these.*"

A rattle of pills being exchanged.

The sound rolled down the walls and echoed in the lamps, turning them erratic.

"*Stop,*" Kidan managed weakly as she sank to her knees. She couldn't bear to hear this.

Footsteps echoed closer to her. The shadowy shape had come to take her too. A frowning boy squatted before her. Ice shot through her when she remembered who it was.

Susenyos cocked his head, checking his watch. "Barely a minute."

She hid her face from him. "What are you doing?"

He brushed her braids away, lifting her chin to delight in her pain. "It seems I was worried for nothing. You are not strong enough to master this house."

She slapped his hand away, focusing on his face, her gaze darting from his eyebrow to the middle of his forehead and then to his chin and back—again and again. In a chaos of triangles. Anger repressed the fear.

"Leave Uxlay," he warned. "Or this will only be the beginning."

He walked away, stealing the anger from her, and leaving only thick air. Kidan drowned. Time grew endless, the silence ate away at her flesh, and the world, already bleak, darkened entirely.

This loneliness was so potent, so violent, that she clawed at her beating heart for a moment of reprieve. She had to end it now. Her bracelet, her pill. A soft hiss escaped from the charm as the clasp broke.

Warm hands and soft skin found her, and Kidan felt herself being dragged, led upstairs, settled on her comfortable bed. For a moment, she thought it was Mama Anoet, and she wanted to weep. Her room cleared her thoughts like a wet rag.

Etete returned with a plate of wheat bread. "Eat. You'll feel better."

Kidan chewed the soft crust and whispered, "What's happening to me?"

Etete's tone was heavy. "The house is echoing your mind."

Dean Faris had mentioned something similar, but this? This was far from what she'd imagined.

"Does it affect you as well?" Kidan's voice became haunted.

"Yes. But you two have suffered great loss, and so the house weighs on you more heavily. It returns whatever you feel. Different rooms represent different emotions. It'll get better."

Kidan thought of the observatory, the coldness leaking from it. Susenyos on his knees, in agony even though he was alone.

"Does he go in there often?"

Etete's mouth thinned. "I told him to let me know before he does. One day, I fear I'll be too late. So I'll give you the same advice. Never stay in the hallways for long."

"Hallways?"

"Yes, they hold your pain now."

Kidan would rather climb out her window than do that again. Her brows met. "But why does he go in there?"

"To be a master of a house, there are many steps you must go through. The first is to conquer all parts of your mind."

Her eyes widened slowly. Dean Faris had conveniently left this information out. Probably because she'd gathered Kidan would never have entered this place if she'd known. Kidan's worst enemy was her mind. How was she meant to survive this?

"What's the second step?"

"I believe the house shares its body with you, grants you some of its strength. I'm afraid I don't know details. Only Professor Andreyas knows the true art of it." Etete's voice carried grief then. "Susenyos has worked for years to change the present law."

"What is the house law?" she asked suddenly, remembering Dean Faris's instruction.

"I'm afraid I don't know. Only potential heirs can read it."

If Susenyos was putting himself through hell to master this house, it had to be pretty important.

The law will be hidden in the room you least want to visit.

Skewering her mouth, she stared at the rippling hallway.

"Can you help me? In case it gets too much? I need to find out the law."

Etete's eyes creased, a tone of defeat in her words. "I will. Just like I helped your mother."

Kidan's head jerked up. The portrait of her mother flashed before her. High forehead, sharp eyes, and hair like June, soft in texture and curling at the end. A resigned, careful look leveled at every observer as if she had walked through life with undeniable purpose. A cold wave of numbness spread through the room.

Kidan averted her gaze from the kind woman. A part of her wanted to ask more, but what point was there in that? Her mother was dead. And knowing if she was a gentle singer like June, horrible at cooking, or good with her hands like Kidan would only make the loss more potent. Her chest already ached enough.

She tightened her jaw and cleared the image. Refocused. This house law, whatever the hell it was, held Susenyos's secrets. Perhaps it even held June.

13.

FOUR MINUTES. THAT WAS HOW LONG KIDAN COULD BEAR THE HALL-ways and her demons before she needed rescuing. She tried for three miserable days, and all she could manage were those embarrassing few minutes.

"It takes more time for some than others," Etete would say, bringing water to Kidan's parched lips. "Be patient."

Frustration gnawed at her. Susenyos knew what the law was, and he was actively trying to change it. Kidan needed to know it too.

With her bruised mind, sleep was the only thing that brought relief. Escape from June and her warm eyes that turned into flinty stones. Accusing, punishing. Kidan slept deeply, escaping into the dark.

Only this morning, her ears were ice-cold. She drew her blankets up, still in the realm of sleep, but the wind found her ankles next. She tucked her legs in, but just as she settled into warmth again, a bird cawed close by. She groaned. She must have left her window open. She tried to open her eyes, but it was unbearably bright, like she'd been slid under a magnifying glass and fluorescent light. She eased her eyes to the light, propping herself up. Trees swayed to the morning wind, all around, under the blue sky. A dream, she thought. Then her hands rested against something resembling a dragon's hide. She took note of her position, her body sitting at an odd forward angle, before she slid, slowly at first, then with an abrupt jerk. Her stomach plummeted, and she screamed, before coming to a sudden stop.

Her socked feet plunged into chilled water, and she dug her fingers into the dragon-hide tiles, trying to break her fall. The gutter had stopped her, and the collected rain seeped into her. There was also something slimy, which she refused to think of, brushing against her ankle.

Kidan, along with her blanket, was on the roof.

The roof.

"Help!" she called, but it was too soft. Her heart was beating inside her throat.

How had Susenyos managed to do all this without waking her? She would never sleep again.

She braced herself and called out louder, "Help! Someone, please!"

Kidan dared a glance down and saw her books and clothes scattered all over the front yard. She would be livid if she weren't so terrified.

Then a miracle happened. A girl wearing a checkered dress and cream-white sweater stumbled onto the path. She had some of Kidan's things gathered in her hands, and it seemed she had followed the trail here.

Her curly-haired head tilted upward. "I know the stars are lovely at night, but aren't you cold up there?"

It drew Kidan in slowly, the innocent lilt to the girl's voice. She squeezed her eyes shut, trying to dislodge it from her mind. It was easier in her apartment, to cut off the world and avoid the temptation to rescue pretty, helpless things. Through her window, morning and afternoon, she'd track her neighbors, skin itching, wondering if they'd make it home safe to their families. If they were late even by an hour, Kidan tortured herself imagining a shadowy figure feasting on them, that she'd let it happen again.

In every defenseless human, she saw *her.* June. Shy smile and honeyed eyes, trusting nature. And the painful urge to protect rose like a violent tide, devoid of reason. Like now.

Kidan searched for a way that wouldn't lead her to the girl, but she could see none.

"Check the shed for a ladder," Kidan managed. "Hurry."

The girl spotted the garden shed. She disappeared and returned with a ladder. It took Kidan a great deal of effort to remove her leg from the gutters and find the top step. Once she had the comfort of the solid steel under her, she breathed and climbed down.

Kidan gathered her things into her bag, eyes on the ground, ears warming.

"I'm Ramyn, by the way. Your tour guide? We were supposed to meet an hour ago."

Kidan shut her eyes. Of course she'd forgotten. "Right, sorry."

The girl hesitated. "It's okay. I'm not really supposed to be here. If you didn't mention seeing me, that would be great. My family lives close by. I just come here to watch the...house sometimes."

That gave Kidan pause. She faced her fully, taking in her large eyes and light brown skin, the glittering septum piercing shaped like a flower. How odd. Watching houses was for those uninvited, unwanted, and Kidan wanted to know why Ramyn watched. But she forced herself to turn her back, breaking the spell.

"Do you want a raspberry candy?" Ramyn's lips were already slightly pink from the sweet.

"No, thanks, Ramyn. Can we do this tomorrow?"

Ramyn was not really listening. In fact, she seemed in a world of her own, walking toward the front door.

"Why are you sleeping on the roof?"

"I wasn't sleeping there by choice." Kidan gritted her teeth. "My house dranaic did this."

Ramyn's eyes widened. "Is...is he here?"

"Who? Susenyos?"

"Yes." Ramyn swallowed, and Kidan tensed.

"Do you know him?"

"Only by name." Ramyn chuckled, but it was an odd sound. Her thick, expressive brows shot upward. "But if you're Kidan Adane..., where have you been this whole time?"

"I grew up...somewhere else, in another town."

"And your house dranaic doesn't want you?" Ramyn's voice strained. "Why?"

"Who cares? They're all vile."

She gaped. "How can you speak about them like that? Aren't you trying to be his companion?"

Kidan was having a hard time answering her questions. She was studying the girl's pinched expression. Ramyn rambled on, now a nervous ball of energy.

"It's silly, isn't it? All these years, waiting until we're older to meet them at the Introductory Dinner, and when we finally do, it's...not what we expect. What I'm trying to say is, it's important to make a good impression, you know? You'll be working with them, well, for a long time if you're lucky."

Kidan saw her opportunity. Ramyn was distracted, gnawing on her bottom lip.

"Thank you for helping. I need to go."

Kidan hurried into the house and closed the door. She parted the curtains carefully to watch the girl. Ramyn frowned, then walked off by herself, her nose ring twinkling in the pocket of sun that seemed to appear over her head.

Susenyos strolled by then, shirt opened at the collar, same book in hand as the day they met. *Ebid Fiker*—that was the book's title. It was Amharic, but she still made note of it.

"Ah, there you are. I thought I heard rats on the roof. Someone should really clean out those gutters."

"I could have died," she said, seething.

"A touch dramatic. You would have fractured a bone at best. But death by falling is such an uninspired end for you."

His eyes darkened at those words, sliding to her exposed throat. Kidan's nightshirt was loose, its neck cut wide. Disgust pulsed through Kidan.

"Stay away from Etete," he warned, making her eyes crease.

"Why? Afraid I'll discover the law?"

"Great and worthy heirs and heiresses are able to read a written law the first moment they enter the house. Reading a law is the easiest part of this process." His cruel grin stretched. "Yet here you are, unable to. Why should I be afraid?"

Kidan's eyes fell a little before her jaw hardened. "I must be getting close, though. Why else stoop to a childish prank?"

He raised an eyebrow, his expression brightening. "You're judging my attacks now? Perhaps I should get more inventive."

She lifted her gathered things higher to cover her neck and tracked wet marks to the stairs, her socks squelching.

After she touched the first step, she paused, voice colder than ice. "You will bring down my things by the time I leave the shower, or you'll be the one sleeping outside."

"Is that a command?" Susenyos spoke very carefully, and it occurred to her that he was managing himself as well.

She faced him. "Yes. I like the laws of this place. And the law says a dranaic that physically hurts a human will suffer great consequences—"

"Wait, I did not touch you—"

Kidan slammed her head into the stairway wall. Sparks danced in her vision, but she fought through it, wanting to capture his shock in every frame of her mind—and God, was it delicious.

She would have a bruise clear as day tomorrow, but finally the vampire understood who he was dealing with. Kidan walked away, blood trickling down her forehead but smiling nonetheless. When she reached the top of the stairs, she snuck one more triumphant glance, but the sight chilled her to the bone.

Susenyos Sagad crouched low, touching the few drops of her blood and bringing them close to his lips. Their eyes locked, hers wide with horror, his eclipsed by hunger.

"You bleed red, little bird. I'd think it was black with that hatred of yours."

Kidan rushed to her room, locked the door, and breathed against it. She traced along her forehead and winced. The cut was deeper than she had intended, the blood running down her fingers.

Slow footsteps echoed closer, making her body seize. He didn't open her door, but his shadow flickered under the slit. Her heart pumped painfully.

He shuffled, and a solid black line stretched on her floor. Was he...sitting out there? A cap twisted, and the sound of drinking traveled.

His voice was rough and angry. "You're making the whole house reek. You need to stop bleeding."

She gritted her teeth. "Sure, I'll get right on that."

This time, the voice was quieter, almost a breath. "Hurry."

"House Ajtaf and House Adane, older than all, one
was the hand of tradition; the other, legacy. House
Ajtaf took wood and stone and built their way from
mud huts to flat-roofed houses to buildings that
tore into skyscrapers, onward to the future. House
Adane took its elders, gathered them around a fire,
listened and carved history, dug at the earth, and
burrowed into the past.

One built itself a golden throne; the other buried
itself in caves. They are the Gold House and the
Dirt House."

—*History of the Acti Houses*
By Yohannes Afera

The Gold House bastards never concerned themselves
with us, but for the past few years they've wanted to
play in the dirt. Ajtaf House wants to buy our Axum
Archaeological Project, begun many years ago to discover
the Last Sage's old settlement. Your parents have refused
to sell; so have I. It is the only thing we're in complete
agreement on. Ajtaf House will continue to pressure you,
but do not be swayed.

14.

KIDAN HAD A STALKER. SHE WHIRLED AROUND FOR THE SECOND TIME that day as she walked on campus, finding a dark-haired boy in black clothes standing by the trees, watching her. Her scalp prickled with the possibilities—he could be the messenger who had brought Aunt Silia's journal, he could know about June, he could be a reporter. He disappeared into the morning crowd of shuffling students before she could find out.

She shook her head, probably being paranoid. Not for the first time, she fiddled with the bronze pin on her sleeve. House Adane's sigil was two mountains eclipsing each other. Kidan guessed it was an homage to their archaeological past. She wanted to take it off, avoid anything linking her to *him*, but Dean Faris had said it was mandatory. Bronze pins for new initiates, silver for those who graduate Drànacti, and gold for those who've mastered their houses.

All students and vampires of Uxlay displayed their house sigils with a pin either worn on the sleeve or secured to the chest. Kidan found herself tracking students' arms or shirts, playing a game of matching who belonged to who, learning the symbols.

"Adane! Help up here!"

Ramyn's black, low-heeled shoes dangled from a high tree branch. Her red plaid skirt was paired with a simple white shirt, and her stockings were torn. A pastel bag with a *Save the Wild Foxes* badge remained under the tree.

Kidan whispered under her breath. "You've got to be fucking kidding me."

She considered walking away and alerting someone else, but the seeming impossibility of finding Ramyn in a similar situation as hers rooted her to the spot.

Kidan rubbed her temple. "What happened?"

Ramyn laughed nervously. "You know how I told you a dranaic and an acti should have a good relationship? I told my house dranaic about what happened to you, you know, as a joke to break the ice, because she doesn't like me very much. I said at least she didn't put *me* on the roof, because I'm terrified of heights. Then she invited me for a walk and...she put me up here."

The creature inside Kidan's belly extended its claws in fury.

"Are you going to report this?" Kidan asked.

"No, no, it's fine."

"Why not?"

"I don't want to cause trouble." Ramyn looked down and quickly fixed her gaze straight ahead.

Kidan had many questions. The most obvious was why were the humans afraid of the dranaics if the dean preached so much about peace.

"There's no ladder, Ramyn. You'll have to get down without one."

Ramyn shook her head firmly. "That's okay. I'll just stay here."

"I'll coach you through it. I'm not leaving until you get down."

Ramyn didn't move. Kidan remembered what she used to do with June whenever she was afraid. A game of finding something worse to take the fear away. Kidan studied the stack of books spilling out of the pastel bag.

"Look, Ramyn, today is my first day for Introduction to Dranacti and I can't be late. I'm sure you don't want to be either."

Ramyn's eyes swept downward to the books.

"So let's go, okay? Before we fail for being late."

Reluctantly, Ramyn agreed. They took it slow. Finding her footing on the bark proved hard, so Kidan instructed her to take her shoes off. With her ribbed stockings serving as extra grip, Ramyn scaled down, blowing curly hair out of her face when she finally reached grass.

"Thank you. Thank you." She hugged the ground.

Kidan shook her head in amusement and helped her up.

"What happened to your face?" Ramyn frowned, worry filling her eyes.

"Oh." Kidan touched her forehead. It had hurt but did what it was supposed to do. Susenyos had barely glanced her way since then. "I hurt myself forcing open a stuck door."

They entered the sprawling courtyard, and Kidan stretched her neck, taking in the old buildings.

"I guess I could give you a tour on the way," Ramyn said.

"There's no need."

The girl dimmed. "But I practiced."

Kidan stifled a sigh. "Fine."

Ramyn beamed, fishing out something from her bag. "Also, here. Your full schedule and course list."

Kidan took the paper.

Uxlay University

Semester 1
Student: Kidan Adane
House: House Adane, Department of Archaeology and History

Course List
East Africa and the Undead, _School of History_
Introduction to Dranacti, _School of Philosophy_
Mythology and Modernity, _School of Philosophy_

Texts Required
Migration: A Dranaic History by Nardos Tesfa
Introduction to Dranacti by Demasus and the Last Sage
Black Gods and Their Children by Wesfin Alama

"There are many departments in Uxlay but the Department of Arts has four branches. The School of Art, School of History, School of Languages and Linguistics, and School of Philosophy. Together, they form the Arat Towers," Ramyn explained, stopping in the middle of the grassy court.

She pointed to the towers boxing the lush field, each located at one corner of the huge square.

"They were designed to indicate time and schedule. For decades, Uxlay's art students followed Resar's education circle. When the sun faced the first tower, of the School of Languages and Linguistics, students filed into the building for its teachings. They would be there until the School of History's tower lit up, and then they'd move on to the next ones in turn. Resar said philosophy had to be held at dusk—only after the mind was supplied with the appropriate sustenance of art, literature, divination, and history could it engage in insightful discussions."

If Kidan squinted just right, she could fool herself into thinking she was attending a normal place of education, with normal human beings.

But her first glimpse of the dranaics on campus snuffed out that hope. They emerged in groups from the Southern Sost Buildings, which were identifiable by their black iron gates and spine-curling spikes. Dean Faris had made it very clear humans were prohibited from those three buildings without invitation, and trespassing there was cause for expulsion.

One of the vampires Kidan instantly recognized from her first day. She was still dressed like a gentleman of high society, strikingly beautiful. Her name was . . . Iniko. One of Susenyos's friends. The dranaic slid Kidan a deathly gaze.

Kidan matched it with her own hard stare, wishing she had a weapon. Her skin itched with how powerless she felt. She thought about the Last Sage's Three Binds keeping the vampires in check. Her lips twisted upward. *They* were also powerless. Fairy tales and myths had always been more June's thing, though, which was why Kidan made her that three-pointed charm. Her stomach tightened. She had to get that bracelet back.

Iniko flashed her teeth at them. At Ramyn, to be exact.

"Do you know her?" Kidan asked.

Ramyn averted her gaze. "She's one of my house dranaics. She's the one who put me up the tree."

"You could have been seriously injured."

"It was my fault anyway," Ramyn said, walking fast toward the School of Philosophy. Kidan followed. In certain moments, Ramyn seemed so much like June, weak and waiting to be taken. Kidan clenched her jaw. The humans of this place were surrounded by wolves.

The School of Philosophy glinted in the afternoon haze as students climbed its stairs. Kidan shared the elevator with nervous students, then kept her distance from them until they reached Room 31. Ramyn disappeared when she got called over by some smiling girls, leaving Kidan to enter alone.

The classroom was as dead as an old photograph. It featured seven windows with glass drenched in sepia tint, all dimmed as if they were in mourning. At least forty desks and chairs were placed in concentric circles, and in the middle of it all waited a funeral of a man.

The only indication of life on Professor Andreyas was his cornrowed hair. Four thick lines falling neatly across his scalp before reaching his mid-back, fastened by a black clasp. Hair implied growth, some humanness. Yet, as he surveyed the students with a quiet regality only found in ancient paintings, Kidan retracted that thought. Humanness had no place in this room.

"I see many of you did not take my advice to pursue other subjects." Displeasure fit itself well around his voice.

All the chairs were occupied, and all their occupants shifted and squirmed.

Kidan wanted to disappear into the back, but it was already taken. The high windows and their muted brown color minimized the effect of the sun, making the desks cold to the touch.

Kidan studied her book. Dranacti. It was a combination of two words—"dranaic," meaning "vampires," and "acti," meaning "humans."

"A few rules," the professor said. "Dranacti does not follow traditional teaching, schedules, or grading systems. The schedules and times of our classes will vary depending on the events of the day. Each of you is allowed two absences based on medical exemption or some other nonmedical life-threatening circumstance. More than those absences will mean instant dismissal."

No one objected. Kidan lifted her pencil to a straight angle, piercing her notebook. She'd thought she'd last longer, but the command of authority and the meekness of her cohort made her skin hot. She was meant to suffer through this for a whole semester?

"At the back of the room, you will find phone numbers for counseling and psychological services. I implore you to use them. The loss of life that can be preventable should be prevented, lest it impede on all our futures."

Kidan skewed her mouth. Even their good intentions eventually served their own purposes.

The professor continued. "Introduction to Dranacti offers the theory and groundwork for the coexistence between dranaics and actis. It was written by Demasus and the Last Sage during the ancient civilization of Axum. One of you will graduate this course. At the companionship ceremony, you will choose no more than two dranaics, if they'll have you, and be eligible to study Mastering a House Law next year to finalize your induction into Uxlay society."

"I'm sorry, sir," a voice said. "I think I heard you wrong. Did you say only one of us will graduate Dranacti?"

It was a soft-faced boy with freckles, who appeared to be the youngest here. Did he belong to any of the houses Aunt Silia mentioned? Kidan needed to befriend some students if she wanted to find out more about Susenyos. But she lacked the patience for surface-level conversations that made strangers feel at ease. She jumped straight into interrogations and made people uncomfortable. That was her specialty.

"The university forbids me to fail all of you. At least one of you must pass so the program can continue."

The student swallowed, looking to his friend in apprehension.

"Do not view one another as competition. Dranacti is written in a difficult language, one you must take care to translate. You will need to form study groups that compensate for what you lack." He swiped chalk from the board. "Now, moral theory found in Dranacti can be sectioned into three parts. If one of you knows what they are, grace us with the knowledge."

A sound came from the back, a soft but horribly flat voice.

"Relativism, Quadrantism, and Concordium."

Kidan turned to find the girl, but there were three circles, and she could only glimpse a large jacket.

"In Aarac, if you can," the professor said.

The same girl answered. "Sophene, Arat, and Koraq."

His eyes sharpened with interest. "Sophene, Arat, and Koraq. Nicknamed the three poisons. One of these subjects will become incomprehensible to you during our study. When that happens, you will be dismissed."

He walked to the curved walls and wrote the three topics to be studied.

"Some relief, or perhaps a stress point, is that I do not test by the written word. Your understanding is measured by informal questions, formal discussions, and private tests. You will defend, recommend, and challenge one another's ideas in these meetings. Silence is death during these circles—do your best to avoid it. I'd encourage you to read to broaden your minds, but if you are not already aware of that basic requirement, I'm tempted to watch how deep a hole you dig for yourselves." The professor observed them, a hawk in front of prey. "Shall we begin?"

Kidan could hear her own breathing in the absoluteness of the silence.

"Here is your first task, actis." He sat on the edge of his desk, his mahogany skin bronzed by the window light. "Each of you knows why you want to pass this course. I'm not speaking about your family and the pressures of legacy but yourself, personally—what do you want to achieve? Write it on a piece of paper. Articulate it to one word, no need for exhausting sentences."

A flock of papers took flight as students rushed to complete the task. Kidan didn't lift her pen. She had no word to encompass her reason for being here. At least not personally. June was always the answer. What did she want to achieve from a course about humans' and vampires' coexistence? How to kill them would be nice to know. She guessed that was her answer. Murder. Revenge. Fire. All leading to death. She had no future anyway, so she wrote nothing.

The professor asked them to write their names and collected the words. He then partnered the students based on the answers. Kidan's chest pinched. Would she be without a partner?

"Kidan Adane and Ramyn Ajtaf," Professor Andreyas announced.

Kidan became alert, watching the familiar girl in the red plaid skirt and white shirt walk toward her as everyone settled alongside their partners.

Ajtaf.

Gold House. One of the houses Aunt Silia warned against.

"Hi, again." Her voice rang shy.

Kidan regarded her carefully. "Hi."

"You wrote nothing too?" Ramyn whispered, and when Kidan nodded, a tinge of sadness touched her voice. "Join the club."

Kidan's brows creased with questions. She peered at Ramyn's vintage watch. The band featured a pin she hadn't noticed before: a thin golden tower. House Ajtaf's sigil.

"For Relativism, you will be working with your partner. You cannot pass without each other—and no, you cannot change partners," the professor instructed. "I'll give you a moment to introduce yourselves."

Kidan's mind blanked. How did normal people deal with these situations?

Small talk, she supposed. *Are you excited for the year? What's your favorite color? What the hell are you doing studying a course that permanently ties you to vampires?* Probably not the last one.

Ramyn studied her, almost amused, waiting for Kidan to speak.

Oh, fuck it. There was only one thing she wanted to ask.

"What do you know about Susenyos Sagad?"

Ramyn's face dimmed at once.

"Everyone knows him." She tucked a curl behind her ear.

Kidan lowered her voice. "I heard he does something awful to girls."

Ramyn's large eyes widened. "Who told you that?"

"Just . . . rumors."

"Well, they're not true," she said quickly, looking around as if to make sure no one heard.

Ramyn shifted, exposing her collarbone. A dotted red bite mark marred her brown skin.

Kidan tensed. "Are you okay?"

"What?" Ramyn followed her gaze and adjusted her clothes, covering her goose bumps. "Yeah. I'm fine."

Kidan remembered the blindfolded girls and bitten shoulders. Cold sweat broke out along her back.

Her voice dipped to the depths of hell. "Did Susenyos do that to you?"

Ramyn stiffened, then a flicker of anger crossed her eyes. "He hasn't done anything to me, and you shouldn't believe everything you hear."

Her fingers trembled as she reached for her book. Warning bells rang even louder. Without thinking, Kidan reached out a hand to calm Ramyn's nerves. An icy cold shocked her at contact.

"You should wear something warmer," Kidan said, gesturing to her outfit.

"Yeah." Ramyn sniffed. "I always forget."

They settled into an odd quiet, neither knowing how to move on to the discussion they should be having. Were Ramyn and Susenyos connected somehow?

Ajtaf House had more than two hundred dranaics, according to Aunt Silia's journal. It brought up a niggling question that had been in the back of Kidan's mind. What had happened to the house dranaics sired to House Adane? Why was Susenyos Sagad the only one left?

Before she could ask more, Professor Andreyas called attention back to himself.

"Let's begin with a primary question. Is morality influenced or innate?"

Not a single hand rose.

"If you show courage, I might refrain from dismissing you all in the first class." His tone of condescension made her skin prickle. "No one? What little thoughts you must have."

Ramyn shrank when the professor's ancient eyes rested on her. Before she knew it, Kidan was speaking, her attention fixed on her desk.

"Humans are a product of influence. We are at the mercy of our family and those we've loved and lost. The world decides what we become without their control. So, influenced."

His shadow climbed on her desk. "That makes you no different from an animal."

She lifted her head, met those unmoving orbs, hatred boiling from the proximity. "An animal kills and feels no remorse, no loathing," she said. "The only human morality there is, is reflection and regret."

"Interesting hypothesis. What are your sources?"

Kidan's gaze dropped slightly. She didn't have any.

"Thoughts if not dissected and proved are meaningless. Find those that can support your ideas before you voice them."

The sting of his response mounted with each second. After a moment, the same monotone girl from earlier spoke. "I agree as well. Influenced."

"Source?" The professor lifted his chin.

"The first law trial of Ojiran."

"Interesting time period. Go on."

"Ojiran was imprisoned after being accused of seducing his friend's wife and murdering her. Before he died, he left his friend a poem."

"Do you know the poem?"

"I do."

The girl had a colorless speech pattern, no intonation or rhythm. A sort of tone that shouldn't be allowed to bring a book to life, let alone a poem. Kidan's gaze was carried to the trees outside, yet she didn't make it far. Her attention snapped back with the first crack of the verse.

"If the source of all hate is this eye, blind me. But if it still lingers, take my second. If it still speaks, cut my tongue. If it still writhes, unhinge my bones. If it still lives, then look at your hands. If it's in your skin, not mine, in your very soul, then purge yourself. Purge yourself, my friend. And hope you can join us in the clouds."

The words fell with tremendous impact. For the briefest of moments, the voice slipped into a different cadence. It turned haunting, shaking, and alive, as if the speaker was pleading the case herself.

"Driven with doubt over sending Ojiran to his death, the friend went mad with never knowing the truth about who seduced and killed his wife. He became known as the Hand of Infidelity, pursuing and ridding the world of harlots and adulterers. As such, his sense of morality was very much influenced by the letter left for him."

The lead of Kidan's pencil broke into small chunks. She snuck a glance over her shoulder, ever so slowly, eyes tracing along the floor. The girl's shoes were black-laced combat boots. Kidan outlined their shape, imagining the hard ridges of their bottoms pressing like the rubble of a road.

At least this girl didn't appear to be fragile. Fragility was a sickness to Kidan. It infected her from within, driving her wild until she could find a way to cure it.

A pen bounced near the boots, sending an unusually loud ringing to her ears. Kidan glimpsed something else and already committed it to memory—fingerless gloves, graceful hands.

"Who's she?" Kidan whispered to Ramyn.

"Oh, that's Slen."

Slen. Even her name cut across the tongue, and Kidan had the urge to touch her lips, sure she would find blood there. Or maybe it was her words, the poem.

"Her family are the Qaros," Ramyn was saying. "They own the music conservatory."

Qaros. Another important family her aunt warned about.

Kidan lowered her voice, eyes going to Ramyn's bruised shoulder. She needed more answers. "Meet me tomorrow at the East Corner Coffee for our project? Around noon?"

Ramyn appeared uncertain before nodding. When Professor Andreyas concluded the lesson with the first assignment, on the Scales of Sovane, Ramyn was the first out the door. As if she couldn't wait to get away from Kidan.

Kidan exhaled. Her social skills were rusty. But spending an entire year talking only to furniture would do that.

She busied herself with a new plan. Form a study group with Ramyn Ajtaf and Slen Qaros, and hope to uncover how their houses were involved in the decline of hers. And more importantly, why? Was it jealousy, revenge, or a grab for wealth? What wealth did House Adane even possess to garner such hatred?

Aunt Silia would probably advise her to stay clear of them all. Stay alive. If these established houses discovered she was sniffing around, it wouldn't be difficult to make sure House Adane went extinct for good. Kidan released a slow breath. All she had to do was keep some students close, try for a smile instead of a grimace, work on her tone. A groan slipped out of her.

If they didn't kill her for whatever agenda they held, they surely would for her lovely personality.

"House Qaros, the wool makers, the humble shepherds who warmed the other houses with blankets. A family of farmers who knew the land like the backs of their hands, they tilled and toiled to battle Uxlay's hunger. They are the Farm House."

—History of the Acti Houses
By Yohannes Afera

House Qaros has climbed the rank of the families faster than anyone in the past ten years. For generations they ranked at the bottom, but recently switched their businesses to music, broke partnerships with lower houses, and are climbing slowly to the top. They're ambitious, and ambition is dangerous.

The rats of House Qaros steal. They're known for poaching dranaics from the other houses. Ten of our own dranaics defected to House Qaros over the past few years. Watch for them carefully. Their very blood is disloyal.

15.

RAMYN AJTAF RESCHEDULED THEIR MEETING TO BE IN THE GRAND Solomon Library. Kidan arrived early, glad to be far away from that haunting house and Susenyos. Every time she laid eyes on him, all sense abandoned her, the desire to attack him almost maddening. From the way he clenched his jaw and avoided her, she thought he must feel the same.

The library reminded Kidan of a tunnel, a very rich and self-important one. Instead of cracked concrete, smooth gold flooring stretched out, so polished she could pick something from her teeth in its reflection. Instead of unpleasant smells, all scents were removed; not even ink or paper was allowed to disturb the complete absence of odor. Every book held its breath and tightened its lungs to fit in its leather bounds. Lastly, any good tunnel had rats. In Uxlay's Solomon Library, they appeared petrified and set in stone, statues of men and women wide-eyed in every corner. It was a beauty only the undead adored. In the middle of the library space, a three-tiered chandelier hovered over Uxlay's crest, which was etched onto the floor. A banner wrapped around the lions and twin blades read, *Seek mind above blood, and if you must bleed, use it as ink.*

Kidan pulled out a book titled *Weapons of the Dark: A Recounting of the Wars and Battles Fought Against the Dranaics* and learned of two things that killed vampires: silver that had been licked by a vampire's bloodied tongue, and the horn of an impala. The first one intrigued her. A vampire's blood on silver created some sort of chemical reaction and made it deadly. So if red-slicked silver hit a vital artery, the dranaic would die. The second one, though, made her shiver. A horn was a reminder of a life that no longer existed. It was a memento, a treasure of a cruel act.

She settled on the stiff seats and flicked through *Migration: A Dranaic History*, by Nardos Tesfa.

RITES OF COMPANIONSHIP

A human acti's blood is poison until relinquished by themselves at the companionship ceremony. If a dranaic drinks from an uninitiated child or adult, they will harbor reddened eyes for three days, and must face the Law Courts. The companionship ceremony with its blood sharing is only held after an acti graduates Dranacti.

Kidan touched the veins at her wrist. Was her blood really poison? Until it was relinquished at least, whatever that meant. Instead of relief, fear thrummed through her. June's smiling eyes covered the page, then split wide with pain. Would she be tortured to relinquish her blood? Kidan scratched a triangle over the words, using the force to expel the image. Her jaw flexed. Rites and ceremonies. Their pretense at diplomacy grated on her nerves. She loathed anything that hid from what it was, unable to look itself in the mirror.

She skimmed through other headings: "West African Influence." "The First War of Dranaics." "Cossia Day."

In celebration of the concord achieved over years, the lawless Cossia Day was monumental in converting rogue dranaics to Uxlay's customs. Cossia Day serves as a commemoration of the nature of dranaics and the sacrifices they've taken on in the name of peace. Humans evacuate the grounds of Uxlay at midnight, and then all dranaics are free to engage in their anarchic activities.

Kidan read it two more times. Lawless Cossia Day. An entire event when the monsters were not held accountable for what they did. What had Susenyos done during the last Cossia Day? Had he left Uxlay to take June?

Kidan retrieved the public records of all the Cossia Days, which catalogued the vampires challenged, the championed, and the deceased. She gasped when her fingers tracked Susenyos's name toward the very end. During the last five years, Susenyos Sagad had killed almost all of House Adane's dranaics.

The sheer violence and calculation behind it made her fists clench. Every year, slowly, he eliminated anyone that threatened him. The rest of the year he acted perfect, within the laws, so much so that Dean Faris believed he was innocent of other crimes.

Her phone dinged, interrupting her thoughts. She rolled her neck and read the message from Ramyn. *Sorry. Have to cancel.*

Kidan pursed her lips. She needed to ask Ramyn about those bite marks.

On the way out, Kidan asked the librarian for one more book.

"Do you have a copy of a book called *Ebid Fiker?*" It was the book Susenyos Sagad always carried.

The librarian smiled kindly at Kidan's attempt at pronouncing Amharic. "You mean *The Mad Lovers.*"

Mad Lovers?

"Is there a translated copy?" Kidan asked.

The librarian nodded, walking down the long aisles. "It's very famous."

With the book secured, Kidan exited and found a deserted area with a small fountain. The water ran smoothly, free of leaves or gunk. Kidan could make out the shimmering art at the bottom of the pool. Her fingers played with her bracelet as she thought of her sister. June would enjoy pretty scenery like this. Then the rippling water slowly turned red, blood swallowing the tiled art beneath until it spilled over the edge. Kidan staggered back, chest constricting painfully. She blinked—and it was back to normal, clear water. Her fingers trembled, and she opened the clasp of her bracelet, touching the pill lightly.

I'll find you.

"Kidan, right?"

She jerked upright, knowing that voice immediately. A flat tone removed from the world, until it read poetry.

"Up here."

Slen Qaros had positioned herself on the top step of a wide stairway. Her black jacket reached her thighs, but it appeared fashionable, not odd. She held a cigarette between her fingers. Cinders sparked, fueled by the wind, and caught in the frame of Slen's pupils. Kidan blinked, and the wind carried away whatever light brightened the girl's black eyes.

Kidan climbed to where the sun shone, the heat warming her chilled legs. Her gaze traveled to Slen's bronze pin. She liked House Qaros's sigil—an intricate upside-down trophy cup with three musical instruments spilling from its mouth like ruffling gold.

"Everyone thought Adane House would go to Susenyos Sagad, then you showed up." There was no emotion in her tone, only fact.

Kidan tried to relax, glad for the natural lead into her question.

"Do you know him?"

"Not personally. All I know is he's killed all his fellow house dranaics during Cossia, at least the ones foolish enough to stay. That's why no other family will take him as their companion. Savage Susenyos always survives. That's what my father says, anyway."

Kidan slid her a glance. "I heard most of my surviving house dranaics joined yours."

Ten of House Adane's dranaics, to be exact.

Slen shrugged. "The more dranaics sworn to your house, the more power and sway you have on the politics of Uxlay, using them to vote toward your agendas and expand your business. It's not personal."

"I see."

Slen tilted her head. "You're taking East Africa and the Undead."

"I am."

"Is that what gave you your insight? *The only human morality there is, is reflection and regret.* Not many express Dranacti ideas like that."

"Yes," Kidan said, because it was easier to explain than firsthand murder.

"I see."

Kidan took a deep breath. "Maybe we could form a study group."

"I don't form groups with just anyone."

"The likelihood any of us will pass Dranacti is very low," Kidan said, switching tactics. "They say philosophy is underpinned by the four pillars—art, literature, divination, and history. I want to make a study group with those skills."

Slen thought it over. "Resar's education circle . . . interesting."

"I know Ramyn Ajtaf is focusing on literature. I'm sure she'll be willing to join. I can introduce you two."

"Everyone knows Ramyn." Slen's tone lingered with something Kidan couldn't identify.

"Okay, good. We need an art student as well. I know House Umil runs the School of Art here, so if you know someone from there, that would be great," Kidan said, thinking of her aunt's notes and the portrait Omar Umil did.

Slen sighed. "Unfortunately, I know one."

Good. This was all coming together.

"That leaves the hardest of all: divination," Slen continued. "You should recruit the Mot Zebeya I saw following you."

Kidan's neck prickled. "What? When?"

"Before class. He was hiding in the trees."

So, she did have a stalker. "What the hell is a Mot Zebeya?"

Slen raised an eyebrow. "You don't know what they are?"

"I was raised far from Uxlay . . . customs."

Slen considered this before explaining. "They're called Mot Zebeyas in Amharic. Loosely translated, it means 'the Guards of Death.' Their monastery is past the northeast gate, up in the mountains. They're taken there as infants and practice solitude, as the Last Sage did, to become keepers of all our laws."

Kidan glanced in the general direction, but she could only see the University Plaza. "Taken as infants?"

"Those born during the month of August from all households are usually chosen. It's not a desirable sacrifice the Acti Families want to make. The child is prohibited from knowing their family, status, or wealth—anything that could sway them from their faith."

Kidan's lips curled. "Why would anyone agree to give up their child?"

"Uxlay depends on them. Mot Zebeyas perform vampire transformations and companionship rituals. Their secluded upbringing acts as a check and balance. Since they have no affections or affiliations in Uxlay, everyone is their family."

Kidan soaked in the information. Slen Qaros was articulate and devoured knowledge. She would be helpful.

"He'd be a solid addition. They are intelligent and very rare, if unsociable. It would be a victory to recruit him."

"I'll do it," Kidan said reluctantly.

Why the hell was he watching her?

Slen regarded her carefully. "I also want one more thing—*Traditional Myths of Abyssi*. A rare book that'll help with translating the Dranacti principles. Last I heard, it's located in the collectors' section of Adane House's library."

Kidan nodded, keeping her voice light for the next part. It was important that Slen said yes so Kidan could investigate House Qaros.

"So, should we meet at your house for our session?"

Caution crowded Slen's words. "And why not meet at your house?"

Slen Qaros wasn't Ramyn Ajtaf. A different type of approach was required, one that made Slen see Kidan as a worthy challenge. Those flat eyes...They burned colder than blue flame. She held them with her own burning fire.

"Because if I'm forced to spend another second with Savage Susenyos, I might just kill him."

Kidan didn't inject any humor into the words, yet...no flicker of fear or worry crossed the Qaros girl's face. How interesting.

Slen tucked her gloved hands in her pockets and stood. "Tuesday, four p.m., at my house. Don't show up without the Mot Zebeya."

16.

KIDAN FOLLOWED THE MOT ZEBEYA BOY THROUGH THE CAMPUS
grounds. He stuck out like a sore thumb with his formfitting black clothes
and the pure white chain draped along his pocket. He walked with purpose,
winding through an area of little buildings, past a formidable gated enclosure
shrouded with dark, ominous clouds. Kidan paused to read the words branded
above a silver-maned lion holding a long sword—*Sicion Training Grounds*. Uxlay
had its own elite vampire army, but Kidan hadn't seen any of the Sicions yet.
She shuddered, hoping she never would, and continued on until a clearing
sparkled in the distance. It was a field featuring various tall stone structures.
Gravestones.

The boy bowed in the shadow of a stone angel, clearing something on
the ground. He was focused so intently that Kidan moved closer to him, then
stepped behind a monument, watching. He opened a holy book stained by
scented oil from a purple flower.

"It's rude to spy," he said softly.

Kidan's spine stiffened as his reflective eyes found her. "Why have you been
watching me?" she asked.

He was brown-skinned and tall, and he rattled as he came toward her. The
noise came from finger bones fashioned into a very long chain, beginning at his
belt and disappearing into his pants pocket. He had soft dark hair and wore a
black turtleneck and pants.

"I apologize," he said with utmost sincerity, indicating his finger bones. "I'd
like to give you a reading."

Kidan watched him warily. "With finger bones?"

"Bones have vitality, will. They're used in the study of Sageism and foretell who will die next."

A chill ran down her spine. "You think I'm going to die?"

His forehead creased. "Whenever I'm near you, they stir, clinking together. They don't usually respond so strongly."

Kidan took a cautious step back. What if he learned about her blue pill, or worse, her murder?

"I came here to ask you to be in our study group for Dranacti." Her voice tightened. "Not for a reading."

A gentle breeze rattled the bells from the nearest monument and swayed the curls away from his face. "Then I will join your group."

She lifted a brow. That was too easy. "Why?"

"All life must be protected, and if you're in danger, it's my duty to protect you."

"But you don't know me."

"Why does that matter?"

Kidan didn't know what to make of him. She didn't trust that anyone from this place did something out of the goodness of their heart.

The boy regarded her in the same manner, like she was a creature he couldn't decipher. She watched him gather his things, and they left the cemetery together.

She shot him a side glance. "I hear Mot Zebeya students are rare around Uxlay."

His lips carried the ghost of a smile, and his eyes slid to the northeast campus gate. Kidan was close enough now to see the thick trees crowding the campus border, as well as the mountains in the horizon. Was there really a monastery up there?

"Yes," he said after a while. "Most of us don't seek a dranaic companion."

"But you do?"

"When you spend a lot of time truly alone, you see how a dranaic's soul feels. Cold and quiet. Solitude teaches us that. Companionship is what I seek, because it's a brighter way to live."

Kidan knew the hunger of being alone. Every part of her had ached when her sister disappeared, leaving her in that apartment where day and night melded into one. Yet it was no excuse. She hated the Last Sage's weakness. He was gifted the power to erase all vampires from this world, yet he chose to settle alongside them. His lack of backbone birthed generations of believers who didn't know any better.

Kidan told the Mot Zebeya to meet at Qaros House and studied him walking away. Other students parted around him as if avoiding a ghostly creature. He was the only one here without any house sigil on him. His air of loneliness pulled at her core. She swallowed the feeling away with a touch of her bracelet.

She glanced at West Corner Tea at the edge of the small courtyard. Maybe she should grab some doughnuts. Across Sheba Square, she spotted Ramyn's familiar curls. Kidan's hand rose to wave, then froze. Susenyos appeared, exchanged quiet words with Ramyn, and guided her to one of the Southern Sost Buildings with a hand at her back. The very place Dean Faris told her was off-limits to actis.

Kidan's heart slowed, limbs going numb. She forced herself to put one foot after another, bolting to the door they'd disappeared into. She pulled on it, but it was locked.

"Ramyn!" she shouted, kicking against the iron door.

A large dranaic approached and hissed at Kidan to leave. She swallowed her rage, rounded a corner, and touched her forehead to the cool wall, trying to shake the image of Ramyn as June. She wasn't June.

Quickly, Kidan dialed Ramyn's number. No answer. She didn't want to frighten the girl, so she bit her lip and left a voice message, telling her to meet at Qaros House on Tuesday.

She retreated, only to spot Susenyos Sagad watching her from a high window. The corner of his lips tilted upward in an arrogant smile.

17.

EVERY NIGHT, KIDAN HEARD SUSENYOS'S LOW HOWLS OF PAIN AND Etete's soft footsteps hurrying to rescue him. She listened to their gentle conversation drifting up to her room from the lounge. The light trace of laughter and familiarity made her brows furrow. Etete would scold him like a mother, tell him not to push himself, instruct him to be kinder toward Kidan, and he would fall silent as if he listened. She didn't understand their bond.

She had this gnawing sensation that he was getting closer to changing the set law, and therefore closer to owning the house, giving him yet another advantage.

Not today. No matter how badly Kidan suffocated in her memories of June, no matter how tightly her throat constricted, she wouldn't leave without learning the law.

Kidan made sure Etete had left on an errand before approaching the hallway. She didn't want to be rescued. Her fingers drew squares against her thighs, but she forced herself to walk in. Dean Faris said this would be easy. Her bones shook and grated against one another as June's bloodied face appeared. A hand tore into her chest, squeezing and pulling, snapping the muscles free.

Why haven't you found me yet?

Kidan whirled around to the sound of her sister in the rippling dark. "I will."

Why did you kill me?

This voice wasn't June's. It was different, older, lashing on the sensitive flesh of her back like a whip.

You let me burn in that house. I should have known you were always like them.

The smell of burning flesh wrapped around her. Kidan threw up air, heaving until her throat tore inside. The nausea wouldn't stop, and her open room beckoned her to safety. If she just stepped across the threshold, her veins wouldn't bulge along her skin.

No.

She squeezed her eyes shut, forcing herself to stay.

Show me the house law. Show me the house law!

Over and over again, she screamed it inside her mind, splitting herself open.

Darkness closed over her vision. Her pulse skittered. This was it. She was going to die.

Blue flames began at the tips of her fingers, the sensitive pads peeling away in excruciating pain. Her mouth opened in a scream, but only black smoke engulfed it. Fire raced along her forearms like lightning, cracking and marking her flesh, and collided at her chest in blinding light. She pleaded for it to stop, but there was still so much of her skin left to burn. And this was going to be a slow, punishing death.

Kidan surrendered herself to it.

Let herself burn. Burn and burn.

Hours passed as she drifted in and out of consciousness. Then, when she was no more than a wilting breath, she whispered, *I'm heiress to House Adane. Show me the house law. Please.*

She could no longer feel her flesh, only relentless heat. Her hand rose before her, skinless, bone charred like white wood. Horror pulsed through her. It was too much. She had to escape, live—

Golden thread swirled and moved, forming itself into letters. She whimpered in relief and willed her weak knees not to crumble. To read. She needed to know the law her parents had set before they died. Her teeth cut into her lip from how hard she gritted them. The words imprinted themselves on the wall, seared into her mind.

IF SUSENYOS SAGAD ENDANGERS ADANE HOUSE, THE HOUSE SHALL
IN TURN STEAL SOMETHING OF EQUAL VALUE TO HIM.

She bolted to her room with desperate speed and collapsed inside with a gasp, falling unconscious where she lay. A fading smile touched her lips. She'd done it.

Kidan woke up on the floor with a headache, but she'd uncovered the law. Relief curled through her, all the way down to her toes, and she sent some gratitude up to her parents. If they set this law, they obviously didn't trust him. They were on her side. Susenyos was at a disadvantage. He couldn't harm House Adane. He couldn't harm her *or June.*

But...he had taken June. He'd broken the law, and perhaps he was being punished for it. She needed to know exactly how this law functioned.

Kidan grabbed her victim's confession tape from the bottom of her vanity, stomach tight. She copied it to her phone—password safe—and mulled her plan of attack. Discovering the house law was the best ace she could hope for.

Today, she'd confront him.

She had to push him into a confession without giving too much away. Her heart pounded as she descended the stairs with the recording.

Susenyos was in the lounge that doubled as a study, sitting on the couch with his favorite book.

Kidan's grip tightened on her phone. "If you tell me what you did to my sister, I'll leave. You can have everything. The house, the money, everything."

He regarded her with a bored expression. It was dangerous, this desperation of hers, and it only grew tenfold when she saw it had no effect on him.

"You sounded so much better unconscious."

He'd heard her

"Tell me," she pushed through clenched teeth.

"Accusing me of such a crime...Perhaps I should file a complaint to the Law Courts. We all know how actis enjoy placing blame for their own depraved actions on us." He cocked his head. "Perhaps *you* did something to June. I hear you apologizing a lot in the hallways."

Kidan was stunned momentarily. He settled further into the couch, a rather satisfied expression on his face. He would never take her seriously because he believed she posed no threat to him.

"I'm giving this to the dean."

He sighed and his black brows rose. Kidan approached. Her thumb rolled over the play button and pressed. The recording scratched, and Kidan's throat tickled with the smoke of that day.

"Where is June?"

It was Kidan's voice, but raw, the quality of a mad person attempting to reason. She'd been on her knees, facing the bound and gagged woman.

Susenyos drew closer, interested in the contents of the sick interrogation. Kidan watched him carefully. Was he worried or uneasy?

Music played through the phone. Kidan remembered choosing a thumping bass she'd been sure would drown out the sounds escaping a taped mouth. She'd relished the fear tightening her victim's features. Kidan had brought the end of a lit cigar to her flesh, and the smell of tobacco and melting skin had suffocated her.

"I saw a vampire take her. They'd only find us if you told them where we were. Did you tell them?"

The poison in those words belonged to an animal who only craved the truth. Kidan burned her three more times, watching her skin blacken like paper and then peel before she broke.

Mama Anoet's hair had stuck to her wide, sweating face, her small eyes growing large with terror.

This woman had once clothed and fed Kidan, protected her from this world. She was the only mother Kidan knew and loved. It was that love—and the horrifying act Kidan committed despite it—that made her unforgivable.

"Yes. He wanted you two. You and June," Mama Anoet rasped when Kidan loosened the gag.

"Who? What's his name?"

"I...I don't know."

Another scream as Kidan pushed the crackling end of Mama Anoet's beloved cigar to the back of her neck.

Kidan saw the smallest of flickers in Susenyos's eyes. It disappeared like a wick pinched between two fingers, but she knew it to be anger. He masked his expression, but it was no use. He'd already given her what she was looking for.

Kidan touched her ear, reminding him to listen to the next part.

"What's his name?"

Kidan had teetered on the verge of truth, and finally she would get her confirmation.

"Sagad!" Mama Anoet had shouted. *"His name is Susenyos Sagad."*

Darkness simmered in his eyes. "So, that's your proof."

"Please," her victim pleaded.

The recording picked up the labored breathing of both, one in pain, the other vengeful. This had been the moment the truth shattered Kidan's perfect world. The moment she learned that the one meant to protect her had colluded with the very devils they'd run from all her life.

It had seized every part of her, that rage. It was the sort that slipped into the depths of hell and rose cloaked in eternal flames. She remembered the rest in clipped images. Mama Anoet begging, a match lit, nicotine burning in her lungs from the cigars. Then the house was burning. She'd been too busy rejoicing in justice, too busy extinguishing one evil, to notice that another had slithered past and seared itself into her own eyes. Her neighbors screamed after arriving, terror lingering in their parted mouths, pupils filling black. Kidan had whirled around, ready to vanquish this monster too. The neighbors had stood outside, fire heating their skin, smoke drowning their lungs, but...there had been no other monster. They were staring at Kidan.

Her. The devil that frightened them.

A part of Kidan had died that night too.

Kidan stopped the recording.

"Why stop there?" His eyes were brighter than crushed stars. "Did you try to save her?"

Kidan blinked. What an odd question. Most people asked if she'd survived.

"Did you try to save her, or did you let her burn, little bird?" he asked roughly, coming to stand in front of her. She swallowed, and he followed the movement along her throat. Her heart beat rapidly from his proximity.

"I'm *not* a killer. It was an accident." Her lips trembled. "The fire got out of hand, and I tried to help, but..." She'd been used to these words, practiced for the press and detectives. The catch in her throat was very believable.

He blinked up at her, his interest draining away. "How disappointing."

She glared, hiding her wild beating heart.

Kidan had more than watched Mama Anoet burn. She'd enjoyed every muffled scream, the bulging of her eyes, as Mama Anoet realized the daughter she'd raised wouldn't come to her rescue.

Of course her most volatile act he would find interesting. Disgust stirred in her gut. The urge to burn this house down around them both itched at her fingers.

"I want to know what you did to June. I want the truth, or I take this to Dean Faris tonight."

Kidan's fingers tightened on her device. She refused to let him joke or belittle his way out of this. He was caught.

He folded his arms, leaning back against the edge of the table. "Oh, I think that's far from the truth. You want blood. You seek it in a glorious way, for a human. So even if I did tell you the truth, I don't think you'd rest until I was quite dead, yené Roana."

Yené Roana. Another nickname. He wasn't taking her seriously. She needed to change tactics.

"I know the house law you so desperately want to change," she bit out.

He stilled, the dancing light of his eyes punching out.

She smiled. Finally.

"'If Susenyos Sagad endangers Adane House, the house shall in turn steal something of equal value to him.'"

His fingers twitched, body tensing like a rope eager to snap. *Good.*

"So, I'm thinking one of two things on why you want to change the law. One, you want to endanger the house without consequences, or two, you've already endangered the house and have had something stolen from you." His breathing stilled, and Kidan's eyes brightened. "Two it is."

He remained quiet, emboldening her.

"You took June or hurt my parents, and now the house is punishing you." She couldn't keep the delight from her voice. "This is too good."

"You don't know what you're talking about," he warned, teeth gritted.

She got close to his face, within an inch of his chin, and craned her neck to meet those burning eyes.

"No? I think I'm getting pretty close."

He wrapped long, warm fingers around her throat, squeezing until her heart thundered and she stiffened. "You're wrong."

He was so close she could count his thick lashes. Her pulse raced.

His other hand reached for the recording tightly grasped in her palm. "You've had this for a long time. I assume the reason it isn't already with Dean Faris is that it implicates you more than me."

He cocked his head, almost pitying her.

She focused on his chest. "I don't care what happens to me."

"Yet you care about the truth. You care about what happened to June, and going to prison would certainly mean giving up the search."

Kidan suppressed a scream when his large hand crushed her knuckles, her bones pressed hard against the recording device.

"This is what you'll do. Tomorrow, you will resign from Dranacti, hand Adane House over to me, and go back to your life."

He kept squeezing until the device fell from her grasp and clattered to the floor. She tried to crush it under her feet, but he moved with unnatural speed. He shoved her aside, sending her into the cabinet of liquors and glasses.

"Maybe a few years in prison will make you more hospitable." He smirked, and pressed the middle button.

Nothing played. He frowned, touching the button again, but the contents had been erased. Kidan had done so the moment she stopped it. Of course, he'd try and use it against her. She couldn't be rid of it permanently, because she still needed it, which is why she'd made a copy before confronting him.

Kidan straightened unsteadily to match the fury radiating off him, a bitter smile on her face.

"You're right. I'm not leaving until I see you killed for all the sick things you've done."

He took a furious step toward her, then stopped himself, chuckling. "You have such vile expectations of me....I look forward to proving them true."

Kidan dragged her fingers through her hair, the room spinning after he left. She touched the butterfly bracelet that had once belonged to Mama Anoet. Her little blue pill. Her chest slowed. *Breathe.* The room found its center again. Even though it hurt, the pill was her greatest power.

Power because choosing how and when to die gave humans the thing they lost the moment they were born: control. Invincibility and punishment—both were somehow inside her, chained to this bracelet. And she would need them to bring the creature upstairs to absolution, or kill him, whichever she felt like first.

So what if Mama Anoet and her parents had failed to protect her? Kidan always found a way to survive.

18.

QAROS HOUSE HELD ITSELF WITH THE ATTITUDE OF A WELL-DRESSED
butler. Kidan's footsteps echoed on the marble, cold snaking up her spine.
Inside the large living room, rich wooden musical instruments drenched in polished wax were arranged neatly. Kidan felt a pang of disconnect—music held
history, tradition, particular to a country and identity she'd lost.

The Mot Zebeya, Slen Qaros, and…Ramyn Ajtaf occupied one side of an oval
table. Kidan's lungs expanded with relief. The girl hadn't been drained to death.

Ramyn was alive.

On the opposite side of the table, a handsome boy in a burnt-yellow shirt
and dark vest, his sleeves rolled up, was consumed by something on the page in
front of him. Holding a charcoal pencil with soot-stained fingers, he was lost in
his drawing.

Slen lifted her chin to Kidan. "The *Myths* book?"

Kidan had searched the bookshelf of the study but hadn't found it. "I'm
working on it."

Slen nodded and looked around the table. "Introduce yourselves quickly.
We have a lot to do."

No one spoke. Kidan slid a glance to Ramyn's chipped nails and bruised
collarbone. What was the best way to ask "What the hell were you doing in the
vampires' designated building?"

Nothing came to mind.

Ramyn popped in a raspberry candy and offered one with a warm smile.
Kidan took it and suppressed a sigh, enjoying the girl's kindness a little longer.
Because once Kidan interrogated her, Ramyn wouldn't speak to her again.

Her bracelet burned her wrist. *Look what happened to the last person you interrogated.*

Her mouth filled with the taste of burnt skin, and she fought a gag.

"Hello? I said introduce yourselves." Slen waved at the handsome boy.

His house sigil twinkled on his chest: two logs burning with a blue flame shaped into a woman dancing. Beautiful. Slen must have kicked him, because he jolted, blinking as if just noticing them.

"Yusef Umil, everyone. I like long walks on the beach and bad girls that ride motorcycles. Hobbies include failing Dranacti two times, so if you're anxious, remember you're never as anxious as me."

Ramyn's smile faltered. "You really failed two times?"

"It was racism, really," he joked.

Kidan regarded him curiously. Yusef Umil. His father, Omar Umil, was currently held in Drastfort Prison. What did it feel like to be a murderer's son? Had his father's darkness leaked into him? It must leave a deep stain.

"What else?" he continued, thick brows furrowed. "I'm told I have one good hour in me each day to produce quality work. Unfortunately, I don't know when that hour takes place, so please feel free to stay as close to me as possible. With a pen and paper in hand, preferably, so you can take note of my genius when it comes."

Ramyn bent her head toward Kidan. "He's joking, right?"

"No." Slen was unimpressed. "He has the attention span of a needle."

Kidan's lips almost twitched.

"A Mot Zebeya." Slen turned her attention to him. "You guys all have initials for names, don't you?"

They did? Kidan realized she hadn't asked his name.

"Yes. You can call me GK. I choose to follow the old naming traditions. My companion will name me, as Demasus named the Last Sage."

Kidan tried to recall that name from her childhood tales. Demasus, the Fanged Lion. Leader of the vampire army that waged war against the Last Sage and rained down unimaginable terror.

"George," Yusef offered instantly.

GK frowned. "I just said my companion—"

"Yes, yes, but I really think you can pull off a George. No, wait. Giorgis. I like that."

Before GK could protest, a tall boy with similar features to Slen entered the house, a gym bag slung over his shoulder.

He squinted at them, then grinned. "Ramyn? Where the hell have you been?"

Ramyn beamed and stood to hug him, her tiny form comical next to his towering height.

"We suck without you. Are you coming to orchestra practice soon?"

Ramyn bit her lip. "No, not for a while."

His honeyed face dimmed. "Lucky you. If I could quit, I would have been long gone."

"We're trying to study here." Slen opened a thick book of Amharic and Aarac translations.

He smiled and planted a kiss on Slen's temple. "Don't let my sister scare you away. This is the first time she's had people over."

"Hey, I come over. I'm people," Yusef said.

"But I don't invite you," Slen countered. "You're just always here."

Yusef took his pencil and mock-stabbed at his chest. Slen's brother laughed and went upstairs. A coil of jealousy unfurled inside Kidan at the familial exchange. Slen had a brother, a family. Then why did the Qaros girl look like she was drowning? Or was Kidan only imagining the absence of warmth in Slen's eyes?

Slen leafed through *Introduction to Dranacti*. "Our first formal circle, about Sovane, is tomorrow. I want you to gather information about it in your respective fields. The more viewpoints we have on this, the richer our discussion."

Everyone agreed, and they fell into an easy quiet. Kidan read about the Scales of Sovane—a historical anecdote about a prince named Sovane Ezariah who struggled with two minds. Since two souls couldn't survive in a single body, one had to fall. Kidan's lip curled. Why did the professor want them to learn this? Her gaze shifted to her classmates.

Ramyn fidgeted with her broken vintage watch.

GK's mouth moved in soft repetitions of prayer as he read. Yusef munched on roasted pumpkin seeds, ripping out pages rather than drawing on them. Slen's forehead scrunched, a pen pressed to her lips.

Why were these students choosing to tether themselves to vampires? Didn't they know that path was steeped in blood, or didn't they care?

"I need to use the bathroom," Kidan lied. "Where is it?"

Slen spoke without lifting her head. "Upstairs to your left, second door."

Kidan headed up the double staircase, trailing her fingers on the golden handrail. Her Family House appeared a hundred years older than this place.

After discovering a coat closet and gaming room, she arrived at Slen's room. A set of eleven violins shone in their cases, their scents of wax and wood heavier than smoke. Kidan quickly searched through Slen's drawers, her jaw clenching with each dead end. Aunt Silia truly left her a nightmare of a clue—House Qaros had turned on House Adane. Nothing specific. How the hell was Kidan meant to learn about the houses?

The sound of people walking echoed, and Kidan instantly flattened herself against the wall. Her vision tightened, blood racing through her veins. If Slen came in here, she was done for.

She cursed herself for not being more careful. Barely an hour into this plan of hers, and she was going to be kicked out and labeled as some weird lurker. The rumor would spread like wildfire, and no student would go near her. Her stomach turned to water, the sensation too close to the days after news about her murder trial broke. She had almost forgotten how bone-chilling those cold glares were in her neighborhood.

A door opened and closed, cutting off the voices. She exhaled softly through her nose and counted to ten before slowly walking out. The hall was empty. Thank God.

"You can't just quit," a gruff voice snapped from one of the rooms. "We need you."

Kidan approached, pressing her ear to the door and taking care not to make a sound.

"I-I'm s-sorry," Ramyn stuttered. "I can't do it anymore."

"Just leave her alone," a younger boy cut in, Slen's brother.

"She made a commitment."

"Screw your commitments."

A smack rang out. Ramyn squeaked as if she'd been struck. Kidan's breath caught, the sound peeling back a memory she'd buried deep beneath—June hiding in the bathtub after breaking filigreed china plates, Kidan confessing it was her and receiving a burning pinch.

When Ramyn whimpered again, Kidan wrenched the door open without thinking.

An older man dressed in a fine suit stood across from Ramyn, his thick fingers grabbing her delicate shoulders. Nearby, Slen's brother held his smarting cheek. Kidan's eyes narrowed, that familiar violent tide swirling into rage and pouring into her gut.

She forced her voice to relax. "Ramyn. I'm lost. Do you know where the bathroom is?"

The man's sharp gaze fell on Kidan. "Who are you?" he asked roughly.

"Kidan. I'm here for a study session."

"Kidan...House Adane?" Light shone in those pinprick eyes at once. "Nice to meet you. I'm Koril Qaros. Slen's father."

He shook her hand in his thick ones, and Kidan tried not to wrest it back.

Behind Koril, Slen's brother wiped at his cheek.

"Are you okay?" Kidan asked.

"He's fine," Koril dismissed.

Kidan kept her eyes on the boy until he forced a smile. "Yes. Ramyn, show her the way."

Ramyn took Kidan across the hall, to a wide bathroom. She pulled out some makeup from her handbag and cleaned her smudged mascara. Kidan picked up Ramyn's eye shadow case, opened it, stared into its small mirror. Her eyes appeared small, eyelashes hardly visible, dark circles present. How long had it been since she wore makeup? A year ago. The night June was taken. She'd given up everything that brought her joy.

"What was that about?" Kidan frowned, putting the case back down.

"Just orchestra practice. I've been missing sessions lately."

"Did he hit him?"

Ramyn fiddled with her eyebrow brush, but her hand trembled too much. She blew out a breath and rested the brush on the counter. "Yes."

Kidan regarded her shaking form with pity. The tears had erased some of Ramyn's eye shadow. Kidan lifted the brush. "Do you have makeup setting spray?"

Ramyn handed her the bottle, her brow reflecting curiosity. Kidan sprayed some into its cap. Then she collected a lovely shade from the chocolate palette onto the brush before dipping it into the cap, wetting it until she was satisfied.

"Turn to me." Kidan gently adjusted Ramyn's face, no longer surprised at her cold temperature, and began painting her eyelids. The process was oddly calming, like watching a movie with an old friend. "It will last longer this way, and it's more pigmented."

Ramyn gave a small smile, her septum piercing twinkling. "I didn't know you liked makeup."

"Not so much on the rest of the face, but I always loved playing with the eyes."

Ramyn studied Kidan's bare lids, the brown eyes quite large this close. Ramyn's peach perfume tickled Kidan's nose. "So why don't you wear any?"

Kidan's lips twisted sadly. Because she used to practice applying makeup with June all the time. It felt like a betrayal to enjoy it without her. The brush wavered, but Kidan gripped it tightly.

Once it was done, Ramyn thanked Kidan, admiring herself in the mirror.

Kidan steeled herself for what she'd actually come here for.

"We have to talk. I know you know Susenyos."

Ramyn tensed. "I don't know—"

Kidan ignored the pang in her gut as she moved to lock the bathroom door, shutting her eyes.

"What are you doing?" Ramyn appeared no different from a baby doe caught in headlights.

"You're going to tell me what you're doing with him." Kidan's voice slipped into that other place, the voice she had used to leech the truth out of Mama Anoet.

"I-I'm not doing anything with him," she whispered.

"I've seen you two together."

Ramyn's eyes darted to the door. Within moments, Kidan had rescued the girl only to subject her to more intimidation. Kidan hated how Ramyn resembled June, her soft edges, bottomless brown eyes. She didn't want to hurt her. Each time Kidan hurt people, she cut her own life span in half, and she was already living on borrowed time.

She tried a different approach. "Please just tell me."

"Why?" Ramyn's quivering voice struck her soul. "Why do you care so much?"

Kidan's fingers trembled, but she balled them into fists. "Susenyos took my sister. I came to Uxlay to find her."

It fell quiet. Kidan couldn't bear it if another person didn't believe her. She braced for the disappointment. Instead, soft, ice-cold hands reached for her. Kidan fought not to pull away from the tenderness. Her entire body ached. She'd missed the touch of another human being.

"I'm sorry." Ramyn's voice took on other people's pain too quickly. "You're brave for going to such lengths for her. I don't think any of my brothers would even blink if something happened to me. They always say I have no future. I'm inadequate, weak." Ramyn's eyes creased with admiration. "Your sister is lucky to have you."

"Family is supposed to be there for you," Kidan told her, unable to imagine why her brothers would treat her like this.

Ramyn squeezed her hand. "I don't know. My friends have always been kinder to me than my family."

Her voice had a tinge of hope. Kidan pulled her hands free and put them in her pockets.

"What's he doing to you?" Kidan spoke to the floor.

Ramyn fiddled with her broken watch and sighed softly. She pulled down the top of her thin dress to show needle marks along her collarbone. Not bite marks.

"What..."

"I was poisoned as a child."

Kidan's eyes widened. "Who poisoned you?"

"I don't know. It happened so long ago, but there's no cure. I'm...dying."

Kidan burned with an unexpected amount of grief. She had to look away from the weak girl, fingers tapping out a rapid triangle. Why people like her? When there were so many evil creatures?

"It's all right." Ramyn smiled sadly. "I've always known I'd become a vampire."

Kidan's throat constricted. "A...vampire?"

She nodded. "Susenyos is helping me get a life exchange."

Life exchange. Kidan rushed to unravel its meaning, brows pinched. Her knowledge of how humans became vampires was tied to the Three Binds. The Third Bind, specifically, controlled dranaic overpopulation. It forced vampires to sacrifice their own lives if they wanted to give their immortality to human beings.

Life exchange . . . Was that what Uxlay called this process?

Her stomach flipped. She couldn't imagine Ramyn, with her gentle hands, transformed into something so vicious.

"It's not easy, you know. Not many vampires want to give up their immortality. Some ask you to jump through hoops. Susenyos helps me talk to them." Ramyn gave a short laugh.

Kidan's finger burned her thigh, a square and triangle searing her skin. She tried to focus. "Can you help me find out what he did to my sister?"

Ramyn withdrew into herself. "I'm sorry."

Kidan's fists bunched. "Why?"

"You're scary, Kidan, but nothing compared with him. I . . . I'm sorry. I can't help you."

Kidan turned away before she did something she'd regret.

"I really hope you find her," Ramyn called softly.

Kidan squeezed her eyes shut and hurried downstairs, not sure if she wanted to embrace Ramyn or hurt her. Why would Susenyos care about Ramyn? He wouldn't give up his own life, but apparently he was more than happy to find her a match?

And if he was helping her, why was Ramyn so terrified of him?

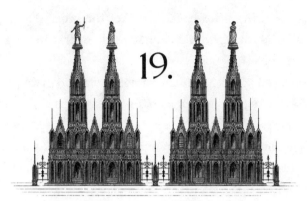

19.

"PROFESSOR ANDREYAS TELLS ME HE ALREADY KNOWS THE STUDENTS who'll fail today," Susenyos said, ankles crossed on the couch armrest. He slid her a triumphant smile. "And your name is on the list."

Kidan's mouth parted. It was?

"It was a toss-up between the house forcing you to leave or Dranacti." He flexed his arms behind his head and settled deeper into the couch, eyes closed. "Well, it's been a true displeasure."

Kidan scowled and slammed the door shut. There was no way in hell she'd fail.

For Dranacti's first formal circle, the seats were arranged in a ring, the windows blinded and the temperature warm. Kidan never thought she'd detest a shape this much. It provided no protection. The arc of it pressed on their backs like an invisible, tightening band, and her eyes could only rest on other eyes, a disquieting violation of privacy. If she could see the sweat gathering on their top lips, surely they could see right through her.

"Welcome to your first formal circle. There will be two components to the test: this discussion and a private test, where I'll speak with each of you alone. You should never entirely agree with someone else's point of view. If you do, you will be dismissed. If you have nothing to say, you will also be dismissed. So, shall we begin?"

Funnily enough, he terrified them all into silence. A twinkle shone in his eyes. "Scales of Sovane—what does it represent? And can it be kept in balance? Be brave, actis."

Unsurprisingly, Slen Qaros spoke first. "I don't believe the scales should exist. The pursuit of balance ensures that one doesn't progress, as the forces of nature plague it. Tilt either to greatness or wickedness, because they are better than indecision."

There was no more pause after that. Each student picked up on others' sentences and wove their own arguments until the hour ended. Ultimately, three students were dismissed.

Yusef sagged in relief when the professor's eyes went past him. Ramyn didn't lift her eyes from her desk. She'd been shaky throughout her talk.

"Well done to those of you present. You'll have a five-minute break. Wait outside until your name is called."

Yusef dabbed at his sweating forehead. He grabbed his favorite snack of roasted pumpkin seeds and started to peel the shells with his teeth.

GK dropped onto one of the lounge chairs and frowned at Yusef. "You kept distracting me."

"I'm a nervous snacker. You want some?"

GK sighed and took a handful. Ramyn appeared meek next to Slen.

Poisoned. Looking for a life exchange. A vampire.

Kidan ground her jaw. How could she save the girl from destroying her soul?

"Kidan Adane," the professor said. "Follow me."

The space had been cleared to provide a single chair. It reminded her of the stale interrogation room she had been taken into after the house fire.

"What have you learned about Sovane?" The professor leaned against his desk.

Kidan took a deep breath. "Sovane was often plagued with a genius shadow that took the shape of a human and spoke to him of war strategies, brilliant power plays, ways to lead a nation. Sovane could never act on them because for every strategy, there would be severe losses. He kept himself balanced for years, trying to please his intelligent shadow and his human heart and lead the country. Until a famine ravaged the kingdom, and the scales could no longer be kept balanced.

"Sovane kneeled before his people and declared he was unfit to lead them. He had to destroy a piece of himself so his shadow self could rise. Sovane described the feeling as sacrificing a childhood friend, their cascading laughter haunting until unbearable silence fell. But only an iron mind could save his people, so his gentle heart had to fall."

"Whom do you choose to fall?" he asked.

Kidan took a deep breath. She had to trust her gut. The professor had partnered them up for a reason. Even when it became clear the only way Sovane could succeed was by surrendering his humanity.

"Whom do you choose to fall?" he asked again.

Kidan met his black eyes. "Ramyn Ajtaf."

Her next words scratched against her throat and tongue, cutting her open. "She's inadequate, weak. She sees no future for herself."

Speaking ill of a dying girl, using those terms...Kidan's insides twisted. A part of her truly hurt, an emotion she thought was long lost. Somehow, Ramyn had brushed awake the pocket of light Kidan had suffocated under mountains of ash. There was a childlike ember of hope. A longing for the future instead of dread. Ramyn must have infected her with it when they touched, her ice-cold fingers and caring eyes brushing aside her blackened soul—and Kidan must have liked it. Wanted more. Why else did this hurt so much? Her chest swelled uncomfortably.

"It's why you partnered us based on our answers, isn't it? To show us how similar we are? So we would experience how difficult it was for Sovane to make that choice. That we cannot be good for all things."

Silence extended between them. She felt like she'd wrenched out and crushed something vital and beating beneath her heel. Like that innocent bird she had wanted to help but instead killed. Blood found her hands no matter what she did. She wiped her palms on her thighs.

The professor still didn't speak.

Her heart pinched in worry. This had to be right. Ramyn and she had both written nothing on their papers because neither saw a future, or rather only saw death in their future.

Doubt crept in. Had she misinterpreted the task? This could be the end of her time here. No more investigations into June. She straightened up, preparing to say more, when Professor Andreyas spoke.

"Well done. You may leave."

Kidan's ears buzzed as she got to her feet. She'd passed. Her relief flattened as she realized what it'd taken. Would Ramyn pass this test?

She got her answer a few minutes later when Ramyn came out in tears. Kidan swallowed bile.

"Ramyn?" Yusef said.

Ramyn's lashes glistened. "I failed."

Kidan couldn't meet her eyes. She felt rotten, her skin scaly and slimy, and rushed to touch her bracelet. Breathed. This was what she did. She hurt those around her.

But she wouldn't feel like this forever. After she found June, this would all end.

Ramyn sniffed and left.

Yusef ran a hand through his soft curls. "I hate this part."

The test continued. GK, surprisingly, came through. Kidan had thought his religious views might be a conflict.

"How was it?" she asked him.

"Hard." His eyes were troubled. "I didn't expect this."

Slen came through next, eyes black and sharp. No surprise there. Yusef passed as well.

Seven students failed.

The professor faced them, one hand in his long coat pocket. "It's more than I expected, but do not congratulate yourselves. Soon, we will have our first practical test at the Acti Gala. Dress in your most decadent style. You will be presenting yourselves to the dranaics in the hope they choose you."

Back home, Kidan waltzed into the study. Susenyos was at his desk, working with some books and scrolls.

"No need to pack." His lip quirked. "Etete did that for you."

Kidan dragged a chair to him and crossed her ankles on his desk, shoving aside his books with her boot. He leaned back, furious at the dirt on the pages.

"What the hell are you..." He drifted off, studying her pleased face. The piece of paper in his hand crumpled into nothing. "You passed."

Her smile was smug. "I told you. I'm not leaving until I see you dead."

Eyes boiling, he knocked her feet from the table, sending her flying off the chair.

It *hurt*. She swept her braids back, glaring from the floor.

He tidied his desk. "I guess I need to make it clearer just how unwelcome you are in this house."

20.

KIDAN STIRRED IN HER SLEEP, STRETCHING HER FINGERS AND FINDING damp sheets. Cold seeped into her with a vicious bite. Her eyes flew open. Her bed was...wet. Heart galloping, she switched on her bedside lamp and screamed.

Blood was *everywhere*.

She shot out of bed but slipped in a puddle of red. Kidan shouted again, trying to get up but failing. She caught her image in the mirror and froze. Ropes of blood drenched her like a deranged monster. Kidan tried to wipe it off, but it only spread along her skin.

"No, no." Her pleas rattled in her throat.

Had Kidan killed someone in her sleep?

Please, no.

A low rumble of laughter pulled her frantic gaze to the shadowed corner. Her insides twisted. Susenyos was there, lazily leaning against the wall, eyes gleaming.

"What— Whose blood...?" she started, unable to finish the sentence.

"Oh, I think you know."

June.

Kidan squeezed her eyes shut and shook her head. This was a nightmare. The house was playing tricks on her.

Her legs trembled as Susenyos crouched before her. He touched the puddle and smeared the blood on her face, making her flinch. He then brought his fingers to his lips, tasting. His eyes remained a flat black, hair unchanged from before, but his lips curved dangerously.

"This is your last warning." He left, tracking red footprints out the door.

Kidan's thighs shook, and she pressed her knees closed, unable to move.

This wasn't June's blood. It couldn't be. Kidan dared a glance at her reflection, at her ruined face.

Immediately, she grabbed her phone and called Dean Faris. She picked up on the third ring.

"Kidan? It's late—"

"Help," she croaked.

Dean Faris rustled, as if sitting upright, yet her voice remained calm, strong. "Kidan. Where are you?"

Kidan made her voice shake. *"Help."*

She hung up and readied herself for the next part, her stomach coiling with dread. She balled one of her ties and shoved it in her mouth. Then she positioned herself flat on the floor beneath the shadow of her large chest of drawers, making sure only her arm was in the line of impact.

Kidan kicked the heavy bottom of the chest, making it rumble and jerk. She kicked again. It teetered back and forth, a mountain, her heart launching with it.

You have to do this.

Dean Faris needed proof.

He had already set the scene for her. She only needed an injured body.

Kidan kicked violently. The chest swayed back, held itself for the length of a heartbeat, and tipped forward. She closed her eyes as the very sky descended on her left arm. Pain unlike anything she'd ever experienced thundered through her. Her scream was absorbed by the tie as her mind went dizzy. The loud crash swallowed the *snap* in her jaw, her toes, her very core. It took all her strength to pull her broken arm out and hold it. She dragged herself to the front of her bed, pulsing all over.

Then the front door was being pounded on. Spots danced in Kidan's vision, but she forced them away. Through the ringing pain, she could hear Susenyos's startled tone and rushed words as he tried to keep Dean Faris and whoever was with her from climbing the stairs.

When they entered her room, Kidan's head was hung, braids falling over her face, as she cradled her arm.

"My God," Dean Faris whispered, then ordered with a snap, "Help her!"

Strong arms lifted Kidan onto the bed, making her cry out. But she could see them now—two armed dranaics, Dean Faris, and Susenyos's shocked face.

"Whose blood is this?" Dean Faris's features contorted in a frightening wave. "Answer me, Sagad."

It took Susenyos a moment to speak, his confused gaze pinned on Kidan. "It's red dye. A harmless prank. Taste it."

One of the armed dranaics did, nodding. Dean Faris's anger eased a little. With a shaking hand, Kidan touched the blood on her face, running it through her hands, noticing its consistency. Too thin, and almost...grainy. It wasn't blood.

Both relief and fury swirled inside her.

Susenyos sidestepped the others, coming to the bed by Kidan.

"This is all a big misunderstanding. She's fine." He grabbed her arm—and she screamed. He let go at once.

She could still use this opportunity.

Kidan didn't have to fake the pain in her voice. "He broke my...arm."

"*What?*" he snarled.

"Step away from her."

There was pure command in Dean Faris's voice. When Susenyos didn't move, a dranaic pushed him aside.

"Hurry, feed her your blood," Dean Faris ordered.

Kidan tried to fight off the dranaic pushing his wrist to her mouth. She'd heal on her own. His terrifying strength brought his metallic blood to her lips, and she whimpered helplessly as it slid down her throat.

Stop.

At first swallow, the pain broke like a fever. The dranaic ignored her limbs writhing under him, feeding her a couple more drops. When he eased a little, she shoved him aside and turned over to hurl. Strings of blood and saliva dribbled out of her lips. Her stomach cramped in revulsion, and she gagged again, but nothing else came out. Kidan wiped angrily at her mouth.

"I didn't need help," she growled at him.

"There is a short period of time vampire blood is effective in healing bones." He spoke formally, giving a slight nod of apology.

Dean Faris's attention was on Susenyos, voice straining to be calm. "Harming an acti, especially one in your household, is a great offense."

Susenyos's fangs threatened to show with how far he pulled back his lips. "I didn't touch her. She must have slipped and knocked the chest over, or injured herself on purpose..." Even he sounded like he couldn't believe it, taking in the collapsed furniture.

Dean Faris looked at it, then at Kidan's sweating face.

Please, Kidan silently pleaded. *Do something.*

"This is the bracelet all over again." Susenyos raged, eyes blazing. "She plans to frame me."

Kidan's mouth fell open. Did he say *she* planned to frame him?

"Are you kidding? You had June's bracelet in your drawer!" Kidan roared, ignoring the twinge in her arm.

He released a disbelieving breath. "I'd be an utter fool to do that."

"Yeah, you are!"

Dean Faris shut her eyes like her head hurt.

Red fury sank into Kidan. "He's going to kill me."

Every muscle in Susenyos's jaw twitched. "This is ridiculous. Listen to her accusations. Out of all places, why would I put my *victim's* bracelet in my drawer?"

Kidan didn't miss a beat. "Maybe you're just sick that way."

He took a menacing step toward her, fists flexing, but the vampires stopped him.

Then, in a voice cruel as death, he said, "If I left her bracelet in my drawer, I might as well have hung her corpse in my closet."

Kidan flinched like he'd truly struck her.

"*Enough*," Dean Faris snapped with iron authority. "The matter of the bracelet will be investigated, but Kidan, know this: Only your fingerprints are currently on it."

Kidan was at a complete loss. "You have it?"

"Yes. Susenyos brought it to me at once."

Her throat closed. "That's not...possible."

Susenyos crossed his arms smugly. Then she remembered. He'd been careful not to touch it, using a napkin. He'd been several steps ahead.

"It's because I touched it without thinking!" Kidan grasped for words. "He must have planned for me to find it."

Dead silence.

They didn't believe her. Just like the detectives when she told them June had been kidnapped.

"You have to believe me," she pleaded, looking around wildly.

Susenyos gave her a pitying look and turned to Dean Faris with a harsh tone. "Why are you letting this go on? Send her away."

Dean Faris narrowed her gaze on him, then browsed the bloodied room. She knitted her fingers before herself. "If anything else happens to Kidan Adane this year, if she comes to harm or, God forbid, *dies*, Uxlay will strip you of your chance at inheritance and imprison you."

Susenyos's eyes grew wide, his tone venomous. "You cannot enforce that."

"Would you like to go to the Mot Zebeya Courts? They will not offer you the same mercy."

"You cannot *enforce* that. The dranaics won't stand for it. Uxlay will be thrown into a riot."

Dean Faris stepped closer, her voice a lethal blade. "I have watched too many Adanes die."

Susenyos was still as a grave statue when he said, "As have I."

Dean Faris studied him closely. She was quite small before his muscular build yet undeterred.

"House Adane will not go into extinction on my watch. I will not allow it."

"Then send her away." His voice was close to the earth, unreadable.

"No, this is her legacy."

His mouth took on a cruel shape. "You will do anything to block my ownership of this house. Going to such lengths to find a loophole in the inheritance law. Why dance around the edges? Why not kill me now?"

His harsh tone made the guards pull out their weapons halfway.

Dean Faris held up a hand and they sheathed their blades. "You have served House Adane for years. I never forget loyalty. But do not test me."

Susenyos's chest rose and fell, his nostrils flaring. "Send her away before—"

"Before what?" Dean Faris cut. "Before you harm her?"

His jaw tightened. "I didn't say that."

"Good." Dean Faris stared him down. "Because no harm shall come to her. Am I clear?"

He nodded slowly, fists clenched so tight that green veins shot along his dark arms.

Kidan sagged in relief. "Thank you—"

"No, I'm not finished." The dean's tone made the house tremble. "If you falsely accuse Susenyos again without proper, *irrefutable* proof, you will be expelled and stripped of access to our legal resources."

Kidan's face drained of color. Susenyos's smile was a curved knife.

"Am I clear, Kidan?"

Kidan nodded. *What just happened?*

"Good. The vampire blood will help for tonight, but visit the infirmary tomorrow morning. You may need a salve for the ache."

Kidan said nothing, still trying to understand. Had she won more than she lost? She'd hoped he'd be arrested and investigated, but this wasn't too bad of a second prize, was it?

"Good night." Dean Faris touched the wooden frame of the door as she passed. "And please, for the sake of the ancestors who paid too much blood for this legacy, do not run House Adane into the ground."

Susenyos waited until the front door closed before he gave a dead, unbelieving laugh and clapped slowly. "Well done. You've trapped us both. Are you satisfied now?"

"I warned you not to fuck with me."

He took a dangerous step toward her. She held up a finger, shaking it slowly. "No, no. Not one scratch on me."

Susenyos forced a hand through his thick hair, nearly pulling it out.

At least there was one silver lining—Susenyos couldn't touch her. She grasped her bracelet, which hid her blue pill, and felt the irony of it all. Her death was always the answer.

"Why are you smiling?" He watched her with caution.

Her smile grew cruel. "Because you've lost, and you don't even know it."

He glowered and left, slamming her door so hard, one of its hinges hissed and broke.

This poor house wouldn't survive them.

21.

UXLAY CAMPUS ONLY HAD ONE SEASON. IT BORROWED SUN ON RARE days and hail on others, but the wind never relented, whistling through bricked corridors, ruffling braids, and stinging exposed necks. The bottoms of Kidan's ears were like small ice chips, burning into her jaw whenever they touched. She knew cold, but this was something else. A cold preserved for the dead of the morgue.

Kidan tucked her chin into her blue sweater and the dark tie under her shirt's collar. She rushed to the campus store, which sold scarves. With the crest of Uxlay's lions and twin blades emblazoned, they were quite popular, with stock running out every day. She got the last one and rushed out, running straight into Ramyn.

Ramyn had a light sweater on, hair blowing wildly, cheeks pinked because of the cold. Kidan got goose bumps just looking at her. She sighed, took off her scarf, and draped it around Ramyn's throat, dressing it with care. Her own neck protested immediately, but she gritted her teeth against the icy air.

"Oh." Ramyn widened her large eyes. "Thanks. I always forget."

"I know."

Ramyn's fingers lingered on the scarf, her eyes cresting with light. "I heard...them talk about your sister in the Southern Sost Buildings."

Kidan's spine locked. "What? What did they say? Is she here? Where—"

"They didn't say much," she said in a rush, to calm her down. "I only heard them mention her name."

Kidan's heart was pounding like a drum, blood rushing through her ears. "I need to know more."

"I know," Ramyn said softly. "But you're not allowed in there."

"I don't care—"

"They will suspend you. I can get in. I'll try to find out more."

The roaring in her ears calmed. Kidan stared. "You will?"

Ramyn bit her lip, averting her gaze. "I should have helped you when you first asked, but I was scared...."

Kidan couldn't believe it. Someone finally believed her. Wanted to help her. Lost for words, she hugged Ramyn tightly, surprising them both. Ramyn gave a small laugh, squeezing her back.

Kidan inhaled her scent of sweet peaches. "Thank you. And I'm sorry... about Dranacti."

"It's fine. I'll see you later, okay? We can talk more then." Ramyn's piercing eyes remained bright as she waved goodbye.

Soon, June.

Kidan clung to that thought and hurried across the courtyard. On the twelfth level of the School of Philosophy, a rectangular space framed by eight rooms waited. Kidan knocked on the door of Room 3.

Yusef waved her in. Slen was illuminated by the bright window stretching almost wall-to-wall.

"The Mot Zebeyas are for protection of life. It's what we uphold higher than any belief," GK was saying.

"One life is nothing," Slen dismissed.

GK stared at her in awe. "It's everything."

Kidan settled next to Yusef, who appeared bored to death.

"It's human nature to protect those close to us. People die daily, and you don't see strangers mourning them," Slen continued.

"This is the issue with our world. All life is equal, and each death should hurt the same. The loss of one finger should cut as deeply as a hand," GK said, more animated than ever.

Yusef yawned. "I don't know. I think everyone wouldn't mind losing the ring finger. I mean, what does it really do?"

They all stared at him.

Yusef blinked. "Well, we can't lose the middle finger. It would be a tragedy."

"Let's just read," Slen said.

Yusef brightened, leaning in to Kidan. "You're welcome. They've been at it for an hour."

Kidan almost smiled.

Yusef ran a hand through his closely cropped hair, glancing at the far window, which doubled as a mirror.

"The wind is wild today."

After fifty minutes of silent work, Kidan stood to stretch her neck, enjoying the view. The Arat Towers met in a quadrant style; black stone statues perched on each spire bowed their heads, pitying the poor students crossing Resar's lush courtyard to enter their halls. If Kidan tilted her head just right, the spire statues almost mirrored an arrangement of peaceful murder or fervent prayer. What an odd choice to place as decorations. But perhaps this was how the residents of Uxlay chose to exist, between the divine and the evil, using one inexorably to conceal the other.

She half turned when a shadow caught her eye from the opposite tower. She squinted, trying to make out the shape. Dread seeped into her core. It was a person, head whipping wildly, dangling in the air by a hand around their throat.

Kidan's instincts screamed. *June.* She lurched forward, finding a hard surface blocking her path. Kidan pounded against the glass, eyes jumping back to the figure suspended in the air. She looked down desperately, but no one had noticed. An Uxlay red scarf unfurled from the victim's neck, billowing red in the wind. Kidan's pounding eased. This wasn't her sister. June had no reason to wear that scarf.

Kidan stiffened at the presence of someone at her shoulder.

"What's wrong?" Yusef said, alarmed.

He followed Kidan's gaze and shouted, giving voice to the horror unfolding inside her. The others rushed to them, watching the struggle in panic.

Someone left Kidan's side in a rush, and the door banged closed a second later. GK. He must have been running in desperation.

Yusef was on the phone, shaking and breathing hard as he spoke with the campus authorities. Slen remained as still as Kidan.

Moments later, GK appeared in the courtyard. He pushed through a group of students, who collapsed like bowling pins as he tore past.

The person writhed in the terrifying height. The attacker had to be unbelievably strong. *Vampire.* Kidan's body turned to liquid. Here she was again behind a glass, powerless.

GK entered the Languages and Linguistics Tower, and she imagined him taking the stairs two at a time.

Please make it.

"He won't make it," one of them finally said.

The hand let go. The figure fell, weightless, a rolling piece of body and limbs trailed by red before— Kidan shut her eyes. The crunch resounded in her spine and along her skull. When she opened her eyes, it was done.

Yusef slumped forward. "Who...is it?"

Although there were hundreds of students with similar clothes, figures, and heights roaming the grounds, Kidan knew that scarf belonged to the girl who smelled like sweet peaches. Just like she knew the day had tasted of death. Kidan's fingers twitched against her bare neck.

"Ramyn."

22.

RAMYN AJTAF'S BODY HELD GRACE IN ITS FRACTURE. HER NECK LAY to the side, her arms folded on her chest like she was cradling an infant. Her legs, which should have bent unnaturally, were covered with her scarf, curling around her delicately. If Kidan hadn't seen the fall, she would have believed Ramyn's body had kissed the ground instead of plummeting toward it.

Yusef's eyes were glassy. "How...who...?"

As the campus authorities lifted her, the hair shifted from Ramyn's face, revealing her lips. Earlier today, they'd been a lovely shape, a heart with a rounded bottom shaded in brown honey. Now they were dry of their moisture, cracked, and most of all, stained with *red*. Kidan's vision narrowed. She wasn't imagining it. Ramyn's lips were painted as if she had been blood-kissed before being thrown off the tower.

Kidan rushed forward, breaking the perimeter drawn by campus security. One officer caught her, but she fought, elbowing his gut until the man swore and let go. An image pulsed in her eyes. June lying under the moonlight, neck twisted at an angle, lips bloody.

Kidan seized the stretcher and turned Ramyn's head forcefully. Distraught gasps echoed around her. Ramyn's throat was punctured by two bite marks. Kidan swiped her thumb across Ramyn's wet lips. A few students turned sharply away, aghast. It was blood.

Kidan snapped her gaze to the crowd. Was the murderer here?

"Get her away," someone barked, and Kidan was dragged away.

They took her to a tall Black man dressed in a white shirt tucked into gray pants. He wore a badge next to the Uxlay crest. CHIEF DETECTIVE.

"What's your name?" he demanded.

Kidan stored a specific dislike for all authority figures. They'd failed her at every turn regarding June, forcing her to take matters into her own hands.

"Look at me when I'm speaking to you," he ordered.

Kidan did, and his nail-like eyes hooked into her soul. They brimmed with intensity, a raw darkness that told her he'd stared into death's eyes and lived to tell the tale.

"Kidan," she bit.

"What were you doing with the victim?"

"I was checking something."

"Why?" he spat.

Kidan ground her jaw. Why should she trust him? Her gaze traveled to the crowd. Nearly everyone stared at her instead of the crime scene. Her neck prickled at those harsh eyes, their glare meant for something foul and horrific.

The chief detective noticed and indicated for her to follow him. Glad to shake off those accusing whispers, Kidan followed. They entered a colorless one-level building and sat opposite each other in a cramped room.

The ground rippled under her, morphing into the prison cell they held her in until her bail was posted. Wet cement mixed with dried vomit, and alcohol filled the space. She tried not to focus on his badge.

You're not there anymore.

He questioned her again. Holding her breath, Kidan explained how the case mirrored June's. She told him she had seen Susenyos with Ramyn in the Southern Sost Buildings, but the chief detective's face gave nothing away.

She squirmed under his blank expression, wondering if he'd bring up her case.

Professor Andreyas interrupted them, taking long strides into the small room. "The Sicions will be here soon. They're being pulled away from an important task. I hope you have a lead."

"Head Andreyas, as always, I appreciate your knocking."

"A name, chief." The professor's voice wavered in impatience.

"I should ask *you* for a name. The dranaics fall under your responsibility. Is it possible you missed signs of insurgence?"

The professor's demeanor darkened. "Are we so certain it's my department at fault? Throwing someone off a tower reeks of human desperation."

The chief narrowed his eyes. "There were bite marks. Kidan here and her study group were in the Philosophy Tower. One of them even ran into the Languages and Linguistics Tower, a young man by the name of GK. Kidan says she saw Susenyos Sagad with Ramyn Ajtaf."

Her gut tightened. Professor Andreyas was Dean Faris's companion. Would they consider this a false accusation?

"I'll let the Sicions know," the professor said evenly. "I want this closed before Acti Gala week."

Once he left, Kidan turned toward the chief. "I can help."

"No, go home. Be safe."

"Home," Kidan repeated in disbelief. "With the vampire that did all this! Please, let me help."

She fisted her hands as a minute ticked by. Her shoulders shook.

"Listen." He sighed. "We need solid evidence pointing to Susenyos. Anything that can be tested and connect him to some crime. Bring me something like that, and I can do something about it."

Kidan blinked, relief stirring in her. When she was free to go, she spotted the scarf in a tub, set aside on a desk. Her neck warmed, then went cold as if it was coiled around her. A hole expanded in her chest.

Had Ramyn been targeted because of her?

The officers were occupied with different duties. She quickly swiped the scarf, tucking it inside her sweater, and exited. Holding on to it was an unbreakable promise. Kidan would bring Susenyos to justice or die trying.

23.

"R AMYN." KIDAN GLARED AT SUSENYOS IN THE LIVING ROOM.

"Yes? Do you want to accuse me of something?" Susenyos lowered his book, eyes filling with light and anger.

No. Dean Faris had been very clear. She clamped her lips together and shook with the effort not to scream.

His gaze took on a satisfied glint. "Good. Dean Faris won't be happy about this personal vendetta of yours. We can't have everyone thinking I'm capable of such a grotesque murder. But perhaps you are, yené Roana."

That name again. From Kidan's limited knowledge of Amharic, she now knew "yené" meant "my," and she'd learned that Roana was the lead character in the twisted *Mad Lovers* book he was always reading.

Roana was abandoned outside a church for her unholy thoughts. She'd sought men and women with the hunger of a starved wild animal. Caught after a murder, she'd been dragged to the priests to be purged. She pleaded with the night stars for a new heart, and the heavens granted it. She left to live in an abandoned village, smothering any traces of her violent urges with solitude. It didn't last. The story truly kicked off when she hid a young man wanted for massacring a nearby village. His name was Matir, and he carried his own darkness.

Kidan didn't understand why Susenyos was so fascinated by this story. It was grotesque—and worse, he associated her with it.

My Roana.

Her eyes turned to slits. "Don't call me that."

"Why? Do you know what it means?" His voice was teasing.

"It's not my name."

"I see, little bird."

"Don't call me that either." She gritted her teeth.

A shadow of a smile curved his lips as he turned to the fireplace, warming himself. "If you're going to kill an acti, there are many more pleasurable ways to do it."

Her voice threaded with horror. "You mean drain their blood."

She didn't need to see his face to know he was smiling. He opened his golden flask and drank.

"Only a fool wastes precious acti blood. There are so few of you."

Kidan's vision became transfixed on that flask, a new panic launching her heart. Whose blood was that? Susenyos had no companions, and Aunt Silia was dead. Could it be June's blood?

Her fingers became erratic, her vision blurred. Evidence. She had to get that flask to the chief detective.

For a couple of days, Kidan studied Susenyos's drinking pattern. She noted exactly when and where he drank from the flask. He drank whenever she walked into a room where he was, insulted him, and, especially, brushed past him. They gave each other enough space to avoid the matter, but sometimes they accidentally reached for a doorknob and touched, at which point he'd glare and drink. Then he'd return the flask to his chest pocket. The only time he lost possession of it was when he went for his daily "soak" in the prohibited Southern Sost Buildings. At that point, he'd leave it on top of his dresser. Every single day, this was the routine.

Kidan carefully stole it on the third day, making sure her fingertips weren't on it.

She gripped it so tightly that if she was one of *them*, it would have dented. Her nose moved toward it as if, like a hound, she'd be able to smell her sister's blood.

The chief detective took it with a gloved hand and deposited it in a sealed bag.

"It will take some time," he told her.

Kidan nodded. She didn't know if she wanted it to be June's blood or not. Either way, she'd have an answer soon.

24.

THE SUDDEN DEATH OF RAMYN AJTAF BROUGHT WITH IT A MOURN-
ing like no other. Black billowing curtains hung across the Construction
and Engineering Departments that her family ran.

The funeral took place on a dreary Tuesday. Closed casket. Ramyn's eight
brothers lined up in dark suits and solemn faces.

Kidan tried to imagine growing up in their shadows, a little dove among
hawks. Did they know the truth about Ramyn's hope for a life exchange?

Midway through the service, the sun came uninvited. The sullen clouds,
which had hovered over them for days, parted, revealing rays that danced on the
coffin, and on the skulls of the attendees. Ramyn's brothers maintained their grief,
but their eyes caught traitorous light when they knelt to toss flowers into the grave.
Kidan shook her head, searching again, only to find heartbreak. All of their House
Ajtaf pins were painted red in grief. Not every family was as broken as her own.

"Excuse me," a light-skinned man with muted green eyes said to her.

Tamol Ajtaf, the eldest sibling of the main Ajtaf family, introduced himself.
He came up to her height and was dressed in a sharp suit.

"This isn't the place for it, but I've been trying to get in contact with you."

"You have?"

"Yes. You have yet to respond to my letters."

She hadn't gotten any letters. "What did you want to talk about?"

"The Axum Archaeological Project. I'm impressed by your family's dedica-
tion to finding the Last Sage's rural settlement. Ajtaf Constructions helped with
targeted excavation and made great progress. We're interested in taking over
officially. We would compensate you well, of course."

Kidan grew cautious. Aunt Silia had warned her about the Ajtafs. Why was he talking about work at his sister's funeral? Shouldn't he be asking if Kidan knew Ramyn?

"Why the interest in an old settlement?" she asked.

Tamol's smile was thin. "It's as mythic as the Lost City of Atlantis. Hunting for the Last Sage's treasures and history lost in that settlement is a rewarding endeavor."

He brought out a business card and gave it to Kidan. "Dranacti studies are difficult to pass. Call me if you want to discuss other options."

Written on the back of the card:

We are here to help.
The 13th.

Kidan frowned. Dean Faris had mentioned that many groups existed within Uxlay and most would benefit from recruiting a Founding House heiress to back their agendas, but Kidan had thought no one was interested.

After he left, Kidan tried to cry for Ramyn. She bit on the inside of her cheek, willing something to come out—one tear, and she'd know she didn't carry a black heart.

Cry, she begged in her mind.

It was no use.

Kidan removed herself, walking through the cemetery and taking note of the names and dates. Most of the graves were of young people. There had been one death last year. Two the year before that. Five years ago, four students had died.

That stopped her cold. Kidan wondered what, or who, had killed these students. Her stomach knotted with the growing realization that Uxlay either could not protect students or didn't care.

Her contempt for Dean Faris returned. Uxlay wasn't a place of law and protection at all.

A group of protesters who shared Kidan's thoughts crowded Dean Faris when she arrived. They accused her of failing to change the acti protection laws, leading to this. One House Delarus girl even tried to attack her with paint before being escorted away.

Kidan nodded in support. It was good the students were fighting back.

Despite her lack of tears, Kidan reached home exhausted and desperate for bed. But when she arrived, she found the study in chaos. This was the last thing she needed. Drawers hanging out, cabinets wide open, glasses shattered, liquor bottles empty. Susenyos was on the carpet, shirt disheveled, three empty flasks around him. He faced the fireplace, in a trance.

She drew forward carefully.

"Susenyos?"

No response.

Kidan touched his shoulder. He winced and shot to his feet at once, rubbing furiously where she'd touched him. Kidan stared at her hand. It was clean, a little scarred, but nothing to warrant such a reaction.

"What—"

"Don't come any closer." His hoarse voice was laced with exertion. "Did you take it? My flask?"

"What? No."

"Don't lie to me," he growled, making her stiffen. Sweat broke out along his forehead.

"I'm *not* lying."

He stared at her with scorching eyes and shook his head, gripping the edge of the chair until it creaked.

Kidan cursed internally. "What's going on?"

A vein tightened along his temple as he let out a stilted breath. "I'm out of blood."

So he couldn't leave and get June's blood from wherever he kept her?

"Why can't you go get more?" Even saying the words made bile rise in her throat.

He gave a brash laugh. "I have restrictions. And Silia's blood is running out."

Silia? Did she donate copious amounts of blood before dying?

Shit. Even if Susenyos wasn't lying… it was clear that if he could get blood, he would. It suddenly occurred to Kidan that she'd taken all the blood away from a vampire. Her body went cold.

A pained groan tore out of him as he pressed a hand to his temple. He snapped the wooden chair into ugly splinters and, with a piece of it, skewered his palm to the table.

Kidan flinched, shouting, "What are you doing?"

"You need to leave," he panted, briefly catching her eye. The blackness of his pupils expanded like an animal's. Fangs slipping in and out.

Kidan staggered back. "What's happening to you?"

He laughed miserably. "If I remember correctly, every nerve in my body will seek out my potential companion's blood no matter where I go. *Your* blood. Your face, smell, and touch grow excruciating with every second. So, for the millionth time, I suggest you pack your things and *leave*."

Kidan glanced at the door but didn't move.

His labored breaths echoed around the house, the smell of violence gathering like thunder. A deep scratch, like the sound of a blade against a tree, made her turn. Broken wood was between his teeth. His fangs scraped like knives, leaving deep gashes.

"Fuck," he whispered.

His eyes had become colorless. But it was his lips, stretched and bloody, cut into pieces with his own teeth, that collided with her nightmare. June might as well lie by his feet, her own lips bloodied, still as death.

"Why are you still here?" he breathed, snapping the wood. "Leave!"

His shout sent a crack through the house.

Kidan straightened her spine and grabbed a butter knife from a tray.

He laughed. "That knife isn't going to help you, little bird."

Her grip tightened, voice cold as ice. "Rites of companionship. If a vampire feeds on a human without a vow, their eyes will remain red for three days so they'll be found and imprisoned. So come on, feed on me."

He whirled like a god of death. "I can make you take a companionship vow."

Did that mean she didn't have to pass Dranacti to make a vow?

Her back locked for a second, remembering she was dealing with a creature both ancient and lethal. She recovered quickly. "Red eyes or not, feed on me and I'm at Dean Faris's house."

She wielded the knife higher, daring him to take a step closer.

He threw her a hateful look and grabbed his jaw. "My fangs are aching, pulsing like throbbing bone. I'm going to bite through everything in this house, including you, just to please them. I won't just feed on you. I'll kill you."

Kidan's eyes dropped for a moment. If she let him, Dean Faris would definitely arrest him. But what about June? Would she be found?

Kidan had to make sure June wasn't lost. Dying here would serve no purpose.

She lifted her chin to him. "Then I guess you're going to have to control yourself."

His eyes swirled with breathtaking fury before he said through clenched teeth, "If you won't leave... There are pliers in the shed. Bring them now."

She froze in confusion.

His jaw barely moved, so quiet were his words. "You're going to defang me."

Kidan's eyes widened. That sounded deliciously... painful. She walked backward, exiting to find the pliers. More sounds of furniture shattering exploded from the house. She returned, pausing at the door.

"Come here." Susenyos braced against the wall. "It'll be hell itself, but they'll grow back." He seemed to be talking to himself, preparing. "They will."

She marched toward him, and he flinched like she'd hit him.

"Slower," he barked.

She softened her steps. It was both strange and delightful to see him so frightened, when he was the monster. He turned his face, eyes shut. "Your smell... It's fucking intoxicating."

"Look at me," she ordered.

"Stop speaking."

"How will I—"

He let out a guttural sound and seized her jaw, bringing her face close to his bloodied one. Kidan's instinct was to resist, but she faltered when she glimpsed the craving that was rioting in his body. His bone-white fangs sharpened to an incredible point against glistening dark skin. Her breath quickened like a trapped bird.

"Stop breathing."

She did.

He let her go and guided her hand holding the pliers to his mouth, opening wider. Blood pumped in her forehead. He positioned the pliers at his teeth.

"Now." He inhaled a shuddering breath. "Quickly."

Kidan kept twisting the pliers in her hand, still not touching his tooth.

"What are you waiting for?" he snarled.

She shook her head. Positioned the pliers again and touched his teeth. He hissed, shoving her away from him. If her just touching it hurt, how would pulling it out feel? A smile played on her lips. He saw it.

Fuck.

In a swift movement, he pinned her against the wall.

"You're enjoying this," he panted, caging her with his arms, muscles contracting.

Say no.

"Yes."

Venom cut through his pain. "Do you want me to show you how I drank from June?"

Kidan's body stiffened, her smile thinning out. "What did you say?"

"I had her like this, between my arms, she was so defenseless. All I had to do was lean in—"

Kidan seized his shit-spewing jaw, jamming the pliers inside. His eyes grew into saucers. She clamped onto his sharp tooth and in a furious motion wrenched back. The force made her shoulder pop, and blood sprayed her face.

The pliers came out with the fang and some of his gum.

Susenyos banged his fist against the wall, puncturing it close to her ears so all sound faded. She hurried to pull the other one. Once it was done, Susenyos sank to the floor, pressing his head to it. Kidan breathed like she'd scaled a mountain, staring down at him.

Something had torn free inside her, a release of the ferocious kind that made the world a little brighter.

He was pure evil. One she would keep defeating.

Kidan crouched low, grabbing his chin like he'd done to her in the hallway. His skin was burning, eyes wet without tears.

"Where is June?" she asked.

The pain from his lost fangs vibrated into her cradling palms and slithered into her veins. He was in agony, leaning into her unconsciously to seek relief from the pulsing ache.

"Tell me." She lowered her tone. "I'll give you anything you want."

His lips parted. She was close enough to inhale his shuddering breath. The entire room throbbed like belted skin. She brushed her fingers along his cheek, feeling him wince at her feather-like touch. He was so close and in so much pain.

"Did you kill them?" Kidan's voice was velvet soft. "Did you kill June and Ramyn?"

It was the wrong thing to ask. Like a gust of icy wind, it chased away whatever pull she had on him. He shoved her hand away and staggered into the shadows, hiding his face from her.

Kidan closed her eyes in frustration.

The front door clicked open.

Etete came in, shaking at the scene. "Dranaic Susenyos! Acti Kidan! What happened?"

Kidan walked to the stairs, closing her fist over his fangs.

Let it take a month or year, she'd pull the truth out of him one by one.

25.

MYTHOLOGY AND MODERNITY CLASS WAS HELD IN ONE OF THE THE-aters located inside the Qaros Conservatory of Music.

This course was another requirement for Kidan to stay in Uxlay. She had to earn a satisfactory grade for her two electives and absolutely pass Dranacti. So far, this class was the most enjoyable.

Ramyn's absence, however, was a needle under the skin. Yusef had lost his easy smile and drew a continuous line on the edge of his paper. Slen stared ahead, unreadable as always. Kidan had found her in the Philosophy Tower late last night. They both couldn't sleep, so they'd studied without speaking, well into the yawning dawn. Kidan usually hated such a complete silence, her skin prickling in the same way it had in her cramped apartment, but it'd felt oddly natural, warm instead of bone-chilling. In those witching hours, they grieved Ramyn without mentioning her name.

GK had reported what he saw to Professor Andreyas and the chief detective. A glimpse of brown leather shoes, and some metal bands.

He rubbed his tired face again.

"There was nothing you could do," Kidan said softly.

"I could have reached her faster." His reflective eyes swam with questions. "How long did you watch her struggle?"

Kidan's ribs contracted sharply. She heard his silent accusation. Why hadn't she shouted out the moment she saw Ramyn?

A pang of disappointment rolled through her. In less than a week, he was already seeing her differently. Perhaps he was realizing she wasn't worth saving.

There were these people Mama Anoet had called carcasses. Her husband was one.

"They live only for themselves and die alone."

It was such a violent thing to call a living human. Kidan and June had asked how to avoid being one, and Mama Anoet said, *"Have people you care about. Otherwise, you're not worth existing. Look at how many of you I take care of."*

Kidan heard what she didn't say. *Look at how many lives I have.*

Kidan observed her study group, human and vulnerable. If someone like Mama Anoet could be forgiven by taking care of others, could Kidan be forgiven too? She had that love once—with June, her chest tight with so many years ahead of her, giddy on the edge of youth. Until her sister's absence left Kidan hollow, close to death. Perhaps she could shelter new souls, find a way to breathe again. She'd do it even better than Mama Anoet, never punish or risk harming them. Something punctured her wrist, her bracelet digging in sharply for the selfish thought.

"Good morning, class," Professor Soliana Tesfaye greeted them, wearing a long, patterned dress. In this class, they studied the myths that birthed the creation of dranaics and actis, the relationship between the Last Sage and Demasus, and, of course, the famous Three Binds, analyzing the effects of those stories in relation to current society. "Today, we begin with a performance, as our legends have always been passed down through oral storytelling."

The lights dimmed. The tragic play was about the Last Sage and Demasus the Fanged Lion, from Aarac myth. It was adapted from *Traditional Myths of Abyssi* and loosely translated to fit the structure of Crusade of Pantagon, a war-style story, according to Slen.

The stage lit up on a group of masked people who wore curved impala horns—the hunters, Kidan realized. These were the villagers who protected their families against dranaics: blood drinkers, or as the West knew them, vampires.

The human hunters traveled to a cave and found the Last Sage dressed in a cracked mask, wearing a ruby ring, and holding twin blades. They pleaded with him for weapons to fight against the dranaics.

Demasus, leader of the dranaics, wore a lion's mane as a crown and led armies to butcher Axum country. The next scene recounted horrible casualties as the massacre mounted.

Kidan shifted in her seat. How powerless they were against speed and fangs. If vampires chose to rise again, what hope did the rest of the world have?

In the second act, the Last Sage arrived at the battlefield. He seized Demasus by the shoulders and disappeared into a smoke of shadows. They woke inside a cave, sealed off from the world. For all his might, Demasus couldn't break through the stone to free himself.

Years passed, marked by the seasonal changes of the tall grasses near the cave.

The villagers came to express their gratitude, and the dranaics scattered without their leader. Still, no one knew what transpired in those years.

The stage lights shuttered, focusing intimately. The Last Sage and Demasus appeared on their knees, facing each other. Demasus, in growing distress, howled and buried his face in his own hands, his crown of lion's mane thrown aside. The entire auditorium watched the silent struggle. A blade fell between their hands, grazing the chest of one, only to be wrenched away by the other.

Kidan couldn't tell assailant from victim. Each portrayed the role in a graceful dance, neither willing to kill or be killed, live or die. It slipped into a repetitious loop but didn't break its power. They must have suffered, Kidan thought. Alone in that cave trying to forge a path made impossible by their nature.

The blade finally found its mark. There was a release, a puncture, in the audience as they stared wide-eyed. The Last Sage had cut into his own palm, pouring it into a scattered bowl.

"Swear loyalty to me, Demasus, and my blood shall be yours."

Kidan was convinced the actor had cut his palm. It dropped not too quickly, like a true cut; it glided into the gold plate like forbidden water. Demasus growled like a wounded animal, eyes flickering between the growing puddle of blood and the Last Sage's neck.

He didn't want to harm him. What had caused their impossible friendship?

"Swear to me you will not harm another but merely ask me to quench your thirst," the Last Sage proclaimed.

"You grant me what I seek, to torture me," Demasus replied. "Your kindness is poison, and I should have your heart for it."

"Let me bind you to water, sun, and death," the Last Sage said. "Drink from those I choose for you. I will teach them to care for your kind. Abandon your strength that makes them fear you as beast. Take life only at the cost of your own, so you may know how precious it is."

Through blinding hunger, Demasus delivered his famous line: "You riddle me with sacrifices, but can you bear what I will ask of you in turn?"

Kidan leaned forward.

"I will. And in return, you will not leave my side. You will remain as the wind by the sea and the stars by night. Your companionship, Demasus—that is what I will receive, until the day I die."

Then, upon twin blades, a red ring, and a shattered mask, they created a bond. A bond that would be inherited by eighty families and carried down like sacred tradition. A bond that created the Three Binds of the Dranaics, also called the Water, Sun, and Death binds.

First Bind: Vampires could no longer drink from all humans, only from the Eighty Families. Second Bind: Their original strength and powers—there were rumors they could once compel, disappear into shadows, even fly—were all weakened and repressed. Third Bind: If they wanted to turn a human into a vampire, it came at the cost of their own life.

The last one Kidan loved the most. There could never be mass armies of vampires. *Still*, she thought, touching her bracelet. *You don't put a leash on evil. You kill it.*

The scene closed with the Last Sage's three objects scattered across the world. Those artifacts, if discovered, were rumored to have the ability to break the binds, so they were hidden, far apart. In the unforgiving seven seas, the mountains that reached the heavens, the shifting sands of an endless desert and beyond.

Finally, the two men went out to the villagers, to teach them their new way of life—Dranacti.

The actors were brilliant. She'd almost felt compassion for Demasus, and understanding instead of anger toward the Last Sage.

GK had leaned forward, wrapping his chain around his palm.

"It's not all accurate," he murmured. "The cave they stayed in isn't in Axum. It's in the Semain Mountains."

"Those mountains don't exist." Slen adjusted her gloves repeatedly.

GK frowned a little. "They . . . exist. They're just hidden. I hope to visit them one day."

Yusef laughed softly. "Can I come? I've always wanted to scream from the top of the world."

GK wiped his face in exasperation. Kidan's small smile faded when she glimpsed the empty seat next to her. Ramyn's septum piercing would have twinkled, a curve playing on her heart-shaped mouth. She shouldn't have died. But Kidan couldn't dwell on Ramyn or the fragile beginnings of their friendship. If she didn't act soon, who else would die?

She focused only on the facts. Ramyn had visited the dranaic Southern Sost Buildings with Susenyos for a life exchange. It was there she overheard dranaics of Uxlay talking about June.

While Kidan waited for the blood results, she'd infiltrate the dranaics' private building and hope she wouldn't be expelled from Uxley.

"House Umil, the perfect house of art and beauty. They began with charcoal, capturing African people and culture on smoothed walls, acting as our own historians, and documenting the migration. Today their legacy has been refined, their collection expanded to thousands of works, and a museum is dedicated to them. They are the Art House."

—*History of the Acti Houses*
By Yohannes Afera

Omar Umil was arrested fourteen years ago for the violent murders of ten of his dranaics. His only son bore witness to the act and testified against his father. He was only six. House Makary oversaw the case, and Omar now resides in Uxlay's Drastfort Prison.

Omar was once a close friend to us all. It would break your parents' hearts if they knew he'd fallen to such a state a few months after their deaths. Go to him and share what I've shared with you.

26.

KIDAN STALKED THE SOUTHERN SOST BUILDINGS FROM A DISTANCE. The three buildings were huddled together like shouldered brothers, timeless in red sandstone and promising blood to anyone who crossed their iron gates. It was four o'clock, and according to her observations, this was when Susenyos arrived for his daily soak.

She took quick strides in that direction and stopped when two familiar boys on a stone ledge outside the left building caught her eye.

GK and Yusef meditated in silence. Yusef drew, earbuds in, and GK read his Mot Zebeya book.

"Kidan!" Yusef waved.

GK closed his book slowly, sighing. "You're supposed to notice the music only."

Kidan approached. "What are you guys doing?"

"GK is teaching me one of his Mot Zebeya lessons, being one with nature and stuff."

"It's called Settliton," GK said under his breath. "You should all practice it."

For two people who often complained about each other, they seemed quite content.

"Here, listen," Yusef said.

Kidan took one earbud out, bringing it to her ear.

"Nina Simone?"

"She was playing the first time I painted. It helps me get unstuck."

She leaned against the pillar, looked out over the freshly mown Sheba Square, and listened to the soft jazz and soulful vocals. Kidan didn't know the last time she had enjoyed music for the sake of it. It felt disconnected from everything she knew.

"So, do you come here often?"

Yusef touched the patterned walls of the hall in appreciation. "These corridors are a tribute to the oldest existing educational institution."

There were arches above their heads, as if each column supported an invisible moon between it and the roof. Kidan's fingers traced the geometric work that continued onto the wood pillars.

"Andalusian architecture and art. Breathtaking, isn't it? Imagine being a companion to a dranaic who lived through those times. My father spent eight months away with his dranaic just creating work. His dranaic would dictate about his life, and my father would capture it all."

With those words, Yusef's face looked pinched, and his eyes fell a little. As soon as Kidan read about Yusef's father, she was a fan. He'd killed ten of his dranaics. The only person in this hellhole who had any sense. She wanted to know how he'd done it. With an impala horn? Was it all at once, or one by one?

She had tried to visit him at Drastfort Prison once but wasn't allowed access. It wasn't the prison that had blocked her request. Omar Umil didn't speak to anyone. So Kidan had decided to write him a letter. She chose her words carefully to disguise their meaning, since the officers read everything first, and wrote out a brief introduction, mentioned Aunt Silia's death, and asked to see Omar Umil. He had yet to respond. Maybe in her next letter to him she would mention that her study group included his son. Hopefully that would persuade him to see her.

Yusef sighed and took back his earbud. Near his feet, a few crumpled pieces of sketch paper had gathered. He collected them, stuffing them in his pockets.

"Let's go into town," he said suddenly, voice bright.

GK sighed, then turned to her. "Come with us."

Kidan's lips lifted sadly at the invitation. What she wouldn't give to just be normal, go off and have fun. Breathe and relax into the little things.

"No, you guys enjoy."

Yusef waved and walked away, but GK remained. He studied the imposing Southern Sost Buildings shrouded in the swelling clouds, then shot her a pensive look. "Are you sure?"

She blinked at his tone. Did he see her walking toward it? "Yes."

He nodded slowly, touching those finger bones again. "Be careful."

Once he left, Kidan worried her bottom lip. Did those chains tell him she'd die in there? She eyed the black iron doors. A small metal plate read,

ACTI STRICTLY PROHIBITED WITHOUT INVITATION. ENTER AT YOUR OWN RISK.

There was no other choice. She entered the jaws of the beast.

Dim filtered light broke through the high windows. The Southern Sost Buildings were eyes made of mirrors. Portraits gazed out through glassy, haunted eyes and undressed her. They removed her clothes and flayed open her naked body, taking the wayward parts of her being. Kidan saw pieces of her soul everywhere. The violence of a collapsed bloodied man, a woman staring with terrified yet defiant eyes, a child's cheeks messy from fat tears. Morbid pessimism clung to every wall.

Then, an odd sound greeted her. A rush of water came from the direction of an ornate door, as if the arched hallway would be flooded any second now.

A tiny engraving above the door read, BATH OF AROWA.

Gently, she eased it open. Warm fog fanned her face immediately and droplets of water stuck to her eyelashes. Through the haze, a spacious room made of marble stretched out, a large basin pool in the middle. Hot water spilled from the mouths of black lion heads, creating a layer of steam. Through the mist, three figures moved. Kidan ducked low and shut the door behind her. The gurgling water masked what little noise she made.

She squinted. The figures were in loose white robes. One of them shrugged theirs off at the edge of the pool. A smooth leg started to wade into the water—Iniko, elegant and beautiful, her breasts soon dipping into the turquoise water, her short hair sleek along her angular face. The boy Kidan had seen with Iniko that first day entered next, muscled chest bare, a gold-plated headband around his forehead.

If they were here, then ... Kidan didn't finish her thought. Susenyos disrobed.

He was built like one of the statues, deep brown skin fitted not to sag or stretch. She forced her gaze away but still caught the sight of his pelvis forming a perfect shape, mist covering the rest as he waded in.

The three of them spread out to edges of the pool and rested their heads. Kidan crouched there, eyes fixed on Susenyos, and skin unbearably warm.

"Taj, I want you to visit three places tomorrow." Susenyos's voice, low and earthy, drifted to her. "They're urgent. Iniko, you'll have five places."

Taj groaned. "If I'm acting as hero, maybe they should address the letters to me."

Letters? Kidan searched her mind and remembered the scrolls in Susenyos's room. *Letter to the Immortal.* Was it some sort of encrypted way of communicating?

"There's an issue with the Axum excavation process, some problem with the locals. They'll stop the dig if someone doesn't go." Annoyance warped Susenyos's words. "Iniko?"

"Handled. Best I leave before I do something I regret here anyway."

"Why are you looking at us like that?" Taj gave a light chuckle.

Iniko's tone curled. "I told you both to stay away from Ramyn, and now she's dead."

Kidan drew closer, easing the tension in her crouched legs.

"We all had our fun with her. God rest her little soul."

Kidan couldn't identify who said that. The sound of pressurized air deflated in the room, and steam poured from the floor grates lodged every five squares. Heat swept over her body. Her multiple layers of clothing weren't helping. She pulled out her tie and loosened it, wiping the back of her hand across her sweating forehead. Were there coals behind those grates? How hot did they need this place to be?

It was too quiet. They'd stopped talking. Kidan dared a glance but could only see thick fog. Her heart thundered.

She should leave.

Now.

"What are we looking for?" A low and secret voice tickled the back of her neck.

Kidan's spine jerked. Every cell in her body whimpered. She couldn't bring herself to turn, to witness the vampire crouching close.

"This is my lucky day."

He laughed softly against the bottom of her ear. How had he gotten here so fast?

"You...you can't hurt me," she began. "Dean Faris—"

"You willingly entered a *prohibited* area." He cut in with too much delight. "The moment you crossed that line, you voided her warning. There are starving dranaics in this building, accidental falls, drowning. So many deaths you've made possible, and I cannot be expected to save you from them all. I am not God. Although I do enjoy answering prayers."

Her stomach withered away. The steam had thickened, so she couldn't see past the ends of her fingers. Sweat trickled from her temple to her eyes, and she blinked furiously against the irritation.

"So, little bird, shall we stay like this forever or will you look at me?"

Fire scalded the back of her skin, skyrocketing her pulse. She bit the inside of her cheek, using the slash of pain to force her body to turn. If she was going to die, she'd do it while looking at those spoiled eyes.

And what a sight they were, wide and starving. The mist cloaked him like a second skin. His hair was wet and he was naked except for a single towel wrapped around his waist. She swallowed thickly, cheeks heating.

He gave her an appreciative whistle. "Very brave."

"I'll...leave." She made a move back, shoes slippery from the condensation.

He knelt forward, making her freeze. Gently, he grabbed the end of her tie and pulled, rubbing the fabric between his fingers. "I have had many thoughts about this tie of yours."

She blinked furiously and, when he smiled, launched her fists at him. He captured them in one hand and relieved her of the tie with his other. Her collar remained buttoned up, but without that layer of protection, she felt horribly exposed.

"Give it back," she snarled.

Then, to her horror, he was using it to secure both her wrists to the metal towel rack above. Her legs kicked out, but the angle made it awkward, and barely any of her attempted assaults landed on him. She was left in half a crouch, trapped with her arms above her head. Kidan shook her braids clear of her sweating face.

He disappeared into the mist. Her panic shot up. Was he going to leave her here to suffocate? Her nostrils burned with the eucalyptus drenching the wet air. She pulled and tried to gnaw at the tie, but it was no use. Her eyes stung, and she cried out breathlessly for help.

White fog swallowed her.

The Bath of Arowa melted away, and smoke seared her throat. The smell of burning body clung to her hair. No matter how many times she'd wash herself, it would never fade. Kidan choked. Inside the mist, Mama Anoet was tied to a chair, fighting for breath, begging for help.

It's not smoke. You're not at that house.

She squeezed her eyes shut and tried to calm her heart.

You're fine.

A loud whoosh sucked in a breath. Air thinned and Mama Anoet's betrayed eyes faded. Kidan's skin grew goose bumps with the sudden drop in temperature. Relief pumped through her.

Susenyos stood before her, fully clothed. Well, almost. His loose shirt was nearly unbuttoned to his navel. Why even wear it? Susenyos raised a brow at her stare.

Her face burned, and it had nothing to do with the steam.

"Let me go or I'll scream." Her arms shook, her top lip slick with sweat.

"Let you go? You're in my house now. It would be rude to leave without sharing a drink." He licked his lips, pulling his gaze down to her throat, and smiled when she shivered. "Or you can apologize for defanging me and I can let you go."

Apologize?

Kidan's eyes turned to slits. *"Or you can go straight to hell."*

He laughed like he expected this answer and freed her. When she reached for her tie, he held it out of reach, tucking it into his back pocket.

"Your lack of self-preservation, as always, is breathtaking. Let's see if we can wake it."

27.

SUSENYOS TOOK HER TO A CIRCULAR ROOM WITH MULTIPLE LOUNGES along its nooks. Dranaics mingled with one another, some behind the drawn curtains, a few by the bar, and right at the center, lined up like dolls, were blindfolded actis.

"What is this?" Kidan hissed, struggling against his hold.

"This is blood courting. Last time, you rudely interrupted our little gathering. Don't you remember?"

Kidan twisted her face in disgust. He pulled her into a lounge booth and secured her hands to the armchair with her tie.

Susenyos looked into the crowd. "Taj, watch her for me."

Taj peeled himself away from a stunning dranaic and joined her. Susenyos crossed over to the blindfolded group.

Taj gave a bow, chestnut eyes glittering. "Taj Zuri. The person Yos brings to people he hates the most. I wondered when we'd meet again."

His brown face split into a grin, a permanent quirk piercing each cheek. His long, twisted locs were held back by the thick gold-plated band along his forehead. The tail end of the band featured a sigil pin—a cup full of instruments. He belonged to House Qaros.

Kidan silently glared at him.

"Oh, we're not talking. Got it." He settled across from her, on the plush couch, and picked up a magazine from the low table. "Let me know if you change your mind."

After minutes of trying to free herself, Kidan sagged backward, eyeing the drawn curtains around the room.

"What happens behind there?"

Taj met her eyes over the magazine, smiling. "You're thinking horrible things, aren't you?"

"Shouldn't I? With a name like blood courting?"

"Oh, sweetheart. No." He set his reading aside. "Blood courting is for heirs that have graduated Dranacti and taken a companionship vow. Technically, we're only allowed to drink from our companions, but some find a little thrill in letting others have a taste of them, to see if they want another vampire." He let out a long sigh. "Only a taste, though. The once-a-month rule is criminal, but Dean Faris loves her rules."

Well, he was chatty. Kidan kept her guard up, face hard. "Once-a-month rule?"

"Can't drink from the same acti until thirty days pass. The wait is agonizing, and for those of us with little control, pacing yourself is important."

"Why cover their eyes?"

"They request it. Helps them concentrate on the...act. Some choose companions based on business, some pleasure. You can tell which one I prefer."

He offered her a wide grin.

Bile rose up her throat. "That's disgusting."

He laughed, tilting his head so his gaze fell to her neck. "Really? You wouldn't shop around before picking your companion? That's unfair to you."

She shifted in her seat. "I'm not picking anyone."

He raised his brows. "What if you prefer the feel of my fangs over another's? How will you know if you don't try?" Her horrified look made him chuckle. "A shame. There's nothing quite like it."

"For *you*."

He laughed again, the lightness of it surprising her. Kidan hadn't met a vampire who laughed this genuinely, and certainly not this often. She'd thought them incapable of true joy.

"Yes, but there's pleasure in the bite for actis too," he said. "You see things you never would, experience things you never dreamed of."

"What do you mean?"

His brows scrunched. "You've been here this long, and no one's told you how the human body reacts to a bite?"

She hardened her gaze. Why should she care about the violent act? A bite was a bite.

"It's my pleasure to educate you." Taj lowered his dancing voice as if sharing a secret. "Every time a vampire bites a human, there are chemical reactions. One is of the body, and it's *extraordinary*, but there's one of the mind too. A moment when we can look into each other's memories and thoughts."

Kidan gaped with equal measure of shock and horror.

His eyes twinkled. "It gets better. Each body part conjures a different category of emotion. A bite to the wrist takes you into each other's childhood, and the chest conjures violence. I always prefer the neck, though. Nothing like knowing what a person's desires are."

He had to be lying, because what the fuck?

Before she could ask more, she saw Susenyos lowering his head into the ear of a blindfolded girl.

"What's he doing?"

Taj followed her line of vision. "Asking permission. We're not monsters. Wait, no. That's wrong. We're not monsters unless you want us to be."

Kidan couldn't begin to parse the emotions Taj Zuri was stirring in her.

Susenyos approached with a raven-haired girl on his arm. The girl didn't seem frightened at all. He gave a nod to Taj, who left with a wink. Susenyos settled the girl onto the empty couch.

Kidan tried to tug herself free, but his knot was impossible to break. Susenyos bridged the space between them, leaning forward so his damp twists tickled her cheeks. The scent of eucalyptus and rose oil clung to his skin, and the combination was heady. Almost like a drug. She licked her lips and pressed herself as far back as she could.

"You took my flask, didn't you?" he whispered. "What did you do with it?"

She glared. It was her only weapon at the moment, and she'd keep wielding it.

"Then you defanged me." Suppressed anger rippled his words. "Only one other soul has done that. Do you know what I did to them?"

Kidan schooled her expression to flat disregard. "You killed them. Original."

He popped her collar free. Goose bumps spread across her hollowed, exposed throat. Her chest rose and fell in rapid movements.

Susenyos gave her a slow smile. "You indulged in my excruciating pain, it's only fair you watch as I take my pleasure."

Watch as he...

Her heart threatened to tear out of her chest.

He was going to bite her.

"Relax, little bird." He rested a finger on the divot of her neck, and she shivered. "I won't drink from you...yet."

When he stepped back, she exhaled, relief making her dizzy. Susenyos sat on the couch and pulled the raven-haired girl to his lap. He trailed a slow finger down her arched, smooth neck. Kidan's own neck muscles contracted. Hot spikes punched up her veins.

She saw that his fangs had more than healed when they parted his mouth, no different from bone-white blades, wide at the base and sharpened to a deadly point. Kidan's lips parted.

He shrugged the girl's loose strap aside and closed his full mouth over her bare shoulder. A deep, unabashed sigh flitted out of the girl. Kidan's ears warmed. He sucked at the skin in slow, languid kisses. Kidan rolled her own shoulders, imagining his mouth to be warm and wet like the inside of boiled fruit. She pinched the inside of her palm for the disturbing thought.

A whimpered *please* came from the girl next.

God, how could anyone enjoy this?

Susenyos stretched his lips. Kidan needed to look away.

Right now.

But try as she might, she couldn't break his searing gaze. Kidan knew the moment his fangs tore flesh, because the girl twitched and clung to the front of his shirt in a firm grip.

A thin line of blood glided down her brown skin, absorbed by her bunched dress. All through this, Susenyos's black eyes never left Kidan's.

Her teeth rang and her skin stretched tight as the room faded around them.

She could *feel* him on her, arms wrapped along her chest and waist, crushing her body to his as if he'd only be satisfied if he climbed inside her skin. His eyes crested with desire, burning into a tarnished gold, a ring of red around the pupils, the ends of his hair catching brilliant sunlight.

Look away.

Kidan's gut withered to nothing but ash.

Why aren't you looking away?

She would die here watching him.

The girl's hands tapped him, and Susenyos tilted back, fluttering his lashes shut in what could only be euphoria. Drinking from the flask never drenched him in this much golden light, bronzing his features to the point that fire ate at his hair. Kidan's thighs trembled, and she pressed them together to fight the shake. Just what kind of monster was he?

Taj reappeared, placed a bandage on the girl's shoulder, and sent her away. He rested against the wall by Susenyos's side, arching a knowing brow at Kidan. Heat flushed down her neck.

Susenyos hung his head forward for two heartbeats, touched his forehead, then walked unsteadily to her, grabbing both edges of her chair. She kept her attention at his chin and not his wild, shifting irises.

"And to think this will be us every day." His voice had changed, swallowed too much smoke. "Is this really what you want by staying here? To be on my lap for the rest of your life? Feeding me your blood like a good little bird?"

Whatever weird heat had been traveling through Kidan abandoned her. It was an effort not to snarl. "You'll have to kill me first."

He crouched before her, forcing her to meet his starlight eyes. "There's only one way I'll let you leave. I want to hear you say sorry."

Her face twisted. "Sorry?"

"Yes, like that. But without the sneer, and not like it's your first day apologizing."

She flattened her gaze. "Never."

At once, his tone became night, devoid of all calm. "Actually, *I'm* sorry. I don't want to hear your apology. I want you to beg."

"*What?*"

"Beg me to let you go."

He was not serious. Yet the stillness of his face and Taj's tensed shoulders said otherwise.

"Beg," Susenyos repeated with a deathly low tone. "For all you've put me through. *Beg.*"

Laughter bubbled up in Kidan's throat and broke free. Thunder rolled down Susenyos's face. He didn't know her at all.

"All this because I defanged you after you begged me to? What's wrong? Do your teeth still hurt after your little show?"

Taj palmed his face.

Kidan ignored him. "I'm not apologizing, and I'm sure as fuck not begging."

Susenyos only needed four words to shake her resolve. "Taj, close the curtains."

Taj's brown complexion yellowed. "Are you sure? Come on, you still haven't fed on Chrisle."

"*Now.*"

Kidan jerked from the force of the words. But it was Taj's worry that irritated her. Why was he so afraid?

"Sure thing," Taj said. "But first you have to log that you fed from Arwal, before someone else does."

Susenyos didn't move.

"You don't want Dean Faris to ban you from here again," Taj continued carefully.

The small booth swelled with silence, save for the pumping of Kidan's heart.

Susenyos rose slowly, an annoyed tick to his jaw. "I'll be back."

After he walked out, Taj sagged in relief. "You need to do whatever he says to get out of this place. This is about pride now. One of you has to cave, and it must be you."

Kidan bristled. "There's no way—"

He crossed quickly and knelt before her, features tight. "You defanged him. There is nothing, *nothing*, more demeaning to us than that."

Her next protest died on her lips.

"It's more intimate, more violent, than pulling out our hearts. That's why he's angry."

More violent and intimate...so? Let him be angry. Did he expect empathy? If it hurt him this much, then those fangs were a savage reminder she'd taken from him just as he had from her.

Taj's chestnut eyes pleaded with her. "He can't just let you go. You have to help him."

Kidan ground her jaw. "No."

He wiped a hand down his face. "You're both too fucking stubborn."

"Why do you care?" she shot back.

He leveled her with an anxious look. "It doesn't matter if you die here or outside. He'll be blamed."

"You're protecting him."

"I'm trying to help you both. If you two cross this line, there's no going back." Kidan turned her chin away.

Taj remained quiet for several seconds before his soft tone pulled at her. "If you can't beg toward him, beg toward me. Just do and say whatever it takes for him to let you leave."

Every molecule in her body vibrated with fury. By the time Susenyos returned and drew the curtains, cutting all light and noise, Taj was at the back of the wall.

A thin, gleaming knife flipped in Susenyos's hand. "I prefer my silver, but this will do. Now, should I start with your teeth?"

Kidan ground her teeth so hard, he wouldn't need the knife to collect pieces of them.

He stabbed the knife into the side table. With a forefinger on the hilt, he spun it, making the wood groan and creak. "Or maybe that tongue? But then you wouldn't be able to beg. Taj, what do you think?"

Kidan's gaze flicked to Taj, who was still imploring her with those large eyes. Her loathing had never boiled to this point. But Taj's face, patient, worried, quelled it a little. Made her see some sort of reason. Breathe.

She couldn't die without taking him down first. Without finding June.

Taj gave her a small nod.

Thinner than a whisper, she forced out, "Fine. Sorry."

The spinning knife stilled. "Don't stop there. For what, exactly? Ruining my peace? Trying to steal what was rightfully left to me? Destroying my treasures? Defanging me? With a list this long, it's remarkable you're still alive."

Each word was like swallowing acid, and she had to down it in one go. "I'm sorry I took your flask. Sorry I defanged you."

I'm sorry you're the most disgusting creature to walk this earth. I'm sorry I didn't pull out every single one of your teeth. I'm sorry I didn't douse you in gasoline and burn you in that observatory. I'm sorry I haven't found the weapon that will end you.

"What else?" he mused.

"Please . . . let me go."

He laughed softly, putting away his weapon. "Oh no. I want that in public. Taj, bring her."

Kidan was confused as Susenyos parted the curtain and exited.

Grim-faced, Taj freed her hands and walked her to the middle of the room, lowering his voice. "You're going to kneel."

Her eyes grew wide. "You're not serious."

Susenyos took his position by a couple of snickering dranaics, voice loud and bright. "My lovely dranaics, here we have Kidan Adane, who entered our building without invitation. She has something to say before I can let her go."

At least twenty dranaics stared down their nose at her. Kidan's cheeks ignited. She felt like some infestation that had disturbed their peace.

Taj tried to lower her, but her shoulders locked.

"Kidan," he warned.

Her legs were made of pure stone. She would not kneel. Taj must have sensed it, because he applied a little pressure at her elbow, softening her spine like melting ice. The sharp pain of her knees hitting the floor was nothing compared with the embarrassment choking her.

"I forget how pitiful they all look," a silver-haired woman voiced, lips red as sin.

"Yes. Very. But you can't help but want to watch them forever." Susenyos's voice grew rough again. "Beg."

Kidan couldn't stand the sight of his eager face, ready to devour her like a beast. She shut her eyes, took a breath. "Please . . . let me go."

Light laughter bubbled all around, setting her blood on fire.

"Again."

She said it lower this time.

Kidan heard him move toward her, footsteps light, scent cloying. "Once more while looking at me."

She refused to open her eyes. "Just please let me go."

"I love the shape of your mouth when you beg." The delight in his voice was too much. "But don't deny me those dark eyes of yours. They have a language of their own."

Her eyes flew open, raging with a thousand crackling embers.

He drew in a slow breath, tracking one pupil, then the other. "Your hatred burns like ocean ice. And it's entirely...mine. I've never owned something so completely."

Fuck, she was going to lose it. She was going to curse him within an inch of his life. Let him kill her. Let him do whatever the hell he wanted. She was—

"I think she's done," Taj said quickly.

Susenyos cocked his head. "I don't know. I still feel like she doesn't mean it."

"Yos," Taj said. "Look at her. She's shaking."

Oh, she was shaking all right. From the effort not to strangle him with her own tie.

Susenyos studied the crowd, then spared her a bored glance. "I suppose. And you'll leave Uxlay?"

Hell no.

Taj's gaze screamed at her. *Just get out of this building.*

"I will."

Susenyos thought for a long minute, sighed, and stepped away. "Take her home and help her pack. Make sure she leaves."

Taj pulled Kidan to her feet with such speed that she swayed from the sudden change in gravity. As he led her away with quick strides, she glimpsed a look back. The crowd was congratulating Susenyos on his little show. He smirked and welcomed their pats.

She forced her chin straight. He would regret this. She would pay this back twice as viciously.

Outside the Southern Sost Buildings, the lion-shaped lamps broke the night in fanned waves. Had she really been in there for hours?

"You're not going to leave, are you?" Taj said once they crossed the defined border into acti territory.

She ignored him, rubbing her sore wrists.

He released a breath, running a hand through his hair. She tensed, worried he'd do as told.

What she didn't expect was a sheepish grin. "Tell Yos I gave you firm instructions and scared you, okay?"

"You're not going to force me to leave?"

"I don't really do force. Besides, I don't think he wants you to leave."

"What? Of course he does."

"No." His voice quieted. "If he really wanted you gone, he would have sent Iniko with you."

Kidan's eyes creased with distrust. Why was he willingly sharing details about their group? Why was he helping her?

"Well, see you tomorrow," he said.

"Tomorrow?"

Taj smiled secretively. "The Acti Gala. There's a grand assignment waiting for you. One of my favorites, really. Better make up with Yos. You won't pass if he's still pissed."

She bristled and watched Taj lace his fingers behind his head, whistling as he melted into the darkness. If she wasn't so furious, and perhaps was a decent person, she would have thanked him for saving her life.

Make up with Yos.

Like they were a pair of bickering roommates. Like he hadn't made her beg and feel him all over her body. Kidan's shoulders tingled again, and she clenched her fists until her nails tore into her palms. It didn't matter how. She had to get back at him.

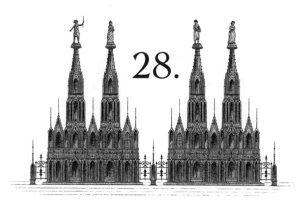

28.

"Welcome to your first Acti Gala. Tonight, your assignment will be to convince a vampire to gift you an article of their clothing," Professor Andreyas said.

Kidan couldn't have heard that right. They were standing amid the swaying grass, under the twinkling stars, dressed in their finest outfits. The annual event was held in the Grand Andromeda Hall, which sparkled in front of them like broken glass under water. Kidan wore a high-collared sea-green dress that Dean Faris had sent for her. The dean had insisted that the heiress of Adane House appropriately make her debut. An emerald hairpin encrusted with the Adane mountain sigil accompanied the outfit, securing Kidan's braids up and away from her neck.

"You want us to take...their clothes?" Asmil, a girl with closely cropped hair, squeaked.

"Not take. Have them gift it to you." Professor Andreyas fixed his cuff links. "Aim for a personal possession—their rings, coats, even dresses if you're capable of it. It must be of great significance. The more meaning to the possession, the higher you will rank. Although I hate repeating myself, I must because most of you choose to let your hearing fail you at this stage: *You cannot steal it.*"

He stared them down with those ancient eyes until they nodded.

Rufeal Makary, a boy with a slippery smile, asked, "Is there a particular rule we have to follow to get a dress? What's the limit?"

He grinned at his friend.

Professor Andreyas shot them an unimpressed look. "No limit. You can do whatever you must. Seduction too. Although I doubt you would be capable of it, Makary."

A line tightened along Rufeal's jaw. Yusef laughed, earning a glare from Rufeal.

"You have until midnight. Enjoy the food, music, and conversation. Make it count, because the entire party will observe what you have been gifted. Good luck."

After the professor left, they stood outside, strategizing.

"As far as I know, Iniko Obu is the hardest target. The last time she gave her clothing was fourteen years ago, I think. Taj Zuri, on the other hand, hands it out like fucking candy," Rufeal explained to his friends a few paces away.

"And Susenyos Sagad?" Asmil asked, voice fluttering. Kidan's ears perked up.

"He would, but no one approaches him. Too much bad house history. Everyone knows he killed his companions. I mean, look at the state of House Adane. How the hell is there only *one* of them left out of—"

"Shut up, Makary," Yusef cut in coldly.

Rufeal crossed his arms, dark gaze sliding to Kidan. "You know I'm right, Umil. Even you didn't choose him last year."

The students' attention heated her face. Kidan cast her gaze to the shifting grass, fists tightening. She couldn't begin to parse the loss of her entire lineage— she would sink right here and never get up. But June was attainable. June she could make sure wasn't lost.

"Ignore them," Slen said next to her. "If you think you can pass, go for Susenyos."

Kidan shuddered against the thought. No way would she ask him.

They entered through the massive doors bracketed by Demasus's golden lion statues. The mythic creatures bared their violent fangs, and students rubbed their sculpted manes for good luck and strength as they walked in.

Inside, the wide, sparkling space flowed with soft classical music, poured champagne, and cascading chatter. Tables around the room were assigned according to status, the current high-standing House determined by business status and how many dranaics were loyal to them. The First Table belonged to House Ajtaf and the last to Adane.

Slen, GK, and Kidan did one round together, discussing who to approach, and they lost Yusef along the way. Kidan spotted Taj talking to Asmil but saw no sign of Susenyos. Not that she wanted to find him. He hadn't come home last night, and she hoped he wouldn't tonight either.

When the three of them paused for a small break, Yusef reappeared with a piece of clothing—a heel. It'd been exactly five minutes. Both Slen and Kidan glared at him.

"What?" He shrugged. "I'm charming."

Rufeal grinned as he walked past them, holding a new coat behind his back, and coming in second.

Kidan narrowed her eyes. "I hate that guy."

"Same," Yusef echoed.

"Weren't you his study partner for Dranacti last year?" Slen asked.

"Yeah, but it's just his energy.... I feel like he's always watching me."

Kidan slid a glance to Rufeal, who indeed was now watching them from the opposite end of the room.

"This year he's my competition for the Youth Art Exhibition," Yusef continued. "He wants to become a talented, cocky little artist. The world can only handle one of those, and that's me."

Yusef laughed softly. When Kidan was being attentive, she glimpsed his laughter stutter and slip off its curve like a speeding car before it crashed. As if it was all a mask. And now she saw it clearly.... He was afraid. Artists and their pursuit of capturing the divine, obsessed with creation, being the best.

"I'm sure you'll be fine," she said.

"Yeah. He's been trying to convince my great-aunt to give him a seat on the Umil Art Museum board. That's what's bothering me. Since when do the Makarys swap their briefcases for paintbrushes? Why would he even switch to the arts? The art museum is ours—it was my fath ..."

Yusef's words faded, and he shook his head. Kidan wanted to ask more, but she worried about pushing him too soon.

"Anyway, you guys should get moving. I'm getting a drink," Yusef said, and left.

"Who do you want to go for, GK?" Kidan asked.

GK's warm eyes settled on someone. Kidan liked his soft movements, the silent guardian quality to his stance, always observant and alert. "I'd like to talk to Susenyos Sagad. No one is going near him, and it's difficult to watch."

"No," Kidan said too quickly.

Her neck prickled, but she wasn't going to look. *So he's here.*

Slen and GK each lifted a brow.

"Trust me. You don't want him as your companion. He's vile."

GK pondered this before nodding. She sighed in relief. She hadn't been able to save Ramyn from Susenyos's clutches. She could still protect GK.

Someone at the next table moved, revealing a familiar red velvet vest and coat as well as sculpted cheekbones. Kidan's stomach tightened. Iniko Obu. From the scathing look she wielded, Kidan understood that she'd heard everything.

"I'm going to browse." Kidan moved into the crowd, rolling her shoulder to shake off Iniko's wrath.

Once she was safely in the middle of the crowd, she loosened a breath.

Taj walked toward her. When they'd glimpsed him earlier, he had on a suit jacket, long coat, and gold chain. Now he was left in a tank top outlining his muscled arms and...missing a belt.

"Really?" Kidan raised a brow. "That was quick."

"I usually try to stop before I'm indecent, but couldn't resist. Prof is not going to be happy. He said I had to pick three."

She studied the gold-plated band that covered his forehead more than his hairline. "Why do you wear it like that?"

He touched it, surprised, and offered a smile that didn't quite reach his eyes. "Got a hideous scar."

"Is the band comfortable?"

"Not for the last sixty years."

Kidan's mouth parted. "Then you shouldn't wear it. Scars are nothing to be ashamed of."

He smiled. "I'll remember that."

She shifted on her feet, not knowing how to ask for what she wanted. "Give me something."

He shut his eyes like the words wounded him. "I wish I could."

"Why can't you?"

Taj's attention traveled to the back of the room. No doubt to who. Gritting her teeth, Kidan finally looked.

There he was, arrogantly lounging in a suit that matched his inky black eyes, red and gold trimmings curling along the collar. Upon noticing Kidan and Taj, Susenyos's expression darkened.

Her blood turned cold. "You're not giving me anything because of him?"

"Got to side with my boy on this one."

GK was right, Susenyos was alone. It was incredible how no actis dared approach him, as if an invisible shield separated him. One student actually changed direction halfway so she wouldn't run into him.

Year after year...was this what he went through?

Kidan crossed her arms. "Why does he even come?"

"Maybe he hopes someone will give him a chance," Taj said with a pointed look in her direction.

Kidan scoffed. "Maybe if your *boy* wasn't such a deranged piece of—"

"Careful." Taj's dark demeanor cut her savage words. "Don't insult him before me. It'll be the quickest way to ruin our friendship."

Kidan blinked. Taj held her gaze with a piercing warning, a new darkness eclipsing his chestnut eyes. Her pulse quickened at the fierce loyalty in them, aged and unwavering. First Iniko and now Taj. What did Susenyos do to garner such protection? Who was he to them?

Kidan gave a slow nod, unsure why....When the hell had they become friends?

Taj smiled again, light flooding his face as if that tense exchange never happened. He wished her luck and disappeared into the crowd. Kidan shook her head, trying to dispel the odd tightness in her chest. Was this fear or hurt? No, it was more disgusting than that. She was jealous of Susenyos.

He'd found people to accept him as he was. To walk beside him as he committed unspeakable acts without flinching.

Kidan glimpsed GK along the wall, regarding the light and sound of the gala with stiff shoulders; Yusef was at the center of it, smiling near a group of girls; and Slen was speaking to her grinning brother.

She found herself wondering if she'd have their true friendship. Something she hadn't allowed herself to consider until now. That sacred bond was for those deserving and worthy of life. But...if Susenyos could have it, why not her?

She shook her head. What was wrong with her?

A loud altercation drew her attention to the corner.

"Give it to me." Koril Qaros loomed over Slen and her brother, voice cold as ice.

Slen's brother held out a joint. Koril looked at it for a second, then back-handed his son. The joint flew out his hand and landed near Kidan, flickering dimly.

Slen righted her injured brother. "Leave him *alone.*"

"This is the last time you'll embarrass this house," their father snarled at both of them before fixing his suit.

Kidan's nails dug into her palms, almost drawing blood, and she marched toward them without a second thought, lifting a drink from a tray on the way. She stumbled inches from Koril, spilling the red wine all down his suited back.

Koril Qaros spun toward her slowly, dripping, face contorted.

She touched her head. "I'm so sorry."

His pinprick eyes narrowed. He opened his mouth but shut it when he realized half the room was watching him. He forced a smile, then swiftly exited to clean himself up.

Slen checked her brother with gentle tenderness. Kidan averted her gaze at the familiar touches. She'd done this exact thing with June many times.

"I'm fine." He brushed her off, embarrassed, and walked away.

The crowd shifted their attention to more interesting things. Slen's fingers curled at her sides, quiet.

"Thank you." Her voice was water losing its ice. Almost soft.

Kidan swallowed roughly. "This isn't the first time your father has done that."

"I know."

Her mouth hardened. "I can take care of him for you."

Slen blinked. The most emotion Kidan had ever seen on her. "What do you mean?"

Shit.

"I mean . . . help report him or something."

Slen studied her like a troubling translation. Kidan regarded her in the same manner, cautious, trying to figure out what went on in that intelligent mind. Here and now, Slen's eyes weren't dead at all, but walled with so many layers they deflected anything from piercing them.

Maybe Slen Qaros was the only person here who understood a family's betrayal, a vicious thorn under the skin. No matter how deeply you dug or scraped at the wound, you could never pinch and pull it out.

They found themselves staring at each other too long, and an awkward silence blanketed them. They solved it by nodding and walking to opposite ends of the room. Kidan shook her head, focusing on her task.

For the next three hours, every vampire she approached gave her the cold shoulder. She grew embarrassed to the point of tearing out her own hair. She didn't want the dranaics, but why didn't they want *her*? They certainly talked about her. Whispered about the last heiress of Adane House. Her gums hurt from caging her tongue.

A House Rojit vampire, short and smelling of peppermint, stopped her halfway into her ask.

"Sorry, not interested."

His eyes darted to the back of the room, widening slightly. He hadn't been the first one to look nervous. Kidan followed his gaze, confused. Susenyos raised a glass, lips curving. The vampire scurried away before she could speak.

You've got to be kidding me.

Kidan stormed toward Susenyos. "What did you say to them?"

His voice flowed like silk. "A life of companionship with you would be a death sentence."

Kidan gaped. He'd blacklisted her. Kidan's features contorted, but yelling would do no good. She had thirty minutes left, so she swallowed her fire. She ran an eye over Susenyos's fitted clothes. He would have to do.

He wore a crisp white shirt with several buttons opened to reveal a dark, muscled chest. Red thread webbed along his collar like veins, and golden rings adorned his twisted hair, catching light his eyes didn't. His suit jacket rested on the chair beside him. So easy to take.

"Oh, I dare you to try."

"Try what?" she said, irritated that he'd read her so easily.

He smirked. Then *he* was regarding her openly, his eyes trailing up her curved hips and full chest before resting on her collared neck. Her body went cold, then hot. His gaze darkened with equal measures of desire and disgust.

Her jaw clenched. "Stop that."

"I will when you do."

"I'm not doing *that*," she said, horrified. Though she couldn't help but notice him a little more since the Southern Sost Buildings. An unwanted image of him in that towel flitted across her mind, drenched in that intoxicating scent. She scowled.

He studied her pinned braids with a growing smile. "Better. Now your lovely neck is on display."

Her eyes turned to slits. "No wonder no one wants to be your companion."

He lifted a brow. "You're running out of time bad-mouthing me. You should really go *court* some vampires. I'll watch this time."

A reminder of yesterday. Kidan's shoulder tingled again with the memory of watching his wet kiss, then his searing bite. Her nostrils flared, but she calmed herself.

"I get it." She sat next to him, lifting his jacket onto her lap and feigning compassion. "No one chooses poor Susenyos, so you want me to know how it feels."

"I love watching you grow desperate."

"I'm not desperate."

"What did Taj say? I saw you talking to him." He snuck a side glance at her. "You looked quite heartbroken."

Her grip tightened on the jacket.

"It's adorable." A low laugh rumbled in his chest.

"What?"

"You thought Taj would side against me. Was his little rescue in the Southern Sost that convincing?"

She shot to her feet. God, she hated him. Even staying this close to him for a few minutes was impossible.

"Ah, wait." He stretched out a muscled arm. "Jacket, please."

It was still clutched in both hands. Gritting her teeth, she gave it back.

"To your final night." He lifted a drink. "You've lasted longer than I expected." Bristling, she stormed off.

Midnight was twenty minutes away, and almost everyone had succeeded. GK was surprisingly talking to . . . Iniko.

Kidan left the stifling heat and breathed in the cold, biting air outside. The chatter faded from her ears, and grass stretched out to the woods, beckoning her.

This was it.

If she failed Dranacti, she couldn't stay at Uxlay. Her heart squeezed painfully, and she leaned against the building, shutting her eyes.

I'm sorry, June.

The clinking of finger bones met her ears. "Are you all right?"

Kidan lifted her head, letting out a deep sigh. "I'm going to fail."

GK's light brown eyes creased. "There's always next year."

She shook her head. "I can't wait until next year. The moment I leave... Susenyos will inherit my house. He only has to live alone for twenty-eight consecutive days."

GK remained silent, listening. Then he spoke. "Why did your parents leave the house to him?"

"I don't know!" she cried out, startling him. "But I can't leave now. I'm here to..."

His brown eyes carried the reflected lights. Patient. Kidan didn't know why she felt a sense of kinship toward him. The others excited her—an aura of desperation, creativity, even danger circled them—but GK was clean. Like the smell of grass after it rained.

Could she trust him? She remembered how he'd run to save Ramyn. How he joined the group because he sensed she was in danger. It wouldn't matter soon anyway.

"I'm looking for my sister." Her voice almost broke with the confession. "Susenyos took her, and no one believes me."

GK's eyes darkened with unbridled concern. It was such a relief to see someone else echo her pain. She wanted to tell him everything.

He was silent for a long time. Then he took Kidan's hand and in it placed a black button from a certain red velvet coat.

Iniko had gifted him an article of clothing.

"Take mine," he said.

"What? I can't."

"There's nothing in the rules that says I can't gift you what was gifted to me."

Kidan's gaze softened. "Even if that works, you'll be forced to leave. You're here to find a companion."

A sad smile captured his lips. "My reasons feel quite weak next to yours. I can stand the solitude of being a Mot Zebeya another year. Take it."

Kidan ached at his kindness. The solitary lifestyle of the Mot Zebeyas was still unclear to her, but it had to be cruel. Leaving your family behind always was. Kidan knew that beast in the dark, spinning her out of control. She'd only been alone for a year, and it'd broken her. The need for people's voices around her, their smell, their touch—she'd started to die the moment they were withdrawn from her.

How long had GK been alone? And yet here he was, offering to return to that abyss. When Kidan thought of good, this was what she wanted so desperately to be. Kind like Ramyn, like June.

"No." She returned the button to his hand and closed his fingers over it. "I'll find another way. Thank you, GK."

He nodded slowly, perhaps wanting to refuse, but he didn't.

A group of drunk boys burst out of the gala, hollering and shoving one another. One lost his balance and knocked into Kidan with his whiskey bottle. She hissed at the sharp pain.

GK caught her and put her behind him with surprising quickness.

"My bad, man." The Rojit boy grinned, sloshing his drink.

"You should pay attention to your steps." GK's voice eclipsed itself, his body unusually stiff.

The Rojit boy blinked rapidly. "Yeah...sorry."

He tried to walk away, but GK blocked his path. "Apologize to her."

The drunk boy worked his jaw. "Get out of my way."

Kidan touched GK's tense shoulder, confused. "It's fine."

He moved aside slowly, eyes swirling. The boy muttered something about Mot Zebeya freaks and hurried to join his friends.

GK's face remained tense, watching the retreating boys like they were still a threat.

"Don't worry about them," Kidan said, trying to ease the tension. "They're just having fun."

"Fun?" He said it like a foreign word. "I think they look like fools."

160

Kidan studied their childlike tussling and wild laughter. "I don't know. They look happy. I can't remember the last time I laughed like that."

He regarded her with a guarded expression. "I'm sorry I didn't realize you were in so much pain."

"Why would you?" She gave him a sad smile. "You should go in. I'll be there soon."

He hesitated for a moment, then walked back inside.

GK's words about the rules had given her a dangerous idea.

Some kind of personal possession, Professor Andreyas had said. She checked her phone: ten minutes left.

Kidan headed to her haunted house to acquire what would drive Susenyos mad.

Oh, he'd *wish* he'd given her his jacket, his rings, his entire wardrobe.

29.

KIDAN MADE IT BACK A MINUTE BEFORE MIDNIGHT, BREATHLESS AND sweaty, just as students were lining up.

"Where were you?" Slen muttered as Kidan climbed onstage. "Did you get something?"

"Yes. It's . . . risky."

Interest gleamed in Slen's features, making Kidan's lips press together with nerves. This could go brilliantly—or be disastrous. Either way, she would go out with one final win.

Dean Faris watched, a turquoise beaded hairpin shining in her sleeked hair. Kidan had overheard that Professor Andreyas gifted it to the dean forty years ago on this day. The cornrowed and dark-skinned professor remained the oldest of all the dranaics here, a companion to the very first dean of Uxlay and serving the house loyally ever since.

"Actis, dranaics." Professor Andreyas didn't need to raise his voice to command attention. "Following tradition, we will now reveal which actis have garnered the gift and interest of companionship from dranaics."

Yusef Umil held up a heel. "Resa Tar, Delarus House."

A stunning vampire with a neck tattoo shot him a sultry look.

Rufeal Makary nodded toward a large vampire with a thick beard. "Asuris Redi, Makary House."

GK held up a button. "Iniko Obu, Ajtaf House."

Awed whispers echoed in the room. Iniko gave a brief nod of confirmation.

Kidan's heart launched into a frenzy when it was her turn.

"Kidan?"

Shit.

She was displaying no article of clothing. Nothing.

"Susenyos Sagad, Adane House."

The professor lifted a brow, as did others in the front crowd, leaning forward. Dean Faris regarded her with a curious tilt of her head.

Susenyos held his relaxed position at the back of the room, drinking with a triumphant look. He knew that whatever she had, he'd say he didn't gift it to her, utterly embarrass her, and that'd be the end of things.

She'd known she needed something he couldn't afford to deny. Something he'd rather say he relinquished than have every soul in this room learn she had *wrenched* from him.

Kidan opened her fingers, revealing a pair of glistening and bloodied fangs.

The crowd gasped.

Susenyos choked.

Kidan smiled.

"The assignment was an article of *clothing*," Rufeal sneered.

"You said something personal, professor." Her voice rang loud in the stunned quiet. "What's more personal to a vampire than his teeth?"

A small roar of laughter echoed, breaking up the shock. The actis laughed. No dranaic did.

"He gifted these to you?" Professor Andreyas's mahogany forehead furrowed.

Kidan lifted her lashes to him. "How else would I get them?"

Every head in the vicinity turned toward Susenyos. He was on his feet. Iniko and Taj were blocking him. When had they gotten there? Iniko had a firm hold on his arm, and Taj was speaking intently into his ear. She could imagine Taj's rushed words, reminding him they were in public, to calm down.

Would he admit she defanged him because he attacked her, almost forcing a companionship vow? No. Dean Faris was here.

Would he say she defanged him by force? No. He had far too much pride. And no one would believe a weak human girl could overpower the great Savage Susenyos.

He'd rather say he gave them to her and save face. It was his only move.

Stop smiling, she told herself.

She really tried.

"Susenyos?" Professor Andreyas called.

Kidan thought the most beautiful expression she'd witnessed on him was after he'd found the artifact room destroyed. How wrong she was. This look could murder all looks. If Kidan could paint, she'd capture his stiffness, curled lips, black eyes catching red, the hands of his friends taming him as if he was a wild beast a breath away from tearing out her throat. He was all her fury, all her hatred and violence, made manifest—and how decadently, how divinely, they fit him, better than the clothes he wouldn't gift her.

Now they were even.

Taj's words must have convinced him, because Susenyos managed a curt nod, barely moving his chin. It sent another wave of murmurs through the room.

Professor Andreyas gave nothing away. "Very well."

Kidan rested her hands, sighing. She'd passed.

"You've seen this year's cohort. Wish them luck and hope they will join us formally at the end-of-year companionship ceremony. Now, as tradition dictates, actis, please join your chosen dranaics in a dance."

The claps were staggered before falling as one.

Wait...Did he say "dance"?

When Kidan snapped her gaze to the back of the room, Taj, Iniko, and Susenyos had vanished.

30.

DEAN FARIS ADJUSTED HER SATIN GLOVES, THEN CAME TO STAND BY Kidan. "Quite the show."

"Thank you."

Her sharp eyes bore down as if she could read Kidan's thoughts. "And you will dance with Susenyos to show this newfound...trust, yes?"

"Um, I don't know the dance. Maybe next year."

Kidan tried to get away, but Dean Faris stepped closer, dropping her voice. "Kidan. Susenyos didn't hide his anger well, and there are many who noticed. You will dance with him, show us this was a *choice*, or I'll be forced to investigate just how he lost his fangs."

An investigation into this wouldn't bode well for either of them. Who would Dean Faris believe?

Kidan's throat went dry. "He left."

Dean Faris pointed down a hall to where two black-clothed vampires stood guard. Silver swords gleamed at their waists, and moonlight daggers were strapped to their thighs. Sicions. The only ones allowed to carry silver weapons openly.

"They're down there," Dean Faris said. "Go fetch your dranaic. We'll wait."

It was remarkable, the power this woman wielded. Fighting a grumble, Kidan crossed the hall that spilled into a small art gallery.

"You have to dance with her." Iniko's calm voice traveled from the side door.

Kidan froze.

"I'm going to *pull out* her black heart." Susenyos's voice sounded burnt, much too guttural. "Get out of my way."

There was a fighting sound, grunting, as if they were trying to control him.

"If you leave now, they'll think she overpowered you," Iniko continued. "But if you dance with her, they'll see you two are serious about being companions, that you chose this. It's not unheard-of."

"Unheard-of? She dangled my fangs like a fucking *trophy*."

Another wild tussle of a fight. Kidan's lips twitched.

"You need to calm down." Taj sounded like he had a knife in his gut.

"You allowed her to." Iniko's voice tightened. "Everyone knows she could never take them without your permission. We all know, Yos. Pretend like you wanted it for your own sake."

"Wanted it? Wouldn't it be easier if I knelt and lapped at her feet?" he snarled, making Kidan's smile grow.

Yes, that would be easier.

Taj spoke through labored efforts. "If you'd let me give her my shirt—"

"I dare you to finish that sentence."

Kidan flinched from the bite of those words. Yet there was no way she was going to miss this. She kept approaching, keeping her feet light.

"It's only a dance," Taj implored.

"Don't let them think you're weak, Sagad," Iniko added. "Remember what you're fighting for. Why we're all here. She's just one person."

Two words pushed through his closed teeth, promising violence. "She's here."

The door wrenched open, and they loomed over her like gods of wrath. Her bravado nearly buckled at the expressions on their faces. If she was ever going to die, this was the time.

Susenyos seized Kidan's hand in a bone-crushing grab, drawing a cry from her, and dragged her across the polished floor.

"M-my hand!" she half shouted. "What are you doing?"

"Let's dance, little bird."

31.

THE BALLAD OF EYES WASN'T A SIMPLE BALL DANCE. THE DANCERS didn't face each other. The dranaic stood behind the acti, and neither was allowed to glimpse the other's eyes.

Mirrors served as walls, boxing the dancing space and reflecting soft light on mortal and immortal alike. Three stunning chandeliers descended from the ceiling, their crystals hovering high above Kidan's piled braids.

Susenyos slipped into the space of her shadow, fingers splayed on her stomach to pull her closer. The material of her dress was thin, and the ridges of his fingers imprinted distinctly. Her stomach contracted, heat flushing through her gut. She straightened her spine, careful not to let her back touch his chest. The awkward space between them could have fit another person.

"You kept my fangs?" he hissed for her ears only. "What is wrong with you?"

Her lips curved. "You have your treasures, I have mine."

He gave a low, dangerous growl, making the hair on her neck stand. The orchestra began, and his hand seized hers from behind, again with crushing force, but she refused to cry out. He didn't so much lead her into the routine as drag her like an annoying weight he was shackled to. It was slow at first, slow enough that she could keep her spine straight and away from him.

The tempo picked up, an explosion of furious violins and piano, and her feet faltered, barely grazing the floor as they turned and stepped and bowed. He spun her and her back slid, gravity throwing her onto him. A sound vibrated deep in his throat at the impact.

"I will never forgive you for this." His voice swam with the chandelier lights. "I should have fed on you. Let you truly feel my fangs."

He traced the curve of her neck, sending a new current thrumming down to her fingers. He pulled at the emerald hairpin, and her pile of braids cascaded like black waterfalls. He used it to conceal his face, lowering his mouth to fan her pulse point. Terror gripped her.

"Don't," she warned.

His voice was wet with thirst. "Why? Isn't this what you want? To expose me as a monster in front of them all?"

The spins of the dance, mixed with the rush of adrenaline, made her head fog, and thinking became difficult.

"Why haven't you left?" he whispered, fanning her ear. "Are you here to torment me? What else must I do to make you leave?"

His grip tightened, and a slash of power shot through her. She liked him this way, weak and wanting. It would be easy to use against him. Expose him.

"Do it," she dared him, pushing her body backward and ignoring how the current between them became electrified. "Drink."

His groan deepened with the music, building to a dizzying crescendo. They traveled in wide arcs until she could no longer tell where she started and he ended. At this speed, if he drank from her, no one would be able to tell them apart from the refracted lights. She needed to slow down. But they'd cut into a pocket of the universe where only their flesh and its desires mattered. And they had to hurry. The music would fall soon, and their minds would snap back into their bodies.

Hurry. Turn. Hurry. Turn.

Still, he didn't bite.

She wanted them to see him for the monster he was. Vision swirling, she reached for his neck and drew blood first. Nails scratched his dark skin. His teeth grazed her neck. Sharp electricity shot through her. He was almost there. His restraint was fraying like a thread under fire. Any moment now. She closed her eyes, giving in to the delicious pain—

He twirled her with such quickness that she crashed into another pair before stopping in the middle of the dance floor. Their eyes finally met. One mirrored the ocean, dark with hatred; the other the desert, burning with heat. Head still spinning, Kidan couldn't tell who was who.

He broke away first, turning and exiting quickly. Kidan breathed heavily, stepping out of the way as the dance continued.

Her heart pounded, her fingers strained, trying to find the right emotion to evoke.

32.

THE HOUSE WAS SILENT WHEN KIDAN MADE IT HOME FROM THE GALA.
She fought past the hallway as June blanketed her shoulders, whispering foul things about how Kidan had almost let him drink from her. Kidan stumbled to her room. At once, air stirred in her lungs, and the blanket was ripped away. It amazed and horrified her how each room stirred different emotions. Her room always offered relief.

She took off her heels and changed before sinking into bed. Soft light from her desk lamp turned her golden.

Her plan of keeping Susenyos in line by using Dean Faris wouldn't work forever. She needed to get back into the Southern Sost Buildings. Learn what other clubs existed besides blood courting, and how Ramyn became wrapped up in their sick games. Hopefully Ramyn would lead her to June.

But there was no way Kidan could sneak in without getting caught again. How had Ramyn done it? Kidan's mind churned away. It wasn't Ramyn's sweetness that got her in. She'd been dying. Looking for a life exchange.

If only Kidan was dying.

Her neck snapped down to the bottom of her vanity. Kidan did have something. Ears roaring, she fished out the wooden box taped under the furniture and retrieved the clear liquid. Her aunt's words resurfaced.

In case you choose to run, ingest the fake poison enclosed in this book.

Her heart drummed. How had she not thought of it until now? If she played her part well—a girl afraid for her life—could she retrace Ramyn's exact steps, make it deep into those restricted groups? Possibility thrummed in her veins. Yes. It was dangerous, but it could work.

Kidan opened the lid, hesitated. It smelled like vinegar and acid. June's voice slithered in from the hallway.

Drink. Find me.

Kidan downed it in one go. Only after she got under the covers did she consider the possibility of it being real poison. Still, she slept deeply.

The sound of her door creaking made Kidan blink one eye open. She switched on her lamp, and Susenyos's silhouette stretched along the floor.

She buried her face deeper into the pillow, groaning. "Can't you torture me in the morning?"

He said nothing.

Kidan sighed. "What disgusting thing are you putting in my bed this time? A snake? Maybe a—"

"Something's wrong."

His tone held no trace of amusement. She sat up and studied his stiff posture, two fingers rubbing her hairpin.

"Your smell…" His eyes settled into their unnerving blackness. "Are you sick?"

Oh. The false poison worked quickly.

Kidan cast her gaze to the floor for a heartbeat. It was difficult to act out the role. She tried to imagine what a person who feared for their life looked like. Uneasy, parted mouth, slow to respond.

"Kidan," Susenyos called. "Are you ill?"

She lifted her lashes. "No."

She could see his brain trying to piece together her reactions.

"You're lying."

Aunt Silia had thought very carefully about this life-threatening illness. It needed to invite no clinical treatments and exhibit no symptoms. It needed to move through the body silently, with a sudden rupture that would take her away in a few months' time. It also had to be incurable.

"Tell me," he demanded, furrowing his brow. "I know this scent. It's Shuvra's plant. That can't be right because it'd mean you're…"

Quietly, cast in the thin glow of the lamp, she said, "Poisoned. Yes."

His eyes split wide. The urgency in his voice surprised her. "Who? Who poisoned you?"

"I...don't know."

It was strange, almost beautiful, to see the fear on his face. She felt like she was granted a peek into one of nature's secrets. That the sun was never in the sky but drowning underwater.

Yet he wasn't looking directly at her but more above her head, as if a ghost only he saw stood near. She blinked, coming to her senses. Of course. This fear wasn't for her. Her pride bled at the realization. Had she actually wanted his concern?

He feared what Dean Faris promised him if any harm came to her.

Kidan crossed her arms. "Why do you look so surprised? I think it's you that poisoned me."

He blinked like she'd slapped him. It was only a matter of time before her coldness called his, the same way the devil called on hellfire.

"You believe I poisoned you?"

She shrugged. "It's no secret you want me gone."

"Poison is a coward's weapon," he bit out. "If I wanted to kill you, it'd be while looking you in the eye."

Hate festered between them. The familiar deep gut feeling that all her demons would be vanquished if she killed him threatened to overpower her. Each day Kidan spent in this house, she was mirroring him, matching his violence, matching his desire. He was absorbing her entirely, but Kidan couldn't break her promise. She had to destroy them both.

Kill all evil.

His distrustful eyes searched her face. "You have a few months left if it's Shuvra. If you think I poisoned you, why are you still here?"

When she said nothing, anger vibrated through him. How little it took to raise the monster curled inside him. She'd read somewhere that all dranaics were a host of dead faces. They'd collected souls they found bright and lovely, and grafted the essence of them onto their very skin. It was why, during a conversation, their smile would turn foul, light would leach from their eyes, or a biting sorrow would engulf them. They were a collection of a hundred lives, and on a whim, on a bad day or hour, they could kill them all.

Her voice held the command of steel. "You have to help me."

"Have to?" he snarled. "I didn't poison you."

His fangs made an appearance, causing Kidan's pulse to skip.

"You *will* get me a life exchange."

He shook his head in disbelief, gave her a long pitying look, and...walked away.

As if he was done. As if she was nothing. How dare he leave her alone in this?

Kidan shot out of bed and followed him into the hallway. "Help me, or I'll tell Dean Faris *you* poisoned me."

He froze like lightning had struck him. In an instant, her back was pressed against the wall, his forehead against hers.

Words of rage flitted out of him. "You will not blackmail me into *caring* for you."

Her heartbeat was in her throat, but her voice didn't tremble, and her lips almost curved into a smile. "I think I'm doing it quite brilliantly."

"This has gone on long enough." His voice dragged with something she couldn't identify. "Enough, Kidan. You need to leave. You're done."

What did he mean by that?

Was he finally breaking? Perhaps tired of this back-and-forth? If that was the case, she needed a different strategy. As if the house sensed her, it wrote the restrictive law in golden thread on the wall.

Searching his roiling eyes, she softened her words with great effort. "You will have the house. If I'm a vampire, I can't fight your inheritance. I'd no longer be considered a human descendant of House Adane. The moment I turn... you'll win."

His wild expression shifted like thunderous clouds breaking, possibility shining in those wretched eyes. Yes, this would intrigue him.

"You will help me," she demanded.

Muscles shifted in his jaw. "Ask me properly. Don't order me."

"What?" she barked, forgetting her strategy.

"Ask me to save your life."

This was about pride for him again. Her fingers twitched with fury. She'd just gotten the upper hand, but he was determined to win. Although...would this be a win for him? She still pulled the strings.

"I need your help," she muttered.

"That's not going to do it." His features remained hard. "Louder and more specific."

"I . . ." Her voice fought out of trapped vocal cords, asking for something more intimate than two souls becoming one. "I want . . . to . . . live. Please, help me."

He brushed her braids away with cruel gentleness. This time she didn't flinch, allowing the burn of his fingers to sear into her flesh.

"And you'll tell Dean Faris I didn't poison you?" His words were sweet poison themselves.

She hated herself as she nodded.

He'd been bored the first day they met, his expression long dead, but something was awake in those pupils now, a startling brightness.

"Are you truly ready to be a vampire, little bird?" A concealed emotion lurked in his voice as his gaze dropped to her full lips. "Can you survive it?"

She breathed in sync with him. "I don't want to be a vampire."

He considered her words, stepping back and letting her relax. "Sometimes, to survive, we must be made something entirely new."

33.

HE GIFTED YOU HIS FANGS." SLEN STUDIED KIDAN INTENTLY. "I STILL can't believe it."

They'd met extra early, at West Corner Tea, and fresh pastries now filled their table. Slen's gloved hand wrapped around a mug of black coffee.

GK didn't eat, choosing to fast most days like all Mot Zebeyas. A touch of concern lingered in his words. "Even in the Last Sage tales, fangs are often a symbol of pain and loss, never an offering of companionship."

Kidan popped in a cinnamon mini doughnut. The taste always brought memories of a flustered June baking with serious concentration, fussing over her journal as she experimented with different ingredients. "Guess he wanted to make a statement."

Yusef ran his hand through his hair, using the back window to double as a mirror. He was particular about his appearance, wanting his thick curls to sit at a certain angle.

"And boy, did he. Everyone's been talking about it." He frowned. "Makes the heel I got look like a consolation prize."

"Enough with the jealousy," Slen said, touching her temple. "You're not his type. Get over it."

Yusef looked offended, then grinned. "It's okay. I'm your type."

GK flipped through his book. "I think to be her type you'll have to focus on a page longer than you do on your own reflection."

Yusef's mouth dropped, Slen's mouth twitched, and Kidan burst into an unexpected laugh. She touched her lips, surprised the sound had really come from her.

GK raised a brow at her and smiled, chin bowed.

Yusef shook his head. "It's always the quiet ones."

"Like GK said, focus, please." Slen turned her laptop to them. "Quadrantism. Our new topic. The Aarac translation for Quadrantism says that *the four quadrants of a dranaic produce a paradise, of which the human is a mirror.* Yusef, do you want to share?"

Yusef folded his legs on his chair and unwrapped a chocolate muffin. His flared brown pants and rolled-up white sweater made him look effortlessly handsome.

"Quadrantism is a theology that says to live a good life, a human must keep all four pillars intact," he said. "I practice it."

"What do you mean you practice it?" Kidan asked.

"It's a way of life. Metaphors for good behavior. To obtain optimal quality of spiritual, mental, physical, and material well-being."

"A lot of artists practice it," Slen said. "They believe it brings them closer to creation, saving four hours every day, each dedicated to strengthening the four pillars."

"Then you can help us pass?" Kidan asked Yusef.

He winced, rubbing his neck. "Ironically, I failed Dranacti at this stage."

"Oh," Kidan said.

No one spoke for a while.

"It's similar to the Last Sage's principles like Settliton," GK finally said.

Slen tapped her chin with a pen. "An interesting lens. Are you able to deliver your exegesis without personal bias?"

"Exegesis," Yusef said absentmindedly. "Put a dollar in the jar."

Kidan watched in amusement as Slen sighed and took out a crumpled dollar from her jacket pocket. Yusef retrieved a small glass jar from his bag and slipped the money inside. It was labeled on Scotch tape in his block writing: WORDS THAT MAKE ME FEEL SAD.

He held it to the light. "I'm going to buy a new charcoal pencil set soon."

"Really?" Kidan had never thought Slen would engage in this.

"It's fair play. I have a jar for him too," Slen said.

Yusef's jar was labeled in Slen's cursive writing *Debilitating Creative Rants* and was half-full.

Yusef leaned toward Kidan. "Funny thing is, she owed me a dollar for the word 'debilitating.'"

Kidan's lips curved with mischief. "GK, do you think you should get one for Yusef? For the times he checks himself out?"

"I did." GK's warm eyes danced, catching her meaning. "It became too heavy to carry."

Yusef could only stare at GK, then at Kidan, wonder breaking his voice. "Okay, what happened to you two? I'm the funny one."

Kidan laughed softly, absolutely loving this and feeling *normal* for once.

They worked quietly for the next two hours before deciding to meet again in the afternoon. Kidan left with the required readings.

GK followed her out of the room, his light expression fading. "Are you all right?"

"Yes. Why wouldn't I be?"

He shifted, his chain clicking. "It's just you told me Susenyos did something to your sister and then you showed everyone his fangs. . . . Did he hurt you?"

His eyes filled with turmoil. He must have been worried all this time. Kidan squeezed his arm, surprised she was initiating human touch at all. It felt . . . nice.

"I'm okay, GK. Really. I shouldn't have told you."

He traced his finger bone chain, jaw tight. "But first your sister, then Ramyn?" He shook his head. "I'm worried."

Ramyn had died after getting close to Kidan. Now Kidan was spending time with GK. She swallowed. She needed to keep him safe.

"How about Mondays before class, you and I go for a walk around the grounds? We can look out for each other."

The tension seemed to leave him. He nodded and opened the door, then paused, looking back at her with a small smile.

"It was nice to hear you laugh. Even if it was only for a moment."

Kidan's chest lightened, though she was unable to understand why he was so good to her.

"Thank you," she said.

She clung to the weightless feeling, refusing to touch her searing bracelet. For a few minutes, she'd almost enjoyed herself in a world without June.

Guilt knotted her from the inside out.

Later. She'd punish herself later.

Kidan lay awake in bed. The house pressed in on her like a boulder, crushing her chest and determined to grind out the sliver of joy from the day. June and Mama Anoet swarmed her in cycles, their voices more vivid than ever, crossing from the hallway into her room. She dressed and left the house in a hurry, barely closing the front door. Grabbing onto her knees, she inhaled clean, sharp air, dizzy with the emptiness of her mind. Her neck prickled with the feeling of someone watching. Her eyes darted up to the window. It was dark and no one was visible, but she could have sworn the curtains of Susenyos's room had fluttered.

She shook her head and walked on campus, illuminated by the lion-shaped lampposts. It was midnight, but one room in the Philosophy Tower glowed soft orange. Kidan took the elevator up. Slen was there, as expected, and the two nodded at each other, settling in. A single thin candle burned in the middle of the table.

Slen inched a book titled *The Sage's Quadrant* toward Kidan, who opened the thick cover. It spoke about the four principles the Last Sage practiced in his seclusion. Settliton. Kidan highlighted the values in relation to Quadrantism, hoping to decipher the topic. They worked in a practiced quiet of shuffling papers, light typing touches, a cap twisting in Slen's teeth. Her usual piney scent mixed with the lingering aroma from several empty coffee cups. Kidan should tell her not to drink so much. It was probably why she couldn't sleep.

The room grew hot around their second hour there. The sensor heaters turned on, and Kidan took off her scarf and opened her collar. Slen shrugged off her large jacket and slipped free of her gloves. Three lines of deep welts—no, scars—ran along her palms, the almond color of the flesh broken up with dark lightning bolts. Kidan's hand froze on her turning page.

Slen didn't notice for several seconds that Kidan had stopped working. Then she caught Kidan staring, blinked, and quickly reached for the gloves, frowning.

"I almost forgot you were here."

"You . . . don't have to put them back on."

Slen hesitated, then gently set them down, not looking at her. Kidan didn't ask. But the warm space swelled with the expected question. Slen shut her eyes like she'd come across an inconvenient piece of Aarac to be translated.

"The bow of a violin can cut flesh if you swing it hard enough. My father doesn't like errors."

Kidan's lips parted. Then, almost as quickly, her teeth rang with fury. She looked away, veins tight. "My foster mother didn't like errors either. Whenever my sister and I spoke Amharic, we were punished with a painful pinch."

The sharp twist of skin between hardened fingers burned hotter than a lit cigarette. Perhaps that was why the language still tasted like iron on Kidan's tongue.

"Let me help you." Kidan moved her jaw with great effort. She wasn't sure exactly how she would, but she wanted to do something.

Slen stared deeply, a curious glint to her gaze. "Passing Dranacti will help me. It'll make me the next heiress to House Qaros. An heiress can make all the errors she wants and still be valuable."

Kidan's mouth soured. "You shouldn't have to be an heiress to be valuable."

Slen faced the gentle flame. "In a place where houses are power, there's nothing else we can be."

Those cinders caught in her dark eyes again. Kidan could almost imagine them crackling, daring her to burn this place to the ground—or perhaps it was her own thoughts pounding like a drum, wanting to shake the girl and scream, *We don't have to wait for the houses to give us power. Power can be a match and a lighter, a gun, a fire. I can kill him for you.*

A chill like no other swept over her. She touched her forehead. What was wrong with her? She really was getting worse.

"Maybe you can be honest with me now too," Slen said.

Kidan's brows rose. "About?"

Slen's words were low, unexpected, and almost dark. "Did Susenyos Sagad poison you?"

Kidan's mouth opened, but at first no sound came out. "How did . . . you—"

"Taj Zuri belongs to my house. He talks a lot."

Right. And Susenyos had obviously told his friend. Still, it surprised her. She didn't want anyone to know yet.

"And if he did poison me?" Kidan asked, sliding her a side glance.

Slen fixed her with those flat black eyes. The flame bent close, as if listening too.

"I can take care of him for you."

Those were Kidan's words. Sharp with an underlying bite to them.

Her eyes widened. Her heart pounded close to the surface of her skin. Did Slen mean it the way Kidan had at the gala? Did she mean . . . *kill* Susenyos? The tower room became sweltering again. Why was the thought that they could be alike so exhilarating yet horrifying? Kidan wanted to say yes. Wanted this girl to experience what taking a life felt like. Let them spiral into a fit of violence and shared misery. But that couldn't be what Slen was hinting at, could it?

"What do you mean?" Kidan asked, desperate to stop her buzzing thoughts.

Slen stared into the flame, brown skin iridescent. "I mean Susenyos can be one more task on my list once I'm heiress. I never fail my assignments."

Kidan found herself transfixed, desperate to crack open Slen's thoughts and truly understand. Slen brushed her short braid away, tucking it behind a pierced ear. The sight of those graceful, scarred palms poured ice down Kidan's back. Shook her free.

Slen was already in her own version of hell. Suffering.

Kidan bit the inside of her cheek, using the pain to anchor her. "No, he's helping me find a life exchange."

Slen's brows drew together a little. "I see."

Kidan's chest squeezed at the withdrawal in her tone. There wouldn't be another moment like this with Slen. Vulnerability was a flaw, a thing to be corrected. But as much as Kidan wanted to find a partner in all this, what she wanted more was for Slen to survive. She couldn't bear it if Slen was the next person to dangle from a tower by the neck. Some sliver of light had to exist for girls who were punished just for existing.

All that lurked in Kidan's revenge was guilt and self-hatred and eventual death. Taking a life would only inflict a deeper permanent scar on her.

No, she promised herself. Kidan wouldn't be selfish with Slen. She'd help her keep her soul, not destroy it.

There were other, more depraved methods Kidan could use to feed her loneliness before she met her end.

34.

ADANE HOUSE HELD DIFFERENT PARTS OF KIDAN'S MIND, AND SHE became many souls as she traveled through it. The front door pulled anger, the kitchen pulsed with longing, the hallways crowded with grief. Sometimes she leaned against a wall and let sadness engulf her, pouring into her like a relentless waterfall, before a creak from elsewhere reminded her to keep walking.

There were good thoughts too. The corner bedroom indulged her fantasy. She imagined a kind woman's smile in the vanity, felt the invisible suits in an empty closet, replaced the scent of wood and dust with skin and perfume. It unsettled her how deeply she longed for her dead family.

Then there was his room. She sat across from it when he wasn't there, like now, and stared it down like a stubborn pet. Shadows from his scrolls rested against her feet, the stories of many women calling her in. Kidan reached out a hand and touched the door. Unlike the first day she entered it, there was now a horrifying yet distinct absence of hatred in its space.

Why? This room had killed hundreds, this room took June, this room... invited her in.

She had a sense that if she simply crossed into that room, the weight on her chest would ease.

See? June's voice echoed. *It's because you are like them.*

Kidan shuddered at the coldness. This wasn't the real June.

On the wall, the house law shimmered, taunting her.

IF SUSENYOS SAGAD ENDANGERS ADANE HOUSE, THE HOUSE SHALL

IN TURN STEAL SOMETHING OF EQUAL VALUE TO HIM.

What did "Adane House" mean to her parents? Etete said Susenyos was desperate to change the law, and by how persistent he was in his suffering in the observatory room, Kidan assumed that something of value had been taken from him. It left her circling around to the same question.... What did Susenyos value the most?

"What are you doing?" A low earthy voice echoed.

Kidan startled. Susenyos stood at the end of the hallway. She hadn't heard him come in.

"I was just leaving," she replied unsteadily, but made no move to stand. Her legs were still heavy. How long had she been here? Time warped itself here.

Susenyos approached slowly, studying her for a moment before taking a seat next to her. He felt solid, a sudden wall against the dark hallway, so her grief ebbed and flowed like a current. Warning pulsed through her. Perhaps it wasn't only his room. *He* affected the spaces of this house. The spaces of her mind.

"Don't sit next to me," Kidan said, sliding away from him.

"I'm afraid I must. Etete won't forgive me if I walk away from a dying girl looking so pitiful."

"I'm fine." She stared ahead, eyes glassy. He, on the other hand, kept watching her.

Time stretched into eons, and she sank deeper into the loss of it all. She let her eyes shut. There would be no end to this pain.

"I didn't drink from June." He sighed, making her lift her lashes. "I don't know how her bracelet got in my drawer. I don't know why your foster mother evoked my name. So I will say this once and never again, because I have spent my entire life accused and judged and I refuse to prove myself to anyone." His unwavering coal gaze held hers. "I did not take, harm, or kill June."

Her body went numb with the words, blood pumping in her ears. He'd never said it this plainly before and never this genuinely.

Kidan stared at the floor. "Why are you telling me this now? After all this time?"

His expression was unreadable. "To ease your mind, if we are to work together."

A wave of suspicion rolled through her. June's eyes flashed with warning.

The carpet rippled under her. It grew wet, and she lifted her hand to see blood. She wiped it furiously on her lap, but after a moment, nothing was there.

"I don't think it's helping," she admitted, knees shaking.

He studied the light curtains swaying in his room as if he could hear them speak. "It's normal to feel the house more the longer you reside in it. It heightens your emotions, so you must work to control them."

He shut his eyes, lashes resting against smooth skin, as if he was doing just that.

Kidan's head lifted to the flickering hanging lights above them, souls on the verge of being extinguished. She was back there, in her apartment, in the unbearable silence, with the scratching of paper and the stove being lit. An unending loop with no way to break free. The world grew dark around the edges again, her lungs working twice as hard.

The scrolls of his room grew longer shadows and stretched along her feet with a new wave of moonlight. The tendrils wrapped along her ankles, gentle as a mother's touch, and encouraged her to speak without her will.

"I can feel June here. Mama Anoet should have protected us." Kidan's voice shook with the effort to keep the words to herself.

She felt it again.

That unbearable need to cry and cry until she dissolved into nothing but water. It built inside her like a volcano, but her eyes couldn't find the emotion. She hadn't cried since Mama Anoet's death. What kind of monster didn't mourn their mother?

Susenyos watched her intently; the weak lamp above them flickered again, washing them in extreme dark and light. Silence yawned between them.

Kidan met his eyes slowly. They had gathered the lamp's glow. He blinked, and they settled into their darkness.

"Those we expect to protect us often fail us," he said, jaw hard. "We must find a way to survive on our own."

On our own. Kidan thought about being on her own. Without June. Alone in that apartment. Even the thought wounded deeper than any blade. There was no life in that loneliness, was there?

Behind his shoulder, June's face shimmered. Her lips bled red, and blood ran down her chin, her face cut in fear. The dying lamp fought like hell overhead.

The shadowy man came again, hovering by June's neck. Kidan's face contorted in pain, a sudden force squeezing her body. Air faded from her lungs at once, and she gasped aloud.

Take me instead.

The light switched on and off. On and off.

"Kidan?" Susenyos sounded too close.

Take me. Take me.

The lamp struggled and she struggled with it. Kidan's breathing followed. On. Off. On. Off.

She clawed at her chest, digging at her hummingbird heart, but the tension only tightened and tightened. The lamp became erratic, ready to burst. Kidan wanted to scream, but her mouth could only gape soundlessly.

Off.

Susenyos led her into his dark room. She swallowed huge gulps of air, but it didn't reach her lungs.

"Kidan," he said urgently. "You need to breathe."

"My chest... It's too tight." She gasped in painful bursts.

"Kidan, if you don't calm down, you'll pass out."

She started to scream.

A wretched, agonizing scream that poured out of her in earth-shattering waves. It was a scream for Mama Anoet and June. A scream for all the blackened parts of her soul. A scream for someone dying—because she was.

Her nails dug into flesh, tight around his forearm, the same way she had killed that bird and drained its life away.

Susenyos tensed at the contact but remained in place, solid and unbreakable, so that all of her assaults landed on him.

Breathe.

The house allowed her mind another fantasy, a moment to trick her body into calm waters. This wasn't Susenyos Sagad she braced against. It was reprieve, in the shape of monster or human, it hardly mattered. It was her fault to have let it get this rampant. Back home, she'd listened to June's videos to control her panic attacks. She could never predict them. Months would go by where she was completely fine, then she'd be keeling over in a grocery aisle. But in this house, she suffered alone with nothing to alleviate her pain.

"Kidan?" His voice reached her through the pocket of the universe they'd cut into.

He still hadn't stepped back, his form towering over her.

"Why... why are you helping me?"

"You need to control your emotions," he said, voice burning low. "It's starting to affect the house. Me."

She was glad the dark hid his face. For all she knew, she held on to death itself. Yes, death. This way, she could rest her body a little longer. Death was warm. She'd expected it to be like the ocean at night, cold and unforgiving.

35.

IN THE SOUTHERN SOST BUILDINGS, SEVERAL GATHERINGS WERE HELD. Almost all were after-hours and by invitation. Every Friday night, dranaics mixed for an evening of enlightened conversation and gambling. The moment Susenyos guided Kidan into a dark room curtained with red tassels, sneers were directed at them. Clearly, they were both incredibly popular.

Kidan waited for him to bring up last night. Her body tensed, ready for the discomfort, but he made no mention of it. She couldn't help but feel relief. He was letting it go.

They stopped by a man with glasses and a gray suit.

"Ah, Yonam. May I introduce you to Kidan Adane," Susenyos said.

The man looked Kidan up and down. She was dressed in a simple black dress that rested above the knees.

"This building is for dranaics," he said.

"Yes, well, she's dying," Susenyos replied with a smile. "We can have compassion for a dying girl, can't we?"

The man's eyes widened with interest. Kidan shivered at his gaze.

Susenyos turned, spotting someone in the crowd. "Keep her company for me. I'll be back."

Kidan tried to follow where he went, but the room had a single lamp, positioned in the middle. The outskirts were entirely dark, probably for nefarious business purposes.

Yonam gave her an unkind smile. "What will you do with your new vampire life? I assume you're here for a life exchange."

The question made her brain fog. Her high school counselor had once asked about her aspirations. Junior year, Kidan had enjoyed a woodworking and metal shop elective and discovered a new love. The joy of carving something out of nothing, the feel of hard and soft materials being torn, broken, welded, and remade, with endless possibilities so nothing was ever in its final form. It'd given her true peace. But the counselor had crinkled her nose when Kidan explained she wanted a job where she would get to destroy things and make them whole again.

"Hello?" The vampire Yonam frowned. "Did you hear me?"

She cleared the ball in her throat. "I haven't thought about it."

He tsked. "Of course you haven't. Will you push for change? Fight in a war? Start a revolution? Or will you whore yourself out and be drunk on blood for eternity? Most women do."

Kidan curled her fingers into a fist.

"Ignore him," a familiar light voice said from behind.

Yonam's lips puckered. "Speaking of whoring yourself out. How are the women, Taj? I hear you give yourself to anyone that gives you a sliver of attention."

Taj, dressed in a fine dark jacket, seemed entirely unbothered. "Even if that's true, you still won't be one of them."

Yonam's disposition darkened so quickly that Kidan almost laughed. He squeezed his glass in anger and walked away.

Taj studied her for a minute. "You're not going to ask me to give you my life?"

She slid him a glance. "Last time I asked you for something, you said no."

His eyes danced. "A choice I'll regret for the rest of my life."

She straightened her arched lip and changed the subject. "Did Ramyn Ajtaf also come to these events?"

Taj shifted his shoulders inward, crossing his arms suspiciously. "She did."

Kidan kept her tone casual. "She comes here in search of a second life and loses hers first. That's dark."

"No one in their right mind would ever harm an acti. Even a dying one is still valuable."

He was referring to their blood. Kidan's throat closed up.

"Maybe she stopped being valuable. Saw something she shouldn't have?"

Taj was about to speak when Iniko appeared at his shoulder. "Yos is looking for you."

He sighed and left with a nod.

Iniko and Kidan faced the crowd, neither speaking. Unease bloomed between them.

"Susenyos shouldn't have brought you here." Her clipped voice made Kidan tense.

"Why?"

"It makes him look weak. Bringing the girl who waved his fangs like a war prize, admitting the last heiress of his house has been poisoned under his watch. No family will take him on now."

"Maybe someone from my study group will make him their companion. If he saves my life, that is."

Iniko's lip curled. "Actis playing God. You only need us when a bad cold renders you sick."

"You talk like you weren't once human."

A dangerous fire burned in Iniko's eyes. She moved closer, her large red collar tickling Kidan's neck.

"I fought for my immortality. It has cost me more than you could ever imagine. *You* hope to ask nicely and receive it."

Kidan stared into ancient eyes that would cut her down if she said the wrong thing. Her lungs stuttered for air.

"I can smell unwillingness on you." Iniko's breath fanned Kidan's cheek. "You already carry a dead heart."

Kidan's throat bobbed. Even as Iniko melted into the crowd, her words echoed close, cruel, and true. Kidan knew it was impossible for her to want to live. To continue this wretched existence and loathe herself to the point of exhaustion. It would only be a matter of time before Susenyos noticed it too.

She ordered a drink and sat down, wondering what Ramyn must have gone through, parading for these vampires to give her their life. A card slid onto Kidan's table, interrupting her thoughts. On the front, *13th* was printed. On the back:

If you want another chance at life, come alone.
Building 34, Level 2, Room 1.

Kidan gasped softly. Tamol Ajtaf had given her a card about the 13th.

She searched for Susenyos but couldn't find him. She slipped the card under her glass and left. If Susenyos was a member, it wouldn't help, but if she didn't return from Building 34, at least there was a clue left behind.

It took her five minutes to reach the room. A pretty young girl from House Delarus opened the door. Kidan recognized her from Ramyn's funeral—she was one of the protesters asking for protection law changes. She'd been the one to confront Dean Faris and be escorted away by security.

"Come in," she said.

A quiet gathering was taking place at multiple low-lit tables, with whiskey and cigars present at each station. The smell of cigar smoke turned her stomach—too close to Mama Anoet's burning skin.

A familiar pair of pinprick eyes across the room startled her.

Koril Qaros approached and took her hands. "I'm very sorry to hear about your illness."

Slen's father... was here. She fumbled trying to hide her surprise.

Breathe, smile. No, not smile. She was supposed to be sad. Afraid. Dying.

"Thank... you."

"How are you holding up?"

Kidan wanted to yank herself from his calloused hands. All she could see was how roughly they had grabbed Ramyn and slapped Slen's brother. Marred Slen's palms with painful cracks. The flat dissociation in Slen's eyes struck her again. Kidan had seen her fair share of horrors and still didn't float by as invisible and untethered as her study partner did. She understood why now. Her mouth soured, imagining several ways of relieving Slen's father of these troubling hands.

"I'm staying positive," she said instead. "Hoping for a life exchange."

He nodded compassionately. "I hope you get it. I hear the list is particularly long this year. Let's have a drink."

Kidan wiped away the dark energy of his hands when he turned.

They sat down at a table. "I heard you went to the Southern Sost with Susenyos Sagad."

Already?

"I had no other choice." She adopted meekness. "I...don't know anyone else."

Koril Qaros sipped his whiskey. "Unfortunately, Susenyos is not welcomed by many dranaics, given his violent history. I'm afraid being seen with him hurts your chances."

So Susenyos wasn't welcomed here. But what exactly was "here"? What group was the 13th, and why were Tamol Ajtaf and Koril Qaros members?

"I think I know of a dranaic that would be willing to give their life for you."

"Really?" She made her voice rise an octave.

"It won't be easy," Koril said, almost grim. "Every afternoon, I want us to meet here, see if we can help each other. Gradually, I'll introduce you to other members and see what we can do about your situation."

"What exactly is the 13th?"

"Oh, I wouldn't worry too much about that. There are many exclusive groups formed within Uxlay. The 13th aim to help indebted or failed graduates and, now, sick students like yourself."

"Did Ramyn come here?" Kidan asked without thinking.

The easy smile he'd plastered on strained a little. "Yes. Tragic what happened to her. We'd almost found her a life exchange."

Her stomach contracted with rage.

Breathe. Relax.

She'd almost managed it when he said something that made her want to smash his glass across his skull.

"I've heard about your sister, June. It's a dangerous time for young girls. Let me know if there's anything I can do to help you find her."

Kidan drew triangles along her thighs and forced out, "Thank you."

Koril stood, fastening a button on his expensive suit. "If Susenyos gives you trouble, the law is there for you. Don't hesitate to protect yourself from him."

Odd, Kidan thought as he escorted her out. A day ago, she'd have loved to have anyone by her side against Susenyos. Yet Koril Qaros was a beast of his own making.

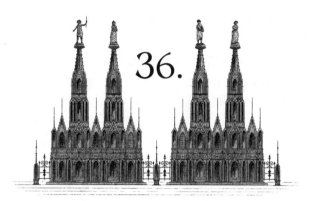

36.

WHEN KIDAN RETURNED HOME, SUSENYOS HAD SETTLED BEFORE the fireplace. He poured a few drops from his new blood flask into a glass of liquor and drank. Then he held up a card between two fingers.

"The 13th invited you?"

He watched, expression guarded, as she took off her coat and kicked off her heels. "Who was there?"

Kidan took her time putting away her scarf, walking across the polished floor, pouring herself a glass of water, and finally sitting next to him.

She ignored his raised brow and her body screaming at her to move.

There had only been one suspect as to who took June. Susenyos. But the 13th... Could they have some play here? Was Susenyos part of their group and pretending? She had to be careful. Play a very different role. Be nice. Being rough and callous had gotten her nowhere.

"Koril Qaros," she said, carefully watching him over her glass.

His calculating gaze burned into her. "Did he offer you a life exchange?"

Kidan hesitated, considering what to share. "Not yet."

"It definitely won't be from his own house. He doesn't share his dranaics."

Interesting. "He said I shouldn't trust you."

Susenyos's mouth twisted into a sardonic smile. "I'm not surprised."

"I don't trust you."

Susenyos tilted his head to the ceiling, brown face catching light. "Let's consider the facts. If you die, I inherit the house. If you become a dranaic, I still inherit the house. You have nothing to fear from me."

That appeared to be true, but it would take far more to trust him.

"Furthermore, you'll need my aid. The 13th only allow a select few to earn a life exchange."

"Such a hero."

His lip almost quirked. "In exchange, I want you to tell me everything they say about me in that secret group of theirs."

She raised a brow, both surprised and not. "Why?"

"I want to know all my enemies. And I get quite nervous when they start inviting each other to tea."

Kidan rolled her eyes. "Stop being paranoid. They're not after you. They just don't like you, and that's very valid."

Susenyos let out a low rumbling sound, surprising her. A...laugh that seemed genuine instead of cruel. How odd.

"Come, let's get to work," he said, walking toward the artifact room.

Curious, she followed him. The door handle was still broken, courtesy of her axe. Her breath fogged inside the metal shelving. Of the three shelves Kidan destroyed, one had been entirely restored. Her eyes widened at the sight, admiring how carefully Susenyos had pieced back together the many trinkets. But there were still boxes of shattered pieces by the working station in the back of the room.

Kidan's attention rested on the massive portrait of the goddess. Her axe slice was still imprinted, not yet repaired.

"I guess I should apologize?" Kidan said when she saw him looking at it with longing.

"Yes, you should. You ruined something dear to me."

"Who is she?"

He hesitated as if deciding whether he wanted to share this piece of himself. When he finally spoke, reverence crowded his words together. "I saw her when I was young, or at least I think I did. She saved me. I tried to capture her best I could. It's one of the things that reminds me of joy, life."

She never expected him to be the religious type, but the tone in his voice could only be reserved for worship. Kidan studied the woman's dark skin, all aglow. The power in her arms. The silver weapons, red ring, and cracked wooden mask. An angel or a goddess, she couldn't tell.

"What did she save you from?"

When he remained quiet, she gave him a sidelong glance. His eyes were dark and tumultuous as the ocean, endless as the beginning of time. He blinked, and whatever memory had possessed him vanished.

He turned his back to the portrait. "Over here."

Kidan frowned and surveyed the slit eyes of the mask, and a pulse echoed in the walls of the room. For a moment, she could have sworn the goddess moved, shimmering like the surface of water. Kidan blinked, and the image settled. She joined Susenyos by the ruined remains of the artifacts. He retrieved two sets of white gloves.

"So why are we in here?" She rubbed her bare arms against the chill.

"This is how you're going to convince the 13th to give you a life exchange."

"With old artifacts?"

"With your history."

They settled at the station where various tools and machines sat. An illuminated lamp and a magnifying glass were present.

"When they ask you why you want to live, you'll say to continue House Adane's legacy."

He handed her the five broken pieces of a brass ring and held out the gloves.

"You're not serious?"

"Entirely serious. You'll speak about preserving African history, your love of reclaiming stolen artifacts that represent not only a country but its generations of natives all over the world. That it is the only thing in this world that's immortal."

Under the soft glow of the lamp, his skin melted into a richer shade of brown and his brows were drawn tight in concentration. With his loose, revealing shirt and the light casting a bronze filter over him, he could be an old photograph tucked in her grandmother's hatbox or carried in her chest pocket, faded and worn, as she reminisced about her young lost love.

He was history itself.

Kidan did want to play with the artifacts. She missed working with her hands. The smell of old metal and sawdust from her elective class filled the space, making her muscles tense with excitement. Still, she hesitated.

Susenyos's true age showed in his displeasure. "You still don't trust me."

"I just didn't know you were...like this."

He regarded her with an expression difficult to read. "What do you really know about me? Besides the assumptions and stories you've cast? You made me your nightmare the moment you heard my name. And nightmares aren't allowed to have likes or dislikes. We're only allowed to haunt."

Kidan's brows creased at the resigned tone of his words. But there was also a thread of something else, although she wasn't sure what.

"And now?" She searched his eyes. "What's different now?"

"You're becoming one of us." His voice nearly tugged upward. "A vampire doesn't shy away from learning the truth."

If he learned that she was lying about her poisoning, that she would remain human with a very good chance of taking this house from him, their fragile alliance would crumble.

She took the gloves slowly and slipped them on. He nodded, and they began her lessons. With each artifact they mended, Susenyos recited its origin and importance.

"Ethiopia, 1823. An empress wore it on her wedding day."

His lips carried a ghost of a smile. Kidan's favorite ones, though, were the artifacts stolen back from colonist countries with the help of Adane's Department of Archaeology and History. The sense of justice that ran through her was unbelievably sweet. And she felt true guilt that she'd irreparably damaged most of these treasures. No matter how carefully they were put back together, they'd never be untouched as they had been.

Susenyos, of course, was a frustrating teacher. He'd say no before she even lifted a piece to glue it back on, hover like a shadow until her own vision was obscured, examine her work and find twenty faults with it, strip it down and ask her to do it again. Kidan wanted to tear out her hair, but she complied, absorbing his teachings.

"What about the crown I took that day?" she asked, carefully piecing together a broken chalice. "What's the story there?"

"Do you have it?"

"No," she said. Technically, it wasn't a crown anymore.

"Then I guess you won't know."

He didn't sound angry, only bemused. As if he knew she'd done something irreversible to it.

They talked about historical books too, including *Traditional Myths of Abyssi*.

A book Slen wanted to help decipher Dranacti. It was here, hidden in the alcoves of the shelves, a thin book with red stripes. Susenyos held it out carefully when she asked to borrow it, eyes hesitant.

"I want it back after."

There were many books here in Amharic, and she strained to read the blocky letters before giving up with a sigh. Her mouth tasted metallic. How could something she once knew be entirely gone? Her speech was limited to a few useless phrases. She touched her hand, the memory of the pinches making it tingle. Mama Anoet should have let them keep their language. It made Kidan feel at sea, forcing her to battle tides on a tiny raft when she was meant for the trees and shores. Left her with not enough ground to stretch herself.

"These are my favorites," Susenyos said, pulling her from her thoughts. He held several books in his hand.

Kidan wanted to ask him about *The Mad Lovers* but hesitated. She didn't want him to know she was reading it. At its heart, the book was a twisted affair between two broken souls gearing for tragedy. Something she never thought Susenyos would repeatedly return to. Kidan had become so engrossed in the story, she'd begun staying up reading till three a.m. every night.

After their conversation, Kidan retrieved classics, tragic poems, and devastating lines that brought to life her most intimate thoughts. Never had she found beauty in misery before. Yet in the hands of centuries-old writers, even murderers were woven a tale of forgiveness. In those stories, Kidan was...the hero. They gave her solace, and she quickly grew obsessed with finding writing that confessed evil as if purged by holy water.

On those cold nights when she couldn't sleep, her window would come awake with light, and she'd recite passages of books speaking to her soul. The buzzing of every winged creature in her mind would then settle to hear the words, keeping warm by the lamp before the heat incinerated them to dust.

Fed on the language of greedy and monstrous men alike, she knew just what to take to Koril Qaros to gain his trust.

37.

KIDAN HANDED KORIL QAROS AN ORNATE WOODEN BOX WITH engraved Amharic text the next time they met.

"A gift," she said. "To thank you for your invitation."

He set aside his drink and took the box. Inside was a fourteenth-century washint flute crafted of a native wood only found in Ethiopia.

Koril lifted it gingerly, admiring its length. "This is an impressive find."

"I think it'll look lovely in your Qaros Conservatory."

New interest flickered in his eyes. He rested the flute on the velvet bedding and noticed the ring. Set with a large ruby that had a noticeable crack at the base, it twinkled like sunset. He shot her a surprised glance.

"Ah, that," Kidan said casually. "I must have packed it by accident."

Susenyos had taught her the value of history and it would be helpful—but not enough against a man who sought to possess art, whether it be music or a portrait or antiques.

"Do you know what ring this is?"

Susenyos would be mad if he knew she'd taken it, but she would worry about that later.

"It's the closest replica to the Last Sage's lost ring artifact, carved from the same ruby stone found in Axum. Rumored to have been used in the making of the Three Binds."

"Then you know it's invaluable."

"Everything has value. It only depends on what you want."

This turned his grin serpentlike. His greedy gaze studied her for a long moment before he said, "There is a gathering tonight, if you're available, that I think will be most fascinating to you."

Kidan watched him slide the ring onto his bony finger. She had the urge to bend his wrist and take it back. Later, she told herself.

Kidan expected the gathering to be a formal event, black dress and cocktails, like before. What she didn't expect was to attend a private viewing of a vampire transformation in the Mot Zebeya Building. Koril Qaros escorted her upstairs to where shadowy figures were already seated, talking among themselves.

Tamol Ajtaf's green eyes shone behind his spectacles. "Hello again."

Kidan masked her distaste with a forced smile. She hadn't liked him at Ramyn's funeral, and certainly not now.

"Kidan here is looking for a life exchange," Koril said. "I believe we can help each other."

They shared a pointed glance Kidan couldn't decipher.

"Perhaps we could discuss safeguarding what truly belongs to you." Tamol's cuff links twinkled, encrusted with the thin golden tower of Ajtaf House.

Kidan's lips formed a line. "You mean the Axum archaeological site."

"It's no secret Ajtaf Constructions would love to do business with Adane House. The search for the Last Sage's settlement must continue. Our company can help."

So it came back to this. No one had to say it, but the price of her new immortal life appeared to be signing over her house's business. Was this the 13th's goal? Total absorption of other houses' finances? Why would they harm Ramyn or June if that was the case? Kidan was missing something.

"Later, Tamol. We have more pressing concerns," Koril said before escorting her to the back.

Once they found a secluded spot, he lowered his voice. "I have a task for you. I know you're close with Yusef Umil."

Kidan shifted on her feet. "I am."

"Do you believe he'll pass Dranacti?"

"I think so."

Koril's mouth thinned. "I see. I want you to keep the boy from passing. Can you do that?"

"I . . . why?"

"The head of House Umil right now is a very elderly woman. She's easier to convince of our great plans than a stubborn boy."

"And what plans are those?" Kidan asked carefully.

"All in due time." Koril smiled before turning his attention to the crowd. "Rufeal," he called. "You have a partner in your task."

Kidan's gut tightened. Rufeal Makary was in the 13th?

"It's his sister, Sara Makary, who will be receiving a life exchange tonight," Koril said.

"And who's the vampire giving up their life?" Kidan asked.

"Someone from Umil House, I suppose."

House Makary was coming for the Umils—in business, in the art world, and now by poaching their dranaics. Yusef wasn't being paranoid.

Rufeal was dressed in a smart suit and offered his slippery smile. "Never thought you'd make it here, Adane. Perhaps we're more alike than I thought."

Kidan wanted to hurl.

Koril grabbed their shoulders. "I want you two to work together on the Umil boy."

Once they nodded, Koril moved on.

"It's not easy making someone fail," Kidan said.

Rufeal adjusted his expensive watch. "I've done it before. And if my plan doesn't work, we'll have to resort to less pleasant options, won't we? There's no failing a 13th task."

Kidan stilled. "What do you mean?"

He didn't elaborate, but the gleam of his eyes made her spine shiver. Was this why Yusef kept failing?

"Please take your seats." A soft sound came from below.

Rufeal crossed to his mother, hooked an arm through hers, and descended the stairs. Kidan stood by the rail, leaning forward to see.

The altar below had ominous black curtains. A young girl who Kidan guessed was Sara Makary parted the curtains, dressed in a loose, ankle-length traditional kemis. Flowers, brilliant white ones, were carried forward and laid before the girl by Mot Zebeyas, faithful servants identified by the finger bone chain wrapped around their neck, wrist, or belt.

One of the Mot Zebeyas lifted his head, making her breath catch. GK set up along with the others, not glancing at the higher deck.

She quickly took the stairs down and slipped into one of the multiple rows of benches illuminated by soft amber light.

GK spotted her, surprised, and came over. "Kidan? What are you doing here?"

"What are *you* doing here?"

He frowned at her tone. "Helping with a transformation."

"Do you know the people upstairs?" she asked, pensive. Was he in the 13th? God, she hoped not.

He glanced up. "No, but there's always a viewing with these things."

Kidan's heart rate slowed. "So how does it all work?"

"You're taking Introduction to Dranacti and don't know how transformations work?" He didn't sound rude, only curious.

She slid aside and patted the seat next to her. "You could tell me. I'm a quick learner."

He glanced back at the altar.

"Come on," Kidan said.

GK appeared torn before sitting down.

Sara Makary sat on the stone bed, and the vampire giving up her life knelt in front of the girl. Kidan glimpsed a familiar shape, a horn with circular ridges crafted into it, from her *Weapons of the Dark* book. Her world stilled, fingers twitching at her side.

An impala horn. If she could somehow steal one, she'd finally have a weapon against them.

An elderly Mot Zebeya took the horn and cut along the vampire's wrist, weakening the dranaic. Sara Makary drank the blood slowly.

Kidan's tongue filled with salt. Was she really going to witness another creation of these creatures?

"So, she drinks from the vampire and wakes up as one of them?"

"Sort of."

"I thought it'd be more complicated."

GK's body stiffened. "There's a forbidden one called death transformation. It's where humans can be changed after they die."

Kidan's stomach turned. After death...

Her voice became hollow. "I didn't even know that was possible."

His eyes hardened. "It can happen only in the early hours after death, before certain irreversible changes in the body take place. If dranaic blood is infused directly into the heart before it's too late, a lawless transformation will take place."

Her throat nearly closed. "That's...awful."

"Rogue dranaics usually practice such a thing. It's a last desperate move, with horrifying consequences." She didn't miss the note of revulsion in his words. "Those changed like that are more bloodthirsty and violent."

Kidan found comfort in his disgust. They were united in seeing evil when they imagined that scenario.

Sara Makary continued to drink from the vampire's wrist for the next twenty minutes. Gradually, the vampire's posture slackened, eyes dimming, before she fell on the stone bed. Dead.

Sara Makary's eyes fluttered awake, then closed, before she slept.

"She won't wake up for two more days," GK explained.

"Why?"

"Everyone says different things, but I believe it's because she's reliving every memory, thought, and emotion the vampire had. The exchange of life is a powerful thing given to us by the Last Sage."

Powerful, yes, but an act that should never exist nonetheless.

One of the elderly Mot Zebeyas approached, crinkling and smelling like an old piece of paper. GK jumped to his feet, bowing slightly.

"What's your name?" the Mot Zebeya asked her in a deep, curious voice.

She blinked. "Kidan."

His thick finger bone necklace jittered along his hunched neck. "You should come to the monastery. I'd like to give you a reading."

Kidan swallowed. This again. Did all Mot Zebeyas sense death?

"She doesn't want one, but I'm looking after her," GK said, and she smiled a little at the words.

The two went off to the side and spoke in quiet voices, eyes sliding to Kidan. Maybe she wasn't welcome here.

On the stone bed, Rufeal brushed his sister's cheek, whispering softly. When his eyes landed on Kidan, his lip curved slightly.

And if my plan doesn't work, we'll have to resort to less pleasant options, won't we?

Kidan rolled her neck, fingers clenching. If he laid one finger on Yusef, he'd join his sister on that stone, with his heart missing so he'd never be resurrected.

38.

KIDAN SHADOWED YUSEF FOR THE NEXT FEW DAYS, DESPERATE TO keep him away from Rufeal Makary's hungry gaze. He went into town with GK on weekends but often chose to spend his time inside the Grand Andromeda Hall, where Slen practiced her violin. Past the left wing, there was a wide vacant room, perfect for the beautifully haunting sounds drifting up to the curved domes.

Only Greek and Roman statues, noticeable for their expensive white marble, crowded the edges of the space as Slen played and Yusef sketched, sitting cross-legged in the middle of the floor.

Kidan sat on the cold stone too, mesmerized by the music. She glanced over at Yusef, taking note of which piece of creation possessed him. Today, it was Slen, head angled and chin resting on her violin, fingers on display, arm pulled back in motion.

Yusef already had an eraser in hand.

"Her eyes." He rubbed furiously at the spot, and in a silvery slash, Slen appeared blindfolded. "I can't get them right."

Kidan was swept away by the low and high waves of the notes. Slen appeared to love the art of it, her eyes shut in the swelling and ebbing of a mournful tune. Kidan's eyes almost misted when Slen played the final note, ringing it with a never-ending intensity until Kidan was sure the strings would snap. It vibrated right through her body, the marble, the earth's core.

Once finished, Slen breathed heavily and lifted her lashes to them. "What do you think?"

"You're incredible," Yusef and Kidan said at the same time, and smiled.

Slen packed away her violin and came to sit next to them. "Hopefully, I can be a soloist by next year."

Kidan regarded her curiously. "You love it, don't you."

She nodded.

Kidan's eyes fell to Slen's scarred palms and the gloves she was putting back on.

Her forehead creased. "Still?"

It occurred to Kidan too late that it was a rude question. Yusef froze next to her. He must know too.

She tried to apologize, to take it back. What the hell was wrong with her? But Slen answered.

"If I hated it, he'd win. He'd take far more than a little skin."

Yusef's eyes became downcast, his grip tight around his charcoal pencil. Kidan studied the marble, letting Slen's words wash over her. Slen was stronger than Kidan thought. It took an incredible amount of strength to love a poisoned piece of yourself. Slen was sucking out the venom every time she played. What would that be like? To fill your mouth with toxin and spit it out instead of swallowing?

Kidan's lips curved sadly. "I like that. Not letting them win. My sister...and I tried to hang on to Amharic for as long as we could but lost it eventually. Our foster mother made sure. It didn't used to bother me, but now..."

She trailed off, unsure why she was telling them all this.

Yusef gave her a compassionate look. "I'm sorry."

Slen, on the other hand, held her gaze with determination. "I can teach you Amharic."

Words of gratitude stuck in her throat, and she could only manage a nod. The tension melted like ice, and Kidan found herself a little more at ease.

Yusef redrew Slen's eyes, then abruptly grabbed the eraser again.

Kidan shook her head. "Will you never be satisfied with your work?"

"Not when everything exists to remind me it's not good."

"Really? Everything?"

"I'm trying to achieve something I can only master with a decade's worth of experience. My future self knows every error, angle, and technique. I'm competing with his skills, and I hate my work now because of it."

What an awful way to feel.

He sighed. "But I know I can be great. It's like a pulse under my thumb. It's miserable knowing your own potential. Every day feels wasted if it's not in pursuit of it."

She tipped her head to the cathedral-like ceiling.

"The pursuit of perfection is a reminder we will always be imperfect." She was impressed she remembered a quote from Dranacti so clearly. "Freeing, don't you think?"

"More like a curse." He scratched out an eye shape. "Makary House is making an offer to buy the Umil Art Museum. If I don't pass Dranacti this year and receive some ownership shares, I'll lose it."

She'd heard that ever since Omar Umil's arrest, the status of the Umil Art Museum had declined, but the fundraiser of the Youth Art Exhibition would mark a new artist in society as well as raise millions. It was a prestigious event that the Umils held regularly. Rufeal Makary's entry was no doubt adding to Yusef's mounting pressure.

Silence stretched for several minutes. Slen reached for her bag and inched Yusef's *Debilitating Creative Rants* jar across. Kidan released a breathless laugh. Yusef shook his head, smiling, and placed a crumpled dollar in it.

Kidan was beginning to understand their dynamic. How the arts brought them closer.

"We can start your lessons tonight." Slen slung her violin bag over her shoulder and stood. "Philosophy Tower?"

Kidan nodded with a small smile. "I'll be there."

Yusef watched Slen leave. "She doesn't tell anyone about what happened. I like that she trusts you. I don't think she would have told me if I hadn't found her right after it happened.... There was so much blood." He clenched his jaw, then held her gaze with a seriousness unusual for him. "Help her. She won't let me, but maybe she'll let you."

Kidan nodded, instantly liking him even more.

Yusef flipped backward to a page. A charcoal drawing of familiar hands in motion appeared—delicate and manicured. From the slender wrist dangled a vintage watch.

Kidan caught her breath. "Is that...Ramyn's?"

Yusef traced it with swimming eyes. "Yes."

Kidan could almost hear the broken watch—tick-ticking, but stuck in the same position. Her chest hollowed.

"She would have liked it."

Yusef flipped again. This time the hands were larger, holding an old book, with a finger bone chain dangling between the pages. The details, to each vein and blemish, were incredible. GK.

When Kidan saw the sketch of herself, the room faded away. Nothing extra-ordinary about her hands—they were rough, nails still healing from the repeated scratching of her symbols—but it was the action he'd caught her in. She'd been playing with her butterfly bracelet, fingers pinching the compartment where the blue pill waited. He hadn't realized it, of course, but it shook Kidan to her core that, somehow, he'd captured her entirely by only drawing her hands.

A ball formed in her throat. "Why . . . why did you draw this?"

"It's my application for the Youth Art Exhibition. I've always found the hands to be more expressive than the face."

Kidan touched her bracelet, and its coldness burned. She wasn't sure this was how she wanted to be captured.

Yusef continued, unaware of her turmoil. "I think it started with my father. He always had this thing about keeping his hands clean. He washed ten times a day, even while painting. He didn't like his fingers stained." He released a dead laugh. "His hands were perfectly clean—until he slaughtered half our dranaics. Then they were covered in blood. Our parents are all sick."

His pain was a visceral thing, making her own heart ache. How had it felt for Yusef to testify against his father? To witness something so horrific about his own family? She had the urge to travel back in time, reach young Yusef, and tug him free from Omar Umil. The same way she longed to free Slen from Koril Qaros.

"You don't have to talk about him," she said honestly.

"There's nothing to talk about. He's a murderer. A disgrace. How can I ever inherit my house when this is what it's known for?"

When his face found hers, it was unbearably bleak, and she wrapped her fingers inward to keep herself from hugging him.

"Keep making choices your father wouldn't. Like Slen said, we can't let them win, right?"

She tried for a smile.

He sniffed and nodded slowly.

Kidan studied Slen's blinded eyes in Yusef's sketch and couldn't help but think this captured the essence of her gaze more. There was a deadness to Slen's expression now, a steely armor no one could penetrate. The very thing that pulled Kidan in like a violent tide.

Perhaps the key was to realize that peace lay in survival, past the scars and pinches and among righteous revenge, not surrender. What a dangerous, dangerous thought.

39.

"TENUOUS" WAS THE WORD FOR THIS NEW ARRANGEMENT BETWEEN Kidan and Susenyos. Susenyos would help Kidan acquire a life exchange, and she wouldn't go to Dean Faris and accuse him. But her investigation had opened doors to places she hadn't expected, and she still wasn't sure how he was caught up in the 13th.

They trudged carefully around each other, almost diplomatic in the way they shared the house, waiting for the other to exit before occupying a room. Sometimes, when they'd brush past each other, she'd remember the night in the Southern Sost Buildings, and her skin would feel feverish, as if his mouth and fangs were on her shoulder. The thought unsettled her so much that she'd escape to the nearest room to get away from it. They were careful not to slip into their old habits. But it grew boring, and so, instead of leaving the study when he was about to walk in, she stayed.

Curiosity glinted in Susenyos's dark eyes. Cautiously, he settled at his station opposite hers. "What are you studying?"

She hesitated, unsure how to navigate this new peace. "Dranacti, but I'm stuck."

After growing desperate to decipher Quadrantism, Kidan and the others had tracked major historical moments of dranaics, following the theology and how it affected political, social, and economic changes. They were the most agonizing reads of her life.

"Slen and GK think the task is to learn more about our house dranaics." She studied him.

He suggested she visit the Ajtaf Contemporary Library across campus, an odd quirk to his lips. "The Gojam Period, nineteenth century, should prove interesting."

She lifted a brow, curious. Willing to try anything at this point, Kidan located the second library of Uxlay, on the northern side of its layout. Unlike the main library, this was decorated in sleek furniture and modernized with tech assistant guides.

On every white surface, a small screen, accompanied by a pair of headphones, winked black. She sat in the chair facing one of them and listened to a summarized history of dranaics through East Africa's dark period of colonialism preceding the celebratory creation of the Pan-African movement in the twentieth century. She found some interesting facts. Ethiopian emperors were given a new, throne name upon ascension. It was customary for military officials to don a lion's mane as a headdress. Then under a category titled *Hidden History,* she came across a familiar name, of an emperor who ruled Gojam Province, and shot to her feet.

Susenyos III.

"No way," she said loudly, receiving dirty looks from other students.

Mouth agape, Kidan stared at the striking picture, the image leaking into her eyes.

When she rushed home, Susenyos was in his room, enjoying the glow of the afternoon sun. He wore his favorite shirt, taut chest muscles soaking in the rays. She hadn't entered his room since the night of her panic attack.

"You were an *emperor*?"

The question left her in wonder, and the full impact of history and what it meant to defy it hit her all at once. A deeper part of her wondered what else he was hiding.

She pulled up her phone. "Susenyos Sagad the Third. Your throne name was Malak Sagad the Fourth, which means *to whom the angels bow.* You're kidding me, right?"

He stretched out on his chair, dark eyes dancing. "Well, you should have known you were in the presence of royalty."

She studied the regal portrait on her screen, then him. Impossible. But clearly, possible.

She shook her head. "Tell me."

He motioned for Kidan to sit, and she hesitated. This invitation marked a distinct line she didn't want to cross. She searched for a way to justify this. More research into him would help her investigate better. It was a thin excuse, but she needed it, to justify sinking onto his soft bed.

She traced the portrait, over his hairline now missing a crown. "How did you go from being an emperor to a…"

"A dranaic? It's a long story."

She gasped. "Wait, the crown I took?"

The corner of his mouth lifted in a half smile. "It was mine. I wore it on my coronation day."

Kidan could hardly believe it. Would he kill her if he knew she'd fashioned a necklace out of it?

"What happened?"

"It's as tragic as any tale, I suppose." His forehead creased. "It began with rumors about raids, villagers crossing into other people's properties and stealing young girls, blood being drained from animals. We had no idea what kind of plague it was, how powerless we truly were, until rogue dranaics seized my court. They wanted me turned so they could make a home in my empire."

Kidan kept blinking. *My court.* But even more surprising was that his story began like hers: Vampires had attacked him, come to steal what was precious to him.

"Did you fight back?"

His gaze simmered when it rested on her, untouched by centuries. "Yes, for a while. Then I realized how incredibly weak humans were, so I joined the other side."

He chose immortality. Kidan's mouth soured. She'd been so caught up in the story that she nearly forgot his true nature. What had she expected him to do? Cling to his humanity and die? Only the luckiest of souls chose that dignified path.

"What happened to the rest of your court?" Kidan asked, body coiled tight.

He was silent for the length of five heartbeats, his gaze mirroring a fog.

"They're dead. All that remains of them is what you see in the artifact room."

An unexpected wave of guilt hit her. Those artifacts… weren't just a collection of history. They belonged to people who once surrounded him. She'd destroyed them, and he visited each day to continue mending them.

His room morphed slightly, peacefulness streaming through the windows and scattering the darkness. She shook her head, trying to dispel the uninvited calm expanding in her chest. When Kidan returned to her room, she found it robbed of all sun, no longer offering comfort as it once did.

40.

SHOCK AND RUMORS RIPPLED THROUGH UXLAY DURING THE FIRST rainfall of the year. Koril Qaros was taken into questioning by campus authorities. Evidence of him physically restraining a distressed Ramyn from leaving his house had leaked onto the campus's website. The public nature of the evidence left no room for debate as Slen's father became the primary suspect in Ramyn's death.

Understandably, Slen was missing from their study group meeting. There were no books opened as they sat in silence. The only sound came from the video that GK played on his phone.

"Finally." He sighed, brows furrowed. "Ramyn will get justice."

Kidan couldn't muster any pity for Koril Qaros. But this raised more questions than it answered. Who threw Ramyn from the tower? They all knew it was a vampire that delivered the final blow, coloring Ramyn's lips and biting into her neck, so which vampire did it? And how did it connect to June?

At the next gathering of the 13th, the absence of Koril Qaros was the topic of conversation. Kidan stuck to the shadows, listening.

"Throwing a person from a tower feels a little performative, no?" a gorgeous dranaic with black lipstick said. "It seems like Qaros wanted the entire world to see. Quite odd for as private an act as murder."

Her thin, mustached partner said, "Why would he want that?"

She shrugged a delicate shoulder. "Perhaps he loves the art of it, or he's redirecting attention like a masterful play."

"Redirecting attention?" Kidan said suddenly. "To what?"

The woman blinked her thick lashes. "To the tower, of course. A spotlight shone so every head would look up while the mastermind hid in the shadows."

Another dranaic in an impressive burgundy suit responded, "But that's what made Koril a suspect. He had no one to corroborate his whereabouts at the time of the girl's death. It would have been more intelligent to neither hide in the shadows nor take up too much light."

The woman flashed a beautiful set of teeth. "I do love your reasoning, Sacro." Sacro gave a little bow.

Kidan frowned. She didn't like how they spoke about the matter without any empathy, but the cold assessment did raise a good question for her: Why *did* Koril make Ramyn's death so public? Kidan saw no benefit in this.

At the front of the room, Tamol Ajtaf stood and fastened his golden button. "May I have your attention. I know this is a shock to all of us. Koril Qaros was a beloved member of our group. I assure you the proper investigations will be carried out. If any of you have personal concerns, please come see me."

Kidan regarded his cool green eyes. He didn't mourn Ramyn, not openly at least. Here he was again, calm and collected, without even a wrinkle in his suit, announcing that his sister's murderer had been found.

Rufeal Makary came to stand near her. "They must really like you," he said. "No one gets in here this quickly. Then again, you have it easy. Being the only heiress and all."

Kidan fought not to move away. "Getting in doesn't seem hard."

His smile strained. "The rest of us born with fourteen cousins have always had to prove ourselves."

"What do you mean?"

"Do you think the 13th found my sister a life exchange out of the goodness of their hearts? I had many tasks to complete, including ours."

Kidan's neck prickled. "You don't need to worry about Yusef. I got it."

He raised a doubtful brow. "If he passes Quadrantism, I'll have to deal with it. And you might not get your life exchange."

He had a sickly determination to his eyes, a predator hunting for prey. She forced a nod.

On the other side of the room, Tamol slipped through a side door with a new member Kidan hadn't seen before. House Delarus, for sure. Their sigil was red silk stitched into a rose, appropriate for the Fashion House.

"Out with the old, in with the new, as they say," Rufeal continued. "The 13th love trading up. Members here change as quick as Sacro's suits. You always have to be useful. When Umil lost his mind, Makary joined. When Qaros stumbles, Delarus is ready—"

"Wait, Umil? As in Omar Umil?"

"Who else?"

Kidan's temples hurt. How did she not know that Omar Umil was in the 13th? Because he was imprisoned and an outcast, she had assumed he was excluded.

"I need to go."

Rufeal held up his glass of liquor. "You do whatever you want, Founding Heiress. Let us fight among scraps while you eat your lion."

Kidan's shoulders relaxed as she put distance between them. She knew what to include in her letter to get Omar Umil's attention. Swiping a pen, she mentioned the number 13 twice. Once about her biological mother's birthday and another mentioning a random date. She hoped it was enough.

After delivering the letter, she returned to an empty home.

She considered getting some work done on Quadrantism, but her stomach cramped. The kitchen stove held a pot of siga wot and a platter of injera flatbread. Kidan opened the lid and inhaled the soft-cooked meat and rosemary. She sent a silent thank-you to Etete and heated the stew. A note on the marble countertop caught her eye.

Suseynos, I'm visiting my children. Don't go into the observatory alone.

Kidan set down the note. The house was unusually quiet. She wandered through the hallways, bracing against the wave of knives that tore at her, and reached the observatory. Carefully, she opened the door, letting the stream of blue light fall over her feet.

Susenyos was slumped on the floor, utterly still.

"Susenyos," she whispered.

He didn't move. She took a step forward and froze. He'd warned her multiple times—*my bloodlust is uncontrollable in that room.*

She spotted a mantel to her side and reached over to gather the fake fruit sitting on it. A few cherries rolled into her palms. Without thinking, she started throwing them at him, hoping to wake him up. They bounced off him, his dark skin glowing like obsidian under stained glass.

"Hey!" Once the cherries were done, she grabbed the apples and grapefruits, hitting harder.

Three made contact, but he remained unresponsive.

June's voice swept over her, a hurricane of fury.

"Leave him to suffer!"

Kidan's feet staggered back.

"He deserves it," June whispered, growing stronger. *"You have him vulnerable. What are you waiting for?"*

Kidan trembled. How did she sound so real? "I need his help. I'm still searching for you. . . . I know I'm close."

"He must die. Kill all evil."

Kidan stared at his body while her mind warred with itself. She recalled the night he'd pulled her from the hallway. The pain unbearable after a few minutes. How long had he been in here? All day?

Susenyos had to die . . . and yet, she couldn't help but see a boy king losing his court and the people he loved, with only their artifacts to keep him company. A key to which he kept around his neck. His story softened him against her will, the outline of his profile shifting from an assailant to victim.

And his chest was so still.

Oh, fuck it.

"Don't!" June screamed.

Kidan rushed inside the coldest room of the house, goose bumps rising along her neck despite her sweater. June's thunderous eyes faded into smoke by the door, so angry at Kidan that Kidan forgot to breathe.

She shook the image and knelt before him, tapping his cheek and startling away when his icy skin burned her.

"Hey!" She shook him by the shoulders. Hard. "Snap out of it!"

His eyes flew open.

He scrambled away from her like she was a spider, a film of terror over his eyes. Kidan's heartbeat jumped to her throat.

She held up her hands and got to her feet slowly.

He stood as well, moving into a fighting stance.

"I'll leave now," she said.

She took a step back, but he rushed at her, pushing her against the window so her back cracked. A sharp corner dug into her wrist, cutting her slightly. Pain pulsed from her hand to her spine.

"It's Kidan!" she shouted. "You're seeing things!"

His deliriousness cleared a little. "Kidan? What are you doing here?"

Relief broke through her ribs. "Helping you."

She hid her bleeding wrist, but it would be no use. He'd smell it and, in this room, attack her. Panic beat in her chest as blood trickled down her palm.

Shit.

Instead, he stepped back, touching his veined temple, voice thicker than thunder.

"I told you not to come in here."

"You're welcome—"

"*Out.*"

"Excuse me?"

"Get out!" he roared, and the glass window splintered behind her.

Kidan's cheeks burned with fury. She clutched her wrist and stormed out, checking her hand once she was outside the observatory. The cut was small, but a few drops of blood coated the blue floor. Yet Susenyos still hadn't noticed. He hadn't knelt down to taste it like that first time. He hadn't reached for his blood flask. It wouldn't be so jarring if the one thing consistent about vampires wasn't their reaction to blood.

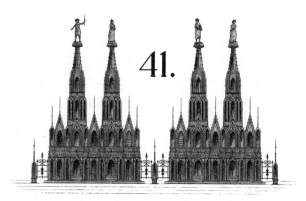

41.

SUSENYOS EMERGED AN HOUR LATER, SHOWERED, HIS HAIR DAMP AND color returned to his face. Kidan ignored him, focusing on her studies by the fireplace.

He ran his fingers through his damp twists. "You can't just come inside that room again—"

"Why?"

His jaw locked. "It's dangerous."

Her eyes narrowed. She didn't believe that. Not anymore. "I was bleeding."

"What?"

"You say your bloodlust is uncontrollable in that room. I was bleeding in there. You didn't react."

His brows drew tight, then smoothed out. "I was doing you the courtesy of not attacking you."

He moved into his seat, preparing his letters, pulling out gloves and ink.

Kidan's ears thrummed. There was something pulsing under her thumb, like she'd discovered a piece of treasure but couldn't tell what it was. The house law stated that if he endangered the house, he would lose something of equal value. Night after night, he suffered to change it. What did this house steal from him? It had to be powerful. She recalled Dean Faris's tea law. What were the limits to such a punishing law?

Her eyes narrowed further. "Where?"

He didn't look up. "What?"

"Where was I bleeding?"

"Why does it matter?"

"You always notice blood. You noticed my scent was off when I was poisoned."

"Leave it alone." The bite to his tone startled her.

"Why...," she began, but drifted off when his dark expression struck her. He was furious, yet underneath it, the same fog of fear from the observatory room lurked. Why did he change so much whenever that room was brought up? "Why are you afraid?"

"Kidan." He said her name very carefully, almost like a threat. "Leave it alone."

The lamp in the study flickered, and the walls rippled with violence. It was as if the hallway stretched out its fingers here, clawing at her throat. *Do not speak.*

She left her side of the room and went to his desk, leaning forward, unable to fight the pull of this thread. Why hadn't he reacted to her blood?

"If Susenyos Sagad endangers Adane House, the house shall in turn steal something of equal value...." She looked in the direction of the observatory and back to his thundering face. "Something *you* value the most...something you fight for, something that saved you from death when it came to your court..." She trailed off, her eyes widening. "But that's not possible."

He rose, resting his palms flat on the desk. He was inches from her nose, barely restraining himself. "Don't."

How could she not? He might kill her for giving life to his secrets. But she had to expel the truth from her body, let it wreak havoc on everything she thought she knew.

"There is a reason." She breathed. "A reason why you warn me against that room. Not because it's dangerous for me, but because it's dangerous for *you*."

The lamp's light became erratic, a bird caged and fighting its incoming death.

"Go *back* to your seat." Each word pushed through clenched teeth.

The lack of reaction to blood, how utterly weak he was in that room, almost...human.

She understood. Oh, she finally understood, and was it glorious. A slow smile spread across her face.

Kidan drew close enough to identify the streaks of his alert eyes. "This house is stealing your immortality, isn't it?"

He shut his eyes slowly, swearing under his breath. "You just couldn't let it go."

Her chest filled with incredible light. "I'm right, aren't I? The law in this house is already in effect? That room steals what you value most—"

The desk was shoved to the side with a speeding screech, slamming into the bookshelf and raining books. Kidan jumped back in shock. Susenyos loomed over her and seized her hand.

Her legs turned to water. "What are you doing?"

He wrenched her forward, a sudden force robbing her breath as his grip tugged the center of her gravity. They were moving at extreme speed. Her stomach twisted, and bile flooded her throat. She would retch if he didn't *stop*. When she finally gasped for air, Kidan was on cold stone, inside the wine cellar under the house. She whirled around, touching the damp walls. Susenyos grabbed the gate and locked it.

"No. No! Susenyos!" She banged on the gate furiously. "Don't!"

He stayed back, shoulders rising and falling, watching her with a dark expression. "You were never meant to know."

Fear tightened her gut. "I won't tell anyone. Just let me out."

He backed away and climbed the stairs, shutting the upper door.

"Susenyos! Fuck!"

She searched around the space for an exit, but there were only bottles of deep red and brown liquor. Kidan sank to the cold floor, trying to breathe through the panic. If he was going to kill her, he would have. This was good. He hadn't decided. She just had to convince him she was no threat. But still . . .

Susenyos.

Human.

At least in the observatory.

Her palms spread on the hard stone, the weight of this house and its laws fully sinking in. House laws were powerful—but this? To change the fabric of life and death, strip an immortal of power, grant a mortal unbelievable strength. Was this why the children of this place killed themselves trying to inherit such a legacy? It was proof she still had much to learn.

Her family had known exactly how to punish Susenyos for endangering Adane House. Where did the term "house" extend to and stop? What did it protect? It was too vague to pinpoint. She let her thoughts eat at her, turning every interaction over and over until the web became too tangled. Exhausted, she slept on the floor, teeth chattering. With her ear pressed to the old stone, she imagined the belly of the house breathing fire so she wouldn't freeze to death.

The upstairs door opened again. Kidan brushed away tiny gravel from her cheek and shot to her feet.

"Susenyos?"

The legs descending the stairs were leaner, below a familiar red brocade vest and sharply cut hair. Icy water trickled down Kidan's spine.

Iniko Obu stood behind the bars, with a cool, unmoving expression. A second set of footsteps revealed Susenyos.

Kidan focused on him. "I want to talk to you."

"I'm sure you do," Iniko cut in. "But I'll be dealing with you."

Kidan held his gaze imploringly, but he shook his head, going back upstairs.

"Wait, please."

Iniko dragged an old chair with her and sat behind the gate, cocking her head. "He doesn't know what to do with you. I, on the other hand, have a very clear intention."

"I'm not going to tell anyone," Kidan's voice scratched.

"That's not something he can risk."

Kidan glared. "If you do something to me, Dean Faris will arrest you. Do you really think he'd risk his life for you?"

Iniko's smile was a thin, humorless curve. "He's our leader. My loyalty cannot be shaken, and you trying to do so tells me more than you know."

Kidan fought not to cower under her wrath. "Where's Taj?"

"Taj doesn't want to see what's going to happen here."

Kidan backed away and sat on the floor. She was screwed.

"How are the nightmares?" Iniko tilted her head.

"Nightmares?"

"They say Shuvra poisoning infests the mind, brings horrible deeds to the surface."

Kidan focused on an old wine. "They're fine. I'm used to nightmares."

Not true, but June was an expert in them. She went just one day out of the year without waking up terrorized and frazzled. Parasomnia, they called it.

"Yos tells me he listens for your heartbeat. It grows more irregular each night. Your breathing is strained as well. You don't have much time."

Kidan hesitated. "He said that?"

"Yes. He wishes for you to live. He's seen enough Adanes die."

Her ears perked up, and she snuck a glance at Iniko to see if it was a twisted strategy to make her confess. Kidan cast her attention away. It had to be a lie. Susenyos cared for one thing only—changing this house law so his secret wouldn't be discovered.

"Tell me about your nightmares," Iniko continued.

"What?"

"I'm curious."

"I can't think of one right now."

Iniko rose to her feet, her shadow lengthening like death's scythe. "Not many people know this, but Shuvra originated in West Africa. It was given to wailing mothers after the loss of their children. Do you know what it does? It voids sleep of dreams and regulates the body for rest. Most believe their loved ones are dead because they sleep quite peacefully. No nightmares."

Kidan's stomach hitched. "My strain must be different."

The gate unlocked. Kidan jumped up. Iniko walked inside slowly, so confident in her ability to overpower Kidan that she left the door wide open.

Kidan reached for a wine bottle from behind, wrapped her fingers around its neck and hurled it at her. Iniko's arm shattered the glass, drenching her in violent red.

She frowned at her clothes. "That was a mistake."

Kidan bolted.

She made it three steps before her arm was wrenched back. Her wrist was suddenly lacerated. Iniko brought Kidan's hand to her mouth, tongue snaking out to lick the drip. Her fangs emerged next.

"What the hell are you doing?" Kidan screamed.

Iniko bit her. Pain erupted through her veins.

"Stop—"

Iniko's iron hand closed around her throat. The room swirled in a dizzying dance and settled in a different location. Kidan was on a...ship. No, Iniko was on a ship, in chains, dismembering attackers with a ferociousness known to a panther. They called her the Water Demon, the one who sank pirate ships. But it was more than watching Iniko's past. Her rage bled into Kidan's skin and boiled to uncomfortable heat so when Iniko finally let go, Kidan slid down, gravity spiraling.

Iniko crouched, sleek hair catching fire. "Your blood is clean."

Kidan still rocked on a boat, lips dried of thirst. She recalled Taj's words about the connection between a vampire's bite and memories. The wrist revealed...childhood. Had this been Iniko's youth? Had Iniko glimpsed into Kidan's childhood?

More footsteps pounded down the stairs.

Run, she told herself, but her legs were drained of all energy.

Susenyos appeared at the gate. He wrenched Iniko to her feet, voice urgent. "Tell me you didn't drink her blood. What the *hell*—"

"She's not poisoned. I had to prove it."

Time itself froze as Susenyos stilled. "What?"

"She lied to us. Shuvra didn't touch her." Iniko spat, lips stained with blood.

Susenyos skewered Kidan with a menacing look. She rose unsteadily to her feet. She would die here if she didn't move.

Run, her mind screamed. With a desperate bout of strength, she bolted past them and made it through the gate. Hope bloomed in her chest. She was almost at the foot of the stairs. All she had to do was climb.

A solid body slammed into her. Taj, who mirrored a wolf without his usual smile, loomed before her.

"This hurts me more than it hurts you."

Taj grabbed her wrist and held her still as Susenyos bridged their gap.

"Wait." Her voice hiked up in terror. "Let me explain—"

Susenyos brought her wrist forward, inhaling the scent of her blood. His stiffness confirmed it for the others. He straightened, face drained of all light.

"Taj." Susenyos's voice was ice itself. "Take Iniko and feed her blood from her own house. You two were never here. Hide her until her red eyes fade."

Iniko's neck veins contracted. Her large, golden pupils would soon bleed. When a vampire drank from an uninitiated human, they became ill, their eyes reddening for three days. Long enough to be caught and punished by death.

It took Taj a long moment to release Kidan, but he did, chestnut eyes heavy. "I'm sorry."

His apology launched her heart into a frenzy. She was going to die.

The two disappeared with unnatural speed. Suddenly, the last thing she wanted was to be alone with Susenyos.

"Make no mistake, Kidan." His voice slipped, unhinged. "If anything happens to Iniko because of this, I'll put you out of your misery myself."

His fangs emerged, eyes trained on her bleeding wrist. She staggered away, closer to the stairs and freedom, hiding her hand. He shook his head, worked his jaw, and pulled out his flask, downing it in an instant and crushing the metal. His hair and eyes caught fire, burning a striking reddish gold.

He held the cellar gate open. "Inside. Now."

Kidan looked to the stairs. She was *so* close.

"Run." His voice thickened with hunger, canines stark against dark skin. "I dare you to run and ruin us both."

Kidan's pulse jumped to her throat. She walked toward the cellar, to him.

"Slower," he barked, grip twisting the gate.

Her footsteps eased, and when she moved past him, he turned his cheek sharply as if her scent was too potent. Kidan moved until her back reached the rearmost shelf of wine. He locked her in quickly, hesitating with his attention on the lock.

"You lied and used me," he said in a low, dead tone. "And it's entirely my fault. I believed you too quickly because I wanted to. For one weak moment, I wanted that poison in your body to be the answer to everything. It meant I wouldn't have to kill you, it meant you were no longer a threat, it meant you'd become a vampire and you and I could be...at peace."

An unexpected lump formed in her throat. "Susenyos—"

"Thank you for reminding me where we stand."

He left. Kidan sank down slowly. She reached for her tie and undid it, wrapping it around her bleeding wrist. The pressure swallowed the burning pain and she fought to think.

What the hell was she going to do?

It was over. They knew her secret. *He* knew. Susenyos's face flashed through her mind, the slash of shock and betrayal followed by those haunting words.

Kidan shut her eyes and reached for her sister.

I failed. I'm so sorry, June.

June didn't answer. She was mad at Kidan for helping Susenyos, for going against her promise. Kidan drowned in the smell of fermented wine, her head growing heavy. The shards of glass called to her. Maybe she was done.

The upstairs door clicked open, and light footsteps traveled closer.

Etete's warm face rippled with worry. "Kidan? Oh dear."

"Etete?" Kidan rushed to the gate, grabbing the bars. "Please, let me out."

Etete had a large set of keys and began trying each one.

"Where are they?" Kidan's words came out hoarse.

"They've gone to help Iniko. We have to hurry."

Kidan shut her eyes. She could still make it out alive. The sixth key clicked and turned. Kidan embraced Etete's soft form, inhaling her scent of warm bread.

"Thank you."

"Go, and never come back."

Kidan ran upstairs. She had to get her bag and leave. The hallways scratched at her brain with needles. She clutched her head, fighting through the pain. June's image appeared at the end of her path.

You can't leave.

The power of June's voice slammed into her chest, knocking her off-balance.

You promised to find me.

The world shattered, but someone supported her at the waist. With Kidan wincing, they made it to her room, where she could breathe.

Etete wiped Kidan's tears with her scarf. But they didn't stop. For the first time in months, they gushed out of her like a deep wound.

"I can't leave," she whispered. "I have to find her."

"Susenyos will kill you if you stay." Etete's face tensed. "He never allows this secret to live."

So Etete knew the house law. He trusted her this much. The Adane dranacics . . . Had they discovered it? Was this why he'd killed them?

The hallway light flickered. June's honey-brown eyes were sharp as a sword.

"She wants me to stay. Even if I die trying . . ."

Etete nodded soberly.

One last try. Kidan owed June that much. If Iniko was caught for force-feeding, everyone would learn Kidan wasn't poisoned. It would mean the end of her investigation. Today was her last chance to learn something useful.

Miraculously, her phone lit up with an email from Drastfort Prison. Omar Umil was ready to see her. She hugged the phone to her chest, whispering thank you to the universe.

42.

DRASTFORT PRISON REMINDED KIDAN OF HER OWN ARREST. SHE stood at the entrance, finding it hard to cross. She was back there again, the night of burning skin, handcuffs on her wrists, throat raw from smoke inhalation.

She'd been human up until she crossed the threshold of the police station, at which point she became an animal, pushed, goaded, and thrown in a cage. Hair frizzed, body dirty, soul scarred. Wide-eyed and waiting within cramped walls.

Kidan had never loathed herself so potently as she had in that cage.

"You coming in?" an officer called from within the dim chamber.

Kidan shook herself and crossed the threshold, lungs constricted. "I'm here to visit Omar Umil."

The officer had the eyes of a hawk. "Purpose of visit?"

"He's an old family friend."

"You can sit inside the waiting area."

An hour later, she was allowed in. Omar Umil was a man of sixty, brown skin dotted with blemishes and a gray beard. He sat across the table, attention on the ceiling corner.

"Hello." Kidan glanced at the corner. There was an elaborate spiderweb, nothing else. "Thank you for finally seeing me."

He said nothing.

"I have some questions for you, if you don't mind. I know you were—"

"That web," he cut in, voice rougher than sandpaper. "Bring me some of it."

"Sorry?"

Omar Umil stared at the corner again.

"Why?"

No answer.

"This is really important, if you can give me a minute of your time—"

"The web first."

Kidan tightened her jaw. She stood, dragged one of the chairs to the corner, reached high, and shook her fingers through the web, wrapping it like cotton candy before depositing the tattered mess into his large hands.

She rubbed her hands clean. "So, my questions. I want to talk about the 13th."

This time, he lifted his attention from the ball of web. Something like recognition flickered in his heavy-lidded eyes. "Kidan Adane. Silia's niece. Mahlet and Aman's daughter."

Kidan blinked in surprise. She thought so infrequently of her biological parents, it was a shock when others brought them up. The sadness of it, she didn't like. The distance of it, she didn't like.

Omar Umil studied her features, taking note of her eyebrows, hooded eyes, the straight slant of her nose, different colored lips.

"Where is your sister?"

Kidan straightened. "June?"

"Yes, June," he recalled. "Your family was the smallest in Uxlay, so much canvas space. Easy to paint, but difficult not to feel the lives lost. Two grandparents, two parents, two children."

"Only the two children now," she said quietly. "The rest of the family is dead. June is missing. That's why I'm here."

The frown on his face appeared genuine.

"I think the 13th or Susenyos Sagad had something to do with June's disappearance. I just don't know how they connect." Kidan leaned in. "Please, if you know anything, tell me."

Umil fell silent, rolled his web ball back and forth, back and forth.

Kidan pushed. "I need to know what they want. You were part of their group. What happened?"

His face shifted like the surface of a black lake. "The 13th promise a new structure within our society. A man should be able to set his own laws within his house, to protect himself and his family first, not Uxlay. That's what they spew."

Kidan's brows drew together. Dean Faris had spoken about the importance of all houses uniting as one, with the same protection law so no outsider could infiltrate Uxlay. So the 13th wanted each house to be a separate entity...but why risk making the university vulnerable?

"They are a poison, and Uxlay is infested from within." He spat, startling her. "Loyal houses are falling to their movement, and dranaics are scheming."

The pressure increased on the ball of web, flattening it entirely.

"I know what they call House Umil: the Slaughterhouse. But they were spies, almost all of them. They infested my house, where my wife and son ate and slept. I had to remove them. They swore companionship but plotted against me."

Kidan understood the madness that clung to him. That need to remove the stain of those who betrayed you. It visited her often.

"What happened after?"

His tone only soured as he spoke. "They needed me to be the butcher. To prove their principle that the laws should first protect every member of a household and its dranaics. That the threat was greater inside Uxlay than from outside it."

Kidan's skin prickled. The 13th were appealing to both actis and dranaics, reeling them in for a revolution, promising them a chance to wield the powers of houses. This had to be why they hated Susenyos. He was named inheritor of a Founding House and wouldn't listen to their agendas.

"How many houses have joined now?" Omar Umil asked.

"Four, as far as I can tell—Ajtaf, Makary, Qaros, Delarus—but the 13th seem to want more."

He laughed, a rough, gutting sound. "The House Makary vermin. Of course. They've been after my house for years."

A sense of injustice ballooned in her chest. Rufeal Makary's gleaming eyes flashed before her mind. Did Omar Umil know they were coming for his son?

"Do you think the 13th took June?"

Umil's eyes darted around the room, corner to corner. It wouldn't be unsettling if Kidan hadn't displayed the same pattern with the taps of her fingers. Like her, he was disbelieved, a murderer, abandoned by his family. Was this where she would finally end up if she wasn't careful?

"The 13th need an heiress for House Adane," he said. "A house by itself is useless. It can't cast powerful laws or pledge allegiance. If they have your sister, she's alive."

An heiress for House Adane. If that was why they took June, had Kidan somehow ruined their plan when she arrived in Uxlay?

"Where would they keep her?" she asked urgently.

"It could be anywhere."

Kidan dug out Aunt Silia's journal and the patterns and lines Kidan had drawn herself. At one end was Ramyn Ajtaf and at the other was Koril Qaros. She needed help connecting them, making sense of everything. She showed it to him.

"Ramyn Ajtaf was sick and looking for a life exchange. The 13th came to her rescue, saying they'd get her a life exchange—before they killed her."

His eyes held grief, fingers gently touching the words of Ramyn's funeral address. "Helen's daughter."

"No, Reta's daughter." Kidan had studied the Ajtaf family tree carefully.

Umil said nothing. After a moment, Kidan continued. "I was thinking about why they'd kill her. Ramyn was innocent, liked by almost everyone. A lot of houses were outraged by her death, and some, like House Delarus, even joined the 13th, thinking they needed more protection."

Umil's lips twisted. "Each death is calculated by the 13th. It needs to serve not one but two purposes."

What had Ramyn's death achieved besides luring in other houses?

"Here's what I don't understand. Koril Qaros was arrested for Ramyn's murder. He's a 13th member. Why turn on him?"

Umil shook his head. "Koril has inherited Qaros House. The 13th need that slippery snake. They'll get him out before the day ends."

"But they haven't let him out. He's still in prison."

At this, Umil drew his elbows inward. "When did they arrest him?"

"Three days ago."

"Days?" He studied the name on the paper as if it held the secrets. "That can't be right."

"That's what I thought. Why would the 13th abandon one of their own?"

Kidan's frustration returned. She was on the tip of something, but every time she tried to grab on, it slithered out of her reach.

Umil drew the journal forward, muttering to himself. "Koril is one of their strongest. Cunning. Smart enough to kill while standing in a room full of people. Why abandon him now? What are they planning?"

Kidan's ears perked up. "Wait. You said a house by itself is useless, that it needs an inheritor, right? If the 13th only care about true owners...what about Koril's children?"

"The siblings?" He mulled this over while Kidan's throat grew parched. "Have they passed Dranacti?"

"One is in my group. She's intelligent, on her way to passing."

Umil's black eyes pierced hers. "Then they'll have their Qaros heiress."

That would mean...She stared right at Yusef's father. Breathing became difficult as she leaned back. He had said something else that now pulsed in her ears. *Smart enough to kill while standing in a room full of people.*

Slen had stood with them in that tower as Ramyn Ajtaf plummeted to her death. A death that imprisoned Slen's abusive father.

"No." Kidan ruffled through the journal. "I must be wrong somewhere. Slen wouldn't—couldn't—be part of their group."

She went over her past suspicions. There could be other reasons why the 13th needed Koril framed and arrested. She just had to find them. But her handwriting became difficult to read, her fingers tapping. Square. Square. Triangle. Square.

Umil studied her quietly, reaching over to stop her jittery hand.

"Leave."

"What?"

"Leave Uxlay. Today. They'll know we've spoken, and they will kill you."

Kidan withdrew her hand. "I can't leave. My sister, my classmates. They're in danger."

Miserable silence suffocated them.

"I wrote that I'm in a study group with Yusef....You haven't asked me about him," she said quietly.

Umil turned his head away. "There's nothing to ask."

"Why do you all do that?" Kidan's voice lashed out. "Why does every parent I know harm their child? Why give birth to us, why raise us, only to abandon us? You can't blame us when we try to hurt you in turn—you're meant to protect us. Yet..."

She bit the inside of her cheek. Slen's father had led Slen to this. Mama Anoet had led Kidan to this.

"Family loyalty." Kidan's nostrils flared hot. "What a lie it all is."

It was possible she wasn't angry at him but at her recent discovery. The safe space she'd foolishly found was losing its very gravity.

Slen.

Out of everyone, why did it have to be Slen?

She gathered her things quickly, the need to know for certain unbearable.

"Kidan," Omar Umil called out when she reached the door. "Protect my son. If he passes Dranacti, he'll be first in line to inherit. Yusef will refuse to join the 13th, and they won't let that happen. Do you understand?" Umil waited until she nodded. "In my house, under the basement floorboards, five squares from the top left corner, there's a box with a lock on it. The key is under it. There are some weapons. Use them. Destroy all silver from your house first. It gives vampires too much power if it touches their blood."

Kidan was stunned and grateful. "I . . . will."

Yusef would always be safe with her. She didn't abandon those she cared about.

The problem was Slen Qaros. Slen's flat eyes struck Kidan, followed by Ramyn's soft brown ones. Her heart ripped in two. One half led to destroying all traces of evil and earning forgiveness. Everything Kidan came here to achieve. The other led to a slippery, dangerous hope that her torn, wretched soul had finally found its twin. In a girl who wore fingerless gloves, no less.

43.

KIDAN NEEDED SLEN'S CONFESSION MORE THAN AIR ITSELF.

Fiddling with her phone in her pocket, she settled on the secluded steps where she'd first met Slen and thought of Mama Anoet's confession. The last rays of sun hit her eye, and her leg bounced with anticipation. She hadn't seen Susenyos or Taj anywhere. Hopefully, they were too busy taking care of Iniko to come hunting for her. Her best option was telling Dean Faris about Susenyos's immortality, and that he'd kill her for discovering his secret. The dean would offer protection—but what if... Kidan was wrong? What if Susenyos was entirely innocent?

A breeze snuck under her sleeves, chilling and taunting. If she was in the house, the hallway would punish her for such a thought. Of course he wasn't entirely innocent. He played some part. He'd simply mastered concealing it, like his stolen immortality.

Now Slen might be just as guilty. If Slen was a new member of the 13th, did she know anything about June?

Kidan's brain hurt. She wasn't thinking straight, needed time to come up with a plan.

Short, thick braids curled around Slen's aggressive jaw, the sun a harsh glare behind her. She climbed the stairs, with hands tucked into her large pockets. They were positioned like at their first meeting, with enough space between them for two people. The wind whistled and tickled Kidan's ears.

Kidan's voice carried in the shifting gust. "Have you heard of the Green Heights foster case? A girl burned down a house with her foster mother inside. She discovered that her foster mother was behind her sister's disappearance."

"Parents can be cruel."

"Yes, but children? Children can be merciless." Kidan studied her profile. "You don't think it was wrong?"

"In regard to whose interpretation?"

"I'm not discussing Dranacti, Slen. This is real life."

"You believe there's a difference."

If Slen knew Kidan's secret, she was doing an impeccable job pretending otherwise.

Kidan sucked in a breath. "What if I told you it's not just a news story, that it's about me and my sister?"

"So why aren't you in prison?" Slen asked.

"Why aren't you?"

Their eyes met, and for a moment Kidan glimpsed a muscle curving slightly on Slen's mouth before it disappeared.

"Your father is a violent man," Kidan said.

"Yes."

"He was arrested."

"Correct again."

Kidan's hand shook in her pocket, rolling back and forth on the play button. She couldn't bring herself to press it. It was like jumping into an abyss and hoping a giant net was at the bottom. Slen wouldn't confess without demanding something in return. But what would it feel like to finally tell someone? Someone who'd taken a life because of an unforgivable betrayal? Her bracelet twinkled with caution in the fading light. June wouldn't want her to.

"Did you know your father was a member of a group called the 13th?" Kidan asked softly.

Slen tilted her head to the purple and orange sky. Her profile was beautiful, even though it was obvious she didn't want it to be.

"Slen. Answer me. Did you know your father was a member—"

"I know *you're* a member of a group called the 13th. I know you're here looking for June. I know you're a killer, Kidan. I know."

Kidan's vision faded around the edges, her mouth parting. She tried to speak but couldn't.

Slen spoke to the sky, oblivious. "I even know your next question. Where is June? I don't know if the 13th took her. For that, you'll have to ask the older members."

Finally, a strained question slipped out. "Why...why did you join them?"

Slen placed a cigarette between her graceful fingers and lit it.

"Isn't it obvious? My father loves two things: power and music. The 13th protected him well. For years, no one could touch him. There's no defeating the 13th, only joining. I approached them when I turned eighteen, and they refused. I tried again this year, and I received my first task. Get other houses to join the 13th cause. In exchange, my father would be removed. Surely you can understand that."

Kidan couldn't speak. Her temples hurt, and her forehead creased. "But why go after Ramyn?"

Flints of fiery ash lit Slen's flat eyes. "Only a true threat within Uxlay would move the houses into action."

"I don't understand."

"Think about it, Kidan. Why do you look so upset even though you knew Ramyn for such a short time?"

Kidan didn't know the answer to that. She just cared for Ramyn. It had been as natural as breathing.

Slen's eyes lost their stolen fire as if she understood. "Almost everyone loved Ramyn Ajtał, and so everyone would mourn. When the most darling, beloved student dies, most houses would sway. Her death would change hearts."

Kidan grew breathless with the cruelty of Slen's actions. Even more disturbing...it sounded like Slen truly liked Ramyn too.

Why? she wanted to scream. *Why ruin your soul?* Kidan had wanted to spare her this. The despicable act of taking a life.

Slen focused on the fountain below them. "I needed her death. Because of it, I'm able to live twice the life I had."

It'd all been a performance. A disturbing play meticulously planned to eliminate and manipulate. If Kidan distanced herself, she could appreciate its sick brilliance. They'd all been too blinded by the tragedy to suspect the killer among them. Why look at a defenseless girl when the obvious monster bared its teeth? She'd forgotten that terrifying creatures were often wronged girls. Wasn't she proof of that?

"Is human life worth so little?" Kidan whispered.

A question for them both.

Slen lifted her lashes. Her gaze half-lidded with a shade of darkness so pure that Kidan hurt just watching her.

"Was your foster mother's? I did what I needed to in order to protect my brother. Just like you did for June. We aren't so different."

Kidan bunched her fists. That was precisely the problem. Being similar to Kidan was a death sentence. There was no future here.

She cleared her throat, bringing steel to her voice. "Who dropped Ramyn from that tower?"

"A dranaic inside the 13th loyal to me."

"Ramyn's blood-stained lips. Did you tell the dranaic to do that?"

Slen blinked. "What?"

"Answer the question," Kidan demanded.

Slen gave a slight raise of the brows. "It was the dranaic's decision."

Kidan wanted to believe her. To believe she still had something worth saving. Never had she seen someone play with human life as casually as Slen. Was this not what she loathed about the vampires? They weaponized human vulnerability and exerted their power. This went past the admission of guilt, this was…evil. So why was Kidan still here chatting instead of following her promise to cleanse the world of such darkness?

Because a prickle of twisted satisfaction had torn through the awful noise. Slen had taken care of her abusive father. She had survived. Kidan touched her bracelet, hearing Mama Anoet's scream as fire ate her flesh.

Kill her, June's voice demanded.

Spare her, Kidan pleaded back. *She's only trying to free herself from her father.*

June punished her with a violent, endless quiet. Kidan squeezed her eyes shut. Every time she disappointed her sister, the fissure between them cracked wider, impossible to bridge. Kidan's hand moved to her constricted chest.

"Kidan?" Slen asked, making Kidan open her eyes. "Are you all right? You just went somewhere."

"I need to speak to the dranaic," Kidan said in a rushed tone, dropping her hand. "What's their name?"

"I can't tell you that."

"Why?" she demanded.

"Because I have one more task. I need your help."

"You already got your father arrested. Why are you still working with them?"

"I must prove myself until I graduate." A hint of tension tightened her voice. "There's no leaving the 13th."

Slen liked control, and the 13th were still pulling her strings.

"What do they want?"

Slen tapped her cigarette of its ashes. "Susenyos Sagad will be arrested today for colluding with my father and killing Ramyn."

Words escaped Kidan for several heartbeats. This revelation meant Susenyos was not only innocent but being *framed*.

She barely heard Slen's next words.

"You need to corroborate the prosecutor's charges at the hearing. Only after he's arrested will the 13th tell you anything about June, *if* they took her."

"W-what do they want with Susenyos?"

"He's a threat. But sacrificing him for your sister seems like the very thing you'd do. Don't let me down."

Sacrificing him . . . Despite everything, those words made Kidan wince.

Her mind raced to why she had suspected Susenyos: Did the 13th give Mama Anuet the wrong name? Plant June's bracelet? Have Slen use Ramyn's death as the final nail in the coffin?

It was all too much. Her fists clenched and unclenched.

Their target had always been Susenyos. And no one had fallen for it as much as Kidan.

44.

WHEN KIDAN ARRIVED HOME, THE FAUCET WAS RUNNING IN THE upstairs bathroom. She bounded up the steps quickly, calling out in the darkness.

"Susenyos!"

The water stopped. A moment later, Susenyos appeared at the top of the stairs, towel slung over one shoulder. They stared at each other, the house falling quiet. His eyes were furious, ominous. She'd lied and accused him. How had their roles reversed so quickly?

Kidan wanted to warn him, but something held her tongue. What did she want to say? What happened to Iniko? More importantly, why did she care at all? Time stretched out around them, both illuminated by moonlight, both silent.

Before she could speak, there was a loud pounding on the door. Etete rushed from the kitchen to open it.

"Don't," Kidan called, too softly.

Professor Andreyas entered with two strong dranaics, who stormed past Etete. They were dressed in black and carried two gleaming silver swords at their backs. Sicions.

"What is this?" Susenyos barked.

The Sicions charged upstairs without asking permission or glancing Kidan's way. They removed their blades and cut their tongues, wetting them in red.

The professor spoke with a tempered tone. "We have found the dranaic who killed Ramyn Ajtaf."

Before Susenyos could move, the Sicions had their silver blades positioned at his neck. Susenyos blinked at Kidan, shocked even though her last betrayal had barely healed. Kidan had the decency to avert her gaze.

She heard his snarl as he tried to break free, and the slash of blade against skin. His pained grunt made her look at him. He was bent at the knee, blood moon eyes latching onto her with rage, a large gash on his stomach. The Sicions' blood-licked silver didn't hit a vital artery, but there was no promise their next assault wouldn't. Susenyos stopped fighting, and they dragged him downstairs. She heard his curse, only for her ears, snapping with venom.

"*Zoher.*"

Susenyos appeared no different from a wounded, shackled beast. Professor Andreyas faced Kidan.

"Come to the Mot Zebeya Courts tomorrow morning. You'll have to testify in detail about why you believe Susenyos took June."

Kidan nodded slowly, and they left.

Etete covered her mouth, stifling her sobs as they dragged Susenyos out into the darkness. The sound of her cries broke Kidan.

She swayed back in the hallway, breathing rapidly. Her fingers touched the wall, seeking the sharp thorns of grief, but there was no ache or ripple. The lamp above no longer flickered. June didn't roam the halls to haunt her.

Her pain... It was no longer here. Kidan traveled through the house in search of it, opening room after room. The house shifted under her, the areas of her psyche rearranging themselves. She'd felt it once when Susenyos nearly opened up about his past—his room had changed, become softer. Now she walked toward something worse, mutated. The observatory waited and its icy blue light washed over her face. Cold as an ocean rock, it drew her in. Her breath fogged at once.

A scream cleaved the room. A woman in torture. Kidan clamped her hands over her ears, but Mama Anoet's voice descended from the ceiling like a storm. Kidan's limbs locked. There was a deadness to this room she'd never experienced. The opened jaw of something endless, reminding her how unsalvageable she was, how with a single breath she could be vanquished.

"June," she gasped out. "Help me."

An invisible hand choked her, intent on drowning her into oblivion. Her muscles squeezed, and she spluttered. Her heartbeat echoed in the walls, the vision fading with the moon.

"You know how to end this, Kid." June's voice finally came to her, and a tear glided down her cheek. *"Keep your promise. Kill Slen. Kill Susenyos."*

"You don't understand!" Kidan gasped out. "It's not her fault. She only wanted to protect her brother."

The pressure grew on her chest, suffocating. She had to breathe or end it now. Kidan struggled with her bracelet, pried it open, and retrieved the pill. It slipped through her trembling fingers. Showing her soft honeyed eyes, June picked it up, holding it out like a poisonous berry.

"All evil," her sister encouraged, beautiful as a summer sun.

Kidan took it, swallowing it as June caressed her cheek, finally smiling. Tears leaked down Kidan's cheeks.

"Kidan!" The voice sliced through the sounds of her frantic heartbeat.

A woman's kind face and the scent of warm bread brought her out of the dark. Etete's touch was salvation, and Kidan gripped on for dear life as it led her into the hallway.

She touched the base of her wrist. Her heart hadn't stopped. Her bracelet remained intact, her mouth free of death. She retched, trying to expel any of it. But it was an illusion. This house . . . Was there no end to what it could twist and manifest?

"Thank you." She shook. "Thank you."

Etete's creased eyes became deep wells. "You've joined your mind with his."

Kidan pulled herself straighter. "What?"

"The house views you as one. The observatory is where you feel pain now too."

"How . . . is that possible?"

"This house needs a master that's true to themselves, peaceful. You two are pulling it in different directions, so it'll never surrender itself to either of you." Etete clutched the tail of her head wrap to her chest. Tears sparkled in her eyes. "You two will be the end of us all."

Kidan averted her gaze. She hated causing Etete pain. "He called me zoher. What does it mean?"

"It means 'traitor.' One who wastes their ancestors' sacrifice and blood."

The house withdrew into itself, dimming. She found herself in Susenyos's room. It was clean and organized, and a calmness settled over her skin like soft rain. *The Mad Lovers* was perched on the edge of his table, in front of the wall of scrolls she'd never asked him about.

She traced the line of the bleeding grapefruit and flipped through the pages. He'd underlined phrases and scratched his own thoughts into the margins. What was it about this book he loved so much? It was a perverted, ugly intimacy. She retrieved her own copy and returned to his room, because her room no longer offered warmth. Shoulders relaxing, she read. Kidan wanted to know their end before the hearing, and once she did, she fell asleep to the sound of light rain.

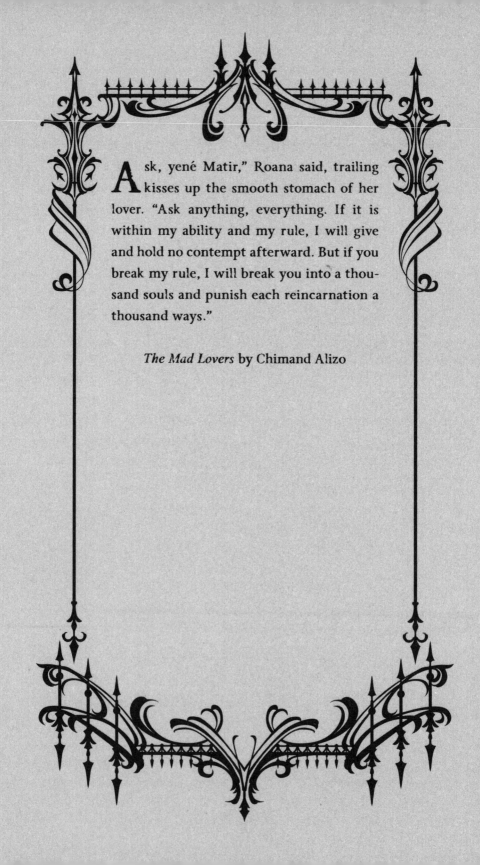

"Ask, yené Matir," Roana said, trailing kisses up the smooth stomach of her lover. "Ask anything, everything. If it is within my ability and my rule, I will give and hold no contempt afterward. But if you break my rule, I will break you into a thousand souls and punish each reincarnation a thousand ways."

The Mad Lovers by Chimand Alizo

45.

THE PRESIDING JUDICIARY BODY OF UXLAY UNIVERSITY WAS COM-
posed of three Mot Zebeya judges and a jury constructed of dranaics and
actis. It surprised Kidan how quickly they had gathered for Susenyos's prelimi-
nary hearing. Koril Qaros's hearing still hadn't occurred. For all the equality they
preached, when it came to matters of murder and wickedness, Uxlay pointed to
its vampires first.

Kidan waited in a secluded area inside the court building, a nervous tick
dancing in her fingers. She didn't know what she'd say. The events of the past
few days needed months to be digested. Slen and Koril Qaros. Ramyn Ajtaf.
Susenyos Sagad.

She shut her eyes and tried to organize them by importance. The answer:
June, always. Yet yesterday, June had fed her the pill. . . . She'd wanted Kidan
dead. Kidan shook her head. *No.* The house twisted things.

Was surrendering everything to the 13th the best way to get June back? If
Kidan complied, became a dutiful, loyal heiress, would June be returned?

Umil's words echoed in her head. *The 13th need an heiress for House Adane.*

It meant, for now, June was alive.

"They're ready, dear." A woman with burgundy glasses stood by the large
doors.

Kidan entered the courtroom, taking the short steps to the witness seat.
Her eyes immediately settled on Susenyos. They had fashioned black handcuffs
on his wrists. The bands were thornlike and piercing his skin. His bowed head
lifted as he sensed her presence.

Anger stole into her chest.

It was supposed to be him. He should have been the source of everything. He should have dropped Ramyn from the tower and abducted June. How many nights had she dreamt of this exact moment? Bringing him to his knees and burning him alongside herself?

Not an ounce of light pierced the blackness of his eyes. They promised death, and she believed them. With him vanquished, her thoughts would no longer press on the soft flesh of her mind like knives. He stirred more hatred, more violence, more wrongness. Even as she sat here, he appeared to see the potential of her own perversion. Darkness stirred inside Kidan, wings spanned, ready to take flight and tear out of her chest.

Here and now, she could kill the wicked part of herself by condemning him. What did his innocence matter? How many others had he killed? Once stained, the hands couldn't be washed of blood, only abstain like a devout person seeking forgiveness, and Susenyos would never repent.

It was either she killed him or he killed any good left in her. June would never forgive her then.

The back door opened, revealing Yusef and GK. The tightness in Kidan's chest eased, the shadows shrouding her vision cleared. She didn't know what drew her to them, this flickering, taunting light. Perhaps it was never having true friends, always keeping an icy distance, being so careful not to reveal her identity that she melted into the back of every classroom. Perhaps she'd finally found a glimpse of the family she lost, or the humanity torn from her when Mama Anoet died. The seeds of their friendship were still growing, yet she felt they were feeding a part of her that was long starved.

Slen appeared behind them, a dark figure in her jacket, chin held high. Kidan's vision tightened once again, unable to untangle her feelings toward her. Slen had had Ramyn killed. She also had gotten her disgusting father imprisoned. Pain and relief spun into a tornado inside Kidan.

Yusef gave her a bright smile crafted from the sun. GK held her gaze and nodded kindly.

We're here for you, they seemed to say.

Her anxiety eased a little. But what would become of them in a few months? The 13th had surrounded her new friends like wolves. If that secret society managed to bend Slen, their strongest, what hope did the others have?

Abandoned as they all were by parents, and vulnerable and desperate for family love, Kidan cared for them more than she thought she was capable of. And maybe, if she succeeded in saving someone this time, her worst sin could be forgiven. She wouldn't be a carcass but someone warm, alive, *loved*.

Out of the bleak darkness came a tiny speck of hope. She couldn't be rid of Susenyos or herself yet. Not when she had work to do. This place would ruin her new friends, brush their souls against old words that would take root inside and manifest in destructive ways. Kidan was already lost, but she could guard them from it—the weakness of a person's psyche, the descent into madness. Just like she'd done for June.

She would set out and take on their every sin until her mind was addled and her skin stretched tight. Then, when she met her end, it would be like in theater plays—as a hero, not a villain.

The 13th wouldn't be scared away if she didn't bare her teeth. Yes . . . she had to delve deep one more time. Like the night of Mama Anoet's death. If monstrosity was what would protect them and bring June home, she could no longer deny herself. She would save Susenyos Sagad. Together, they would bring the 13th to their knees.

Susenyos remained calm, too calm for a vampire awaiting possible death. His head tilted as if he understood she was transforming before his very eyes. Pain crackled along her skull, shooting through her arm and pulsing at her wrist. He'd warned her of this, not so much with words but with twisted books like *The Mad Lovers*. Suppressing her nature would eventually tear her apart.

Taj came in quietly and stood at the back of the room, arms crossed, face hard. Iniko entered from the side door. Her eyes were bloodless as she assessed the exit points. They'd massacre everyone in this courtroom before they let Susenyos see the inside of a cell.

"Kidan Adane," the prosecutor said, annoyed. He must have been calling her. "You reported your sister June Adane's lips were marked in the same way Ramyn Ajtaf's were. Why do you believe Susenyos Sagad took your sister and killed Ramyn Ajtaf?"

Deep breath. "I don't."

A murmur traveled around the room. Those who had come to see Susenyos crucified shifted, exchanging glances.

"You don't believe he took June Adane?"

Kidan exhaled. "No."

Whispers rose to the roof. Susenyos adopted the most obnoxious demeanor she'd ever seen.

The prosecutor read his document, frowning. "And the Axum Archaeological Project deal that Susenyos signed with Koril Qaros? Were you aware of that?"

No, she wasn't. She recalled the picture of Susenyos next to her family in the ruins of Axum, his deep love of preserving artifacts. The warmth in his voice when he spoke about treasuring archives. It didn't seem plausible he'd trade such a gold mine of history.

"That site has been kept up by Susenyos and my family for generations. Why would he sell it?"

"I assume to join Qaros House."

So, this was how they planned to tie Koril Qaros to Susenyos.

"A vampire that killed all his house dranaics suddenly cares for companionship? With a man like Koril Qaros no less?" Kidan waved a dismissive hand.

This sent a startling silence throughout. Susenyos had his head bowed, but she could have sworn she glimpsed a flash of teeth.

The prosecutor lifted a bag labeled EVIDENCE. Susenyos's flask was inside it. The very one she had handed the chief detective.

Shit.

"This blood was collected from Susenyos Sagad's flask. It doesn't match anyone in our system."

Kidan swore internally. The 13th must have had influence in the campus authorities. The chief wasn't here.

"I wanted to frame him...," Kidan pushed out. "So I changed it with my own blood, which I knew wasn't in the system yet."

Susenyos's night eyes twinkled.

"That is a serious offense."

"I know."

"It may even be cause for expulsion."

Dean Faris drew a line with her eyes from Kidan to Susenyos. Kidan couldn't leave now. She was so close to June.

Kidan's palms grew damp and she twisted her fingers. "I know. I'm sorry.

I was—am—still grieving my sister. I wanted to know who took her. I crossed a line."

Dean Faris held her gaze. Would the dean use this chance to expel her? The woman was smart. If Kidan was publicly defending Susenyos, she had to know the threat was elsewhere.

Please believe me.

Dean Faris broke eye contact and spoke to Professor Andreyas in a lowered voice. He relayed the message, and the prosecutor, fixing his tie, returned to the stand.

"Susenyos Sagad," the prosecutor called. "Would you like to press defamation charges?"

Shock rippled through the court. Kidan's eyes widened.

Susenyos didn't lift his head, so she couldn't read his expression. "That won't be necessary."

Kidan loosened a breath, sinking in her chair.

"Very well." The prosecutor cleared his throat. "Kidan Adane will be given an official warning and sign a house release. In the event she graduates and masters her house, she will swear to uphold all laws. If she's found breaking any laws again, Adane House shall be stripped from her and given to Uxlay to be used as it wishes."

Susenyos whipped his head toward Dean Faris with a slash of anger and surprise. Dean Faris stared ahead, collected as ever. Kidan was speechless. She thought the dean was helping her, coaching her as a fellow member of a Founding House. Did she want everything for herself?

"Do you accept?" the prosecutor pushed.

Susenyos met Kidan's eyes, warning etched in his furrowed brow, urging her to refuse.

Kidan's eyes traveled to her classmates. To the 13th members sitting on the edge of their seats, hungry for Susenyos's fall, for House Adane to be theirs. Tamol Ajtaf frowned, and Rufeal Makary hovered near Yusef like a vulture.

"I accept."

Susenyos shut his eyes.

"Very well," the prosecutor said. "Proceed to the office for the paperwork."

Each step down from the witness stand turned Kidan's stomach. She had the sinking feeling she'd done something irreversible. That someday, a week, a month, or even a year from now, this moment would steal everything from her.

But she had no choice. Susenyos knew this place, understood how to skirt the laws to eliminate his enemies. He was a weapon of destruction, and if aimed right, she could make sure she had no blood on her hands for the tasks she planned.

Together, they would eliminate all traces of the 13th. Together, they would find June. Once he forgave her... they were only limited by imagination.

46.

SUSENYOS DIDN'T SPEAK WHEN HE RETURNED HOME, WRISTS BRUISED, pride wounded. He didn't speak the next day either when Kidan tried to engage in conversation. She explained that she hadn't told anyone about his immortality, that she'd saved him when Uxlay wanted to bury him, but nothing. Not even an acknowledgment that he'd heard her.

The house swelled and stretched with his fury, several bulbs exploding whenever he walked past.

Kidan understood he would want her vulnerable, perhaps on her knees again, before there would be any peace. She bit down her anger, thinking of a plan. A place he couldn't keep escaping her.

Kidan arrived at the Bath of Arowa thirty minutes before Susenyos and stripped down. She waded into the large pool, the water gliding along her thighs smooth as milk. Her back rested against a curved corner, head tilted to the ceiling, as she drank in the artwork above. It drew her in, the naked Black bodies intertwined with only slips of silk for modesty. She reached for *The Mad Lovers*, which she'd brought along, and reread the last few chapters. She'd been disgusted by the characters' violence in the beginning, didn't understand it was a unique language lettered in blood, communicating their deepest wants.

"You shouldn't be here."

Susenyos's voice bounced along the cavernous walls. Kidan didn't acknowledge him and kept reading. The lion faucets were on, and she could hear the rustle of his robe falling to the floor, then the ripple of water as he waded in.

When she peeked, Susenyos was half submerged, taut torso dipping into a fog of steam. She allowed herself to indulge, studying the architecture of his body. She couldn't before, clouded by the hatred of losing June, and anything related couldn't be interesting, let alone beautiful.

Yet now, gazing upon his dark chest, the waves of muscles carving themselves along, asking to be traced, she wondered if this was the same person she'd been loathing.

"It's a mistake to be alone with me," he said, voice thicker than the steam. "If I kill you here, I'll have just cause."

His thirst for violence wrapped around her, seeping into her pores.

"I see why you love their story," Kidan said, returning to her book.

His unwavering gaze pierced her forehead like a knife. He said nothing, which meant he was a thread away from snapping. She set aside the book and stood to match his height. The mist obscured her chest, but the sudden breeze pinched at her breasts. His eyes dropped for a moment, then flicked back. Kidan's heart beat in her throat at his heated gaze. The promise of looming danger. Those weren't human eyes—they were coals mined in hell with cinders flaring.

"I won't tell anyone you're human," she said, voice rough.

Susenyos's smile was a humorless curve. His hand shot forward, closing around her neck. Her eyes grew wide. In another second, he plunged her under scalding water. Her nostrils and ears burned, water flooding her mouth as she writhed against him. The aggressive rush of bubbles formed into June's face. Her sister stretched out a hand, smiling, and Kidan struggled against the invisible call to die and leave this world behind.

Come. You've done enough.

Kidan's limbs slowed, then went slack. June's smile broke. She was drowning too.

But then life flooded Kidan's body, and she fought like hell. Susenyos brought her out, her back flush against his chest, brushing her matted braids away from her stuttering face.

"Hush, yené Roana, *hush.*" His warm breath tickled her ear. "You were almost gone."

She coughed and spluttered, rising on her tiptoes to match the length of him and avoid pressure from the squeeze of his arm.

"If you *ever* call me human again, I will end you." He inhaled the scent at her neck deeply. "I can feel your vein pumping blood. If you don't calm down, it'll burst."

"I was wrong," Kidan managed to get out, her nostrils running. "I made a mistake."

"Hmm." He breathed along her throat. Spikes shot through her at the motion.

"I want us to work together." She rushed through her words.

"The problem, little bird, is I can't trust you. You're quite traitorous."

"Then guard yourself," she snapped because she was afraid. "Don't make yourself so vulnerable."

At this, he laughed. A loud, shaking sound that vibrated against her skin and seeped into her own vocal cords. The steam rose higher, and sweat beaded on Kidan's forehead. He traced the outline of her shoulders with the back of his finger. Kidan squeezed her eyes shut and fought against a gasp, her skin standing at attention. She was grateful he couldn't see her face.

"Only you would be naked before a vampire and warn him not to be vulnerable."

"Naked isn't how you have me vulnerable."

"I assume not," he mused, and forced her head to the side. Their eyes met. She'd wiped her expression blank, and so had he. Neither of them would give in. But just like that night in the Southern Sost Buildings, neither of them could look away. Only this time, it was Kidan in his arms instead of the raven-haired girl. Her shoulder tingled with the memory, and desire carved its way through her, traitorous and unwanted. She could see him fighting it too, his black gaze dropping to her lips, lingering too long before springing back up.

He hungered for her blood, but this want for her body was an interesting surprise.... Had it always been there? Had she mistaken his darkened gaze in the past for wishing her dead when it was something else entirely?

She half smiled at the discovery, and he tightened his grip. Kidan scratched the arm around her neck, deep and slow. His hiss was a lovely song, and she craved more of it. She would drown in pleasure when she killed him. It would be the most erotic act, but like any pleasure it would come at the end.

The problem was the waiting. They were two snakes with fangs drawn, the poison turning them mad with the need for release.

"I know you didn't take June," she whispered, staring into those endless eyes.

"Now you choose to believe me. After you lied, used, and humiliated me. Should I thank you?"

Her nostrils flared. "You've done horrible things to me too. Should I list them?"

He chuckled darkly. "See? This is why our partnership will never work."

Something like pointed bone grazed her throat. His teeth.

Kidan stilled. "My blood is poison. I haven't graduated Dranacti or made a companionship vow."

He smiled against her skin. "Ah, didn't you see Iniko at court? What color were her eyes? Your blood is very drinkable."

Iniko's eyes had remained black. Impossibly so. No trace of blood.

"How?" Her voice trembled.

"I could tell you," he said with far too much pleasure. "But I enjoy watching your little mind churn."

"Please, listen. I shouldn't have blamed you. I know the 13th tried to frame you for Ramyn's death. I believe they framed you for June's disappearance as well."

"I know this, and they will suffer for it," he said with a growl, making the hair on Kidan's neck stand up.

"Let's work together," she offered. "I want to destroy the 13th. Help me."

"No."

His mouth pressed on her collarbone, searing and venomous. Every inch of her skin heated with the contact. Her thoughts grew disconnected, and speaking became an exhausting activity, but she had to lay out her terms. He would drain her blood soon.

"I felt it," she gasped out. "I felt pain in the observatory."

His advance ceased. "That's impossible."

"Etete said our psyches have synced. The house views us as one, and we can only master it together."

He didn't kill her, so it was a sign he was listening. He sounded both disturbed and intrigued by the idea. "That's . . . rare."

"We thought I had to leave so you could master the house." She was hurtling through her words, trying to avoid his murderous gaze. "But you felt it too, didn't you? When you told me about how you became a vampire and your people died. Your room shifted, it represented something else."

"No, I didn't feel anything," he mused. "What did you feel?"

He really was going to make her say it. *Bastard.* She slid a side glance to him. "Well, what do you normally feel in your room?"

"Comfort." He shrugged. "It's my room."

"So did I."

A slow grin stretched his lips, breaking the shadows possessing him. "You felt comfort in my room?"

Heat crept along her cheeks. Why was this confession so revealing? Suddenly she was very aware they were both naked under the layer of fog.

"The point is that the rooms are changing, the spaces of our minds are becoming one. You said I needed to manage my emotions because the house was being affected. If you and I are at odds, the house will keep evading us. But if we show the house we're united, it might bend itself to us. It stands to reason—"

"Stop talking."

She did, her tongue dry.

"Have you told anyone about what you discovered?" Something tightened his voice, a form of fear, perhaps anger. He was talking about his immortality situation.

"No."

He hesitated for a minute. "Why?"

"Because it's a weakness for both of us. If the 13th discover it, they can attack you. I need your protection."

"My protection?" His fingers were still on her throat, not tight at all but warm, ready. "And what makes you think you have it?"

She wanted to see more of his face, to gather any information that could help her, but he kept her at arm's length. He seemed at war with himself, but maybe that was a foolish hope and he'd already decided to get rid of her. She had one more thing to tempt him with.

"*The Mad Lovers*." Her gaze drifted to the book swallowed by white clouds. "Famous for loving each other with everything but their hearts, then driving each other to their death. Dark, even for you. But they shared an enemy and worked together to slay the beast. Isn't that what you want, yené Matir?"

His entire demeanor changed at that word. He stepped back. She faced him slowly, mist curling at her neck now.

He regarded her with extreme caution and intrigue.

She quoted the principle of their famous line:

"Ask. . . . If it is within my ability and my rule, I will give and hold no contempt afterward," she said slowly.

"But if you break my rule, I will break you into a thousand souls and punish each reincarnation a thousand ways," he finished, cocking his head, brilliant light finding his eyes. "Fine, I'll indulge your little game. And what is your ability and rule?"

She sighed, breathing in thick air. "My ability is limited by my status and nature. My rule is only one. You never do anything to harm my friends or family."

"Predictable." His finger ran down the side of her figure, the curve of her waist, parting her lips in a soundless gasp. "And what of this? Don't you want to protect yourself from me?"

He definitely wanted her. Her eyes roamed over his wide shoulders, over his skin, which was darker under the domed ceiling and glittering with drops of water. Heat grew in her chest, uncomfortable and uninvited.

When she kept thinking, his fangs elongated past their first appearance, so wide was his smile.

"Are you certain?" he asked. "I can have you on your knees every night if that's my ask."

She blinked, and whatever odd feeling was rushing between her ribs dissipated. This was an agreement. Nothing else. Besides, she wanted his cruelty, wanted it to fuel her hatred from the inside and remind her exactly who he was.

"It's fine," she said.

"What you say and the look in your eyes are two very different things."

"And yours?" she asked, eager to move on. "What is your ability and rule?"

"Ability, endless. Rule, you never do anything that forces me to leave Adane House or Uxlay."

Kidan had expected the house but not Uxlay. She'd thought the first thing he'd want was to flee the place that weakened him. Why stay? What possible reason was there to remain in a place that stripped you of your power?

"Everything else is possible?" he asked carefully.

"It is."

He trailed a line to the middle of her chest, thinning the fog and tracing her scar. She inhaled sharply.

"Scars are rare on actis. When vampire blood is so readily available, wounds close before they're even cut." He frowned a little. "How did you get it?"

"I don't remember."

She guessed it happened the night she and June ran away with Aunt Silia. They'd been wrenched awake in the middle of deep sleep, shoved into cars, and driven away. The violence of the scar made by a blade, as if someone wanted to carve out her heart, made her bare her teeth.

His light touch brought her back, sending whispers of electricity along her veins.

"Do we have a deal?" she asked, trying not to shut her eyes.

"Yes."

She exhaled. "Good."

"Then, if you will allow me my first ask." His voice had transformed, gravel in his tone. "Let me drink from you. I have wanted this from the moment I saw you, sitting in front of the fire, cupping that little bird, calling for help. Do you remember?"

Kidan tipped her neck to the side, giving him access. "Y-yes."

"No, not there. I don't drink from the neck until the companionship ceremony. We wouldn't want you to see my deepest desires, now, would we?"

Kidan remembered what she'd glimpsed when Iniko bit her. Ships. Ocean. Death. Her stomach hitched. She tried to remember what else she knew. The wrist was for childhood. The neck for want. Then where...

He lowered himself and placed his mouth over her breast, drawing a gasp from her. The chest was for violence. How very fitting.

First, he pleasured her with his tongue, making her speak with staggered breaths. This was dangerous. So dangerous to let him touch her like this.

"Change your rule." His breath ignited her flesh. "Tell me to stop."

She didn't.

His tongue slid around her, and an invisible need lanced through her. Her mouth grew parched, her body weighed more than normal, she fought for concentration. She'd long forgotten the carnal nature of her body, and it seemed to hunger for more. More than that, she wanted to peer into his wretched mind.

His fangs grazed her sensitive flesh and bit gently. She cried out, claws digging into his bare shoulders.

The ceiling artwork swirled and melted until Kidan glided into his mind, became him. Raw power coursed through her muscles as Susenyos stormed into a spacious room and killed the remaining seven dranaics of House Adane. They'd all discovered some secret, perhaps that he was human in one room, and all had to die. His hands, her hands, grew sleek with blood, a burning ache in their lungs from the exertion. Body after body crashed around him, staining his clothes in an endless red.

Disoriented, Kidan studied her own hands, braced against his shoulders. No blood. A pang rolled inside her as the image faded too quickly and she detached, the energy draining from her. She was human once again.

Susenyos raised his head, her blood coating the corner of his mouth, and he was the sun itself, blazing with life, fire catching the tips of his twisted hair. Her fingers hesitantly found their way into his thick hair. Light soaked into her.

"What did you see?" His voice was drenched.

She traced along his golden face, and his breath hitched before he closed his eyes.

"Strength," she said. Her chest tightened. "What did you see?"

When he lifted his lids, those flames roared to life in his black eyes. "A woman screaming. A house on fire, and you burning along with it."

That was it, then. He truly knew what she'd done to Mama Anoet. One monster to another. For what would come, this was what they could be to each other, how they'd vanquish their enemies. They would work through each member of the 13th, but those circling her new friends would go first.

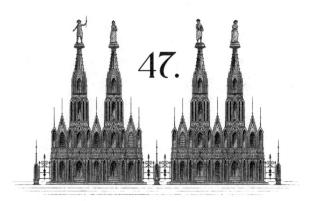

47.

KIDAN FLIPPED THROUGH *TRADITIONAL MYTHS OF ABYSSI* IN THE PHILOS-ophy Tower, waiting for Slen and Yusef. She needed Slen to give up all information regarding the 13th and had brought the *Myths* book as a way to win her over.

Professor Andreyas had dismissed their current approach to Quadrantism. *The four quadrants of a dranaic produce a paradise, of which the human is a mirror.*

They'd tried to understand what, exactly, constituted paradise but failed at every turn. Kidan flicked through stories about heaven and hell in the book. Maybe paradise referred to a higher power. For Yusef, it was creativity, and why he spent four hours every day practicing it.

Kidan stumbled upon a story about the cosmos, the power of a lightning-struck tree serving as a gateway between two worlds. She traced a hand over the illustration at the bottom. It was called the heaven and hell tree, but in Aarac, "heaven and hell" was expressed as a single word—"esat." In parentheses, it read "fire or water."

"Heaven and hell...same word," she said to herself.

The original Dranacti work chose the word "esat," which Slen took to mean "paradise." Not just Slen, but everyone who practiced Quadrantism.

Kidan rewrote the phrase but changed "paradise" to "purgatory" and leaned back, stunned.

The four quadrants of a dranaic produce a purgatory, of which the human is a mirror.

When they arrived, Kidan explained her thoughts. "We were translating it wrong. We're looking at a dranaic's purgatory."

Slen immediately took the *Myths* book.

"That's not possible," Yusef said. "A dranaic's paradise is the balance of the four pillars. Spiritual, mental, physical, and material well-being. When a human mirrors that, they're in tune with nature, able to produce nature's wonders."

Slen studied it quietly, surprise breaking over her face with each new sentence. "Kidan's definitely right. How did I miss it?"

Yusef took the book in his charcoal-stained fingers, reading with a frown. "Purgatory. You're telling me I've been using a meditation technique that brings pain?"

Kidan studied his shaking shoulders. "Are you okay?"

"I need to go."

Yusef left. Kidan wanted to go after him, but Slen was talking, close to deciphering this mind-numbing subject.

"It says the human is a mirror of their purgatory. How do we prove that?"

They started brainstorming, tracking back to the clues the professor may have given them.

Slen's mind ticked away. "What if we have to ask the dranaics? The first task had us compare and choose who should stay in the course, and now we must compare ourselves with dranaics."

"It's possible. Someone's purgatory is personal. The only way to learn about it is to ask."

Slen was quiet for a couple of seconds. "Yes, and compare it with your own."

Kidan swallowed roughly. Why was this their task? It was horribly invasive, no less violating than confessing a murder. The other troubling matter was which vampires would even be willing to share, and at what price. She now understood why Professor Andreyas said only one person would graduate.

Kidan's phone buzzed, a text message from GK.

Please come. Yusef is destroying his room.

She texted back quickly:

Why?

Rufeal Makary was picked as Artist to Watch for the Youth Art Exhibition.

Kidan swore. "Yusef is in trouble. Let's go."

Slen remained by the opened books.

"Slen, come on."

"We don't have time to waste. I'm going to keep researching."

Kidan made sure there was no one in the hallway before lowering her voice. "We need to talk about the vampire who dropped Ramyn from the tower."

Slen froze. "Why?"

"I have a plan. You can trust me."

"You saved Susenyos. Now the 13th are pissed." When Kidan tried to protest, Slen cut her off. "Passing is all that matters."

Kidan swallowed her frustration, staring at Slen's turned back. When another urgent text came from GK, she hurried out.

The Umil House was located ten minutes from where she was. When she arrived, a housekeeper let her in. Kidan hurried upstairs to Yusef's room.

A relieved GK opened the door. "Come in."

Gold and red were woven into the carpet, bedding, and furniture. Yusef, precariously balanced on an open drawer, was struggling with taking one of his charcoal drawings off its nail.

"Yusef?" Kidan called.

He turned, eyes glassy. "I need to start fresh. These are all wrong. I'm heading down the wrong path."

"Okay, but come down. Let's talk about it," Kidan said.

He stayed balanced, looking at the drawing of an older man who shared a resemblance to him. The incredible attention to the wrinkles around his eyes and birthmark on his forehead was impressive. Omar Umil.

"I was wrong, Kidan. Just like I was wrong about Quadrantism. What if I can't create because I'm maintaining all of nature's four quadrants? I'm killing myself trying to keep them all in balance when that wasn't even the point. It's purgatory. I put myself in hell."

"What do you mean?" She exchanged a nervous glance with GK.

When Yusef didn't speak, her worry doubled. He was expressing the off-kilter behavior of his father, just like when Omar Umil asked for that ball of spider's web.

Yusef's opened laptop showed the Artist to Watch display, a sun-bright smile plastered on Rufeal Makary as he posed.

The creature inside Kidan uncurled itself. It stretched and elongated its claws at the smell of threat. She lifted the laptop, studying the curve of Rufeal's upturned mouth. This time, she had no desire to repress herself.

Omar Umil's rough plea came to her: *Protect my son.*

Kidan snuck downstairs to the basement while GK comforted Yusef. She found the slightly marked floorboard, five squares from the top left corner as Omar Umil had told her, and pried it open. She hauled the heavy box up and unlocked it. On top were climbing gear, ropes, and spikes. Kidan dug in, fingers reaching and wrapping around the ridges of a horn. Next to it waited a gun with seven cases of bullets. Power flooded her. There was plenty here. *Good.* She had to prepare for whatever came next.

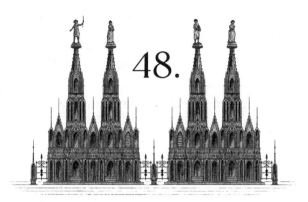

48.

KIDAN AND SUSENYOS LOUNGED ON THE STUDY COUCH, FIRE BURNING close, and talked of all the ways a life could be extinguished without a sound. They had found new ground with this deal of theirs, and it was fitting that planning a murder was their first task together. They channeled all the venomous energy they had toward each other into a specific task, admiring their work like two surgeons over a bleeding body.

Their first target was Rufeal Makary. It was Kidan's first ask.

She shared three ways of stifling murder: an inconspicuous weapon, a covert location, a cohesive story. In her raging state, she'd witnessed the hell that rained down when one of those pillars collapsed. Murder was a gossiping bitch, and she loved to talk. They had to starve her of all information.

Rufeal Makary was a busy student, surrounded by people often, unless he was working. The third room on the second floor of the Umil Art Museum was dedicated to mosaic art—Rufeal's specialty. Shelves were stacked with ceramics and colored stone waiting to be shattered and rearranged into stunning pieces. One small stumble could lead to a loud crash. The room was also in clear view of the elevator, as well as a corner camera. But if Rufeal was to relocate to the west side of the building, where the cameras had a blind spot, they had their location.

The weapon proved much harder. It had to seem accidental so there would be no need for an investigation—or need to move the body, bury it, and lose control of the story.

Kidan tinkered with the idea of poison and liked the potential undetectability.

Something in his mosaic glass or the walls of the room. It would take time, but Rufeal would soon be dead.

Susenyos watched her with a glass resting against his lips. "You're dangerously becoming irresistible."

She reached for the platter of fruit on the small table and bit into a strawberry.

"You're not contributing to our discussion."

"I'm distracted by how your dark mind works."

She shot him a stern look. "Come on, you probably have an easier way of getting rid of him. Share."

"That's a hurtful assumption. I rarely spend so much time planning my kills."

Her lip quivered slightly. He drew closer, his folded leg brushing against hers.

"Was that a smile?"

When she lifted her lashes, there was no trace of it.

"We need to know why the 13th is after you," she said seriously.

His face lost its light, replaced with thundering clouds. "I always knew the families wouldn't be happy with a vampire inheriting a house. It would be a first at Uxlay. But to go to such lengths to frame me...I didn't think they were capable of it."

She understood his frustration. "Omar Umil said the houses want independence, for each to set its own law."

Susenyos straightened. "Are you sure?"

She nodded.

He looked into the fire, expression troubled. "That would break the universal law. Uxlay would be vulnerable." His voice darkened. "What the hell are they planning?"

"What I don't get is why not just directly break the universal law? Why form a whole group?"

"Dean Faris would set her Sicions on any house that dared break the boundary law. If they plan to break it, which I doubt they're even capable of, every house along the boundary must do it at the same time. So Dean Faris won't have enough time to fix the leak."

The calculation in his gaze made her shiver.

"They have June," she said quietly. "Omar said they need an heiress and wouldn't harm her." Her bottom lip wobbled. "What do you think?"

Susenyos thought about it for a long time. "It's likely. Especially since you've made it clear you're not on their side. They will need June to come and master House Adane. If they have her, she's alive."

Kidan released a deep breath, grateful for his confirmation. "But who gave Mama Anoet your name?"

He rubbed his jaw. "Most likely the same vampire who killed Ramyn. Do you know who it is?"

Only Slen did.

"No, but I'll find out," she said with steely determination.

He smiled ruefully. "To think, all this time we shared an enemy. We've been played against each other for too long. Frankly, it's insulting. When I find out who, exactly, planned all this, they will suffer a violent, slow death."

The hair on the back of her neck stood at the lethal promise.

He gave her a careful look. "We must trust each other. No more games."

The house creaked under the statement. Could she truly trust him? It was difficult and would take time. But they could take it slow. She nodded and settled further into the seat, throwing her head back so the firelight cast her golden.

Her body unwound, and her shoulders loosened. Kidan couldn't remember the last time she felt this content in her home.

Her home. What an odd thought, to think of this nightmare of a house as hers.

"Back to Rufeal. I'd think having a vampire as partner comes with certain perks. I know you have strength and speed, but what else?" she asked.

"Am I already failing to meet your standards?" Susenyos replied. Kidan could hear his smile.

"Yusef said you have claws, but I know he's messing with me."

"We do have claws."

She shifted higher, her gaze falling to his large hands. "You do? Can I see?"

With an amused glint in his eye, he held out his hand. Light green veins in the shape of lightning graced the rich brown skin. Then his clean, short nails were growing into wide claws, blackening at the tip as if dipped in coal. Her lips parted, and she traced the inked nails. Sharp enough to slice thread.

"How come I never see you use them?" Her voice rippled with fascination.

"Claws often mean we've let our nature take over completely, become more monster than human. Not many of us like it but...you clearly do."

She withdrew her tracing hands at once. "I was just curious about your powers."

His lip remained quirked. "The ability to create your own law within your home? Now, that's true power." He stretched out his hand. "Shall we?"

Kidan's gut twisted. But this was their agreement. He helped her with the 13th. She helped him master the house. Every evening, they'd try to withstand the observatory. Together. The house demanded peace to be mastered.

They made their way to outside the glowing room. Apprehension tightened Kidan's stomach. The last time she went in there, June fed her the blue pill.

"How long do we have to stay in there?"

"For as long as we can."

Her bones went weak.

"My family...Why did they set the law on you?"

"So I would remain and guard your House forever."

It almost sounded cruel. If he'd stood by their side for decades, why didn't they trust him? As if he read her mind, he spoke in a low voice, arms crossed.

"Your parents couldn't pass down this house to someone who didn't value humans. They needed to cure me of that fatal flaw, and what better lesson was there than to become one?" He skewed his mouth at the word and glared at the pale room. "So this place strips me of my immortality. It brings me face-to-face with death."

"But they only set the law on you. Not the other Adane dranaics. Why?"

He wiped a hand across his face. "Your family found me on the run. They worried that if danger came, I'd abandon them. They wanted to make sure I never leave."

On the run...from what?

"Wait, you can't leave?"

"I did, once. Then I returned to find one of the rooms had changed."

She caught on slowly. "You endangered the house by leaving."

He rubbed his jaw, anger gnawing at him. "The language of the law is purposefully vague, so I never know what action triggers it. I must be very careful. Otherwise, it'll keep taking from me piece by piece. Room by room."

Kidan's brows scrunched. "Why not leave Uxlay and never return? The law only takes place within this house, right? You just have to make sure to never come back."

His face gathered a storm. "No, Uxlay is the only safe place."

Safe? This place was safe?

"Against what?"

He breathed out a frustrated sigh. "I can't tell you any more. I wish I could. But even this might trigger the law and cost me another room."

His fingers closed and released with desperation. Kidan's brows drew. She recalled those nights he lay half dead until Etete dragged him out. He'd convinced everyone he was untouchable, free to do as he pleased, yet was no different from her, bound to a promise, a word.

Kidan walked in, bracing against the dead cold. Susenyos followed shortly after, sucking in a sharp breath. They settled on the floor, the moon beating on their brown skin, and let the swords fall on them.

It began with June. Sleeping, lifeless. Then Mama Anoet, screaming, dying. The entire world afraid of Kidan.

Kidan bit her lip so hard that the flesh tore and bled. Susenyos handled his pain better, eyes shut. The only indication that he was hurting were his fingers tightening into fists, veins streaking along his arms.

The image plaguing Kidan morphed into a familiar face—her own. Kidan with red pupils and a bleeding mouth. This version of Kidan didn't watch June from behind a window—she was the one biting into June's neck, coloring her lips. This Kidan killed her foster mother and rioted with rage, not grief or regret. She held only contempt toward her sister and ached to teach her a lesson for abandoning her. She wanted to tear out of her skin and rain down terror. This Kidan had to die.

June's ghost came to her, a knife in her hand, moons for eyes. Kidan's hand wrapped around the hilt, and June helped her guide it to Susenyos's chest.

There.

Then the knife was turning, Kidan's arm bending to touch her own heart.

There.

Kidan tried to plead with her conscience. They could still serve good, but June didn't listen in this room. Her eyes burned into Kidan, igniting like an inferno. Kidan gasped, the urge to scream climbing up her throat. Pain and scream went together. It was the only release, the only way out. She couldn't keep it in. She had to leave.

Susenyos's eyes flew open. Neither could speak, but his gaze told her to hold on. To stay. She begged him to leave, her cheeks wet now.

Do it now. Kill him. Kill all evil.

June's words thundered.

Kidan lunged, attacking Susenyos with a feral grunt. His eyebrows shot upward as he struggled to restrain her. Her hand was empty of a knife, but that didn't stop her. She clawed and scratched at him, making contact with his cheek and drawing warm blood. He hissed, shoving her aside. The force slammed the illusion and they both bolted to the exit, throwing themselves into the hallway and gasping.

"This is going to be harder than I thought," he panted, touching his cheek and rubbing blood between fingers with disgust. The skin was already webbing itself, healing.

"I don't know what happened," Kidan whispered, eyes blown wide open. "I couldn't control myself."

He nodded like he understood. "You're looking for a way to end the pain. Unfortunately for me, you think killing me is the answer."

He held her gaze, expression unreadable. Not just him. Her too. The knife had pointed to her heart.

"I hear it too," he said, after a while. "That instinct, deep down, telling you to do whatever you can to end the pain."

"What does it tell you to do?"

He hesitated, fisting his hands, then releasing them. "Turn back time and save my people from death."

So this was at the heart of his torture. Kidan glimpsed the key chain around his neck, leading to his people's clothes and treasures. Her eyes creased with the loss of it.

"But you...can't."

"Then you see the problem." He stared at the room with enough flame to incinerate it to dust. "You rest."

She leaned against the wall, grateful. Susenyos walked inside and settled in the haunted room. His face pinched and his palms bled, but he pushed, hour after hour.

Their minds might have synced, but their hearts couldn't be more different. He fought for his immortality. She fought for death.

And the room would be torn apart by their natures.

49.

SUSENYOS WAS IN HIS ROOM, ADDRESSING A LETTER. KIDAN LEANED against the doorframe, watching the sunlight stream into the space. It was refreshingly different from the punishing observatory. Perhaps he had designed it that way. For a moment of peace.

He wrote as he spoke. "Everything is ready for Rufeal. It's just a matter of time."

Yesterday, Susenyos burst the pipes of the toilets near Rufeal's art room. Many disgruntled art students rushed to book library rooms ahead of the exhibition, but Rufeal received a tip about a storage space where the old archaeology department used to keep artifacts. It was quiet enough that the ancient Muses could be heard speaking. By the end of the day, Rufeal had moved his work into the space. There were no cameras there.

Kidan's shoulders relaxed. She wasn't sure about their arrangement, but the moments when Susenyos didn't question murder really made her appreciate it.

"What are you writing?" she asked.

"Come and see."

The room melted away the tension in her body with each step, the sun chasing away the cold. She shut her eyes for a moment, letting it wash over her. Her senses filled with soft rain and earth. Why was this room so calming?

When she lifted her lashes, Susenyos was watching her, a strange intensity in his eyes. She cleared her throat and walked to him, reading over his shoulder.

"Letters to the Immortal?" she said, hoping to break his quiet regard.

Slowly, his eyes shifted away from her face. "Yes, letters addressed to me."

Kidan took in the shelves reaching the ceiling. There must have been thousands of scrolls.

"What exactly is it?"

"A service."

"For what?"

His voice brimmed with surprising light. "For Black women mainly, who historically and today remain the least protected individuals in society. When I lived outside Uxlay, I thought of a way they could request my aid. I couldn't be everywhere, couldn't be inside their homes or their workplaces, but a piece of parchment and ink could. A letter was the most accessible mode of communication back then, and we told who we could find. At first, no one wrote. Now they write every day, every hour. Some requests are immediate, some not; some are simply seeking more to life."

He seemed proud of what he'd created, and it was startling to find him in a new role once again. Kidan couldn't begin to understand which version of him was true. But the magnitude of the letters astounded her, some dating as far back as the nineteenth century.

"You write back to each one?"

"Yes."

"What do you say?"

"I tell them the truth. They may never see me, but they'll feel my presence in their life. Today, tomorrow, ten years from now. Just as the shadow of a cloud or a gust of wind that feels personal, they'll know I heard them."

She leaned over the desk, absentmindedly reaching for another letter, when her bracelet caught on his pen and broke free, cracking open. Before she could catch it, the small blue pill clattered onto the table.

He collected it, question darkening his brows.

Shit. Her heart squeezed.

She had to think fast, but no words came.

"Kidan?" Her name tightened on his lips. "Is this what I think it is?"

"Don't worry about it. It's just in case." She shrugged.

"You wear something that can kill you, just in case?" A thread of unease disturbed his voice.

"I want it to be my choice. In case I get attacked...to end it before it gets bad, you know?"

From his facial expression, he didn't know. Kidan took it from him, walked away, and tried to fix her bracelet. She didn't want his judgment.

She couldn't get it to clasp, and the pain of the observatory crept in. June's presence leaked into this space, reminding her not to break her promise.

Kill all evil.

She didn't feel him move until he reached around her and opened his palm. A piece of the clasp was in his hand. Fingers unsteady, she took it, unsure if her nerves were from his sudden proximity or because he'd accidentally glimpsed her darkest secret.

He said nothing as she tried to fix the metal, hurting her thumb's flesh. The metal wouldn't close. His hands rested over hers. She surrendered the work over to him, and he pinched it closed. It was like their artifact workshop, only this wasn't a treasure they were mending. It was a piece of Kidan, laid bare to be dissected.

He let them sit in silence long after the work was done. The space of time made her racing heart calm down.

She felt compelled to share its history. This room whispered that it was safe to do so.

"It was Mama Anoet's. I made one for her and one for June. Butterflies are a symbol of transformation, she'd say—but never what kind. Some people are better unchanged, don't you think?" Sadness enveloped her. "I changed, and it killed her."

His words were low, serious. "You did what you had to do."

Of course he wouldn't judge her. He didn't see anything wrong with murder.

"You think death will free you from this," he murmured. "It will burn hotter than any sun, that nothingness."

"It's not poetry I want but its punishment. What if I want to burn?"

"Because you are so wicked, so vile, so rotten." Mocking light swam in his voice. "If you are all those things, what hope is there for the rest of us?"

Her voice became hard. "I know what I've done. . . . What I'm capable of."

He was silent for a long moment. "It's a shame that when I finally find my potential equal, she cannot love herself enough to remain in this world." Her brown eyes blinked at him. "How will you ever conquer the observatory when you carry such hatred of yourself?"

Kidan, almost spellbound by his question, couldn't look away. His stillness always struck her, flat black eyes without a natural blink to interrupt their gaze.

"Do you truly love yourself?" she whispered.

He was always so anchored, immovable. She wanted to taste what such certainty felt like. To have lived so long and keep doing so.

He gave her the courtesy of thinking about it. The sunlight danced in waves across his perfect dark skin, and it struck her how violently eternal he was.

"Yes. One doesn't continue to pursue immortality if they don't."

It was her turn not to blink now. Her eyes dried with the need, and water slipped over them like film, but still she kept looking. "How?"

He drew closer, bowing his head and brushing his thumb along her cheek. The sudden intimacy startled her, but she didn't pull back.

"I will teach you. If you let me, I can teach you a thousand different ways of loving yourself." His promise unsettled her very soul.

It was a dangerous thing, loving herself. Because when Kidan loved, she loved entirely. Selfishly.

Ignoring the sudden coldness that seized her, Kidan stepped away, self-conscious. She ran her fingers over the scrolls as she left. Their whispers, pleas, and wants fit neatly into words, all waiting to be visited by him.

Later that night, she found herself writing her first letter to him. The words forced her to concentrate, to choose what to talk about. June. Mama Anoet. Her parents' deaths. The options bubbled up, but other words came out on the page, surprisingly honest.

Letter to the Immortal,

I think I was born to die. Everything I do feels pointless or, worse, hurts those around me. Even the thoughts I believe are good just end up craving blood. There's something inside me that doesn't belong. Something solid and sharp-edged that wants out. It wants to destroy and break the world and rearrange it, shatter it entirely just to please me. The more I fight this hunger, the more I lose. It's taking over my body, my mind, my heart. I can't stand it. I want quiet and peace. I need to end it myself before it wins. Please, tell me how to stand it all.

Her fingers shook, and she fought the urge to scratch it all out. She didn't write her name or country or year. She didn't want him to know it was hers. The next day, when the house was empty, she slipped it under one of the scrolls, burying it entirely. The curtains rippled, and although her words were lost, and her request would go unanswered, the house hummed and listened as if it understood.

50.

LOUD POUNDING WOKE KIDAN IN THE MIDDLE OF THE NIGHT. SHE rushed downstairs, turning on the light as she went.

"Hello? Who is it?"

The knocking continued, and Kidan searched for Susenyos, but his side of the house was dark.

When she unlocked the door, two figures burst in, one supporting the other. Yusef was leaning heavily on Slen and making a low, sorrowful sound. When they stepped into the light, Kidan saw the blood. Ice shot through her veins.

"What happened?"

Slen's eyes were struck with shock, her voice teetering on breathlessness. "It's not our blood."

Kidan stilled.

"Did you mean it when you said I could trust you?" Slen asked, the previous tremble of her voice disappeared.

Kidan was too stunned to speak.

"Did you?" Slen asked, louder.

"Yes, yes. Of course."

Slen hesitated for a moment, then handed over Yusef. Kidan almost collapsed with his weight.

"I need to take care of some things."

"Wait, what are you——"

Slen had already turned, grabbed a jacket off the coatrack, and fled. Kidan tried to move Yusef to the couch, but they both stumbled inches from it.

Yusef shook. Kidan tried to calm him, her fright rising, but he pushed her away and sank into the carpet, head in his hands, mumbling something.

"What happened?" she asked again.

He was whispering something in another language, his voice twisting in painful pleadings that tore at her heart.

"Yusef, please. Tell me what happened."

Over the top of his curls, she saw Susenyos emerge.

"Forgive me," Susenyos said.

"What?"

"Forgive me. That's what he's saying." Susenyos lifted his chin to Yusef.

Yusef continued to rock back and forth as Kidan whispered calming assurances, uncertain it would work but unable to stop.

"Rufeal...," Yusef gasped out.

Kidan met Susenyos's eyes in shock.

Susenyos crouched before them. "What about Rufeal?"

Yusef's tone flattened into cold shock. "He's...dead."

He stared at his bloodied hands.

"Did you hurt him?" Kidan whispered, bringing her voice lower.

"I didn't...think I could."

Her heart collapsed on itself as he quietly sobbed. Kidan had only prayed twice in her life. The night June was taken and the night she'd killed her foster mother. Both had brought her to her knees, profound losses she'd destroy herself to avoid. This loss of Yusef's soul was gutting.

She was no longer praying but cursing all the gods in the universe for taking all the good from her. Why wasn't she enough for them? Why did they have to poison those around her?

Kidan called to Susenyos softly. "Help me take him upstairs."

Placing each of his arms over one of their shoulders, they took him to the shower and closed the door.

"What the hell happened?" she asked, voice cracking. "He can't survive this. He's a good person. What if the 13th come after him for this?"

Kidan went right back to that night, being tossed in a cell like an animal. Her heart squeezed. And it squeezed again.

Susenyos, alert to the flickering lights of the bulb above them, spoke before she spiraled. "Remember what I told you. You will help him, and I will help you."

Kidan clung to those words, nodding.

When they went downstairs, Slen had returned with a covered picture. A spark of fury ignited at her presence.

"Did you make him do this?" Kidan demanded.

Slen stared, ever expressionless. "Yusef is the last person equipped to handle something like this."

Kidan stormed toward her. "What the hell happened?"

"More importantly, where is the body?" Susenyos asked, appearing from behind.

Slen raised a brow to Kidan. "My dranaic took care of it."

"Your dranaic in the 13th? Who?"

Slen refused to answer.

Susenyos crossed his arms, eyes stony with distrust. "Is there a particular reason you don't want us to know? Perhaps you're plotting to frame another innocent for your murders."

The two stared at each other, neither bending nor blinking. Minutes ticked by. Kidan was sure that if she hadn't been there, they would have lunged at each other.

Kidan broke the silence. "Slen, tell us what happened."

Kidan was too agitated to sit as Slen recounted the events of the night. Rufeal Makary had spent his afternoon working on his mosaic of the famous portrait *Woman in Blue*. It was the piece that now stood propped against the fireplace. Upon seeing it, Kidan sank into the couch, softly struck by its beauty. Rufeal had chosen a rich umber ceramic for the woman's skin and azure glass for her robes, which cascaded like waves. The glass reflected the sky, a cerulean shade of blue, and tinted her skin as if she was wrapped in the sea itself. It was a perfect re-creation of the original, save for one small deviation—her creator's blood ran in two distinct stripes across her breast and neck, a shocking spray of red drawing all eyes to it.

Kidan's ears buzzed. She was mortified by the violence, even more so that it had come from someone she thought a gentle soul.

271

The murder weapon was a hammer. The very hammer Rufeal used to shatter glass and ceramic to create the piece.

"Why would Yusef do this?" Kidan whispered.

"He doesn't know either." Slen leaned forward. "You know he won't be able to handle this."

Kidan didn't like her tone. "We'll help him."

"He'll take us all down with him."

"We can't abandon him. The 13th will be after him."

"I know him."

"You know him." Kidan barked out a nasty laugh. "Yet you're the first to throw him away?"

"I'm not talking about prison or the 13th. I'm talking about Dranacti. He won't be able to focus, and that'll hurt all of us."

"You will abandon your friend for a class?" Kidan gaped, searching her face.

"I've been honest about my goals from the beginning."

Kidan's nostrils flared. "We will pass the class *together*."

Slen stood to leave, pausing to look at the picture. "Burn that thing and pray the 13th don't come for all of us."

Kidan stared at *Woman in Blue*. Her striking beauty matched her pearl-like eyes. Kidan was so focused on the image that she didn't hear the shower stop. Only the growing shadow on the couch alerted her to Yusef's presence. She jumped, trying to cover the portrait.

He saw right past her, a haunted and unfocused gaze.

She lifted her hand aimlessly and rested it back against her side. "You should sleep here tonight."

He gave her no response.

Kidan buzzed with questions but couldn't put them before him in his current state. He walked forward and stretched out on the couch, still watching the portrait. Kidan retrieved a blanket from the laundry room and handed it to him. She hesitated, unsure if she should remove the picture. It needed to be destroyed. But she also wanted to study it a little longer. Something about it demanded her attention. She settled on the opposite couch and waited until Yusef fell asleep before moving it upstairs. She slid it behind the space of her vanity. There was a level of calculation involved in Slen's killing of Ramyn, whereas Yusef's was a sudden burst of uncontrolled violence. Actions she had never expected from either of them.

You can't save them.

June's voice slashed at her from the open window, and Kidan rushed to close it with a snap. Kidan's breath fogged.

What if they hurt others? Do you really want more blood on your hands?

The alternative was to remove her new friends from this world. She shook her head. Her friends wouldn't hurt anyone else. They'd made a mistake. A mistake. Yes. She prayed to June.

Let them live.

In her delirious state, Kidan thought June was poisoning her friends on purpose, jealous that when Kidan woke, her first thought was of a peaceful future with them.

51.

RUFEAL MAKARY'S BODY TURNED UP OUTSIDE UXLAY'S BORDERS, limbs scattered in the surrounding forests. A surprising report showed that he'd been mauled by a wild animal; his features were almost unrecognizable. Slen's dranaic had a sick way of handling bodies.

House Makary painted their pins of feather and parchment in red and buried him in the family crypt, next to his aunt Helen Makary.

The campus hosted several opportunities for students to speak with counselors. Besides that, there were no investigations. No outbursts in the community. Kidan had come to understand that deep grief was reserved for the main children of the families, like Ramyn Ajtaf. Rufeal was nothing more than a side branch, thirteenth in line to inherit his house.

Yusef didn't speak for the next three days. They regularly kept him company before Slen suggested they move him to the vacant room in Grand Andromeda Hall. If there were no events on, that space was often empty. She gave him canvas and paint and left. Kidan stayed. Save for eating quietly and painting, Yusef said nothing. Kidan worried as the hours melted into one another. She'd started to get used to the sound of his charcoal pencils scratching on paper, the smell of roasted pumpkin seeds that followed him everywhere.

Yusef stood back from his canvas, paint smeared all over his skin in white, royal blue, and gray strokes.

"It's not there anymore." It was a small, fragile sound—but it was him. Yusef was speaking.

Kidan straightened from her uncomfortable position, resting the book she'd brought.

It was a painting of a Black woman standing on a bed of hot coals. Her face was pinched in pain, and she carried four children around her body. They tugged at her clothes and scratched along her neck and back, biting into her flesh in desperation to escape the fire. Kidan stared, mesmerized by it. It was such a pure expression of maternal love she could neither bear to keep looking nor quite look away. He had titled it *Quad Purgatory*.

"What's not there anymore?" Kidan asked softly, approaching.

He blinked, and a tear slid down his cheek. "I don't want to destroy it. That voice telling me to burn it, it's...not there anymore."

"That's good. Isn't it?"

"Good." His voice tightened in sorrow. "How is it good that I don't loathe myself in the only moment I should?"

Kidan lowered her gaze.

"I...I killed someone, Kidan." He gaped around the room as if suddenly realizing it. "Why am I not being arrested?"

"Slen and I took care of it."

He shook his head violently. "Why are you two doing this? Why are you involved?"

"We know you're a good person. We're not going to let them ruin your life because of an accident."

He stared at her, uncomprehending. "An accident?"

This was the truth she'd reminded herself of over the last three days. He was good. This act couldn't tarnish that nature.

"An accident," she repeated, and grabbed his shoulders. "You need to tell us if there's anything else."

He staggered backward, but she dug her fingers into his shoulders.

"It's done, Yusef. We will help you. I promise."

Kidan didn't let go until he believed her, a small light peeking out of his curtained eyes. She couldn't let him end up like her. How different would her life have been if someone had found her after Mama Anoet's murder? Calmed her and told her it would be all right? Her spine locked with the memory. *Never again.*

Slen appeared by the door, watching them.

Kidan let Yusef return to his work and approached her.

"You're good with him," Slen said.

Kidan slid her a glance. "You are too. That's why you brought him here to paint, right?"

Slen said nothing, but Kidan was beginning to see through her shield. It wasn't that she didn't care for Yusef, she just disliked showing it. And despite her cold confession, she did feel guilt about Ramyn. Kidan had spotted her visiting Ramyn's grave early one dawn, even before morning birds chirped.

Kidan sighed. "I know you still don't trust me, and I'm not sure I trust you, but I have a plan."

"There *was* a plan. Get Susenyos Sagad arrested. One you ruined." Slen's tone tightened.

"I know you want to be free, Slen. But don't let the 13th control you."

This made Slen hesitate, then ask with reluctance, "What's your plan?"

"After you tell me who killed Ramyn, Susenyos and I will eliminate every member of the 13th."

Slen's blank eyes assessed Kidan, checking for any trace of dishonesty, disloyalty. "That's suicide. Almost half of Uxlay is part of the 13th."

"I don't care. They have my sister," Kidan said fiercely.

Slen regarded her cautiously. "My father can't get out."

"He won't. No one understands that more than me." Kidan inhaled. "Now, who dropped Ramyn from the tower?"

An extended silence settled between them.

Finally, in a quiet voice, Slen spoke. "His name is Titus Levigne. I'll talk to him first. He'll meet with you after class tomorrow."

"Thank you." Kidan released her breath.

Slen watched Yusef reach for paint. "Speaking of tomorrow, you do know what you have to do to pass Quadrantism, don't you?"

Kidan sighed. "Learn about my vampire's most horrific act. Lovely."

She'd been waiting for the right moment to ask Susenyos about his purgatory, until Yusef's incident made her forget. Knowing how closely he guarded his secrets, this wasn't going to be easy.

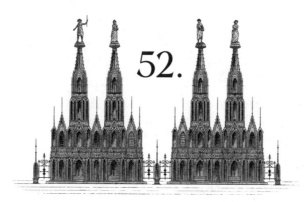

52.

INEED YOUR HELP WITH QUADRANTISM." KIDAN APPROACHED SUSEN-yos's desk, her shadow falling over his letters.

When he focused, he tapped his pen twice on the period ending a sentence. There was a cadence to his writing, a scratch, a scrawl, a dash, dot, dot, that she liked.

"Hmm?"

"Nothing serious," she said casually. "Just wanted to know what your purgatory is?" She traced the edge of his desk.

His hand eased on the pen. "You might as well ask me to split my soul and give it to you."

"Well, if you prefer that, I wouldn't mind."

A playful arch found his lips. He rested his pen and came around, closing the space between them.

Kidan drew in a sharp breath when he touched a hand to her inner thigh. His fingers circled lightly, and her chest tightened and loosened. This new dynamic of theirs was strange, and she hated herself for not being repulsed by it.

"What are you doing?" Her voice became breathy.

"You know about the human body's connection to bite, yes?"

After a pause, "Yes."

"Which of my thoughts would you glimpse if I bit you here?" Even through her pants, the trail of his fingers was sending shivers of pleasure up her spine.

She caught his wrist. "I don't know."

"Sin."

Her eyes widened at once, making his lip quirk.

"So, you see, that's the only way to learn the truth."

She pushed him back slightly, not so much that she couldn't count his lashes but enough so she could think clearly.

"Or you could just tell me."

"No, I much prefer this." His smile was victorious.

She dug her fingers into the underside of the table, concentrating her alarm there. "Because you want to look into my mind as well."

"Always."

"You already know what mine is. What I did to Mama Anoet."

He trailed his index finger along her brows, forcing her to look directly at him. "If I did, there wouldn't be such a look of terror in your eyes. What is it, yené Roana? What are you hiding?"

She dropped her gaze to his chest. "Nothing."

As punishment, he removed the warmth of his hand, and she fought the urge to lean forward.

"It's a pity to fail Dranacti after coming all this way."

"This is an ask."

"Then so is mine."

Her eyes narrowed. "I can imagine your sin anyway. You killed many people."

His smile revealed his fangs. "We both know there are some acts far worse than death."

She hated how his eyes bore into hers, reaching deep and pulling out the mangled thoughts that spoke of her debauchery.

He walked to one of his shelves, continuing with his work. Kidan peered out the window, the haunted outlines of the university buildings visible through the trees of Adane House's grounds. She could hear the corridors rustling with the afternoon wind, the lion-shaped lamps waking to part the shrouding fog. Uxlay held on to its mysteries but demanded that its students peel their flesh apart and bleed. Its ancient stone would only be satiated if it fed on their misery.

Dranacti. A morbid kind of study.

Kidan unbuttoned her pants.

Susenyos's hand hovered by a scroll. "What are you doing?"

She didn't give herself time to think. Thinking hurt, and she only wanted relief. She took her pants off and climbed on the high desk, tiptoes barely brushing the floor.

"Like I said, I have an assignment." That was all this was. An assignment.

Susenyos's lips tilted as he approached slowly. Eyes locked with hers, he knelt between her legs and carried her thighs on his shoulders. Kidan's stomach tightened. This felt different from the Bath of Arowa . . . more intimate. Blood pumped close to her skin. What would they see in each other's minds?

His tongue touched her skin, and her grip tightened on the corner of the desk.

"I want to learn about you." He breathed pure fire on her. "The fact that I can glimpse your mind by exploring your body is one of the few things in this wretched world I'm grateful for."

His words danced in her ear, blurring the room around the edges until the only sensation remaining was his lips on her.

"Don't judge me, yené Roana," he warned.

Her thighs contracted when he grazed along a muscle with his fangs.

"I will always judge you." Her voice came out stilted. "The day I don't, I want you to kill me."

He smiled against her skin. "The day you don't, I'll want you in my bed."

Before she could process his words, he bit into her. Hard.

Kidan hissed, sinking her fingers into his coils. She threw her head to the ceiling. Her skull rang with the pain of the bite. Balls of sunlight spun in a furious streak until her eyes rolled to the back of her head. Clipped images flashed in the darkness.

Susenyos, human, boyish. A crown upon his unkempt hair. A court full of people who adored the new but naive emperor.

An attack on the castle walls by monsters who bore fangs. They'd come to drink the blood of the young emperor. An emperor's death for a country's freedom. Fair trade. Yet the emperor cowered in the face of death.

He ran, cheated death, and resurrected himself as one of them. He took his revenge and stood half-naked in a throne room, reborn with insatiable hunger. Yet it was not for blood. He craved company, eternal company.

He hunted vampires, imprisoned them, tortured each to relinquish their immortality to his people. The palace bled red as Susenyos forced his court to feast on vampire blood, leaving humanity behind. For six days they slept, then awoke one by one.

The first to wake was a boy with a deep scar along his neck and an injured hand.

Susenyos, dranaic, cruel. Older. A circle of blood running down his forehead. A court full of vampires loyal to their new sire.

The image passed by quickly, years melting into decades as they were on the hunt for something. Revenge. Power. An army of incredible strength behind their emperor as they marched into darkness. The darkness reached back, long fingers of shadows eliciting horrible screams. He'd led them to endless torture.

The scene morphed, the boy king's eyes red and fixed as the image faded. Kidan touched her temple, fighting the rush of air that always followed the experience.

"Did you see enough?" His voice came from the ocean, murky and wet.

Kidan blinked several times. She regarded the dranaic between her legs. Same boy, yet entirely otherworldly and cruel.

"You said your court died," she said with heavy breath.

"They did."

"No—you killed them—" she stammered, thinking of the artifact room, a collection of hundreds of items. "Everyone in your palace. You...forced them to become vampires."

His eyes were cut open, unflinching in their truth. Lips slick with her blood. "Yes."

Kidan couldn't comprehend the violence of it. "How old were you?"

"Nineteen."

"Old enough to know better."

"There's that judgment."

She shook her head. "But toward the end...you were all trapped in never-ending pain? What happened?"

"Let's save that for our next uncomfortable violation of privacy."

He retrieved a bandage, ripped it open with his teeth, and placed it on the bite marks. Kidan dressed slowly, trying to read what else he hid. He took out his flask and drank deeply. He must not be satiated. *Then why stop?* Was it because he didn't want her to see any more? Could he control how much she saw?

"Aren't you going to ask me what I saw in your mind?" he asked, wiping his mouth.

Panic beat in her heart, a pathetic bird feeding on her last secret. She moved to the floor-to-ceiling window, a spatter of rain and condensation bringing in a sudden cold, making her rub her arms. In the reflection, she saw him as a sentient shadow, one that was getting too close.

"Are we so different?" he murmured, coming to stand behind her, chest brushing against her back. The goose bumps of her skin evaporated at his touch, a jolt of warmth curling her toes.

Her body kept betraying her. Even now when she wanted to leave, it wouldn't move, reacting to his presence without her control.

"Go on," he said against her back. "Ask me."

Her throat closed, but she pushed against it. "What did you see?"

"You want to stop," he whispered. "You want to let her go."

Kidan braced against the rolling ache. June's long lashes and full smile filled her vision. It no longer brought relief from her anxiety but called it.

"That's not true," she said as no more than a reflex. There was little point in lying to him now. "The 13th took her, and we're going to find her. Rufeal's dead...so that's a good start."

She was *still* looking, doing something. But it had been weeks since she watched June's videos, and in the memory of her she found not joy but punishment. Restriction.

"You targeted Rufeal for June, no other reason?" he asked.

Kidan said nothing.

"You chose to save Slen but punished Rufeal. Slen is complicit in murder and a member of the 13th, so why?"

Kidan's brows drew together. She folded herself inward.

"I don't mean to make you uncomfortable."

"Then stop talking," she said.

He sighed against the back of her head. Kidan relaxed again, following the rain pattern on the window; the swirls and blots of gray mirrored her mind. He was asking her to make sense of it, smooth out the intertwined webs.

"You want to know why I haven't killed Slen." Even saying the words felt like acid.

But even Kidan didn't understand it. Why were these new friends different? Why was she allowing them to mold and fit themselves around her life? At first, it'd been to investigate them, but very soon she'd glimpsed the smudges of darkness that lingered around their souls. The Scales of Sovane test proved that. They'd been willing to let their partners fail to progress. She should have distanced herself then. Yet if these students were a little broken as she was, could they help her?

"The rules of your world bend and break for them. It's dangerous, yené Roana." His voice tickled her ear. "You need to find your reasons. They're the only thing we can use to guide us."

He shifted his cheek against hers, and she loathed how delicious it felt. In his touch, she found herself unraveling one twisted thread, making sense of it.

"If I give in to my reasons, they'd tell me to leave my friends. I can't be alone again." Her brows drew together in concentration. "They make me question what's right and wrong. None of them are who I think they are. Slen is all sharp edges until you see her taking care of her brother. Yusef is light, but every time he picks up a pencil, darkness possesses him. Then there's GK. He views the world in a pure way. I'm curious about his faith. I want to see if he keeps it. I . . . want to see what our friendship becomes."

Susenyos was quiet for a beat. "I've seen the peace they give you."

Kidan turned, almost laughing.

"Peace? No one gives me that. I don't think I'll ever have peace. I'm just trying to avoid more pain."

His expression caught shadows. "No, I've seen you. In the courtyards or cafés, you listen to them talk, and there's this ease to your features that I don't see anywhere else."

Kidan frowned, gazing at him from under her lashes. When had he been watching?

"You and I have looked into each other's minds, yet you still don't feel at ease with me. Why?" As he spoke, he cocked his head, black eyes searching, pulling the truth out of her.

"You don't carry doubt in your violence," she whispered. "You don't question or regret your murders. I'll never feel at ease with you because doubt is the only thing that makes me human."

The backs of his fingers traced the spine of her ear. Letting his voice pour into her like silk, she no longer fought her body.

"You shouldn't fear the madness you keep company during the night, but the chaos of the day. You expect me to hurt you, so you guard yourself—but leave yourself defenseless against others. When will you recognize that humans are the most despicable creatures to exist?"

When she didn't respond, his eyes lingered for a moment, and then he returned to his desk. A chill snaked up her back and along her neck and settled like a noose. He'd given words to the thoughts that found her alone, haunting her with the question of what horror awaited them, and if they could be saved at all.

53.

THE TWENTY-THREE REMAINING STUDENTS WAITED ANXIOUSLY OUT-side Professor Andreyas's class. Many were furiously going over their notes, lips moving silently in recital.

Kidan went first. The room remained dark, and she occupied the lone chair in the middle space, lit by an overhead lamp.

"So, Kidan, how did you find Quadrantism?"

Kidan paused, remembering Susenyos on his knees, dark-eyed and lips bloodied. A monster, yet with a clear, unbending human want. She explained what Susenyos had done, forcing his people into a life of immortality.

There had to be a personal connection to her theory, uncovering how a human mirrored a dranaic. She pulled her sleeves over her palms and explained the hardest months of her life, alone in her apartment.

She stared out the side window. Words felt like pulling teeth. Why was this so hard? "If I had the power to never feel loneliness again...I think...I'd make his choice."

She dropped her gaze, unable to face the truth of her words. But they were out there, brutal and honest.

"Is that correct?" the professor asked.

Kidan prepared to answer but another voice spoke.

"Yes."

She jumped and whirled around. Even before spotting him in the shadows, she'd recognized his even tone, one reserved for dealing with business. Clipped and to the point.

Susenyos approached, dressed in a long black coat, and stood next to her chair. He didn't look at her.

"She revealed it perfectly."

How long had he been there? Kidan averted her gaze, studying the floor.

"Thank you. You may leave."

Susenyos lingered for a moment, then exited through the side door.

"Well done," the professor said. "You've passed."

Kidan glared at him. "Why didn't you tell me he was here?"

"Would that have changed your answer?"

She bit her lip and snatched up her bag.

"Stay in the adjacent room until the test is finished."

She eyed the main door, hoping her friends would join her soon, and slipped through to the side room. GK appeared at the entrance.

"You passed?" Kidan straightened.

"I...dropped out."

Kidan's brows disappeared into her hairline. "What?"

"Iniko's purgatory...She was forced to abandon her people because of an order. I never want to relate to that, leave behind so much destruction." His eyes were troubled. "I never feel anger. It's an emotion we cast aside in our training, but it suffocates me now. I'm changing, and I don't like the person I'm becoming."

"But you told me you wanted a dranaic companion."

"Not anymore. Not if it's a bond steeped in so much anger and hatred."

"Are you sure?"

"I'm saving my soul." His warm smile slowly returned. "This isn't the path I want."

"So, you're leaving."

She couldn't keep the disappointment out of her tone.

He regarded her with light, swimming eyes and lifted the bone chain from his waistband. "The chain still warns me of your death."

She avoided his intense gaze, staring instead at the macabre chain, her throat closing in. Perhaps GK was wrong. Maybe the bones didn't foretell her death but revealed her murders.

"I still hear her choking. Ramyn, I mean. I was close to saving her, and now I feel the same sinking feeling. That I'll be too late to save you all."

There was that echo again, a connection to GK she'd always felt was unique. Almost familial, primal, a need to save and protect others, even at the risk of one's own life. The guilt that ate away at the soul for failing. Ramyn was his June, and he walked around haunted that he'd fail others he cared for.

GK's gaze traveled to the floor. "I don't know how to help you, Kidan."

Her brows creased. "I'm fine, GK. You don't need to worry about me."

He kept playing with the finger bones, expression unreadable.

"And Yusef...Something happened to him, didn't it."

Kidan's blood turned cold. "No, he's just worried about the art exhibition."

He forced a nod, a slash of disappointment crossing his features. After he left, Kidan sank into a chair. She had come to rely on GK's serene presence, but it wasn't safe anymore. Until things settled down...she'd have to keep her distance.

Finally, Titus Levigne came in for Slen's test. Kidan's shoulders tensed. She could barely wait for Slen to emerge. Her fingers tapped away a triangle so loudly that a girl passing by shot her an annoyed look.

When they finally appeared, Slen gave her a nod. Kidan unfurled her fingers, focusing on the vampire who could answer everything. She followed him out—and June fell into step with her, the breeze playing in her curling braids. Her sister's creased eyes had returned to their honeyed color. The fury from the past few days had melted from her face like snow. Kidan was on the right track.

54.

TITUS LEVIGNE WAS A SALLOW-FACED DRANAIC WHO DRESSED IN A large, expensive trench coat. He smelled of cigars and cologne and spoke with a slight accent as he offered Kidan some of his pastry. They'd walked to one of the smaller campus cafés, Axum Buna, and a drizzling rain now dotted their window. This wasn't what she was expecting when she imagined June's attacker. But then again, the same hands that tore the delicate pastry in front of her had held Ramyn Ajtaf dangling in the air by the throat.

"Did Slen speak to you?"

"She did."

Kidan lowered her voice. "The markings on Ramyn's lips, why did you do that?"

He raised one perfect brow. "I can't speak of things that might implicate me outside Cossia Day."

"I won't tell anyone."

"I don't know you."

"Slen does, and she knows I'll keep my word."

"That may be true, but the same compassion doesn't extend to me. What if you report me to the Sicions?"

Her patience was fraying. "Did you have something to do with June Adane?"

"June." He turned the name over on his tongue several times. "I'm afraid not."

"Then *why*—"

Titus leaned forward. Her voice had risen, and the waiter shot a curious glance toward them.

"Attend Cossia Day a few weeks from now, and we can speak freely. Otherwise, don't contact me again."

With that, he left.

Kidan reached home wet and miserable. These delays on a lead about June were irritating. She slammed the front door, shivering as she placed her scarf and jacket on the coatrack. She climbed the stairs to her room and fell backward onto her bed.

She grabbed her earbuds and played June's videos.

"Hey guys," June's light voice cut through. *"You won't believe what I did in school today. I'm so embarrassed."*

It was like coming home. June's voice in the videos was much kinder than the one that visited Kidan here in the real world. At times, Kidan struggled to figure out which one was really her sister. This June was smiling, nervous, and kind. The June inside this house was violent and cruel. Perhaps it was Kidan who enjoyed twisting reality, morphing beautiful things into weapons of evil to punish herself.

"Difficult day?" Susenyos asked, making her jump.

He leaned against her door, head tilted. It was odd always finding him home now.

She pulled her earbuds free. "It's Titus. He offered to tell me more about Ramyn, but only if I attend Cossia Day."

Susenyos's demeanor darkened. "No acti can attend Cossia Day. You're meant to evacuate the campus."

She walked past him to her closet, taking off her sweater behind the door.

"Can you escort me?"

"You shouldn't go."

"Why not?"

"He'll kill you."

She paused at his dark tone and pulled on a shirt. "Well, that's a chance I'm willing to take."

When she popped out, his arms were crossed, dark gaze on the floor.

"I also think you'll see things you don't want to if you attend."

Kidan laughed a little. "After all the things I've seen, trust me, I'll be fine. Besides, it's an official ask."

Even though his face remained tense, he nodded. She liked that he listened to her now. This arrangement of theirs tipped power back and forth between their fingers, yet Susenyos hadn't collected as much as he'd threatened to. She'd hoped his request would be more demanding. It was making her restless. What was he waiting for?

"Do you want to drink from me again?" she asked, pulling her shirt away from her neck.

His eyes shot to her collarbone, pupils dilating. He turned his body away. "No, you'll need your strength."

"For what?"

He retrieved his flask and winced at its light weight. "To face our torture room. Help me master this house. That's my only ask at the moment."

In the weeks leading up to Cossia Day, they spent more and more time in the observatory. During that time, Kidan burst into tears, hyperventilated, and passed out four times.

Each time, she attacked Susenyos with a feral growl. She kept seeing herself kill him, then rip out her own heart so clearly that it was maddening to feel their heartbeats in that room. To feel his breath. June demanded it. And Kidan had to fight back, begging for a little more time, listing the reasons like a prayer. He would help her save others. He would redeem himself. And in turn, she would help save others, redeem herself.

Susenyos would exit the room with deep bites and scratches along his brown face and chest. He'd always touch the blossoming blood, surprised he could be so easily injured, and tighten his jaw.

"I'm sorry," she'd whisper, watching his skin knit closed in the hallway.

"You've dreamed of killing me for a long time. Don't blame your body for still reacting that way." He winced at the large bruise fading along his torso.

She dragged a hand through her hair. "I don't know why it won't stop."

Susenyos had improved, at least—managing to stay in there for seven hours.

"An hour is still good," he told her, frustration lining his jaw. "Tracking time doesn't prove anything. The task is to face your pain, but I feel like all I'm doing is increasing my tolerance to it."

Kidan remembered the source of his pain, trying to save his court from death. Now she knew he'd turned them into vampires by force. Then they'd been caught in some violent thing that tortured them in endless cycles before he stopped her from seeing more.

"Where are they?" she asked softly. "Your court?"

Susenyos stiffened. His body had become so still that she knew he wouldn't answer.

"Are they alive?"

Silence again. His tense face rippled with guilt, but for what, exactly, she didn't know.

Kidan let out a slow breath. "You don't have to tell me, but if you've been trying to master this room for years, maybe you should talk about it."

He got to his feet slowly and stared down the room like a wild beast. "There's nothing to talk about. They're gone, and my immortality is the only thing I have left."

Kidan studied the strong muscles of his back. "Is that really what matters the most to you?"

His head turned over his shoulder, eyes pure steel. "Yes. Always."

55.

"COSSIA DAY IS AN OLD TRADITION CREATED TO APPEASE THE DRANA-ics who claimed that Uxlay laws infringe on their more animalistic natures. They demanded, for a single day, a human-free fighting ring. Those who died on Cossia Day were to be forgotten."

Susenyos adjusted the house sigil pin on his sleeve. The light and dark mountains shimmered like lost stars. His suit jacket was black, embroidered with gold thread, and it fit him well. His lips kept stretching.

"Why are you smiling?"

"I'm smiling because by the end of tonight, there will be fewer of my enemies alive."

She shook her head, turning away to fix her dress at her vanity. His gaze heated her back.

"That dress is absolutely dangerous. Wait—" He took a startled breath. "Is that my crown on your lovely neck?"

Kidan had painted gold on her eyelids, enjoying the bold way it framed her eyes and complemented the liquid-like amber dress and fox mask. But her neck had been unbearably bare until she remembered the old gold and ruby crown crosses she'd fashioned.

"You don't mind, do you?"

He crossed the space between them, tracing her collarbone, and the necklace decorated entirely with the riches that once belonged to his crown. His touch was cool, the backs of his fingers brushing against her jawline, staying there for a beat too long. She tilted her neck, exposing the flesh more, and his breath sharpened, black eyes burning.

She held his stare, reading his plain hunger, heart skipping. "Is there something you'd like to ask? We do have a deal."

He turned away, shutting his eyes for a moment, and when he faced her again, his hunger was restrained. She frowned. She wanted to glimpse more of him, and the neck was where the deepest of desires hid. She pouted, touching her neck softly.

His gaze fell to her neck and swept along her figure. "Stop," he warned. "Or we won't make it to the event."

Their eyes met in the mirror. What an impressive image they cut, she and her vampire. Her...vampire. She waited for the revulsion those words would usually stir, but there was none.

"Titus is going to die tonight." Susenyos's fingers contracted on her back.

Goose bumps spread down her arms.

"I need to talk to him first."

"You will. But he will die tonight."

His lethal tone left no room for reason. She nodded.

"The moment they know who you are, and that your blood is drinkable, they will drink from you until you're dead. Don't take off this mask."

In the reflection, her bare collarbone appeared too human. Her chest rose and fell with her nerves. Inside her dress, strapped to her thigh, was Omar Umil's impala horn. She wouldn't go unprotected.

"Why is my blood drinkable?" she asked. "I haven't attended a companionship ceremony to make a vow."

His tone shifted, amused. "You *have* made a vow. You just don't know it yet."

She lifted her lashes at him, and he studied her with a quirked lip, always evading this question. At least tonight she would finally have an answer about June and Ramyn's connection.

Outside the red sandstone Sost Buildings, Susenyos tucked her hand into the nook of his arm. The lights from the lion-shaped lamps lit the way toward the iron doors of the middle structure. At the entrance, each vampire received a note listing those wishing to challenge them tonight.

Kidan's brows lifted when she saw Susenyos's list. "Twenty-two?"

He shrugged. "I anger a lot of people."

Kidan shook her head.

Cossia Day was the only time silver weapons were permitted, and the dranaics didn't let it go to waste. Iniko wore a choker with silver spikes, two knives along her forearms, and an axe strapped to her back. Taj's curved blade swung at his hip, and Susenyos had twin dragon blades. Dragon, he told her, for the way their edge was like textured hide, jagged like a wave.

Dark skin and silver. They were forsaken gods who'd stolen the teeth of the devil. And hell if they weren't breathtaking.

Kidan liked the cleverness associated with silver in the myth of vampires. The brilliant Demasus planted seeds of misinformation, claiming the metal was toxic to vampires. As such, every town he passed through brought silver to defend against his armies. He acquired their foolish weapons and melted them to forge the most powerful blades. To this day, humans brandished the metal in the presence of vampires. Kidan herself had carried silver from some misguided belief of protection as a child.

They made their way into the blood courting room. It hadn't changed since last time. Several booths still circled the opulent space, with red curtains ready to be drawn for privacy. In the center was a raised stage.

Once they settled in a corner lounge, Taj shot her a grin. "An acti coming here on Cossia Day. Do you have nine hearts?"

"Just one. It's pretty dead, though."

If possible, his grin widened. "You do know you look incredible in that dress, correct?"

"Yes."

"Good. Just checking."

Kidan's lip tugged in amusement.

Slen and Yusef, along with everyone else, were taking a break between terms for a week. There were no actis on the campus grounds. Kidan shivered. She might as well be the sole human in the world with an invitation to hell.

Susenyos leaned into Taj's ear. Taj straightened up and cast his attention around, and his smile faded. A large, bearded dranaic was staring right at him.

"Taj, should I start with you?" The dranaic flashed his wide fangs, approaching.

"If I win, you get to join House Makary and leave the Qaros rats. If you win, I'll join your house."

"So I lose either way?"

"Scared?"

"Only of your mustache," Taj muttered.

The dranaic shoved his face in front of Taj, smelling of meat. Iniko pushed him away with her boot, and he stumbled to the side, baring his teeth.

"Don't touch him." She narrowed her eyes.

"It's no secret who you would have picked. It's great that Foul Child died before she became a true acti," the mountainous dranaic spat.

Kidan's ears perked up. *Foul Child?*

"You're too old to gossip like a teenager, Asuris." Iniko's dismissal only lengthened a vein on his temple.

"Gossip? We in House Makary don't forget what Helen Makary looked like. No one forgets hair like midnight waves and that heart-shaped mouth. That Ajtaf child resembled her more every day."

"Insult my house again and I will wet my blade." Iniko reached behind for her axe.

Iniko was in House Ajtaf. Were they talking about Ramyn?

Asuris pulled out one of the two large blades strapped to his thighs.

"A simple test should tell us the truth. If House Ajtaf is innocent, its leader shouldn't fear for his head."

Iniko stood so quickly that a sharp wind cut into Kidan's shoulder. Susenyos seized her hand and brought her closer to his seat. Kidan stilled for a beat at the sudden gesture before settling beside him.

"You should mind your tongue, Asuris. Iniko hasn't wet her blade in years," Susenyos said.

Asuris showed no fear. "You remember what we did to the Foul Children back then. The point is, be glad Koril killed that girl before she inherited her houses, or I would've—"

Iniko backhanded him into the open space. The force of the blow rippled Kidan's dress and ruffled Susenyos's collar. Asuris sprang to his feet, snarling, and freed his weapons. The chatter around the room died immediately. Every dranaic leaned forward, the scent of violence making them bare their teeth.

Death wasn't given to them easily, the laws of Uxlay restricting them from open murder. But even now their lives weren't wasted. The dranaics defeated tonight would be taken into the Mot Zebeya Courts at once and give their lives to whomever was next on the life exchange list. The process of it all was impressive. How carefully they made sure immortality continued.

"Isn't it bad she's out of practice?" Kidan asked, almost worried.

"On the contrary, she's stronger for it. Each time we use our blood to coat silver, it takes a long time to become potent again. Iniko tempers herself and unleashes her wrath in spectacular fashion. Watch." Susenyos's voice dripped with delight. "Blood-licked silver never misses its mark."

Iniko slipped out a knife from her forearm, brought it to her tongue, and cut. Red glided along its gleaming edge. When she flicked it, the weapon shot forward with incredible aim. But Asuris dodged, and it skewered the opposite wall. Iniko tilted her head, and the knife that was planted in the wall teetered and loosened itself, spinning and throwing itself into Asuris's back, making him growl. Kidan's mouth dropped. They could control blood-licked silver without touching it.

When she gaped at Susenyos, his eyes twinkled. "Told you."

Asuris pulled out the knife like it was an annoying tick and licked his large blade.

He threw in a fast, whizzing arc. Iniko deflected it with her axe, but the force sent her back a couple of steps and cut her hands.

"Shake it off, love." Taj clapped from the sidelines. "Knock that caterpillar off his face!"

"Be *quiet*," she grunted, throwing her next weapon with terrifying precision.

Their match made Kidan incredibly aware of her mortality. How soft her flesh was, sinking with the press of a finger and hurting at the prick of a needle. Was skin truly the only protection humans had? Even her hard parts—skull, bones, teeth—needed to be on the outside if she ever stood a chance.

"What are you drawing there?" Susenyos murmured.

She hadn't realized it, but she was tracing a square on his thigh. He took her hand and stretched out the fingers.

"What do these symbols mean, little bird? It's not the first time you've drawn them."

"Nothing," she whispered back, making his lips quirk.

"He said the head of House Ajtaf had to pay the cost," Kidan said, thinking. "That's Ramyn's father."

Kidan gathered that the dranaics knew a lot about the families' affairs but chose to keep quiet. Even at the 13th meetings, it was communicated with a smirk, the exchange of loaded looks. She'd heard them call Ramyn's father Tesasus, though that wasn't his name. Tesasus was a seventeenth-century king with fifty-five wives. Marriage was rarely between one man and one woman in acti tradition. Yet the head of House Ajtaf took it further, marrying five wives. Most of Ramyn's brothers were her half-siblings.

Kidan turned to Susenyos. "So, what are Foul Children?"

Susenyos hesitated before speaking, face dark. "Marriage between actis is forbidden. Actis are supposed to marry and procreate with humans from the outside world...Foul Children are the result of that law being broken. In the past, Foul Children were given to vampires to be enjoyed and killed. Their existence threatened to end a bloodline, and they had to suffer to deter others. Now the parents are punished instead."

Her eyes widened as she pieced together Asuris's accusation. "Ramyn was born from two houses?"

"We are prohibited from spreading such rumors outside Cossia Day. Iniko might still kill me if she knew I was telling you."

"Being heiress to two major houses would have made her powerful." Kidan voiced this idea out loud—and another crystallized, cruel and cold. "Everyone would see her as a threat."

This got her a rueful smile, not as fully formed but there, in the arch of the lips. "Hell, isn't it? The politics of the families."

"You know something else."

The clash of blades came from behind her ear, silver dancing in his black eyes. His gaze dropped for a moment, giving her the answer.

"Is that why she was poisoned as a child? Who would...do something like that—" Kidan stopped, her understanding settling like a sour drink. "Her brothers."

Kidan *had* glimpsed something at Ramyn's funeral, a disquieting gleam to her brothers' eyes. She clenched her jaw so hard that her gums vibrated. Ramyn had had no clue that the monsters were her own family. Kidan's fingers tapped out a triangle shape erratically.

"Easy, yené Roana." He unfurled her fingers.

Kidan knew which brother would be responsible for it all—Tamol. She'd smelled his greed and ambition the day he'd asked about the Axum Archaeological Project instead of mourning Ramyn. Of course he wouldn't let his sister inherit two houses. But Kidan still needed confirmation.

"It's Tamol, isn't it?"

"That's who Iniko suspects, yes."

She relaxed a little, but her rage didn't dim entirely. They watched Iniko perform a thousand slashes with her choker necklace until her opponent was nothing but writhing flesh. Kidan's thighs trembled. It would be the last time she pissed off Iniko.

Taj put his fingers in his mouth and whistled. "Iniko Obu, everyone. Don't *ever* fuck with her."

He jumped onstage, seized her face, and kissed her temple. Exiting, she handed him the axe, her lips curving slightly.

Iniko retreated into one of the corridors, and Kidan followed.

56.

KIDAN PACED OUTSIDE THE BATHROOM, WAITING FOR INIKO TO EMERGE. If Tamol poisoned Ramyn as a child, why the hell was he still alive?

A growl built in her throat. The sound of clashing blades interrupted her thoughts, and, curious, she returned down the corridor.

Susenyos stood center stage. He'd removed his suit jacket, twin blades spinning in hand. Directly across from him, aiming a short sword, was Titus Levigne.

Her stomach hollowed out.

In the blink of an eye, the two lunged at each other. Sparks came from the rub of their blades, exploding around her vision like fireworks. They gripped each other, blade to throat. Titus held a sneer as he spoke. Susenyos was utterly still.

He will die tonight.

Titus couldn't die without telling her the truth.

She tried to bolt to the center, but Taj materialized before her, holding out a muscled arm to stop her. The tails of his gold band wavered at his back.

"Not yet."

"I have to—"

"He's not ready yet." His tone was robbed of all light.

Kidan's brows pinched. What did that mean?

Susenyos knocked their weapons to the floor and slammed Titus down. The stone beneath cracked in lightning bolts, and tremors shot through the bottoms of her feet.

Titus groaned.

Everyone had gone still and silent—even the curtains didn't dare sway.

Susenyos spoke in a voice that could only belong to death, rolling up his sleeves. "I dislike people who play in the shadows. Working so hard to frame me. Why not face me directly?"

A chilling cold slipped under Kidan's clothes. Susenyos pulled Titus's lolling form upright, spun him so they could see his face, and anchored him with a hand on the shoulder.

From behind, Susenyos's fingers shot out, blackened claws extending and tearing from the roots of his nails. Kidan inhaled sharply. Her vision pulsed around the edges, so her world became only him.

Susenyos shoved his knifelike claws into Titus's back. A horrifying squelching sound bled into her ears.

Titus screamed…a scream that couldn't belong to a powerful vampire. Several dranaics around the circle shuffled backward. Kidan remained frozen, blood pumping in her ears, her mind unsure if she was in a nightmare, her fingers twitching pathetically.

"Let's see if you have a spine." Susenyos spoke close to his ear, utterly calm.

Titus jerked and coughed up dark blood, pupils blown wide. It took Kidan a long time to comprehend what had happened. Her mouth parted and stuck in horror.

Susenyos had grabbed his spine.

From the inside.

Titus broke into soft, unintelligible pleas as Susenyos moved his hand upward, the skin breaking like overheated bread, muscles and bones tearing in chunks, and blood—so much *blood*. It poured onto Susenyos's shirt and formed a puddle beneath.

"Then you invited her here. What did you plan to do?" His voice slipped from its calm, snarling. "Did you think she'd come alone?"

He was talking about Kidan.

Something must have pinched or pulled inside, because Titus's eyes rolled to the back of his head so all that remained was white.

Kidan staggered back.

She could feel Susenyos's black hatred in every cell of her body. She had to run. Get away from the suffocating death and power radiating off him. If this was the kind of power vampires wielded with the Three Binds, what were they like without them?

Titus jerked with the next twist.

"Yos," Taj called, once and final, arms crossed. "Enough."

Susenyos's murderous gaze flicked up, and its unconstrained fury slammed into Kidan. Her knees wavered, and all at once she remembered why she'd hidden from their kind most of her life. The instinct to drop her own gaze, to *bow*, overwhelmed her bones.

She could taste it in her throat, the air dense with his bloodthirst, and she couldn't breathe, couldn't move, couldn't think—because if she did, if she made one single error, he would kill her.

He would kill them all.

She stared at her feet. Her knees buckled, and any moment now they would hit the floor.

"Kidan." Taj's soft voice was meant only for her. "You're fine. You're safe."

She couldn't stop shaking.

"You can look at him. His anger isn't toward you, it's for you."

Kidan tried to lift her head, biting her trembling lip. What was wrong with her? Since when did she fear for her life? She craned her neck slowly, glimpsing his red shoes, his broad rising shoulders, and, upward still, his spoiled eyes. They were fixed on her.

Everything else fell away.

She'd thought she knew the shape and color of Susenyos's anger—when she destroyed his artifacts, when she showed his fangs publicly. Those moments of his rage had been...nothing. A watered-down version, bound and repressed by the laws of Uxlay, only leaking at the edges. Had it been his loyalty to the Adane family that stopped him? He could have removed her heart without blinking, if he wished it. But he hadn't...Even now, his true wrath stretched and enveloped her instead of cutting her down.

For her.

Susenyos wrenched out his hand. Titus gasped and crumpled to the floor. Taj left her side, grabbing a towel from the side panel, and escorted Susenyos to the corner. The two interacted in a practiced manner, Taj cleaning his hands, speaking softly.

Titus's twitching flesh pulled Kidan's attention. He was alive and, surprisingly, healing fast too, gouged-out flesh coming together.

Kidan's fear dimmed, and her spine locked. She walked to Titus and squatted, voice hard.

"Where is June?"

The vampire's eyes bled pain as he snarled. *"You."*

"Tell me what you did to my sister."

Before she could blink, Titus was on her, a shadow blanketing her from the shoulders. It was remarkable that he could move so quickly with his back torn to shreds. He was still unsteady, though, and he put all his weight on Kidan, crushing her. She fought to shrug him off but then a sharp claw at her throat stopped her.

He laughed, teetering back and forth. "I'm taking you with me."

Susenyos and Taj froze at the end of the room.

"You hear that, Sagad?" Titus shouted to the ceiling. "How loyal you are to this girl. Did she break you in the day she claimed your fangs? Leashed you like a feral dog?"

Susenyos wore the face of pure rage. "Let her go."

Kidan reached for her weapon slowly.

"No." Titus's manic laugh scratched on her ear. "I will gift her to the Nefrasi. Isn't that what you want, to reunite with your sister? You stupid, stupid girl."

Kidan stilled. "The Nefrasi? Is that who took June?"

Titus glared only at Susenyos, barely hearing her. "I would have given her a merciful death. They will pull out her spine and wear it as a belt."

"Don't move, little bird." Susenyos approached slowly.

"Kneel!" Titus shouted at him, cutting into Kidan's throat until she winced. Blood ran down her brown neck.

Susenyos's muscles rippled with anger, but he lowered himself. His closed jaw moved as if he was trying to speak without opening his mouth, to tell her something, but Kidan didn't understand.

"Susenyos the Third, Malak Sagad, the Great Emperor. To whom the angels bow, kneeling before me?" Titus trembled with wild delight.

Kidan began hiking her dress up gradually, reaching for the impala horn.

"How far you've fallen from your glory days, Malak Sagad. If we'd all started with your monstrous army, we wouldn't be bowing at the feet of the actis. Yet here you are, a lapdog for the same house for decades. How *pathetic.*"

Susenyos's eyes turned to slits, a twitch lengthening in his jaw.

Titus added a second claw to her neck. She flinched. "Did he tell you about his court? What he turned them into? The savagery of his—"

"Technically," Susenyos cut in with a flat tone, "it's not considered a true bow if the knee doesn't touch the ground, but since you were raised in a barn, I'll forgive your ignorance."

Titus snapped his gaze to where Susenyos hovered several inches off the floor.

"And *I* kneel for no one."

Susenyos spat before Titus could tear out her throat. A stunned choking burst across her ears. Titus stumbled back at once. Something had flown out of Susenyos's mouth, sharp and bullet-fast, nicking her neck before finding its target.

Titus wavered, tried to reach for her, then fell. A silver nail was lodged below his Adam's apple.

"Who are the Nefrasi?" Kidan demanded.

Titus stared upward, blank and unseeing. Susenyos approached the still dranaic, removed the silver nail, and wiped it thoroughly before pressing it into the roof of his mouth.

"You shouldn't have killed him." Her words trembled.

"I offered him mercy. He pushed me."

His right arm was still slick with blood and guts. It had been inside someone. *Mercy.*

"Take her," Susenyos said with an unreadable expression.

A hand pulled Kidan to her feet. She began to protest, but Susenyos was already turning away, facing the next challenger. Taj led her across a hall and pulled her to a secluded corner.

Kidan reeled from it all. Susenyos's wrath, the information she'd uncovered. Had Titus taken June at the instruction of these Nefrasi?

"Who are the Nefrasi?" she asked Taj urgently.

"I don't know. We've never heard of them."

Taj reached for her cut neck, and she jerked away. "You're bleeding."

It was supposed to be tonight. She was supposed to finally walk away with solid information on June.

Kidan leaned her head against the wall, frustrated tears blossoming. Since when did she cry this easily? "Am I ever going to find her?"

Taj's eyes softened as he opened his mouth to say something. A challenger tapped on his shoulder, stealing his words. He worked his jaw and told her, "Stay here and clean your neck. I'll be back."

They disappeared down the hall.

Kidan felt powerless. Stagnant. She needed to act. Tonight. Get justice for Ramyn until she could get it for June. Rufeal Makary was dead, but Tamol Ajtaf lived. She would ask him about the Nefrasi first, and if he knew nothing, she'd kill him. Yes, she needed to regain control.

Kidan was walking to the bathroom to clean herself when a couple of dranaics blocked her way.

"Sorry." She tried to go around, but they blocked her again.

Shit. She hid her neck, but the dranaics stepped closer, smiling.

"Unmask."

Her limbs went numb. A circle had formed quickly, figures peeling themselves from the shadows.

"You smell that? We have a pure acti among us."

One of them withdrew a silver claw and cut along the middle of her dress. She hissed, clutching at the thin rip and the blood emerging. He cut her arm, sending another painful slit across her skin. Then he brought his finger to his mouth, and his pupils bled hunger.

"Clean. We can drink from her."

Kidan pulled out her impala horn and whirled around in a circle. "Stay back!"

A gaggle of laughter followed her. Someone pushed her, and her entire body rocked. Another powerful shove made the room spin, and she stumbled. They jostled her from one side of the circle to another, laughing at her petrified state. Crowding in.

Her arms became pinned from behind. Kidan kicked off, stabbing the horn into a thigh. The vampire howled and let go.

"You're going to pay—"

A dragon blade tore through his thorax, spraying blood all over Kidan's face. She wiped it away quickly to watch the dranaic stiffen and fall.

Susenyos's shirt was barely on him, tattered from more fights. Iniko and Taj were close behind, silver weapons slick with blood.

"That was a nice distraction, but you're going to have to do better than that," Susenyos said, chest rising and falling.

Shaking, she tried to hide the slit in her stomach. But as Susenyos studied her from head to toe, his wide fangs became elongated, the ends of his twists inflamed.

"Who cut your lovely dress?"

His tone sent shivers down her arms. It was a strange sort of relief, being the one rescued. Kidan forced herself to stand a little straighter and faced the bastard who started all this. Susenyos turned his lethal gaze on him. Some stepped back and walked away. A couple stayed. Kidan grabbed the horn and returned it to her thigh strap, stepping out of the way.

"Well?" Susenyos roared, extending his powerful arms. "What are you waiting for?"

Taj and Iniko remained outside the circle, ready to assist if necessary.

It was an unparalleled dance of death. Susenyos dismembered every hand that had dared touch her. The brutality of it, the carelessness of his blows—she'd never seen such true unbridled power. He didn't belong in a university, caught between law and order, but on a battlefield, facing the ends of a thousand swords and daring them to strike. Why had he chosen Uxlay as home? Why did he allow this place to rule him when he could make them all kneel? Kidan couldn't make sense of it.

With each dranaic who fell, Sicions dragged the body away to a draining room. Blood had to be poured before the body was cold for a life exchange.

Susenyos's silver blades became an extension of him, the wavelike edge splitting flesh and eliciting screams. Kidan winced and flinched as their cries became pitiful, begging for mercy. Yet she didn't interrupt him or tell him it was enough. In a macabre trance, she watched the floor turn from white to red.

This was the rage that had engulfed her when she set Mama Anoet's house ablaze. Kidan had to become a shield the moment she realized June was too kind for this world. She needed to be the unbreakable armor every blow fell on, to find some divine balance in the lashing and bear it, because June didn't deserve it.

She was never the one worth protecting. Worth all this blood.

When Susenyos finally came to her, leaving a trail of bodies behind him, his hair had matted, and his dark skin glistened like he'd stepped out of a red sea.

Whispers of "Savage Susenyos" echoed around the room, yet no one dared raise their voice.

"Are you hurt?" His voice was rougher than usual, eyes transfixed on her.

When she didn't answer, he stepped closer, worry, out of all emotions, replacing the rage that possessed him.

"Where?" He traced her cut dress.

Her stomach ignited at the contact, and she closed her eyes, savoring the wetness of his blood-slicked fingers. When he touched her, he felt human in the way a glass teetered on the edge of a table—blinding when the sun scattered him, lovely when he slipped into unimaginable ruin.

"Am I scaring you?" His voice rumbled like mountain rocks. "Do you want to leave?"

The muscles of his shoulders tensed as if he was preparing for another blow. He was mistaking her accelerated heart rate for fear. But it was thrill, the over-whelming rush of scaling a mountain. She lifted her lashes to him and rested her hands over his, coating her palms in red. His gaze dropped to their joined hands in a question, then flicked up, light piercing his night eyes. His strength seeped into her, and she tasted the immortal dark, wet and wanting her. It had been waiting a long time, and damn her, she could no longer deny it.

Just for tonight, she wanted him without the noise of her guilt and self-punishment. A night as he was, and most importantly, as she was.

Cossia Day. A day to be free of laws, of promises. Of June's haunting memory and her vow to end it all.

One night. She would have him for one night.

Kidan broke from his burning gaze, spotted the lounge closest to them, and pulled him inside with surprising force. He loosened a sharp breath, warm yet biting. She stripped off whatever remained of his shirt in one motion, revealing his sculpted torso, and pushed him backward.

He stumbled onto the single couch, eyes wide, as if he was imagining it all. "Easy, easy."

Kidan drew the curtains and hiked her dress up to her thighs, watching his gaze darken. She ripped off her mask.

"Ask," she said, voice thick with need. Unrecognizable. "I want you to ask."

In the truest sense, she now felt like his Roana, and him, her Matir.

Once he realized she had the very opposite intention of leaving, he flashed her a crooked grin. "I'm not the one who pushed me into this dark room. You want, so you ask."

"Why are you being difficult?" She gritted her teeth, impatience exposing her.

He tilted his head. "Why is it difficult for you to ask for something you want?"

"I've asked you for many things."

He grabbed her waist and pulled her to his lap with sudden speed. She gasped. Her fingers braced against his solid chest, admiring its rich color past the blood, a shade darker than her brown skin.

"You've asked for things that serve the purpose of others," he said. "To protect your friends, find your sister. I haven't heard you ask for yourself, for your own pleasure."

She opened her mouth but couldn't do it. This ask felt impossible. How could she enjoy herself at a time like this? *Especially* at a time like this?

Kidan hid her face from him. Suddenly, she was cold. Dirty. What the hell was she still doing here? She didn't know what she wanted from this. To forget the death encircling her wrist? To think about herself for once?

Susenyos's chest pressed against hers, flushing her with delicious heat and forcing her attention back on him. Only his eyes were illuminated in the dimly lit room, and they refused to let her go. Her shoulders relaxed into his frame, loving the trail of his hand up her thigh.

"Repeat after me," he whispered, voice labored. "I."

"I," she breathed.

"Want."

She sucked in a breath. "Want."

"You."

After a heartbeat, then another, she was brave.

"You."

He stained the gold dress with his hard grip and maneuvered her onto one of his thighs. The new angle made her lips part in surprise. His eyes gleamed with intention.

She moved before she could think. Her dress rode higher as her thighs straddled his leg. He trailed biting kisses along her bare neck, teeth scratching her skin, and yanked her dress down to her shoulders. But her braids got in his way. He made a sound of frustration, then gathered her hair in one hand, a tight pressure against her scalp, and used one braid to tie back the rest. Cold air licked the back of her neck. She fell forward onto his chest, almost brushing his lips.

"Don't let go." Her voice hovered between a plea and a demand. "Tighter."

He obeyed. She wanted him to bite at and scar her skin until the outside of her mirrored the tangled ruins of her soul. There was nothing worse they could do to each other, plenty they could do *for* each other.

She braced against him, palms finding skin and muscle only, and began a steady back-and-forth movement, savoring the friction it caused.

His finger trailed a line to her collarbone, and the contrast between his feather-like touch and his hard grip made her bite her lip.

"There you are, yené Roana."

Kidan closed her eyes at this new name he had given her. On this lawless day, she could admit she loved how he rolled the sound on his tongue, the possessiveness attached to it, and more so, the loaded intention every time he used it.

She sensed his canines before she ever saw them. Their pointed strength surprised a gasp out of her. His head buried in her throat, he trailed two lines with his teeth, hard enough to be painful but not to break skin.

"I thought you didn't drink from the throat." She was too out of breath to be convincing.

He swore and turned his face, warm cheek pressing against her collarbone.

"I can't remember why at this moment," he grumbled.

She brought his mouth to her bare shoulder. "But you do drink from here, yes?"

He trembled under her. "You're killing me."

The words thrilled her, and she imagined this scene from a different time, the first night he'd brought her here and made her watch as he fed from another girl.

"I hated you so much that day," she whispered, shuddering.

He pressed a gentle kiss on her shoulder, immediately understanding. "Because I made you beg?"

She shivered. "Because I couldn't stop picturing your mouth on me."

Kidan swore he groaned. She tugged her fingers through his thick twists, loving the coarse texture against her soft palms, and lifted his head.

She stared into those endless, ruinous eyes. "I still hate you."

Why he had to know, she was unsure. But it felt good, so she said it again.

"I hate you, Susenyos."

His brows melted into reverence as if she'd told him the opposite. "As long as hating me leaves you on my lap, I can bear it. Hate me for eternity."

She pressed her forehead against his, letting his supplication tug at her lips, sharing the same hot, staggered breath.

"Eternity...I could do such awful things to you."

"More than what you've done?"

The tug in her mouth turned into a stretch. "So much more. And you'll keep forgiving me?" She rolled her hips deliberately, making him suck in a breath. "As long as I end up here?"

"God yes."

She grinned, unable to help it. "You confess such dangerous things when you want something."

He traced her curved mouth with a finger. "Pulls the truth right out of me. I hold up better under torture."

Kidan ignited from the inside out at his hungry gaze. He was admiring her like she was the blazing sun itself.

More. She wanted so much more. She continued her dance again. His hand moved, firm on her back, sliding a little downward, providing the anchor she needed. Lips parted, heavily breathing, she took her pleasure how she wanted it. He met her rhythm from underneath.

"Slower," she whispered in his ear, borrowing his favorite word.

He smiled and hoisted her higher, slowing. She shivered when his mouth devoured her shoulder, kissing and tugging at the skin. An odd little thought cut through her jumbled mind. She'd been right back then. His mouth was hot and wet as boiled fruit. How would it feel against her lips?

His fangs rubbed in a steady movement, shooting a spear of lightning through her. Still, he didn't bite.

Her breath became choppier. "What are you waiting for?"

"You."

God, she wanted to kiss him.

She moved to do just that, but he grabbed her chin, stopping her inches from him.

She lifted her lashes in a question, biting her lips. He used his thumb to free her bottom lip, and his intense gaze alone made her lips tingle and swell.

He inhaled sharply. "Don't let me kiss you. It will be the last thing you ever do."

She wanted to protest, but he was already hiding his face from her, pressing his mouth to her cheek, then down the curve of her neck and lower to her shoulder in slow, knee-weakening kisses. Her thoughts disassembled, and her eyes fluttered shut. She was pure energy, about to crash into another.

When she did feel the familiar tide rising inside herself, she couldn't say his entire name—it rang entirely too long and she only had a sigh in her, so she gripped his bare arms and whispered, "Yos."

He sank his fangs into her. Dull pain and sharp pleasure collided and vibrated as her body ascended to the heavens. But her mind remained here...in this room, watching this scene through his obsidian eyes. Kidan's full lips were blushed and caught between her teeth, her dress messy and yanked low, her face radiant with glow. The image rippled away, and she returned to the earth, sagging upon him.

He breathed harder, the force of his inhalation lifting her up and down. Sharp pressure poked at her back and thigh. His claws had reemerged.

"The shoulder...," she managed through her delirious wave. "What type of memory does it show?"

His voice, glazed with desire, was thick and breathy. "Not sure. What did you see?"

A lie.

All vampires had to know what memory each body part conjured. They'd never bite carelessly. But...she found she didn't want to know either. It wasn't an old memory she glimpsed but the formation of one. This moment they'd shared must have claimed the space of what the shoulder usually evoked. Whatever that feeling was, she wasn't sure either of them was ready yet.

"Nothing clear," she whispered. "Too distracted. What did you see?"

His eyes swirled, and he seemed grateful for her lie.

Had he seen himself in her memories as well? Her fingers in his wild hair, his otherworldly eyes flaring, lips glistening with blood?

She swallowed thickly, preparing.

He traced the line of her throat, making her knees squeeze around him.

His slick lips stretched. "I saw nothing too."

Kidan's pupils glittered. They were understanding each other without words, as if they shared the same mind.

Susenyos peered at the impala horn scattered at their feet during his touch. The one weapon that could kill him, and she hadn't noticed him remove it from her thigh.

"I wonder," he murmured. "Who was that for?"

She brushed over his taut pectoral where his iron heart would be. "What if I said you?"

He caught her wrist lightning-fast, making her gasp, and cocked his head in near wonder. "It's a shame I can't tell if that's true or not. Even worse that I don't seem to care much right now."

Kidan smiled. He truly confessed such dangerous things.

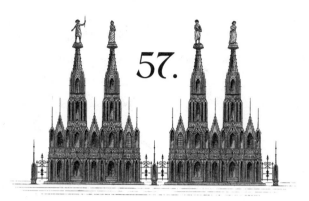

57.

THE ESTATE THAT TAMOL AJTAF OCCUPIED WAS PERCHED ON THE west border of campus, near the main Uxlay gate out to town. Its splendor and magnificence made Kidan's blood boil. This should be Ramyn's. But the world would keep taking unless its hands were singed.

Susenyos and Kidan parked several streets away. She unbuckled her seat belt.

"Easy, yené Roana," Susenyos said, studying her focused gaze. "The Ajtafs have hundreds of dranaics. It won't be easy to enter—"

She unlocked the door and got out. Susenyos swore in Amharic and followed.

"What, exactly, is your plan?"

"Give me your keys."

He balked. "I've never seen you drive. Do you even know how?"

"Well enough to crash it."

Susenyos blinked as if he'd heard wrong.

"I'm crashing the car with Tamol in it," she explained. "You need to get back to the house, so they don't blame you."

His jaw remained open. "And you'll be in the car?"

"Yes."

The look of astonishment on his face would have been comical under any other circumstance. "That's absolutely—"

"An ask."

He stared at her like she was an alien, and held up a hand. "Forgive me for this, because there's nothing I hate more than the following words, but *did you forget you're human?*"

She gave him a thin smile.

"It's dangerous." His face darkened. "We have time to plan better."

"Planning is what made me miss my chance with Rufeal. Besides, you said yourself that spending time planning murders isn't always the best approach."

"Again, forgive me, but you're *human*. The rules are entirely different."

She narrowed her eyes at him. "I'm not scared."

"We can make sure you don't get killed—"

"Do you know who the Nefrasi are?" she cut in.

His jaw snapped shut. Under the diffused light of the nearest lamppost, his face appeared grim, almost torn. "No."

"So, questioning Tamol is the only way to find out," she explained. They didn't have time for this. "An accident is our best option. No one will suspect me, because I'll be in there with him."

"And if you die?" He let out a frustrated breath. "What then?"

This made her hesitate for a fraction of a second. "Let's see what the fates decide."

An exasperated laugh burst from him. "You're still determined to dance on the edge of death." When she didn't respond, he shook his head. "Try not to die, little bird. The house might just be unbearable without you."

Kidan glimpsed their reflection in the car's window and wondered how they'd reached this point. They truly appeared in sync, partners.

"Make sure you leave," she instructed. "Be somewhere public so the 13th can't blame you."

She took the keys and entered the sleek black sedan. Susenyos remained a shadow in her rearview mirror. A sad smile touched her face. Perhaps he'd never understand why Kidan had to keep pushing herself, inching toward death again and again so she could stand the feel of her own heartbeat. Just a taste and she'd be good to go.

She dialed Tamol's number, all thoughts narrowing on her plan.

"It's Kidan."

"Kidan?" He didn't sound asleep. Perhaps he was working. "It's late."

"Sorry." She ruffled her voice to the tune of embarrassment. "But I'm leaving tonight. I can't stay here any longer."

"Is everything all right?"

"Not really." Her voice shook. "You said you could help me with some money? I want to talk about the Axum Archaeological Project."

The crinkle of papers echoed. "Are you home?"

"I'm leaving Uxlay tonight. If you want to talk, I'll be passing your house in a few minutes."

He paused for a moment, then said, "I'll be outside. Don't leave without talking to me."

She ended the call. Kidan rolled her shoulders, the rush of adrenaline pumping through her veins. Night air from the rolled-down window swam in her braids and iced her cheeks. The corner of her lips arched. Finally, she was in control.

When she arrived, Tamol Ajtaf, dressed in a large jacket and pajama pants, fixed his glasses and squinted at her.

"We can talk inside."

Tears came to her eyes. "No, I'm not spending another second at Uxlay. I'm going into town."

He moved his jaw but forced a nod. Surprisingly, he'd brought a briefcase, which he held close as he got in the car. She tried not to smile when she pulled out.

"What happened?" His green eyes ran over her. "Was it Susenyos? I told Dean Faris he should have been removed from that house."

She slid a glance at him. His eyes were bright with eagerness. "It's everything. Not just him."

He injected compassion into his tone. "Dranacti is difficult. I don't blame you."

Kidan's grip tightened on the wheel as the gilded gates of Uxlay swung open. They took the winding road bracketed by trees to Zaf Haven.

"You said you could help me with the Axum project."

"Right." He clicked open his briefcase and brought out papers.

"A vampire has no business owning a house. Especially one such as Adane House. I don't know what your family was thinking leaving it to Susenyos. Officially, you can't sign away your shares until you graduate, but thankfully, you're the last of your line—"

"I'm not the last of my line." Fire raged in her eyes, and the road slipped in and out of her vision. "My sister is. June."

He cleared his throat uncomfortably. "Right, but she's not here, and you are the oldest, capable of signing away your house."

"You know, Ramyn gave me the opposite advice. To stay and fight for what's rightfully mine."

He avoided her eyes, gathering his contracts. "Well, sometimes the best thing to do is stand aside."

Kidan's foot pressed on the accelerator. Just a little. She didn't understand how family could turn on one another for trivial things like money or power. Tamol had been so terrified of Ramyn's potential, he'd sabotaged her without knowing what she'd become.

Her knuckles turned white. "Who are the Nefrasi?"

The papers pinched in his grip. "What?"

"The Nefrasi. I know they support the 13th. Who are they?"

"I've never heard of them."

They took a very sharp turn, and his body swayed, the suitcase smacking against his door loudly.

A tendril of fear tightened his voice. "You should slow down."

"I know you poisoned Ramyn and ruined her chance of inheriting Ajtaf House. I'll tell Dean Faris if you don't tell me who the Nefrasi are."

He blinked, shocked, then—as most men did—called her bluff. "*I* will have you arrested for defamation."

Kidan pressed harder on the gas and gave the wheel a little shake. Their shoulders swayed violently along with the car.

"What are you doing?" he shouted.

"I don't think you understand what you've walked into."

His words came slowly, fluttering like wings. "Stop the car right now."

"Tell me about the Nefrasi or I'll end it." When he said nothing, she added more pressure to the pedal. "You don't think I'll do it? Test me."

He fisted his fingers, and for a moment she thought he'd grab the wheel, but then he relaxed.

"Okay, okay. Slow down. I'll tell you."

Kidan eased up. Only a little.

Tamol loosened a breath. "All I know is it's a group outside Uxlay. They fund our initiatives when we don't want to use our Uxlay accounts."

Outside Uxlay. "What do they want?"

"The same as the 13th," he bit out impatiently. "A new structure of inheritance and rights to ownership. The ability to set our own laws inside our houses, like the Founding Houses. Of course, you wouldn't understand."

"The universal law protects Uxlay's boundary."

"*We* are what the outside world needs protection from." He glowered. "Why should we give up that power?"

"And Ramyn? Did you poison her because you couldn't stand that she might command two houses one day?"

He stared ahead, eyes unreadable. He was too smart to confirm or deny.

Kidan gritted her teeth. "Where's June?"

A frown twisted his thin mouth. "Your sister? How should I know?"

"I know the 13th or Nefrasi or whatever the fuck you call yourselves have her."

He stared at her, brows drawn. "I don't know what you're talking about."

"That's right. You don't understand familial love."

Twin headlights flashed bright, blinding them as they nearly collided with a passing car. Tamol gripped his seat belt tightly.

"You need to slow down!"

"Tell me where June is."

"I don't know!"

Fine.

If he was done talking, so was she. The thundering roll of the accelerator vibrated under her feet. Kidan could have spared his life if he'd had a true reason to betray Ramyn. If he'd been protecting someone else. But his choice to sacrifice his family was nothing but an act of greed. Mama Anoet might as well have been sitting next to her.

Kidan swerved off the road and launched into the thick trees. As the world exploded in twisted metal and glass, his scream rose and abruptly cut, failing to reach whatever he'd been praying to.

When Kidan's eyes fluttered shut, her body was crushed under something. She was ice-cold, the night moon burning her face. The fresh earth beneath reached its ashen fingers toward her, trying to draw her into its belly for warmth. It promised rebirth, a second life, if only she sank inward. Her bleeding lungs stopped working.

The gates of death were adorned with fresh rosemary, as in Mama Ano-et's garden. There was an irritating sound, faint as butterfly wings but growing sturdier, pulsing like a heartbeat, then like a lion-skin drum. It was a warning, calling for Kidan to return to the surface. She couldn't see who or what it was. Didn't care. She was at the end.

Still, it beat a manic rhythm like the devil was at its feet. Without her will, it guided her back, away from the fresh-smelling gates and back to the sky, pounding all the way. It stole into her body, beating inside her like a second heart.

Kidan opened her eyes. A figure hovered across her face. Susenyos's edges had blurred like Yusef's charcoal drawings, brows furrowed.

"I could have sworn your heart stopped," he whispered, lifting his bleeding wrist from her mouth.

The taste of his blood pooled under her tongue. She wanted to ask him what the hell he was doing here, but her jaw wouldn't move. None of her limbs listened to her command.

"Easy, Kidan. No need to speak. Your eyes have a language of their own."

He searched behind him, a background misted with dust and broken lights. When she drifted again, his strong fingers slipped under the crook of her neck.

"No, keep those eyes open," he ordered. "Tally all the faults with my perfor-mance, outline your revenges on me, imagine your perfect murders upon my heart. But keep those eyes open."

It was difficult to do so. Her lashes carried heavy snow, demanded to close. But every time she tried to leave him, he brought her back with the scent of violence. There was no need for promises of love or for quiet tenderness. Nei-ther was allowed to feel the smallest spark of those afflictions. But perhaps their souls were made to be in eternal company. In devotion, in worship, in lust of brutality.

58.

I N HER MYTHOLOGY AND MODERNITY CLASS, KIDAN HAD RESEARCHED
a selfish and lonely god. To decorate his empty heaven, he scoured the earth
for the purest hearts that shone like stars and collected them into his pockets.
He left the wicked and corrupt to rot among themselves on earth. To ensure
that they wouldn't join his heaven, he gave them three lives instead of one, as
death was the only way to be free of their world. They survived miraculous
feats, these vile men impervious to death, and rained terror upon innocents.
Her paper had explored evil's tenacity, its ability to survive.

But Tamol Ajtaf would have served as a much better study. Crushed lungs,
broken collarbone, head injury. Alive.

Well, mostly. A coma had to be induced because of the excruciating pain,
but it was hoped he would eventually recover with the gradual aid of dranaic
blood.

Both of them lay in Uxlay's Rojit Hospital. Kidan's body hurt like bruised
fruit but was healing. She'd be out that night. The nurses told her several times
how lucky she'd been. All she felt was out of luck.

"We need to talk to Yusef." Kidan stood next to Slen in the cemetery. "We have
a common enemy. So we need to tell one another everything."

Slen had iced Kidan out, ignoring all her calls, since she learned that Titus
had been killed.

"Confess to Yusef?" Slen said, incredulous. "No."

They stood there until the waking sun dipped behind a cloud, casting shade on their skin and lengthening their shadows. Ramyn Ajtaf's grave was littered with fresh flowers. Kidan had come here on purpose so Slen couldn't escape her.

"I was thinking about why I don't hate you, Slen. For days after you told me the truth, I waited to feel a sense of rage, disgust, anything. Out of everyone, you deserve my hate the most for what you did to Ramyn."

Last night, Kidan engaged in one of her secret rituals. She'd pulled out the *Woman in Blue* picture, Rufeal's blood casting two dried, morbid lines across it, and curled Ramyn's scarf around her fingers, smelling the girl's peach perfume. She needed to get rid of these mementos but couldn't. She'd lain Mama Anoet's bracelet next to them, wondering if these objects were true companions of one another, losing herself in the violence of it all.

Susenyos had made her see it. The traitorous peace to be found in violence. The path forward.

"I want to hate you, Slen."

Slen's focus fell on the headstone's epitaph—*Death is not the end*. "Why don't you?"

Kidan released a defeated sigh. "Because I understand you. I know you don't enjoy what you've done. You were desperate. Willing to do anything to save yourself and your brother." Her voice tightened. "Because you are me, Slen."

Kidan's chest tore open, spilling her soul.

"You're an anomaly, Kidan." Slen's brows drew in. "I don't know what to do with you."

Kidan's lips lifted in a ghost of a smile.

Slen tipped her head skyward, softening her cheeks. Wind picked up, chilling them. "All right."

"All right?"

"Let's try it your way. Death seems unable to touch you. Maybe we can all survive this."

Gathered in their private tower room without GK, the three of them appeared insignificant against the weight of the bricks and stone of Uxlay.

After Rufeal's murder, Yusef had shrunk into himself the most. For instance, he'd taken to washing his hands longer than necessary yet always smelled of disinfectant. Without an anchor, his erratic actions would swallow him into the depths of a sea he couldn't swim against.

Kidan didn't really know how to say her next words. Her confession would undoubtedly puncture a hole in his world. Unlike Slen, there was no telling if Yusef would survive it.

She inhaled deeply. "Before I came to Uxlay, I burned my house down with my foster mother inside it."

This was the first time Kidan had given voice to the story trapped in her bones, and it was painful, slow.

"She was meant to protect me and my sister, but instead betrayed us. June was taken by a vampire because of her. She was kind before that, though. Raised me, clothed me, fed me, and I . . . killed her."

Yusef stared, blinked, and stared some more. Kidan waited, heart pounding. He had to process her words and decide on his own, without her encouragement or pressure. She wanted to create something here, a place where all their demons danced above their heads and gave them reprieve. Each of them had to see the beauty in absolution.

Once enough time passed, she continued, "There's a group here inside Uxlay called the 13th. They want each house to pledge allegiance to them and back their new reforms. I believe they took my sister."

Kidan's chest rolled into a tight ball. She prayed this would work. She didn't know what she would do if it didn't.

Yusef rubbed his hands. "Susenyos told me Rufeal made me fail last year. That my father was manipulated by the 13th to murder his house dranaics, leading to his imprisonment."

Kidan gaped. *Why would Susenyos tell him that?*

When Yusef lifted his eyes, they were gripped with horror. "You killed someone, Kidan."

She studied the table. "Yes."

The tremble in his hands returned.

Kidan faced Slen, who wore a warning in her eyes. They must have stared at each other for a long moment, because Yusef called uncertainly, "Slen?"

Slowly, she told him about Ramyn's murder and her father's arrest. The shock breaking over Yusef's face was raw.

"You're a member of the 13th?" Betrayal thickened his voice.

Slen's gaze dropped to the table for a moment before it hardened. "It was the only way to get rid of my father."

He stared at her with an emotion Kidan couldn't place. It had an effect on Slen, making her adjust her fingerless gloves repeatedly.

"And now?" he asked. "Are you still a member?"

Kidan didn't trust Slen to answer this properly.

"She's helping me eliminate them," Kidan said quickly. "We need to protect ourselves—that's why we're doing this. You're not alone in this, Yusef."

Yusef placed his head in his hands. "This is hell. We're murderers. We're ruined."

Kidan shut her eyes. Afraid of this.

"No," Slen said strongly. "We are tragedy itself. Nothing can ruin us unless we let it. *I* won't let it."

Slowly Yusef lifted his head. Slen's unwavering gaze fixed on him, clearing his wrought expression like streaming sun through fog.

Kidan could see it. Finally. Her life beyond this year and the next. This space they'd create, sharing their awful truths and cleansing themselves, would fulfill her deepest craving. For humans, not vampires, to see into her soul and not flinch.

Under the table, Kidan snapped her bracelet free, and something dislocated inside her. June's voice rushed at her but was severed at once. Kidan's lungs expanded with clean air, breathing deeply.

They'd help each other eliminate the 13th. Live an honest life from this moment on. She didn't need her blue pill right now.

Finally, Kidan asked for help. "A group called the Nefrasi controls the 13th. I need your help finding out who they are. If we destroy the Nefrasi, the 13th will cease to exist. I can't do it...alone."

In the stillness, she found them united, ready to redeem themselves.

59.

THE THREE TRAGEDIES OF UXLAY THRIVED IN THEIR NEWFOUND MIS-
ery. Nothing could touch them, and everything was for the taking. In the
weeks that followed, their work and their analyses of Dranacti took on a grayer
tone, no longer solid but made of water so they could live through it, find its
reflection in their own hearts, and pour themselves into its teachings.

For the last topic of Dranacti—Concordium—Professor Andreyas asked
what price was paid for the peace forged between dranaics and actis. When the
Last Sage asked Demasus the Fanged Lion to tether himself to the Three Binds
and abandon his nature, what did Demasus ask for in return? It had to be an
equal sacrifice. The answer appeared to be a silver mirror—but an interpretation of this eluded them, dancing out of reach.

They spent hours in the Grand Solomon Library, consulting old texts as
well as tracking the Nefrasi's movements throughout history. It was remarkably
small, their find, so small that it had to have been plucked and erased. As the
days wore on, Kidan grew agitated at the slightest false lead. This had been her
life for the better part of the year, goaded and herded like a sheep while someone
kept the information out of reach. A master playing with its favorite toy.

Slen read a brief news article from the 1940s under the table lamp. "'The
Nefrasi pursue enlightenment from the suffocating existence of the mundane.
They trade in worldly treasures from the continent of Africa and pay hand-
somely to all those that bring forward such treasures. Gathering to be held at
noon, next to Lotus Apothecary.'"

"They were in Britain?" Kidan asked.

"Not just there." Yusef brought his laptop closer. "This is an advertisement from Mogadishu, 1960. I can't read it very well, but I believe it translates to 'We will be rid of the famine with water, blind the sun so harvest is plentiful, and triumph over death.' They were a movement, and these ads were posted at universities to lure in new initiates."

"I think they're talking about the Three Binds. Look at the keywords they're using—'water,' 'sun,' 'death,'" Kidan pointed out.

Yusef's phone rang, startling him. "It's GK."

Slen dismissed Yusef. "Tell him we're not getting together today."

"I hate lying to him."

"Would you rather he know what we're doing?"

Yusef bit his lip and went to answer.

When they could no longer stand the sight of another page, they drank and roamed the campus at night, stumbling through the corridors in fits of nonsensical laughter. They always received disgruntled looks from other students, but they were so far away that these strangers couldn't hope to reach them. Yusef walked on ledges, teetering from side to side. Slen smoked. And Kidan hung back, talking about her failed murder attempt on Tamol Ajtaf, a ray of pleasure radiating through her whenever she earned a smile from Slen. They were as rare as diamonds.

"Slen, catch me if I fall!" Yusef shouted, and nearly did. Slen swore under her breath and moved quickly, reaching out a hand.

Kidan walked to the grass and sat, watching the stars. A night breeze washed over her, carrying the scent of sweet flowers. She exhaled. This feeling...she wanted to bottle it and drink from it forever. It was more fragile than anything she'd cupped in her hands.

"Solve a problem for me. Who's more beautiful, Andromeda or Resus?" Yusef asked, collapsing by her side. Slen sat on her other side.

"Andromeda," Kidan said, smiling.

"See?" Yusef winked at Slen.

"Don't do that." Slen drew her large jacket around herself, looking unsettled, voice unusually husky.

Kidan caught a thread of something there, too faint to pinpoint exactly what. She cast her attention to her bare wrist. Her body buzzed. These people she'd met at this haunting university, had they truly been the cure? All this time? Her mind raced, calmed, and burst with unsaid words and feelings. She needed her fingers to translate it all.

On the grass, Kidan traced a shape she'd long thought impossible. The last time she drew it was a week before her and her sister's eighteenth birthday. June always liked to celebrate things early, to take the pressure off the actual day. Neither of them was allowed to invite friends over, so they celebrated alone, always gifting each other five presents to make it look like a real crowd. A party.

"To the saddest sisters in the world," Kidan would say, grinning.

June would beam back. "Truly pathetic."

It was the only night in the year June didn't have her night terrors. Kidan would stay up till dawn, watching her sleep peacefully, drawing this exact shape.

A slow, shaking circle.

Joy.

Their bubble of delirium and controlled chaos collapsed on Saturday morning. They were at their new favorite place, East Corner Coffee, waiting for Slen's order and discussing Demasus's war campaign as it related to Concordium.

Slen and Kidan had annotated seven classics and referenced the possible interpretations. They'd expected Yusef to crack from the workload, but surprisingly he pushed on, and he was at the coffee shop that morning before Kidan and Slen, brimming with new insights, his third coffee of the day already in hand.

"If this is what it takes to acquire focus, maybe we should host murders every month." Slen watched Yusef's focused state with an unusually heated gaze.

"God, you're sick." His brown eyes shone. "Come to my studio later?"

"No."

He grinned. "I won't talk. You'll just watch me annotate stuff."

Slen opened her mouth to refuse but hesitated, seeming to consider the invitation. He grinned wider. Kidan shook her head, hiding a smile.

A café worker walked over and set down a coffee in front of Slen, and when Slen grabbed the cup to drink from it, she felt a note taped to the side. She stiffened. Her flat eyes scanned the crowd at once.

Kidan noticed, alert. "What's wrong?"

Slen held out the note.

> ## What if your own blood fell out of a tower? —
> ## Ramyn's sister

Yusef pushed aside his books, leaning over to read. "Ramyn's sister?"

Slen got up from the table and threw out the coffee like it was poison. "Ramyn didn't have a sister. Someone's messing with me."

"Is it the 13th?" Yusef's complexion yellowed.

"Probably," Slen said darkly.

"What do we do?"

"Nothing. They want us to make a mistake. We just attend all classes, and pass. If they believe we're on our way to graduating, they won't hurt us. They need heirs, remember."

Slen's words were reassuring, but her eyes translated differently. Kidan saw the shields return to them, a guardedness that had briefly dissipated but was now on high alert, and no one was exempt from suspicion.

Slen didn't join them for their afternoon session. Kidan worried her bottom lip, listening to Yusef share his findings on the Nefrasi but thinking about how, if the 13th got to Slen now, Kidan's path to June would be ruined.

"Here's what worries me." Yusef rubbed at his temple. "This Nefrasi group creates the 13th to, what, take over Uxlay? That means they're not part of our twelve houses. They can't enter Uxlay land without being detected. So we can assume they're rogue houses."

In her East Africa and the Undead class, Kidan researched the Separation of the Eighty Acti Families and their different factions. Only twelve houses had chosen to join the institution of Uxlay, founded by the Adanes and Farises. But sixty-seven houses existed outside those tall gates, and none of them practiced the Last Sage's teachings. One house had gone extinct.

Yusef shivered. "If that's the case, I've heard stories about how they feed on their actis."

Kidan swallowed. She prayed June hadn't gotten caught up with them.

A loud, heated argument traveled from the courtyard. Through the open window of the library, Kidan and Yusef could see Slen's brother shouting at her. He was visibly upset, and they could hear him using colorful words. Slen remained quiet, dwarfed under his tall figure. He slammed her against the nearest pillar.

"What the hell?" Yusef was already rushing through the door. Kidan was close on his tail.

When they reached the evenly cut grass, they heard his pleas.

"Make this right. Tell them what you know."

Slen met her brother's gaze, calm as a silent storm. "I can't."

Her brother gaped, fists forming. Yusef and Kidan sensed his fury and stepped between them. The look he directed at Slen was so heartbreaking, Kidan's own chest ached. It was a familial break she knew all too well. She snuck a glance at Slen, who focused on the grass.

After her brother left, they stood in the winter cold, dazed.

"What was that about?" Kidan asked.

Slen's brother had received a letter of his own.

Your sister knows who killed Ramyn Ajtaf.

Kidan's world tilted just after it had found its balance. She scrunched up the letter into a tight ball. The 13th were making their threats. Soon, they'd act on them.

"What do we do?" Yusef whispered.

Slen appeared lost, so Kidan straightened and said, "I'll deal with it."

His face eased into relief, and Slen gave her a small nod of acknowledgment. Kidan found new strength in their trust, a power she'd wield to defeat all who threatened them.

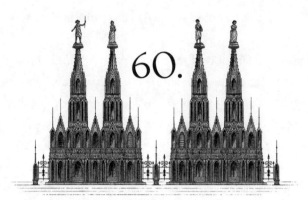

60.

ON THE NIGHT OF THE LONG-AWAITED YOUTH ART EXHIBITION, they appeared in their most expensive outfits. Slen wore a dark pantsuit and a matching set of gloves. Kidan opted for a low-cut dress in forest green, its patterned bursts of flames sending it ablaze. Yusef chose an extravagant suit studded with diamonds at its cuffs and along its collar. GK was more modest, handsome in a simple suit with his signature finger bone chain. That he'd come to support Yusef made Kidan smile.

Yusef's art inside the esteemed Umil Gallery was a collection of fragile humanity captured in the lens of expressive charcoal. His chosen smudge style created the effect of a whirlwind of darkness, a theme carried through each drawing.

His last and most important piece was veiled in the corner, awaiting eleven o'clock. Champagne buzzing on their tongues, they browsed together. Even Slen, who complained about Yusef wasting time during their study sessions, examined each piece. Not surprisingly, there was a drawing of Slen, with a streak of white running through her eyes. But there was another one, a boy covering his face with his arm as if he was weeping and a smattering of daylilies floating behind him.

GK studied it for a long time. Kidan walked over to him.

His attention lingered on the flowers. "He creates such beautiful work."

"He does."

"How are your studies?" he asked.

"Not as fun without you," she admitted.

"I miss your voices. I didn't realize how loud you all were. It's too quiet again."

Her chest ached. No one knew about loneliness more than Kidan and yet . . . how could they include him in their lives right now? He was safer without them.

GK's simmering eyes pulled at her. She clenched her fists to stop herself from inviting him to their next hangout. Slen joined her, warning in her eyes.

"It's time," she said.

The crowd gathered for the final portrait reveal. Yusef stepped forward to stunning applause, beaming.

"Thank you all for coming." Yusef played with his sigil pin. "It's an honor to exhibit in the same place my father did, and his father before him. Legacy is a funny thing. You have no interest in it until it's about to be taken from you. This year, I found out just how much the Umil Art Museum means to me. I want to pay tribute to the man who started it all."

After another booming round of applause, Yusef grabbed the string and unveiled the picture.

The audience gasped. Slen choked on her drink. Kidan's champagne glass broke in her hands.

That wasn't Omar Umil. It was Rufeal's *Woman in Blue*, damning and beautiful as ever, staring right into their souls. She was uncleaned, her creator's blood still staining her chest and neck. Kidan's stomach drowned to the depths of hell.

"Shit," Slen cursed.

"Fuck," Kidan amended.

Yusef remained petrified, staring at the portrait.

"This wasn't part of his collection." GK frowned. "What made him change it?"

The crowd waited for a response, but Yusef could only stare. Sweat shone on his brown forehead, and his lips parted and shut, a fish out of water.

"He's going to crack," Slen whispered.

Kidan backed away, searching for an escape. There was no fire alarm to pull, no sprinklers above since water would damage the works. Fire could only be extinguished by sealing off rooms one by one.

Kidan swore again, this time under her breath.

Think. *Think.*

"I'm going to faint," she whispered to Slen. "Get Yusef."

"What?" Slen asked under her breath.

Kidan threw her hands up and dropped in the most dramatic fashion into the closest pair of arms. The startled man, bless him, caught her. GK was by Kidan's side as the crowd turned to look, eyes concerned.

"Give her space. Move."

Kidan lay on the floor and spotted Slen grabbing Yusef's hand. They slipped into a storage room.

Kidan got to her feet shakily. "I just need some air."

"I'll come with you—" GK started.

"No! I mean, I'm fine. I'm just a little warm."

She walked away from his hurt expression and followed her friends. Yusef was no longer at a loss for words. He was furious, shaking, and looking directly at Kidan. For a second, she tensed up, confused.

The portrait.

"No," she said quickly. "It wasn't me."

"You told me you got rid of it." That came from Slen, gaze calculating.

Kidan thought this room was sealed off, because there was no air in her lungs. The look in their eyes was paralyzing, both familiar and made of the hardest of stones. They'd singled her out and made her nightmares true. How could she explain she only kept the artwork to . . . what? Why *had* she kept it? She wished she could go back and cut off her own hands.

"It wasn't me," she pleaded. "I would never do that."

Yusef turned away as if he couldn't bear looking at her. Slen didn't appear to believe her either.

Slen faced Yusef. "You need to go back out there."

"No way."

"You need to talk about why you chose it. Some people have already recognized it as Rufeal's work. Get out there and explain why you chose to finish his work for him."

Yusef shook his head wildly. Slen grabbed his face, and he froze.

"You can and will do this, Yusef, or I swear I'll kill you myself."

"I'll help," Kidan said.

Slen put up a hand. "No. I think we should all keep our distance from one another. Being together all the time isn't smart."

It sounded logical, but the thread hidden in the seams was plain: distrust.

With Slen's guidance, Yusef managed to go back out. He wove a tale of tragedy for the young artist gone too quickly and spoke about choosing Rufeal's last piece to preserve an artist, to achieve immortality for the mortal. The crowd loved it, but Kidan was on edge, screening each face as a potential enemy.

Were they here, watching them all? Laughing at them? The back of her neck prickled and she whirled around, but there was no clear threat she could identify among the mass of people.

61.

KIDAN TORE HER ROOM APART, SEARCHING FOR THE PORTRAIT BEHIND her vanity. It wasn't there, of course, and neither was Ramyn's scarf. Her drawers were left in a mess, clothes spilling out and spreading all over the floor. Mama Anoet's butterfly bracelet fell out. She lifted it onto her palm gently and cracked open the creature to find the pill inside.

Holding it now was a relief, her old purpose grounding her.

"What's wrong?" Susenyos was by the door.

Kidan hid the bracelet quickly and stood to face him. "Did you take the portrait from my room?"

Her voice grated with desperation, eager to name Susenyos as culprit and have this mania end.

"Are you the one threatening us?" she continued.

"Us?"

"Slen and now Yusef." Kidan paced the small space, wringing her fingers. "Ramyn's scarf is gone too."

Susenyos must have taken pity on her, because he said, "Who was present for Slen's and Yusef's crimes?"

Kidan blinked, stunned that in her terror she'd missed an obvious clue.

Titus Levigne. He'd killed Ramyn, and after Yusef murdered Rufeal, Slen had him clean the body up. She'd dismissed him because he was dead. But dead didn't mean he couldn't have reached the living. Had he told someone? Of course. He must have.

Kidan threw her golden bedside lamp against the wall, shattering it.

"That was from Morocco. A lovely elderly woman gave it to me." Susenyos stared wistfully. "I very much liked it."

"It's the 13th or the Nefrasi again." Kidan continued pacing. "What the hell do they want with us?"

"Your attention, I presume. To scare you."

She gripped her vanity chair and tried to calm her breathing. She stared at a point on the floor, drawing the shapes she'd grown attached to.

"But that's not what's got you ruining my treasures, is it?"

After a long moment, she spoke, voice scratching. "Slen and Yusef think I'm doing this. Why did I keep that portrait?"

"Should I tell you the answer?"

She glared at his condescending tone. "No."

He smiled. "It's quite obvious, little bird. You wanted a reminder of their wrongness so you could tolerate your own."

He left his position and threw a longing look at the shattered pieces.

"Of course, you still think them perfect. Little did you know you acquired them broken."

"They're not monsters." Her jaw hardened, although her voice shook. "They were victims, confused, and had no other choice—"

"You were a victim, confused, had no other choice." His voice echoed back, full of intent.

Her heart pumped painfully at the words. Kidan had been a victim. Even though she'd never allowed herself to claim it. Victims deserved compassion and understanding. Assailants were discarded, severed like infection from the flesh of the world. Her rib cage expanded as uncontrollable tears pricked her eyes. What was wrong with her? Why was she always crying now?

Startled by her reaction, Susenyos reached forward, tracing the tracks on her cheek. His swift change to tenderness made her spine tremble. His thumb tried to wipe the tears, but she turned her chin from him. It was too much. The shadow of his hand hovered, then fell slowly.

"They've done unspeakable things, yet you care for them," he continued, calm as soft rain. "Forgive them and forgive yourself."

She couldn't bring herself to look up. "I know you told Yusef about Rufeal and the 13th. Led him..."

"To kill. Yes."

She jerked up, eyes blown wide. "Why?"

He regarded her for a long time, coal eyes swirling. "To teach you."

I can teach you a thousand different ways of loving yourself.

He had led Yusef to kill...for her. Horror choked her words.

"What are you talking about?"

"To show you that if you love them as they are, for their natural wickedness, you can love yourself for yours."

"What I did and what they did are not the same. They will never be the same. I *killed* the only mother I ever had." Her voice broke, almost gutted from somewhere deep in her soul, and it would leave a scar.

He didn't waver, refused to let her win. "To protect, Kidan. You kill to protect. You even think removing yourself from this world will protect everyone. Your death will not end the violence of this earth. It will only hurt those that care about you."

Kidan shook her head wildly. Unable to speak. But something in his black eyes lulled her to calm down, understand. She was reflected in his gaze, not as she was but perhaps as she could become. In those dark pupils, her form was edged with eternal flames like a goddess of death.

He stepped closer and threaded long fingers through her braids, his head bowing. Kidan tensed when he grazed her ear. His touch both quieted her nerves and sparked them with electricity. She bunched her fists, stopping herself from seizing his shirt.

"The world loves to punish girls who dream in the dark. I plan to worship them."

The words poured into her like forbidden water, making her shiver. The shackled beast inside her hummed back traitorously.

Her heart seized. She relied on her finger to tap out a symbol against her thigh, but it hovered, stuck. Every time she pushed it forward, it froze. There was no symbol to describe exactly what he made her feel. He must have sensed her hestitation, because his gaze flicked to her straining fingers. Gently, he took them, relaxing the stiffness.

He brought them to his soft mouth. Kidan watched. The shadows of her room shifted, cloaking him as part of the unrelenting darkness. After all the things she had done to him, he kept coming back. She'd shown him no good part of her, no forgiving part of her. Yet he bore her hatred, her onslaughts, her anger, her cruelty. Perhaps he was the only one in this world who could survive those parts of her and always...stay.

For a moment, while under his lips, her fingers knew what to do. They stretched toward his cheek, almost tender, feeling the smooth skin. Surprise lit small in his eyes, but he didn't pull away. She marked him with her last finger, drawing a new shape under his jaw. A loop with three cutting lines. It made her brows furrow. She'd never seen this symbol yet knew it somehow. Perhaps from a dream.

A slam from somewhere in the house made her jump back. She rested a hand on her chest, pulse skyrocketing. He moved to lean against her window-sill, an amused lilt to his lips. Moonlight cast silver on his near-obsidian skin. She tried not to notice how his arms corded with muscle as he crossed them, or how the fabric of his shirt drifted and exposed his dark stomach. They'd felt deliciously strong under her palms in that lounge. Her throat became dry and her room filled with the smell of...eucalyptus and rose oil. A curl of steam coiled along her neck, making her so incredibly hot that she had the urge to take off her clothes. Maybe his clothes.

She swallowed thickly. Frowned a little. She hadn't enjoyed him enough during Cossia Day. A day of dizzying freedom she couldn't help but miss.

"You're staring, little bird."

Kidan's cheeks caught fire and she forced her gaze away.

His laughter rumbled low in his throat. "You seem tense. I can help you relax if you'd like. All you have to do is ask."

God.

"Perhaps a bath?" he continued, lips trying not to tug upward. "Eucalyptus and rose oil?"

She jerked her head up, horrified and furious. "What did you say?"

The illusion of the steam thickened, and he wove his fingers through it, curious eyes fixed on her. "Interesting. It appears that pain in the observatory isn't the only thing we can share in this house."

She knew the house heightened emotions, tortured her with memories of

Mama Anoet and June. But this? Exposing her thoughts about him? This was just mortifying.

She willed her mind to focus. To think of the portrait and scarf. The steam cleared gradually, then all at once disappeared.

He arched a brow.

"If you want to help, tell me how to make Slen and Yusef understand," she said seriously.

He sighed, but spoke nonetheless. "I had a friend once, much like your little group. We met in our childhood—a loudmouthed servant and a prince. You can infer who was who. He insulted me, can't quite remember what it was, and I wanted him flogged. But far more than that, I wanted him to serve me whenever I pleased."

"Lovely to hear you were a bastard from a young age."

His lips stretched. "No, what was lovely was how he fed me fruit, clothed me, and sang for me all while carrying hatred in his eyes."

"Didn't you say you were friends?"

"Patience. All great friends start off as adversaries. On my fifteenth birthday, raiders attacked the outskirts of the town I'd been given to govern. They killed his sister and destroyed my image before my father, and for the very first time, we were of the same mind. I bestowed upon him regal armor, and we went after the raiders in a mad pursuit. We found them, of course, and massacred them. There's nothing like being human and killing something more powerful and ancient than yourself."

A shudder climbed up her spine.

"Feasting on violence made us friends. To this day, no one has understood my bloodthirst quite like him. First as human boys, then as young dranaic men."

Of course. If the boy was his servant, he was in his court, and Susenyos had forced all of them to become vampires.

"If he was turned too, where is your destructive other half now?" she asked.

He wore an emotion she couldn't read. Nostalgia, perhaps.

"We parted over a broken promise. I chose this house, your family."

"My family is dead." She didn't mean it to sound crude, but it was. "You have nothing left to stay here for. You asked in your rule that I never ask you to leave this place. There's something else you're staying here for. Something you don't want to tell me."

He gave her a slow, pleased smile. "He would have liked you. Same distrusting nature. To answer your first question about making Slen and Yusef understand, get rid of your friends. You've already used them for their value, but now they're limiting you. They'll eventually become brokenhearted and sour. Fed with your secrets, they'll become the deadliest of enemies."

It sounded like he spoke from experience. Always sharing pieces of his story but never enough.

She shook her head. "That day you stopped me from seeing what happened to your court. You were being tortured. It was awful.... Who did that to you? Did they escape?"

His expression darkened, crossed arms tightening. The shift of his mood came both slowly and all at once, but she didn't budge. He'd said her family found him on the run.

"Tell me," she insisted, stepping closer. "What are you running from?"

His shoulders straightened. "Nothing."

"Fine." Her eyes fell to the floor. "I think I know, anyway."

"What do you know?"

"GK said Iniko was forced to abandon those she loved, following orders. She calls you her leader and only follows your command. You abandoned your court, didn't you? That's how you escaped whatever it was that trapped you."

Susenyos turned to the window, rubbing his jaw. "What if I did? Do you only want to judge me further?"

"I'm not judging."

He looked back and shook his head at whatever he saw on her face. "Your eyes say different."

Kidan bit the inside of her cheek. She didn't want to be right. He'd made his court immortals because he couldn't bear losing them. Then he left them to come and hide in an impenetrable place?

"What?" he said suddenly, making her startle. "Don't fall quiet now. You always have plenty to say."

"What do you want me to say?" Her eyes blazed. "I'd never abandon my friends."

"No, you'd rather die for them. Do you think that absolves you?" His tone was scalding. "Let me ask you something. What is true absolution? Living with

335

what you've done, feeling the pain of your victims on your knees in a cold room, or ending yourself so you can escape your mistakes?"

"I..."

He bled so raw, more vulnerable than ever. They both knew he hadn't meant to share this much.

She swam in the blackness of his eyes, rippling in so many secrets.

"You're punishing yourself too, aren't you?" she whispered. "You regret what you did to them."

He froze like he'd been struck. "I don't need to punish myself. I've done nothing wrong."

Clipped tone and words that told her the exact opposite. She stepped closer, and he sucked in a cautious breath. "Years, Susenyos. You've spent years trying to conquer your pain and master this house. You keep failing because you're punishing yourself."

His jaw moved like he was facing Titus again, touching the hidden nail on the roof of his mouth.

"I didn't see it until now." Her voice threaded carefully. "But it's all over this house. That key you always wear around your neck, the artifacts you visit and piece together each day, the observatory where you fight them off. You miss them, Yos, and it's killing you."

A slight crease formed between his brows. She was close. Closer than ever to whatever he hid from her.

"If they're alive and well, why won't you go to them?"

Susenyos's muscles shifted in his shoulders, fists clenching and unclenching. She tensed, preparing for his outburst.

"Look what she did to you." His soft tone tore at her. "Look what family did to you, yet you ask me to go searching for them."

Kidan's shield vanished like a lamp caught in the wind.

"The more you grow your circle, the wider the areas the weapons come from," he whispered. "Trust me, Kidan. I've felt their attacks. You don't want such a thing."

When she said nothing, he studied the floor with a look of loss, then left. She threw herself on the bed and shut her eyes. The pressure behind them was building to a staggering amount. His words made her shiver. The idea of living alone for years...She couldn't bear it. Never again. Slen's and Yusef's faces flashed before her. Distant and accusing.

She reached into her pocket and put on the bracelet. The pressure eased and faded. *She* chose the length of her life, and if she still wanted, there was a way out. She reached for her earbuds and escaped into June's videos. But she didn't hear the bubbly tone of June's stories; instead the dark one answered.

Kill all evil. Kill them all.

Kidan yanked the earbuds free and threw them across the room. She curled in on herself and rocked. When would this end?

62.

GK INVITED KIDAN ON A WALK THREE DAYS INTO HER SECLUSION from the others. They'd stopped their morning walks after GK had dropped out, and Kidan needed to keep her distance still. But she knew seeing his face would lift this fog of darkness choking her. GK's familiar stance and his black clothes, closely cropped hair, and gentle brown eyes poured some light into her day.

They wound their way through the rolling plains on the edge of campus and to the graveyard. It felt like years had passed since they'd first met here. She'd been so preoccupied with her murderous friends, GK had fallen behind. She'd missed his serene company.

He hiked his bag higher and unlocked a crypt.

"You have a key?" Her voice echoed in the empty chamber as they entered.

"I practice readings alone sometimes."

"Is that what you want to do?" The hair on her arms stood at the chill. "You know I'm not interested."

He cleared the dust in the middle of the room, set his bag down in a corner, unhooked his chain, and placed it in the middle.

"Not you." His words tensed. "The bones have been rattling near each of them."

Kidan walked to him quickly, crouching as well. "Are they in danger?"

He regarded her with a look she couldn't decipher. "You're worried."

"Of course I am."

"You weren't this worried about yourself."

"Don't worry about me. Just see if you'll all be fine."

GK only stared at her, still not touching the scattered bones, as if trying to figure something out.

"What?" She frowned. "Hurry."

"Get my other chain. It's in my bag."

She rushed to open the bag and pulled out a scarf, some books, and a set of the crypt keys, but there was no chain. She returned his things and searched in a different area. Then her fingers froze. This scarf was the standard Uxlay red scarf with the lion crest. She'd never seen GK wear one. She turned it over, and ice spread over her. There in the corner was a spot a shade darker than the rest of the fabric. Like wine had spilled on it. She brought it to her nose. Sweet peach perfume engulfed her senses.

"GK." Kidan's pulse quickened. "What is this?"

"That's Ramyn's scarf."

He got to his feet, watching her with stony eyes.

"What?" she whispered.

"I found it in your room. Along with Rufeal Makary's portrait."

The revulsion in his tone made Kidan stagger back, step onto the keys, and almost lose her balance.

No. It wasn't possible.

"How could you all live with yourselves?" His words punctured knives into her lungs, and she couldn't breathe. *No.*

No.

He kept approaching, cornering her against the wall. "Come with me right now and confess."

"GK…"

"How could you, Kidan? Your own mother?" She crouched as he loomed over and reached for her. "Why would you do this to yourself—"

"Stop!" she shouted with every fiber of her being, squeezing her eyes shut. The yell boomed in the tiny space with a force that cracked her own bones.

GK didn't touch her.

Slowly, she opened her eyes. His hand remained outstretched, fingers inches from her.

Kidan slid to the side, grabbed the bag and keys, and bolted to the entrance.

GK didn't move. Even as she got ready to lock him inside, he remained where he was, warm eyes swirling with emotion.

He whispered, softly and fearfully, a word in Aarac. A word that sounded like both a curse and a prayer. He kept repeating it under his breath, eyes locked on her as if she was a demon he could vanquish.

Her heart broke.

"Just...just sit here and wait, *please*."

GK's eyes stretched more as he sank down to his knees unsteadily, then sat.

Kidan's stomach turned at the look of horror on his face. He was listening to her, and she was grateful.

"I'll be back. Just stay. Please."

He stared at the damp floor, not speaking.

She needed time to understand how GK was involved. How to make him understand all this before he ruined everything.

She ran all the way into the center of campus, stumbling over protruding rocks and skinning her palms. The Philosophy Tower formed a dark, ominous shape in the setting sun. Rain dropped on her forehead, and Kidan touched it. It was blood. She shook her head. No, it was rain.

Concentrate.

She fumbled for her phone, calling an emergency meeting with Slen and Yusef, without saying why. She needed to tell them in person.

Waiting for them up in their designated study room, Kidan paced. The keys in her hand trembled and jingled. She went to put them in GK's bag when a small book—*Traditional Myths of Abyssi*—tumbled out.

She picked it up. He must have taken it from her room as well. Hurriedly, she thumbed through it once again. He had marked different entries and lines. She was not entirely sure what she was looking for—until the name "Nefari" caught her eye. Her heart thundered against her ribs as she read.

The "Nefari," a term used in the nineteenth century, was popularized by the local villagers of Gojam. The villagers spoke of a monster that wore silver metal, bared its teeth like a wolf, and collected cursed objects. There were three forewarnings before the monster would rise. They would be rituals having to do with water, sun, and death. But most claim the creature wasn't a monster at all, but a cursed king with a thirst for blood.

Kidan wasn't interested in the myth as much as in the drawing depicting a Nefari: It was definitely a vampire, with multiple silver hoops and rings along its body. She stared at it for a long time, unsure why it was important. Body decoration with silver was banned at Uxlay, but it seemed fitting that rogues would adorn their bodies with it. She traced the outline of the monster baring its foul tongue. It was long, and something like a pearl piercing shone on it.

Kidan had seen only one person who had defied the silver law successfully by adopting this same tradition. In fact, he had saved her life with it, spitting it from his mouth like a bullet and killing Titus Levigne.

Her chest squeezed, hurt and anger whirling inside her. The Nefari. Local villagers of Gojam.

Susenyos Sagad. Once an emperor ruling Gojam Province.

She shut the book with a snap.

She'd been foolish to trust him, to bend her morals and let him further into her world. She'd asked him point-blank who the Nefrasi were, the same Nefrasi who had something to do with June, and he'd lied.

Why keep playing games? She'd thought they were past the deceit and betrayals. The sound of her heartbeat echoed close to her ears, slow and bleeding. Maybe she'd been foolish to think there could ever be peace between them. Her fingers curled at her sides.

Quickly, Kidan called Slen, told her what she had discovered about GK, and asked her to keep him company until she returned. She left the key to the crypt inside the room and rushed home, planning to drain every drop of secret from Susenyos.

63.

HER PLAN HAD BEEN TO SEDUCE HIM, TO MAKE HIM CONFESS GENTLY and slowly, and it may have worked. He'd said it pulled the truth out of him better than torture.

But when she laid eyes on his relaxed back on the study couch, comfortable, handsome, with an air of triumph that he'd completely led her along blindly, desire abandoned her at once.

Fire caught on the walls of the study, smoldering with her anger. It was just the two of them. Etete was away for the night.

Kidan brought with her the gun from Omar Umil's basement. Ordinary bullets did nothing to dranaics. Grinding down impala horn and burning it, on the other hand, was entirely different. Inspired by her *Weapons of the Dark* book, she'd coated the bullets with the ash. The warriors of the Last Sage had used tar to smear horn ash onto their arrows before shooting them into dranaic hearts.

She fought her hands moving toward the gun secured in the back of her pants. This wasn't what she wanted. She wanted to speak to him. Truly listen and understand.

But the room fed on her rage, and rage saw no reason. She gritted her teeth as fire ate at her in violent bites until her fingers pulled it out halfway. Her other hand bent the spine of the *Myths* book.

"I can feel the room being drenched with your anger," he called out, absorbed in one of his letters. "What have I done now?"

She said nothing.

He kept writing, amused. "Do you want to see what I'm working on? I apologize that my reply to your letter is delayed. You didn't include your name. It took me a while to figure out it was you."

Her forehead creased before her mouth parted. He'd found the letter she hid under his scrolls? Read her tortured, revealing words? Her face heated at once, and she had the massive urge to disappear. But she had a book and a gun in her hands, anchoring her in place. She tightened her grip and threw the book of myths at his back. He snatched it from the air with ease, disposing of her outburst like he would an annoying fly.

"The Nefari, a name created by villagers of Gojam in Ethiopia. Your country." Kidan's teeth ground.

"Technically, it's your country as well."

"You're part of the Nefrasi."

Fire engulfed the ceiling, roaring above her.

Susenyos set down his pen and finally turned to face her. A grin spread across his lips as if he'd finally been caught. "Forgive me, but I never thought you'd discover the truth. Allow me a moment to be proud, will you?"

If he hadn't smiled, she could have contained her anger. She could have walked away and returned calm. But he was enjoying himself.

Smiling at her. Smiling about lying to her.

Her vision went red. Kidan drew her gun out all the way and pointed it forward.

Susenyos's smile broke like glass. Caution brimmed in his eyes at once as he sensed her struggle on the trigger, her shaking form, the fire above. "Don't give in to your rage, little bird."

June had disappeared from her mind the past few days, too angry at Kidan's choice to keep working alongside Susenyos, but now her voice slithered in.

Now.

Kidan's arm jolted as she fired, the force making her stumble and almost drop the gun.

The bullet narrowed her fury into a single point and exploded it out of her in delicious waves. She wanted to do it again and again. Susenyos shouted a string of curse words, dancing between English and Amharic. He gripped his shoulder where the bullet had pierced it, hissing, face caught between pain and pure shock. She could see on his face that he knew something from an impala horn was now inside his body.

More. The room crackled like cinders in her ear. *More. He took me.*

She walked to him, squatted low, found his black eyes, and pressed the gun against his kneecap.

His head eased forward. "You're losing yourself. It's the house heightening your emotions. Fight your rage, Kidan. *Now.*"

"You think I want to do this?" Her voice became a tortured, bleeding thing. "Why did you lie to me?"

His chest rose and fell rapidly, his gaze focused on her anguished expression. "Give me the gun and I'll tell you."

He reached for it, but she lurched back. He bared his foul canine teeth, almost catching her neck, but was weakened from the bullet. She sprang to her feet and took several steps back.

Something shot out of his mouth, needle-fast and coming right at her. Kidan dodged the silver nail by sheer luck. It nicked her ear and punched through the window, leaving the house with a tiny hole.

Her eyes split wide. Had he actually tried to kill her?

"You missed," she snarled. "Try to remove the bullet, and I'll shoot again."

"Fine," he spat.

It had finally worked. There was no trace of amusement in his eyes.

She sat down on the opposite couch, gun resting on the arm of it.

"Now, let's try this again. Where the hell is my sister?"

He glared. "Have I not answered that exhausting question? I don't know—"

Her fingers started to tighten on the trigger. "Stop *lying* to me."

"I can't tell you!" he shouted. "That would be endangering the house, and it will cost me—"

"Don't worry about this house taking your immortality, because *I* will kill you, Susenyos. *Talk.*"

His gaze drifted to the gun and back to her face. He didn't find any hesitation.

He glowered his hatred. "If you cost me another room, *I* will kill *you.*"

She raised her gun higher, defiant. He tipped his chin toward the ceiling, shaking his head.

"I should have taken that impala horn from you at Cossia Day."

"Who are the Nefrasi?"

His mouth twisted. "You still haven't made that connection? They're my court."

Kidan gaped a little. *The court he forced to transition into vampires and then abandoned?*

"We survived, thrived, across Africa and beyond because of me. We were liberated in a way you could not possibly imagine, and drunk on it. I named us Nefrasi, one born of a silver monster."

Her teeth rang. "I should cut out that black tongue of yours."

His laughter sounded half dead. "I have no more reason to lie. You are aware that if the ash reaches my heart, I die. Let me take the bullet out."

He tried to move, but she refused. "No. I suggest you speak faster."

He swallowed, lips parting and closing as if he were starving. Maybe she did shoot him too close to the heart, unknowingly quickening the process of ash finding that vital organ.

He pointed to the book he'd dropped. "How good are you with your myths?"

She didn't answer.

"Weha, Tsay, and Mot. The Three Binds. The Nefrasi's goal was to shatter it. We wanted to be unleashed into our most primal selves. Drink from anyone we liked, harness the power of the sun, and sire our own army without sacrificing our lives."

"You're telling me you chased myths like children, trying to break a thousand-year-old curse?"

"When you have immortality, there's time for everything."

"What does this have to do with June or me?"

"My self-consumed Roana, this is about me. *My* story. You're the unaccounted character that wandered into my play and will eventually be killed off if you're not careful."

She fired at the tall lamp by his head, making his eyes widen. He clutched his ringing ear, howling.

"*This* character gets impatient when she doesn't get what she wants."

"It's your family that's important! Not you or June! Far too intelligent and curious for their own good, your damned parents left a legacy you still fail to see the power of."

She thought for a moment. What legacy did they reign over?

Then she laughed. "The Axum project. The fucking archaeology site?"

Susenyos lowered his hand, rueful. "Fourteen years ago, a rumor emerged that a portion of the Last Sage's old settlement had been discovered. Part of the untouched and preserved civilization from his earliest existence, along with treasures he used in the creation of the Three Binds."

"A rumor," she repeated.

His next words dripped with arrogance even as he sweated along his temple like a dying man. "Except it wasn't. I discovered it alongside your parents. They entrusted me to protect it. I have one of the prophesied artifacts that'll break the Second Bind."

Kidan leaned forward, heart drumming. She hung on every word, the golden truth finally here.

"Go on."

"That very night, an attack was made on this house, killing your family. I remained to protect the artifact."

Kidan pressed the side of the gun against her head. The warm touch accelerated her pulse.

"That's why they left the house to you," she said to herself. "The house law. All this time..." Her eyes creased with the betrayal of it all. "And no one told me."

"I've killed and tortured thousands in protection of the artifact. Lying to you, Kidan, doesn't remotely brush against the horrors I've committed, so stop giving me that wounded look."

She blinked, looking away. The Sun Bind had significantly weakened dranaics. But if this was their weakened state, Kidan couldn't imagine the full extent of their power.

"You're telling me that somewhere in this house lies one of the Last Sage's artifacts?"

"Yes."

"Have you tried it?"

Even in his debilitated state, he gave her a shrewd smile. "It doesn't work like that."

"Give it to me."

He rolled his head back as if it was too heavy to carry. "Come, now. You don't think it's that easy, do you? We're talking about an object that can shift the gravity of our world."

She looked him over. "I assume you don't have it on you now, or you wouldn't be held at gunpoint."

"Quite the poor judgment on my part, believing I didn't need protection from you."

Kidan stood and paced. Her eyes drifted to the artifact room. Was it in there? No, he wouldn't keep it in a place so obvious. Moreover, why would her parents trust him with such power?

And then she realized... "No, you don't have it yet. You wouldn't stay here if you did...."

Susenyos remained still, but the house curtains rippled, the walls hummed, the bulb above her flickered, giving her the answer.

"They hid it in the house." Her voice rose to the ceiling with awe.

Susenyos squared his jaw. She stared with her mouth open. Her parents were geniuses.

IF SUSENYOS SAGAD ENDANGERS ADANE HOUSE, THE HOUSE SHALL
IN TURN STEAL SOMETHING OF EQUAL VALUE TO HIM.

"Adane House" referred to the Second Bind artifact. The Sun artifact.

They never gave him the artifact but nonetheless forced him to protect it. He was here to break one law that weakened him and set one that granted him terrifying strength.

"It all makes sense now. The Nefrasi want to kill you for whatever you did to them. And you want to possess the Sun artifact and hide in Uxlay, safe from harm."

All color leached from his face. "I've been running my entire life, Kidan. Don't judge me because I desire to live. There are horrors waiting in the outside world I never want to face. An immortal is in love with life. I can't bear to see the end of it. Mine or anyone else's I care about." His eyes dropped to her bracelet, simmering. "Unfortunately, not all can be saved."

Kidan touched her bracelet unconsciously. "This danger you keep mentioning. What is it?"

He sank further into his seat, eyes like black water. Haunted.

"I'm afraid you'll have to kill me."

She snarled, holding up the gun. "Tell me."

"I can't. I physically cannot speak of it." He spat. Her brows pinched in confusion. "You only need to know the Nefrasi are messengers of it. They're the beginning of the end."

A line twitched in her jaw, betraying her steely gaze. "When did you know it was your court that took June?"

The question was important.

Had he known the Nefrasi had June from the moment she set foot in this house? Had he known when he'd comforted her during her panic attack? During Cossia Day? She wanted to know which memories of theirs were tainted by his lies.

Susenyos's gaze cleared, serious.

"I thought you came to frame me for June. Then we discovered the 13th... greedy family members going to such lengths to destroy me, but it didn't make sense why they hated me so much." His lip curled. "It wasn't until Titus mentioned the Nefrasi by name at Cossia Day—when he said he'd gift you to them— that I realized who'd been playing in the shadows." He sighed as if exhausted. "I hadn't heard from my court in sixty years. I believed most were scattered or dead. Consider my surprise when you discovered June's bracelet in *my* drawer. Your foster mother mentioned *my* name. All their little signs, games, telling me they were coming, and I was blind to most of it."

He stared at the ground, expression unreadable. Kidan remembered Cossia Day, Titus's manic words as he nearly tore out her throat.

"You killed Titus because he was going to expose you."

"I killed him because he had his hands on you," he dismissed sharply. "Keeping you from discovering their existence was an added advantage."

She wanted to scream, but instead her voice came out strained. "I asked you about them, and you lied to me. Why didn't you tell me?"

"It was too late by then." His eyes shifted like the tides of a dark ocean. "I knew that sending you to them would cost you your life, and somehow I'd fallen into the habit of saving you."

"Don't say any of this is for me," she whispered, more afraid his words could be true than of anything else.

He stared at her shaking form for a long moment. His words slowed as if he spoke through a bleeding lung. "No, you're right. It wasn't for you."

She exhaled in relief. "Then why?"

"What other choice was there? The Nefrasi wanted you to seek them out and fall into their trap, become the dutiful heiress, and surrender the artifact. Spies and tricks. This is how the Nefrasi handle war. It's how they acquired the Water artifact. I can't let them acquire this one."

Kidan drew in a sharp breath. They were already in possession of an artifact. Did that mean two of the Three Binds were at risk of being broken? What would that do to Uxlay? To the rest of the world?

Fear tightened her gut. All this time, it had been some sick game, a web she had no business getting caught up in.

Kidan pressed the mouth of the gun to his forehead, a desperate thought sinking into her. "What if I give you to the Nefrasi for June?"

Susenyos stilled. "You won't."

"I won't?" Only searing pain lingered in her throat. "You don't know what I'll do for my sister, and you've made yourself so easy to be rid of. Lie after lie."

He gave an exhausted laugh, though his eyes were ice-cold. "I lied. I broke your rule. I made shallow mistakes, and your instinct is to throw me aside. To kill me. What is my crime compared to those of your murderous friends?"

She bit her lip and looked away. Unable to think. "They're ... different."

"They're human. And so deserve your *endless forgiveness!*" he shouted, and the fireplace roared to life. With the flames raging behind him and his hair coils loose, he truly became the devil she wanted him to be. Kidan staggered from the white heat, the gun nearly slipping from her grasp.

"You don't loathe my actions, Kidan. You hate my soul, the very essence of what I am. You hate that I live forever, that my damage is endless, my darkness boundless. You will always want to kill me for it, because you haven't accepted yours."

The carpet spread with a dark stain—blood, as if the house was hemorrhaging from the inside. Kidan tried to backtrack, but it was everywhere. Leeching from the walls in ugly tears. The fire climbed around the columns, and the family portrait shattered. The picture of her mother and father became engulfed.

"What's happening?" she shouted, trying to follow the cracks along the wall, her mind.

Susenyos stared at his feet with wide eyes and inhaled deeply. Exhaled. Trying to calm himself. The fire burned lower, retreating like a dragon into its cage. "You have to let me take this bullet out so I can heal. I won't be able to keep my anger at bay for long."

"Your court has June."

He closed his eyes, voice slipping in and out of strength. "And I'm trying my best to make sure they can't have you."

Kidan threw aside the gun and grabbed both sides of his face. He blinked awake, fading gaze focused on her. Startled.

"Where are the Nefrasi?" she pleaded. "Please, Yos. Just tell me."

All fire in the room extinguished, leaving only thinning smoke.

He regarded her with a defeated smile. "You're not afraid of death, are you, my saddest Roana? You have your long-awaited truth. So go and turn over your wrists to the Nefrasi, they'll slit them for you." He pressed his wet mouth to the veins of her wrist, just above her butterfly bracelet. It burned like black lightning. "I won't be the one to do it."

With those haunting words, his head slumped forward as he fell unconscious. She held him out of instinct, cradling him, then stepped away with a start.

64.

KIDAN WATCHED HER VAMPIRE SLEEP. THICK LASHES RESTED AGAINST a still face. She could only describe his deep brown skin as the clearness of water being poured.

He was so close to the gates of death, she was already imagining life without his existence. She'd find the artifact, wherever it was, and save her sister. All Kidan had to do was let him sleep, let his heart slow and beat out a final rhythm.

Yet she remained on the carpet, gun next to her, watching his weakened chest rise and fall. This felt different from the *Woman in Blue* or Ramyn's scarf. Those pieces lured her in with the shock of a horrific unexpected act. This scene of his death was predicted, even prophesied. Perhaps more than her own. And it hurt just like her own would.

It wasn't love. She didn't expect to love him. This world wouldn't survive their version of love. But there was a seed of something here, a mangled cord joining their black hearts, and Kidan couldn't quite sever it.

She traced her kissed wrist, and made sure his chest rose and fell. Her eyes drifted to the pile of papers and the pen. He'd said he was writing her a . . . letter.

Kidan stood numbly and picked it up, reading the careful, cursive writing.

My dearest Kidan,

There are many grotesque evils in this world. Trust me, I have encountered them all. Yet the most frightening of all is the one of the mind. If you can't bear the sound of your own voice, the look of your eyes, the soul of your body, I ask you to do the most difficult thing of all—wait. Wait for the next day, hour, minute, and when it comes close, wait for another. Punish time the way it punished you by promising it your life and taking it back at the last second. After all, why should it win? You make it wait, and when you're busy exacting your revenge, the change will happen in the gentlest of ways. You will find yourself, and you will know you are enough, far transformed and more alive than possible.

Yours eternally,
Susenyos

She stared at the words, vision blurry, her emotions whirling into sadness, anger, and guilt. Her fingers scrunched the edges to tear it up, break whatever horrifying connection this letter extended between them, but she hesitated. She clamped her lips together, willing the tears to retreat. There was care and tenderness in these sentences, and whether it was the beauty of his writing, or because he truly meant them, she'd never owned such a thing. Someone wanting her to live this much.

Hating herself, she folded the paper into a square and put it into her back pocket.

Just then the front door burst free from its hinges, and she jumped. She had barely blinked before Taj had her by the neck, against the wall.

"Please tell me he's not dead." Taj's chestnut eyes flashed, genuine fear tightening his features.

"He isn't. Yet."

He exhaled, loosening his grip. Iniko rushed to Susenyos's side, pushed his head back, and studied his bullet wound.

Iniko retrieved the gun, unlocked a bullet, and brought it to her lips to lick. Immediately, she spat it out, swearing.

"What?" Taj asked.

"Impala horn." Her voice was hard. "Burned to ash."

Taj blinked, facing Kidan in awe. "Where did you get it?"

"I made it."

Taj sucked in a breath. "God, I love women in the twenty-first century."

352

"She shot him. I need to drain him. Now." Iniko heaved Susenyos's limp arm over one shoulder.

With terrifying strength, she dragged him toward the basement.

"Stay here," Taj told Kidan. "I want every detail of your little chaos."

"Let me go."

He did, straightening her wrinkled top like a proud father, and leaned in to whisper.

"Once we sort this out, if you do want to choose me as your companion, I'm available. You are allowed to pick two."

Kidan ignored that. "How did you know to come?"

Taj brought out the silver nail spat from Susenyos's mouth. It glinted in the air with a mocking light.

"We call her Sofia. The fourth member of our group."

Susenyos had never intended to aim for her. He wanted to send a message.

A blood-licked silver never misses its mark.

Kidan had been bested by a bloody nail. She wanted to riot.

"So, about the companionship?" Taj continued with a grin. "I'll be free."

"You lied to me too. You're Nefrasi."

Taj's smile slipped, face crowded with shadows. "*Was* Nefrasi. Let it go, Kidan. If your sister is with them, you won't get her back. Not without losing your life."

Her eyes dropped. His words echoed Susenyos's.

A sudden sharp cramp to her gut made her double over. Taj righted her, alarmed. "What's wrong?"

She gasped, eyes wide. "I...I don't know—"

A second pain pierced her left ribs, like a bullet going through them. Taj settled her on the couch.

When Iniko called upstairs to him, he worked his jaw. "Rest. You must have injured yourself. I'll be back."

He disappeared into thin air. Kidan breathed through her insides, which were being twisted. Was this the house punishing her? It must be, because it wasn't real, and the ache was easing with each second. But the house affected her mind...Did this mean it'd started to manipulate her body too?

She wiped her forehead and looked down at her phone, which was buzzing.

There were multiple missed calls, messages about GK. *Shit.* She'd completely forgotten.

She called Slen back quickly.

"Where have you been?" Slen asked. "GK confessed to everything. He was the one who told my brother that I knew who killed Ramyn."

Slen's tone slid into a dangerous field.

Kidan shut her eyes. "I'm going to his room to search his things, see what else he has on us. Give him some water and wait for me."

There was extended silence on the other end.

"Slen?" Kidan called out. "Give him some water and wait for me."

"Yeah, sure."

Kidan hurried to the men's dormitory on campus. GK lived with a roommate who was also a Mot Zebeya disciple.

"Hey, GK forgot his books here. Can I just grab them?"

The disciple let her in and went to his corner. They both slept on the floor. No decorations on walls or picture frames on shelves. Kidan bent down and grabbed random books while scanning the single drawer. Making sure the roommate wasn't looking, she nudged open the closet, but nothing stood out. On GK's bed was the book he often carried. The first page held the insignia of the twin blades, shattered mask, and bloodied ring. Kidan traced them with curiosity. The Last Sage's lost artifacts appeared everywhere now that she knew the truth. Kidan hid the book under her sweater and left.

She sat on a bench in the courtyard and opened the book. A rush of purple flower scent hit her nostrils at once. There were prayer mantras as well as instructions and rules for a Mot Zebeya in the front of the book. She flipped to the back and saw dated entries, almost like a journal. Hating herself for intruding on his privacy, she went to the date when they all met.

September 1st
 They are loud and argue far too much. In the rare moments they don't speak, they are restless in their studies. Their fingers dance as

they read or to stretch their stiff bones, but none of them make so much noise as he. Yusef calls them pumpkin seeds, small, riotous, almond-shaped seeds he chews on often. There is no discipline to them, he doesn't consume them at breakfast or lunch or dinner. If he did, I would avoid him at those times.

I can only find blissful quiet in the monastery grounds or here in my room. It's a mistake to join this group, but the hand of death hovers over one of them.

I feel this pull to protect and save her. The finger chains have never reacted this strongly before, and it's as if an ancient voice echoes through them, telling me to keep her safe. Even to lay my life down if necessary.

Kidan Adane must live, that voice says. She must.

Kidan's chest swelled at the protective words. What did she do to deserve such kindness?

September 10th

I failed today. A life was taken before my very eyes. I saw a shadow of the man who killed Ramyn—a dark arm glinting with metal bands as he choked the poor girl. I can still feel her scream in the back of my throat. They'd warned us at Mot Zebeya Monastery that death would frighten us. It would suffocate our faith and bring us to our knees, yet we must guard against it. If I felt her loss this deeply, what of her family? I understand now why they raise us in solitude. It's too unbearable to care for souls when they are so easy to extinguish. I must remember the Last Sage's principles, practice my prayers, and remain unattached. A Mot Zebeya has no family and all family. The loss of one finger should cut as deeply as a hand.

September 12th

The professor is not a righteous man. He takes pleasure in dissecting horrible acts in the name of education. He listens to my recounting of the incident repeatedly without a flutter of emotion. He can sense my guilt, I think. Why else would he give me a personal assignment? I want to refuse, but I can't. He instructs me to find the vampire who wears metal bands and study his movements. The professor believes I can move freely between the dranaic and acti courts without suspicion. A man of faith, he says, is respected by the holy and the foul.

November 1st

I'm no closer to finding the dranaic that killed Ramyn Ajtaf. Each moment I spend with the three, I worry for their safety. But time doesn't feel alive in their presence. It is endless, their train of conversation, and easy to get lost in, to miss a joke, and send them into laughter with a simple question. It's what I expect learning a new language would feel like. It's nice to hear their joy, nicer perhaps than the quiet of this room.

Yusef appears at the crack of dawn and ushers me to the highest tower so he can draw me in first light. A personal project. I sit there, cool air fading with each drawn-out light. It's not long before he tears the drawing in front of me, frustrated when his vision doesn't capture reality. I've learned his habits for personal preservation and prepare for what's to come. He follows a particularly bad creative day with a rebellious one. He asks to go into town later that evening. We take his car and I drive, always, because he is too handsome to do so.

November 4th

I found him. The dranaic that murdered Ramyn Ajtaf. The dranaics display all their silver weeks before Cossia Day. All weapons must be registered with the Mot Zebeya Courts. I didn't recognize him at first, not as I was registering his jagged blades, but then three silver bands clattered on the desk. He always wore a trench coat, always covered his arms, until that moment.

Titus Levigne.

I followed him after my classes. He caught me at once, and I offered him a reading. He refused and warned me to stay away. But how could I? Then I noticed him meet with another girl. I'd recognize those gloved hands anywhere. Why would Slen Qaros speak with Titus? He wasn't sired to her house. I worried for her safety and started to follow her.

November 15th

Slen arrived at the School of Art and disappeared into a corner door. It was nearly half an hour before she came out. And when she did, she was holding someone up by their shoulders. They looked injured or weak, and I nearly stepped forward to help when I recognized Yusef.

His eyes were soulless. It was such a striking image compared with who I knew him as that I stood petrified. What had happened? Had Titus hurt him? But that didn't seem plausible. The two walked slowly into the elevator. I almost turned to follow them when the door opened again, and Titus appeared with a canvas bag slung over his shoulder. It didn't carry a portrait. Whatever was in that bag was shapeless, large as an animal, and not moving.

Later, I found out it was Rufeal Makary, when news broke of his animal attack.

Kidan shut her eyes, pausing from GK's words. He had caught them the night Yusef murdered Rufeal. How had Kidan not noticed? Was she so preoccupied with the others that she didn't know another one of them was suffering? She didn't want to read what he thought next but forced herself. She deserved to feel awful.

November 29th

They canceled our study plans. The three of them stayed in Kidan's house. Hiding. I studied them for signs of distress, but Slen and Kidan were calm as the ocean. They were lying, and it sickened me how well they did it.

December 20th

A day before Cossia Day, the campus emptied, many going into town with their families. I waited until the dranaics took their usual

feeding hours and crossed into Titus's room. I found the metal bands
and took them. They felt good in my hands, like I've taken a small
revenge for Ramyn.

I didn't mean to find the rest. Titus had pictures of Slen,
multiple images of the two meeting in town. Evidence about framing
her father for Ramyn's death. Then there was a hammer, sealed in
a bag with dried blood and fingerprints. A newspaper article about
Kidan's foster mother. It made no sense, these things. The mind
would do almost anything not to corrupt something good, but they
were corrupt. Here was proof.

I was wrong. Death doesn't hover above Kidan. She is the hand
of death herself. It wasn't her end my bones predicted, but those of
others.

Kidan's eyes watered, and she wiped furiously to keep reading.

December 22nd

Titus is dead. It's not unusual to hear of many dranaics dying
during Cossia Days, but this one gave me the most pleasure. Death
shouldn't bring pleasure. What is becoming of me? I should tell
the professor about what I found, but how are the others involved?
What would become of their futures?

January 1st

I came here to guard against death, but the very people closest
to me are harbingers of it. I try to make them see their wickedness in
the hopes they will confess. I spoke to Slen's brother. I left Rufeal's
portrait inside Yusef's exhibition.

Yet still I crave their friendship. I still crave to save Kidan. It's
a contradiction that robs me of sleep. But each day I stay quiet,
blood grows on my hands too. If I want them to be forgiven, maybe
I should confess too. If they burn, I'm afraid I'll burn along with
them.

That was his last entry, logged last night. Kidan cradled her head in her hands. She was guilty of many things, but torturing GK with her wickedness was too much to bear. She'd thought him saved, yet he'd drowned alongside them. Kidan lifted her head and called Slen. She picked up on the fourth ring.

There was a prolonged silence on Slen's end that made Kidan check the phone before bringing it close again.

"Slen? Hello?"

A heavy silence followed.

"Slen?" she repeated carefully. "What's wrong?"

"GK is ... dead."

Kidan's vision of the courtyard swirled, finger slackening on the phone.

"What ... what did you say?"

This time Slen's voice was unwavering. "We killed him."

65.

KIDAN POUNDED ON THE BARRED ENTRANCE TO THE CRYPT WITH one hand, the other carrying GK's journal. A frightened Yusef opened the door, face gripped with terror.

Kidan's vision tunneled, darkness swallowing everything else except the figure in the middle of the room. Blood pooled beneath GK's body, the chain of finger bones outlining his head like a crown.

Kidan stumbled and collapsed to her knees, a sob tearing out of her. She reached out to his drained cheek but couldn't touch him.

GK.

The one soul who wanted to protect them, the one soul who deserved all the happiness in this world.

Dead.

His chest wasn't rising or falling.

Breathe, *please.*

Tears flooded her eyes. Two stab wounds, one in his lower stomach and the other along his ribs, poured out dark blood in a continuous flow, fading into his black shirt. Her trembling fingers sank into them.

Her voice came out mangled and raw, almost inhuman. "Why?"

Slen crouched next to her, the scent of black coffee and rosin cutting the damp air of the crypt.

There was a bloodied knife curled in her gloved grip. Yusef had withdrawn into himself in the corner, mumbling, head in his bloodied hands.

"Why?" Kidan's voice cleaved like death. *"Why did you two do this?"*

"There was no other way." Slen held her gaze with brutal intention. In those damned eyes, Kidan's world fell apart. "I had to make sure he wouldn't call the authorities."

She offered the knife to Kidan like poisonous berries. "It's like you said. We share our crime, we share our mistakes."

Kidan didn't understand at first. They wanted her to break GK's skin, complete a third knife wound. Kidan recoiled from the blade, from them, and saw them for what they truly were.

Savages.

She was in league with people who'd cut down a friend for their own sake. There was no redemption here, no forgiveness for such an act. They were hurtling into the depths of hell.

"Take it."

In a storm of fury, Kidan seized the knife and yanked Slen to her feet. Slen's neck stretched under its sharp edge, eyes split wide.

"Kidan! What are you—"

Kidan raged with enough venom that any words of protest from Yusef died immediately. "After everything, you *still* don't understand."

She vibrated with such violent intensity that Slen's soft skin beaded with a pinprick of blood.

"You've killed us all."

Slen blinked, studying Kidan's shaking form. "He wanted to turn us in."

"And?" Kidan yelled, making her flinch. "You robbed him of finding us, of finding himself."

While Kidan's tongue was razor-sharp, her face was in complete anguish, tears coating her lashes. This kept Slen confused and still. The tear in Kidan's heart was unbearable.

Kill her.

Her body locked. The voice was stronger now, and she couldn't fight it off. The blade pushed forward.

"Kidan?" Genuine worry twisted Slen's face.

Kill her. Kidan shook her head wildly. *None of them should leave this place alive.*

Yusef's voice trembled. "Let her go, Kidan."

Kidan couldn't. Tears glided down her cheeks. Slen choked against the pressure. A thin line of blood soaked into Kidan's thumb.

361

"Stop it!" Yusef shouted.

"And you?" Kidan barked at him. "Why did you do this?"

Yusef's eyes were red, voice lost like a child's. "I . . ."

"Why shouldn't we all die here?" Kidan demanded.

He didn't dare speak. There was no answer.

Kidan shoved Slen away with disgust and sank down to the floor. GK's brown face had lost color, becoming a pallid yellow. His warm eyes would never reflect light again.

How could they?

Yusef slid down to a crouch. They stayed there, having no more to say and far too much to feel. For half an hour, maybe more, none of them spoke. They'd torn open something too horrific to explain and lost themselves. Driven by control, creativity, and revenge, they'd lost the only thing that had let them survive all these months.

Kidan had known it first, this power the three of them had, a shield made to protect them. They'd saved her life. Under protection and in defense of their actions, she'd learned not to loathe herself.

Yusef mourned without tears, eyes haunted and absently running his finger along GK's journal pages. Slen played a tune silently with her fingers.

"He didn't fight us." Yusef's voice was a frail, confused whisper. "He just stayed still. As if he always knew we would do this to him."

Kidan fought against this image of helplessness, but it was no use. It would haunt her every dream from now on. They'd murdered him when he wasn't even fighting back.

There was no saving them. No saving herself.

Kidan rose to her feet without control, grip tight on the knife. She'd do it quickly, painlessly, and be done with it.

But she couldn't take another step, an equally strong force rooting her in place. Her bones jittered like they were caught between two rotating walls. The more she pulled, the deeper the snares set in. Her entire body whimpered. She'd remain in this frozen crypt forever, neither dead nor alive, always half of something.

Please. Please, help me. No one heard her plea. Yusef and Slen remained unaware of how close she was to snapping. She wanted to warn them to run like hell, but her mouth wouldn't open.

A pathetic, desperate sound rattled from her lips.

Yusef lifted his head. "Kidan?"

It was a mistake to speak her name with so much familiarity and care. Where was this concern for GK? At once, the snares released and fury set in. She marched toward him, knife shaking.

I'm sorry. I'm sorry. I'm sorry we all have to die—

You think death will free you from this. It will burn hotter than any sun, that nothingness.

She stilled at once. They were *his* words, of all people, drifting into her from the suffocating dark.

She wavered on the spot, shutting her eyes against Yusef's confused expression. Kidan imagined Susenyos close. The shape of his body leached the savage cold from the crypt. Soft rain and burning wood lulled her into his scent. He removed her fingers one by one, gently, whispering along the shell of her ear and sending tremors down her spine.

I don't know what to do, she pleaded in her mind.

Forgive them and forgive yourself.

They killed him.

It was quiet. So quiet she was afraid he'd disappeared.

An immortal is in love with life. I can't bear to see the end of it. Mine or anyone else's I care about.

The knife clattered to the floor. Kidan gasped as if coming out of drowning water. She wiped her nose on her sleeve, the answer coming clearly to her.

"Forgive me," she whispered to GK.

Slen and Yusef lifted their heads. Kidan spoke with a hoarse voice.

"We're going to save him. He's going to become a vampire."

They stared at her like she'd gone mad. Maybe she had. But this death was unacceptable, sacrilegious. One life hadn't been taken today. All of them were fighting to live the moment he stopped breathing.

"It's too late." Slen furrowed her brows. "He's dead."

"There's more than one way to transform into a vampire." She spoke slowly.

"No." Slen straightened at once. "Death transformation? Absolutely not."

Yusef rose to his feet slowly, a tightness that could be mistaken for hope ringing in his voice.

363

"Where will you even find a vampire to give up their life? Uxlay will never let you perform a death transformation."

Kidan had already decided. "The Nefrasi. I'll find out where they are."

Stunned silence descended upon them.

Yusef finally spoke. "What are you talking about? The faction that took your sister?"

"I'll find out where they are," she repeated with force, pulling out her phone. "I don't have time to explain. We only have a few hours before we lose him."

Kidan remembered GK's lesson. He needed dranaic blood infused into his heart before it was unable to accept it.

The others remained still, not erupting into action as she expected them to.

She fixed them with a frightening look. "You're both going to help me save him, or so help me God, I will end us all."

"That's not it," Yusef said quietly. "He'd rather die than turn into a vampire like this."

Kidan had believed that too, once. Choosing death over a wretched life was better, honorable. But fuck an honorable life.

GK would learn to love himself. She'd help him do so.

His spilled blood dried around the edges.

"A few hours," she repeated like a prayer and a curse. "We're bringing him back."

66.

KIDAN RETURNED TO HER HOUSE AT THE ELEVENTH HOUR. SHE LEFT Slen and Yusef to hide GK's body and wait for her call.

She stood in the middle of the living room, guided by the moon's faint touches along the windowsill. The lights had been turned off. A sharp whistle of wind stung her cheek, thanks to the nail that had torn through the window. It was the only fracture upon the house to suggest what had happened.

He was here. By now, she could find him in darkness, taste his thirst for violence like mist.

"If you want to punish me, get on with it." Her voice carried through the rough outlines of furniture.

Something reached for her hand. Fingers, long and hard. They grabbed and pulled. Kidan's heart tugged backward as the world spun. Wind slashed along her skin in tiny scrapes, and her lungs stuttered for breath. She was flying, falling, or both, gravity pulverizing her body in all directions. A sudden and terrifying stop buckled her knees, and bile lurched to her mouth.

She groaned. "Do you really have to do that?"

When her eyes stopped rolling, she was standing on the narrow ledge of the highest tower of the campus, alone.

She tried to scramble backward but found only wall. The courtyard yawned, only splinters of gold light from the lion-shaped lamps revealing its ground. Way, way down below. Her knees turned to water.

"Susenyos!" she yelled against the ruffling wind.

The night didn't answer back. Panic beat in her ears. He hadn't left her here, had he? She splayed her fingers against the engraved wall to anchor herself, but she was entirely untethered. One unintentional step and she would fade from this world.

She squeezed her eyes shut, trying to breathe, think. "Fuck. Fuck."

"For a girl who preaches about death, you look quite frightened."

Relief flooded her soul. She found him a few paces from her, sitting with one leg dangling over the edge, a striking presence under the stars.

"Susenyos," she said, wary.

"Yes, my love?"

"I know you're angry."

"Oh, anger is such a human emotion. I'm dissatisfied. I had a vision for what you and I could become, and you laid it all to waste."

"Look, I'm sorry—"

"You cost me another room." He cut her off, fire betraying his calm voice.

She froze. "What?"

"Another room that I'm weak and vulnerable in because you forced me to tell you about the artifact."

Her eyes widened. She opened her mouth and closed it. Any action Susenyos took that risked the artifact must punish him. He became human in the observatory when he tried to leave the house, and now this.

"You stole many things from me, Kidan. But I won't forgive you for this."

"All I wanted was the truth, to find my sister."

He stretched his arms like a bored cat. "As you've proved countless times. Everything else that doesn't warrant your affection be damned."

"You lied to me."

"And *you* killed me." His response lashed like a whip, indignant. Then he smiled, remembering himself. "Well, almost."

"If you'd told me about the Nefrasi earlier—"

"Do list my numerous faults. It's your favorite habit. If I'd told you about them, all you would have done was run to your death a little sooner. Missed the few months here you enjoyed with your little friends. If I had told you the real truth, the house would have stripped me of my *immortality*."

She felt herself move forward, and it was a conscious and straining experience to keep still. She stared at her shoes, backing them into the wall a little farther. *Appease him*, her mind offered. *Apologize*.

"You were right about them. They killed…GK."

The words were no different from expelling a sword lodged deep in her chest.

This surprised Susenyos into a cruel and mocking tone. The moonlight graced his angular face, casting him half in shadow.

"And for so long you thought me the vile beast. Didn't I warn you of the company you keep during the day?"

"Please."

"Begging, are we? That is delicious." Susenyos stood with an unnatural ease for a person balancing on a ledge. He started toward her, and her heart thudded at the menace in those eyes.

"You can't kill me before I bring GK back," she pleaded.

He stilled. "What did you say?"

"We're going to turn him."

"And whose life were you going to exchange for his?" He bridged their gap in a flash, snarling. "Mine?"

Kidan wavered with his presence, stepping a fraction forward.

Stop, she screamed at herself.

"No." She met those raging eyes. "I want to take one of them, the Nefrasi. For all they've taken from us. I want one of them to give GK his life back."

Susenyos cast her a sideways glance, surprise breaking his anger. "What will you offer them? The Nefrasi will require payment, and it'll be cruel. Most likely, your life."

Her legs moved forward again despite her will. "I won't give them that. I will fight to live."

He watched her feet kissing the very edge.

"My dearest Kidan, you can't even fight a strong wind."

They knew there was no wind pulling her forward—this was something else, deeper than her consciousness, a monster she had yet to slay.

"Here you are again, little bird. Messing with injured souls and giving them three deaths instead of one. Let your friend die."

She shook her braids wildly. "No. Not him."

He cocked his head. "You are a beautiful study. A human girl both in love and at war with death." His next words surprised her. "Fine, I will save GK."

Hope tightened her chest. "You will?"

"Yes. The Nefrasi will not rest until they come for me. I can safeguard against it. The only issue remains you. Your unpredictability and complete lack of consequences."

He stepped away and stared into the darkness, hands folded behind him.

"So, a final ask for such a gift. I want your life."

Kidan's heart sank. This was his punishment. Crueler than a bullet in her thigh, he'd dragged her here to make her reckon with all she had become and finally choose.

Her lips barely moved. "No."

"For what reason?" He gave a short chuckle. "I'll undertake your duties and protect your friends. Better than you, if I might add."

"Yos."

He stiffened as if struck, voice lower than hell. "I'm Susenyos to you. You have lost the privilege of calling me that."

His dark eyes exposed how truly she'd hurt him. It surprised Kidan that she could wound him like this. What could she do? This was her nature. She hurt everyone around her.

"Answer my question," he said louder, speaking as if he was onstage, in front of thousands. "For what reason shall you, Kidan Adane, continue to exist?"

She tipped forward, nearly falling, before she reversed her momentum and it carried her backward.

"Stop."

"Let's end it here, my miserable Roana. Set us both free. What reason is there to fight so hard?"

"You need my . . . blood. My companionship."

"So you exist for me?" He laughed.

"No."

"Then for what reason?"

Her mind splintered with the question. He'd never be satisfied until he wrenched out a final confession from her. Her selfish, grotesque truth.

"What reason—"

"*No reason*," she hurled back, familiar fury drowning her fear. "I don't need a reason. I want to live, so I will. It's my life to do as I please. *Mine*."

They glared at each other as the earth and sun did. Burning and blazing and scorching until her soul ignited.

Finally, he extended a hand. "Very well. Give it to me."

For a moment, she was confused. His eyes fell to her wrist. Kidan unclasped her butterfly bracelet with shaking hands and gave it to him. He wrapped his fingers around it, eyes unreadable.

Then, when he was certain she truly believed her words, and trusted him, he spun them on the narrow ledge. Her back arched toward the waiting darkness, the balls of her feet swaying on the edge. A strong hand around the waist caught her before she fell.

His angry gaze darkened on her lips. For a wild, unreasonable second, she thought he was going to kiss her. Wings clapped in her stomach, and her braids fluttered in the strong gust.

She bunched his shirt tightly, unsure if she wanted to pull him closer or shove him away. "Yos?"

His fingers disappeared from her waist. With nothing to support her, Kidan fell.

Her heart remained on the tower with him. A force had wrenched it out of her skin, and as she plummeted, it cried out for her. In all Kidan's ideas of entertaining death, she hadn't realized the path down would be a pulsing and immediate regret.

Kidan woke on a couch, head spinning. She shifted forward on her elbows, blinking away her drowsiness. She checked her torso, her legs, her arms. All uninjured. He must have caught her.

Susenyos stood by the floor-to-ceiling window.

"I can't come with you. As I've said before, I can't leave Uxlay. Taj and Iniko will go with you. They've been tracking some Nefrasi in town."

Kidan was too stunned by his words to say anything.

He fixed her with a concealed expression. "I can't leave."

"The house law. I get it, Susenyos. And I won't ask you to put yourself at risk again."

He walked to her. "With the lengths you go to for your loved ones, I somehow don't believe you can keep that promise."

She tried for a smile to break the heaviness crowding him. "You sound jealous."

A line marred his forehead. "Of that terrifying love you reserve only for a few? Very."

"We don't need love, Susenyos. We are bonded by something much greater. You're my companion."

He wore an expression she couldn't read, a dark film sliding over his eyes.

"Don't die," he ordered. "Fight to live, like you said."

Kidan's heart contracted in her chest. She offered him a real smile this time. "Haven't you heard? Death doesn't seem to want me."

His attention drifted to her wrist, then settled on her chest as if he could hear its slow, hesitant pounding. "Even death can't resist if you keep flirting with it this much."

Uxlay law was clear on its engagement with rogue dranaics. For students, an immediate suspension pending a court hearing. For adults, an immediate removal from Uxlay society. Dean Faris used the protective universal law to alert her to any mass dranaic movements against the campus. Even if the Nefrasi were in Zaf Haven, they couldn't find the university.

An abandoned community hall on the very edge of town was the sole place to engage with rogues. Kidan and her friends traveled in the back of an infirmary vehicle. Taj drove, unusually quiet. GK's body lay on a stretcher between them.

Iniko adjusted her silver knives along her forearms. "A couple of Nefrasi are staying in Zaf Haven. Taj and I will bring you a dranaic. Act quickly, because if they find us, we can't fight them all." Iniko's eyes creased with disapproval again. She didn't think this was a good plan, but Susenyos ordered it and they obeyed.

Kidan was grateful.

The silhouette of Uxlay's towers grew smaller. Her skin prickled with the sensation of being overexposed.

"You think we won't be able to live with ourselves if we don't revive him," Slen's flat voice came from beside Kidan. "But what if I could?"

"Slen."

Her obscured eyes met Kidan's. "I'm not saying it to be unkind, but I could walk out of here and leave you all. It would be the easiest thing I do."

Kidan sighed. "Well, I hope your ambition doesn't fuck us all over."

"For your sake, I hope so too."

After dropping them off at the eerie hall, Taj and Iniko sped off. Slen retrieved a heavy bag full of supplies they'd need for the forced transformation. Iniko had reluctantly given Kidan back her gun. It only had two bullets left, but it would be helpful.

Their shoes left dusty imprints on the floor as they walked to the empty stage. Moonlight streamed through the stained glass, leaving red and blue hues washing over their faces. The wall had yellowed in the shape of letters that once decorated it.

Kidan checked her phone. They had little time left before GK's body wouldn't be revivable. She settled down on the cold bench, remembering the Mot Zebeyas' ritual as they turned Sara Makary.

Yusef paced, unable to sit as time ticked down frighteningly fast.

"Shit," Yusef said, watching the exit. "What if they don't make it?"

Kidan had nothing but blind hope to cling to. "They'll make it."

She squeezed her eyes shut and prayed.

Suddenly, the door banged open. Taj and Iniko dragged a writhing, gagged figure inside. Kidan jumped into action, giving them more of the horn ash. It wasn't enough to subdue him entirely, nor did they want him so poisoned that he'd die before he transformed GK.

"He needs to be chained upside down," Slen said. "It'll be easier to drain him that way."

Taj and Iniko hesitated. Kidan figured that treating one of their own like an animal didn't sit right with them.

"Please," Kidan added. "Tie him upside down."

They managed it far more easily than expected. The snarling dranaic was suspended from a fixture with multiple curtain ropes. They moved GK's body under the vampire and took off his shirt. Someone needed to make an incision over his heart.

"I can do it," Slen said, and knelt by GK.

They had to slit the dranaic's throat and drain his blood through a tube and feed it into GK's heart. Kidan's fingers trembled as she retrieved the surgical knife from the bag. She tried to think of it as slaughtering an animal—there was nothing else to it. Across from her, Yusef's face turned.

"You don't have to look," she told him.

"No, I have to."

After taking a deep breath, Kidan brought the knife to where the vampire's carotid artery would be. His skin was hot as her two fingers searched for the vein. His eyes widened with fear, he screamed through his muffling gag.

Suddenly, Taj gasped, eyes widening.

"Taj?" Iniko became alert.

Taj swayed, then fell forward, a silver blade skewering his back.

The knife in Kidan's hand slipped. Iniko bolted toward him, deflecting three silver needles spitting from near the dark ceiling. Finally, one pierced Iniko's thigh and she fell, groaning.

Kidan started toward her, but Iniko's yell made her blood cold.

"What are you doing? Run!"

67.

KIDAN'S NERVES VIBRATED IN HER TAUT BODY. SHE FUMBLED FOR HER gun and aimed it at the ceiling. A gaggle of laughter followed her as she spun, trying to find the targets. The dranaic they'd tied up was taken by a whirling shadow. In the blink of an eye, Iniko and Taj vanished as well.

A young man in a suit jacket appeared out of the darkness, hand in pocket. Kidan didn't hesitate. She pulled the trigger. He raised his arm, and the bullet collided with something like metal, bouncing off.

His lip curled at his ruined sleeve, and he peeled it backward. Kidan stifled her horror. His left hand and forearm were entirely coated with silver, button-like holes punctuating its hard spine. When he flexed his fingers, the silver shield shifted like the surface of water. Six or seven vampires stalked out of the shadows, flanking Kidan and her friends. Behind him, vampires waited, dark figures dangling from upper-level benches and fixtures.

Kidan lowered her gun. She only had one bullet left. It had to count.

A mountain of a man brought Taj and Iniko forward in spiked, blood-licked silver chains. Iniko's perfect coat had ripped, and her bow was drenched in dark red. From the various cuts along her arms, it seemed that the dranaic blood on those spikes had penetrated deep, weakening her. Kidan hoped they didn't pierce a vital artery. Taj had lost consciousness. But her choking dread dissipated a little when she noticed his chest rising and falling.

"Kidan Adane. A pleasure to finally meet you," said the young man with the silver arm. He had three thick silver rings on his right hand, which he used to remove his suit jacket. Hardened muscle and several more metal chains were draped along his chest.

Kidan stepped forward, shielding Yusef's shaking form. "Who are you?"

"He hasn't told you my name? That's quite like him."

The vampire approached Slen, pulled her upright, and inhaled the scent at her neck in a sickening gesture. She flinched but didn't protest. Kidan tugged Slen's arm, freeing her from his grip.

The vampire cocked his head. "You can call me Samson Malak Sagad."

"Sagad?"

He was distinct from the rest of the Nefrasi men because of his hair. There was no length, no twists or locs, just closely cropped dark hair that revealed a nasty scar running from the bottom of his ear into his neckline. Kidan gasped softly. She'd seen him in Yos's memories briefly—the first to be turned, a boy with a scarred neck and an injured hand.

Was this the childhood friend Susenyos spoke of? The servant turned friend who massacred an entire raiding party with him?

"So, you do know that name."

"Susenyos doesn't have brothers."

The vampire gave a chilling laugh. "Oh, you're right. Susenyos and I are bonded by something much stronger than blood. 'Sagad' is for royals, it means *bow*—and you should."

Kidan's spine remained locked.

His eyes narrowed. "I see the same defiance in every acti that crawls out of that place you call Uxlay. Trained from childhood to think of us as your guardians. I can't wait to introduce you to true fear."

Kidan's hatred was a sentient being, whispering foul things in her ear. "Where is my sister?"

His smile slithered on like a viper's. "Lovely June is quite safe. I didn't bring her to witness such a violent act, of course. She's quite sensitive."

Kidan's grip on the gun slackened. After months of stumbling in the dark, she'd finally found June. June was within reach.

Her heart beat with a different wild hope. June could come home. All of this... All of this pain would soon end.

He studied each of them with murky eyes. "Let me see if I have this correct. Titus did report well. The leader Slen Qaros. The artist Yusef Umil. The saint

Kidan Adane. Heirs to Great Houses of Uxlay." He tsked at GK's dead body. "Ah, and the miskeen nameless devout boy."

Laughter cackled from the direction of the ceiling, his audience entertained.

Kidan bared her teeth. "What the hell do you want?"

He raised a brow, exchanging a glance with one of them. "You *do* need proper training."

Blood boiled in her eyes, but she kept quiet. They were horribly outnumbered.

"There's a Nefrasi tradition that new initiates partake in to deem their worthiness. Seeing as you're trying to forcibly sacrifice one of us to raise your dead, I think it's fitting you participate."

The air rippled with violence as the Nefrasi shouted in excitement. The cheers echoed from every direction. Kidan tried to estimate how many there were. At least three dozen. Her resolve wavered like grass in wind.

Samson spoke to the ceiling, eyes gleaming. "It's simple, really. The initiate holds a piece of silver and tries not to drop it, no matter the onslaught he faces. As the initiate is already dead, his body will be the silver. So, if you want your devout boy to transform, you simply can't let go of him. What do you say? Give us one more play."

Cruel laughter again. Yusef's forehead broke out in sweat. Slen kept her chin aligned with the floor.

Samson settled in the front row of benches, crossing his legs. "Well, who will go first?"

"I will," Kidan said quickly.

"Such a martyr." His eyes flashed. "But I want the artist first. He looks ready to bolt."

Yusef swallowed but stepped forward. Both Kidan and Slen blocked his path.

"We're not playing your sick game."

The Nefrasi leader tilted his head. Within a flash, Kidan was on her knees beside him, arm twisted so far back that a faint crack at her shoulder sounded. She hissed through her pain, unable to see her faceless attacker.

"You will go last, heiress."

She struggled, watching the others through a curtain of her braids. *Run,* she begged with her eyes. *Run.*

Yusef, the fool, approached GK.

"What are you doing?" Kidan yelled. "Leave— Ah!"

Her arm twisted back farther, making her dizzy.

Samson spoke again, leaning forward. "Remember the rule. If any of you loses your hold on your friend, he won't be transformed."

Yusef studied GK's face with an unreadable expression. Kneeling down beside GK, Yusef took his hand, unfurling the stiff fingers and intertwining his with them.

One of the Nefrasi, a young woman, stepped forward in high-heeled boots. A silver bar was fixed through the bridge of her nose and her hair was sectioned into two Afro puffs. She knelt and brushed Yusef's face with the delicacy that only a lover could bring, whispering something Kidan couldn't hear.

"Arin." Iniko's voice was sudden and strained. "Don't do this."

The two locked eyes. Arin dismissed her, stretching over Yusef like a feline about to devour him. Iniko hung her head. Kidan's panic solidified.

From her pocket, Arin withdrew a small perfume bottle and poured the contents on their joined hands.

"What are you doing?" Yusef trembled.

Arin didn't speak. She only withdrew a lighter and brought it to their hands.

Yusef's voice hiked up in sheer horror. "No, no—don't!"

When the first lick of flame touched his flesh, he screamed and brought his other hand down to squander it. It never made contact. Arin caught it, pinning it to the floor with her heel. Blue, violent flame circled their hands.

Slen fought against the vampires who shot forward to restrain her. Yusef's scream carved itself into Kidan's soul. She wanted to tear out her own ears.

"Yusef!" Kidan shouted. "Let go!"

Yusef refused to let go, his face scrunched up in agony. To stop him from burning alive in front of them, Arin pinched out the fire that reached past his wrist, keeping the flames at their joined hands. Skin bubbled and fell from where the fire ate away at their flesh.

That smell.

Bile rose up in Kidan's throat. She spoke against the floor. "Please, stop. Please."

Samson waved a hand, and Arin stepped away.

Yusef's and GK's hands remained grafted together. Slen broke free of her hold first, running toward them. She took off her jacket and wrapped their hands with it, extinguishing the flames. Yusef stopped screaming and slumped against her chest with a faded look. Slen couldn't separate their hands without causing the skin to break. Her face contorted.

"Slen Qaros, next."

Kidan saw red. She seized Samson Sagad's right hand, the one with flesh, and bit into it. Hard.

Her teeth ground down on bone, gnawing until she tasted blood. He swore and flung her across the room. Her head hit the floor in spectacular pain. But she pushed past her blurred vision, fighting to find Slen. She spat what little flesh she had taken at Slen's feet. Slen, quickly understanding, crawled forward to seize it—and screamed when a heel crushed down on her half-gloved hand.

"These girls," Arin said, voice sweet as malice. "I love their fire. Let me keep them."

"Trying to heal your friend's hand with my finger. Quite poetic," Samson Sagad snarled viciously.

Kidan remained on the floor, cheek pressed to cold stone. Her lips ran with the metallic taste of blood.

Kidan had done this to the others, dragged them to hell because of her guilt. Now she would watch them all die. Her tears pooled onto the floor, bleeding it a darker gray.

Where was Kidan's strength? She'd never felt her humanness so potently before now. So weak and fragile. How could she ever protect anyone like this?

"Enough," Slen snarled, shoving Arin's heel away. She rose to her feet, eyes on fire. "I'll tear out GK's heart right now if you let us go. He's already dead."

The Nefrasi leader lifted a brow. "Such cruel logic. Are you three, then, more worthy of life than the devout boy?"

"We're alive. Our worth is yet to be seen."

He must have liked the answer, because he fished out an object, a knife from his chest pocket, and threw it at Slen's feet.

"Go on. Show me your spine. Cut out his heart."

Kidan propped herself up on her hands. "No."

Slen dismissed her with a turn. She straddled GK's chest and cut into his shirt with a violent rip. Yusef spoke too softly for Kidan to hear, but she could tell it was a plea. He reached to stop Slen, but in his weakened state, he was easy to shake off.

Slen measured from the base of GK's throat to the middle and shifted slightly to the left before making an incision.

It took a very long time, her cut. The blood that spilled out was tar black. Kidan's heart sank. They were too late. Soon, it would be impossible to rejuvenate the heart.

Still, Slen continued to work, with an unnatural slowness compared with her usual speed. There was no need for perfection now. She was stalling, her hand deep in his chest for what felt like hours.

"What's taking so long?" Samson barked.

Kidan understood slowly, the idea fighting past her pulsing headache. Slen wasn't cutting out the heart. She was holding it in place, trying to extend the time in which GK could be saved.

Kidan's vision cleared.

She studied the Nefrasi leader. Samson Sagad didn't want to punish them as much as he wanted to hurt Susenyos. Moving hurt like hell but she did, reaching for her pocket. Someone grabbed her in a steel grip, and Kidan rushed out, "My phone. Call Susenyos."

Samson stilled, shooting his eyes in her direction.

"It's him you want, isn't it?" she said, voice defeated. "Call him and bring him here."

I can't leave Uxlay.

He observed her with the earth's darkest sky, only a speck of star burning in it.

"You would lead him to his death to save your life?"

Kidan stared at the tear-stained stone. "It wouldn't be the first time."

He smiled at this, a truly brilliant smile. "Fine. Let's bring him here."

68.

SAMSON RESTED THE PHONE IN FRONT OF KIDAN, ON SPEAKER, HIS snakelike eyes fixed on her. The Nefrasi vampires leaned and shifted inward to listen as it rang. No sound came from the ceiling.

"Kidan?" Susenyos said, voice urgent.

"Malak Sagad, my brother. How I've missed your voice." Samson studied the upper level of the hall, his friends. "Susenyos the Righteous. The same man that forced an entire court to vampirism, only to abandon them to hell itself. Your loyalty could write sonnets, wendem."

Susenyos didn't respond.

Several seconds passed before Samson let out a long breath. "Very well. I prefer to speak face-to-face. Taj and Iniko are apprehended. I have your pretty companion and her friends in various stages of distress. I simply want the artifact in your possession."

"Petty blackmail? And you were playing at emperor so well until now."

The Nefrasi leader's mouth twitched. "You'd keep hiding like a coward in that wretched campus."

"I quite like this campus. It keeps the rats out."

Samson barked a brash laugh that made Kidan flinch. "The rats will tear your lovely friends into pieces if you don't come."

"The girl means nothing. Her friends even less."

The Nefrasi leader grabbed Kidan's head and slammed her against the nearest bench. Her ear exploded as she cried out. In its shattering, she heard her friends' screams of protest as well. She forced her swirling vision to focus. Slen gritted her teeth against the vampire that was buried in her throat, feeding on her. Yusef struggled uselessly as well.

Stop! Kidan shouted, but no one heard her.

Samson lifted her by fistfuls of her braids, and she groaned, trying to ease the pressure at her scalp.

"Come face us, you coward, or I'll kill her."

Not an ounce of discomfort threatened Susenyos's voice. "Go ahead, I'll listen. Kill her for me."

Samson stilled, then growled like a beast. "What?"

Kidan's head pulsed in agony.

"Kill her for me, wendem. You don't know what a headache it is to inherit houses with so many heiresses popping up. She's in your hands, isn't she? Kill her."

Samson's eyes bled into fury.

Then, in her softest, most wounded part, Kidan called to him. "Yos."

Susenyos stopped talking.

She knew what she asked of him when she called his name and hated herself for it. But he already knew, didn't he? That she was crooked and selfish and would always choose wrong. He saw her. He understood her more than she liked him to. But she also knew him, and this ask—to risk the thing he valued most—would go unanswered. Leaving Uxlay would make the law punish him.

"How lovely." Samson's voice twisted with new light. "None of us here have witnessed your grand protection. Redeem yourself, zoher." He barked. "Let us see if the selfish emperor will sacrifice himself for a girl in distress."

Every soul in the hall waited for the response.

"It's not my job to sacrifice. It is yours." Susenyos's tone remained bored. "And you've done it so brilliantly. I thank you all, truly. I wouldn't have made it to Uxlay without your blood and death. You have served your emperor well."

Anger rippled through the space like a desert heat wave. Arin tightened her fist and brought it down on the floor, making the floor implode and shake through the row of benches, down to the last one. Kidan's jaw chattered from the force.

"I see Arin is there," Susenyos continued once the dust settled. "Always such a temper."

"Come out and face us, Yos." Arin's tone was absolutely lethal. "Or I will tear apart that campus brick by brick."

He really was going to get them all killed, Kidan thought.

"I will finish *The Mad Lovers* for you, little bird," Susenyos said, voice unchanged. "You missed a beautiful chapter. Matir gives Roana her wish. He lets her have Aesdros, and they share a delightful ending."

"What—"

The line went dead.

"No," she said with a moan.

Susenyos had hung up.

Her mind reeled. Kidan had finished the damned book. There was no delightful end. Roana and Matir were ruined when Roana became infatuated with another soul. A human, Aesdros, who didn't play games of rules but only gave pure love. She begged Matir to let the human live with them, and Matir refused before allowing it. The three lived together, finding a balance to their burning hate, until the invited human rose between the two one night and slit their throats. She couldn't unravel the meaning of the story then, and certainly not now.

Samson crushed the phone into pieces. He faced the crowding vampires on the upper level of the hall.

"Do you all see now?" he roared. "Do you hear his words? He would abandon us again and again!"

They were silent as the moon. Arin kept her fists in balls, blood running down her palms from how tightly she clenched them.

Samson's deathly eyes fell on Kidan. Her pulse jackhammered into a frenzy.

Kidan's world became void of sound as she studied Samson's mouth move in furious waves, veins darkening along his forehead. There was only one way to quell a wounded monster.

An invitation. Just like Roana had summoned the stranger Aesdros to her home.

Kidan's eyes widened. Susenyos *had* told her what to do.

Her voice was as uncertain as a baby bird finding its wings. "I can take you into Uxlay."

The Nefrasi leader had run out of patience. She had a second before he tore out her throat. Her heart fluttered but she met his piercing eyes.

"I can be your companion."

He stilled. "Say that again, heiress."

Her voice found its strength slowly. "You will no longer be rogue. You can infiltrate Adane House not only as a spy but as my equal. I can choose you as my companion. You want access to the artifact and my house, right? I'm it. I can get you past the universal law."

Samson was the silence found at the end of the world. Slowly, he spoke. "If I do consider this, you aren't enough. I'll need my people to enter as well."

He tilted his head toward Kidan's friends. Yusef and Slen were no longer being fed on.

"No." Slen, throat bleeding, remained by GK, her hands around his heart. "No way."

Arin, quick as lightning, slapped Slen, making her spit out blood.

"Stop!" Yusef tried to shield Slen with his uninjured arm. "We'll do it. We'll choose you as our companions."

Samson crossed his arms. One dark, one silver. "What of that disgusting philosophy you all study? You cannot take on companions without passing it, can you?"

Kidan's determination was a sharp, vicious thing. "We'll pass. We only have one test left."

He gave her a slight rise of the brows. "So much bravery. And for this generous gift, what will you require of us?"

Kidan's attention drifted to GK.

"Of course." He fixed each of his people with a level look. "We abolish everything that bastard of a Sage teaches. It's why we seek to break the Three Binds. Yet here you are, asking me to sacrifice one of my men for the life of yours."

Kidan willed her fading energy to gather.

"I cannot ask my people to give up their lives," Samson said with surprising hatred. "I won't take their lives like he did."

Kidan hung her head. That was it, then. She hoped they killed her first.

Footsteps sounded in the quiet.

"Leul," Arin called out. "Step back."

Leul was a young man with one steel eye. All the Nefrasi embedded silver throughout their bodies.

"We need to free our people." His voice was softer than anyone else's here. "We're finally close."

"I will take your silver eye if you don't step back," Arin snarled.

He smiled, studying GK's limp form. "You've heard the rumors. I won't entirely disappear. Some part of me will live inside this boy. He's so very young."

He took out his silver eye and placed it in her hand. Arin seized his collar, but he didn't stiffen. His eye healed slowly, settling into a black pupil. He spoke in Amharic, a gentle sound coming from his lips, before removing her from him. He took a silver knife from Arin's hip and nicked his wrist, letting it bleed.

Samson nodded. "Go on. Save your friend."

Kidan crawled at first and then, when the earth solidified under her feet, ran unsteadily to GK. She slid to her knees by his head. Slen was focused on her task, wrist deep in muscle and tissue. Kidan had never seen a human heart before. The flesh was taut as a wrung rose, veins of pale green and blue crisscrossing.

"Slen."

"You asked me to save his life. I don't fail my assignments."

"Slen," she said again, because nothing else expressed the gratitude pouring through her. Ending GK's life permanently would be as easy as leaning back. Slen had to stay very still.

"When he wakes up to kill me, remind him I held his heart in my hands."

Leul poured his blood into the open body. Silence drowned them all. With Yusef anchoring Leul's hand in place, the three of them circled GK to resurrect him.

As Leul's brown complexion faded, the muscle and tissue inside GK knitted and healed. Slen removed her bloodied hands slowly as the skin closed. Leul fell into Arin's arms. Grief and fury were etched onto her brows. Her gaze flicked up to Iniko's, who held it with a quiet sorrow.

Kidan brushed GK's icy cheek, urging him to wake. She needed to see his eyes one more time. All of this would be worth it once he opened his eyes.

His lashes fluttered like fragile wings. She gasped a sigh of relief. He was coming awake. Any moment now.

"Take him."

They were all pushed aside by dranaics. Yusef howled, his hand finally ripping free. GK was collected.

"No!" Kidan yelled. "What are you doing?"

"Ensuring you keep your word. If you fail on your promise to make us your companions, you won't see your friend."

"Wait, please. Let us see him first!"

Samson held her gaze and called, "Warde."

The giant vampire stopped. GK was draped over his broad shoulders. Time tightened her chest as he lifted his head. The brown of his pupils sharpened to golden mahogany, nails extending to blackened claws. His eyes no longer reflected light but pierced like a blinding sun. The anger and power of them stunned Kidan. Both directed at her. She could feel his soul unravel, tearing and molding into something new. Otherworldly.

She opened her mouth, but nothing came out. He looked so furious at her, betrayed beyond belief. Yusef found the words first, weak yet reaching.

"We'll come for you, GK. We'll find you again."

The vampire exited with him. GK was falling asleep again and wouldn't wake for a few days.

Kidan gathered herself and glared at the Nefrasi leader. "I want my sister as well."

Samson laughed close to his chest. "I doubt she will want you. After all, it's been so long."

69.

KIDAN CRADLED YUSEF'S HEAD IN THE BACK OF THE CAR AS TAJ RACED back to Uxlay. Iniko sat off to one side, bandaging herself with a self-practiced ritual. Slen held on to Yusef's unburnt hand, quieting his painful moans.

"We're almost there," she'd say every once in a while.

Kidan's stomach turned whenever she glanced at his right hand, which was raw and wrinkled like rotten almond.

"Drink." Slen placed a bottle of Taj's blood in front of him. In agony, he moved his head.

She managed to feed him a few drops, but his hand didn't smooth. They'd waited too long, and Kidan feared the damage was irreversible.

Slen touched a shaking finger to her gashed throat. "They fed from us. Why didn't they find our blood poisonous?"

Kidan wondered the same thing. "I don't know. Maybe it's all a lie that we have to make a graduation vow first."

"No. A dranaic has fed on me before. They spat out my blood immediately, and their eyes bled for days."

Their eyes met, brows drawn tight.

What had Susenyos said? That Kidan had unknowingly made some sort of vow? What vow had Slen and Yusef made?

Once Taj crossed onto Uxlay land, Kidan's throat expanded, and air moved freely in her body. She never would have thought the sight of those shadowy towers would bring such relief.

Kidan handed Yusef over to Taj, who took off immediately along with Iniko, and Kidan and Slen ran across campus by themselves. A throbbing behind her eyes made her touch the back of her head. Her fingers came away wet. As if awakened by her touch, the pain turned sharp, like a knife had been plunged into the back of her skull.

She didn't stop running, the pain making her vision of the campus walls ripple like the surface of water. And incredibly, her will won. The pain tucked itself away to be dealt with later. Kidan reached the infirmary, and a nurse rushed to treat them.

She escorted Slen away, angling her bitten neck back and calling for more nurses.

Kidan's reflection in the far mirror was monstrous. Her clothes were covered in splotches of red. Some hers, some Samson's from when she bit off his flesh. Her face, especially her mouth, was smeared with blood. She needed to wash. In the glass, she saw Susenyos open the door, storming in like a god come down to rain terror.

He searched the fluorescent hall, voice cracking like thunder. "Kidan!"

She turned, and he locked on her instantly. His eyes were ablaze with a thousand suns, the same wrath from Cossia Day draping him. Then he took in her bloodied appearance, and those eyes lost their intensity, darkening.

Kidan didn't know she was hurrying toward him, running until her body slammed into his, arms tight around his neck. Susenyos made a deep sound in his throat at the impact.

Her tears absorbed into his coat. "I got your clue. Thank you."

He stiffened for a long moment, then embraced her cautiously.

"You're worrying me, little bird."

Kidan stepped back at those words, suddenly embarrassed and aware of who she was embracing.

"Sorry..."

Susenyos touched her head, and Kidan jerked. He swore, pulling back, and studied his red hand.

"Kidan," he said calmly, although his face was anything but. "You're bleeding. Did he do this?"

The throbbing reached across her skull again, pulsing. She stepped farther away and stumbled. Susenyos reached out to right her. Her vision faded in and out, the hospital floor transforming into the abandoned community hall. She searched for the others, but they were gone.

"Yusef...Slen? Where are they?"

His jaw tightened. "They're getting help. Come with me."

She let him lead her to a closet—cleaning products and a strong chemical smell faintly alerted her senses—but she was fading, sliding closer to the floor as he closed the door.

"Hey." He elongated his fangs and bit into his wrist. Blood glided down his brown skin. "You need to drink."

She tried to focus on his eyes, which were sharp with growing alarm. The type of worry she didn't deserve. The type she'd wanted when she told him she was poisoned. Gently, he brought his wrist to her mouth, and she licked, sucked at his skin. It was no different from how her own blood tasted, neither sweet nor sour. But it healed her, cleared her vision, and vanquished her pain. She managed to open her eyes without the need to close them again.

Once she was aware of herself, he took back his hand. He studied her face and mouth, even her braids, where blood had found its way in, brows pinching.

"We need to clean you up."

"He said June wouldn't want to see me. Do you think she's angry I didn't find her sooner?" Kidan stared deeply into those eyes. "He's lying."

Susenyos was quiet.

"He's a liar."

Again Susenyos said nothing.

"Kidan... He hesitated, and it alarmed her. He never hedged his words, even when he should.

"What?"

Susenyos's jaw moved, and he turned away before facing her again.

"Your sister left you a message."

Her stomach pitched. "What?"

He was being careful. "I don't think it's wise to see it now—"

"See it? What do you mean?"

He gave her a conflicted look and sighed. "She sent a video. It's at the house."

A video. The earth cracked beneath her feet. Of course, a video. That was how June always communicated. Kidan rushed out of the closet and out of the infirmary, ignoring his protests.

It took her five minutes to reach Adane House, feet pounding on the gravel like a drum. Breathless, she burst through the front door. The lounge was in utter chaos. Fire had engulfed all four corners. Walls were ripped in deep gashes and impaled by swords. Furniture was tipped and ruined as if a tornado had torn through it. There was *so* much rage, and it wasn't hers.

Susenyos had been livid.

Air faded from her lungs as shattered glass from the chandelier crunched beneath. What the hell happened here?

That thought left her when June's face appeared, projected on the living room screen.

"June?" Kidan whispered.

It wasn't the house playing tricks on her. This was real.

Real.

Kidan rushed to study June's face for any scars or bruises, any mark of abuse. Her clenched fists loosened. June's cheeks were full of life, honeyed eyes bright. Her sister's hair had grown past her shoulders. Relief and confusion flooded Kidan.

She walked slowly to the couch and restarted the video. It was a couple of minutes long.

Her finger trembled over the play button. She had to push her whole body forward to press it, every nerve and muscle working to lend her strength for what was to come.

"Hey, Kid. I don't really know where to start." June's voice had changed, had become less shrill.

She pulled her sweater over her palms, shoulders hunched inward.

"I'm sorry for all of it. I really am. Where do I begin?" She drifted, and Kidan almost smiled at the familiar habit. June always started and stopped a thought in her old videos.

"Mama Anoet shouldn't have done it. We all knew she needed the money, but she loved us. I don't know why she changed, exactly. But I know how she treated you, watched you like you'd do something awful. Maybe it was the night you came home with your fists covered in blood, do you remember? After you fought those boys that put a dead rat in my locker. She was so upset." June shook her head of the memory. *"Anyway, she knew the Nefrasi were coming for you. They wanted the elder child, next in line to inherit. I didn't think she'd agree to give you to them."*

The way the word "Nefrasi" rolled off her tongue with too much familiarity tightened Kidan's gut.

"But I met them first and...something changed. I wasn't afraid of them. Those awful nightmares I always get...stopped. I found the cure for my sickness. I couldn't go back home, to school, making everyone worry. I wanted to see if I could be happy again, and maybe I could in Uxlay, living in the house our parents did, following their legacy." June's eyes found the camera again, staring into Kidan's core. "They haven't hurt me. No one has even drunk from my blood. They're not what we thought they were. They take care of me as one of their own...like a family. I feel safe."

Family. I couldn't go back home. Kidan's cheeks were wet. Silent tears leaked out of her, no different from a candle losing its wax.

"After I left, they started training me. They taught me Amharic and Aarac translations. I can read without breaking concentration and recite philosophy. They even made me fight, so I could protect myself. I was ready. Ready to enter Uxlay, and inherit House Adane. But then Aunt Silia suddenly died and the dean..." June shook her head, a rueful smile present. "She brought you into Uxlay first."

Kidan's knees burned against the carpet as she crawled closer to the screen. June fell silent for ten seconds. It stretched for eons.

"If I'd told you I wanted to go with them, you'd have forced me to return. And I would've listened to you because I always did. For once, I wanted to decide on my own. I wanted you to believe I ran away. So that night, I packed my bags..." She trailed off. "You were never supposed to be home."

As June spoke, pieces of that awful night Kidan had buried away floated to the surface. June had gotten Kidan tickets to a metalworking seminar, but Kidan had returned halfway through her walk. She had the feeling of forgetting something, and that gnawing sensation wouldn't leave her alone, so she'd retraced her steps all the way to their garden only to watch June underneath the moonlight, lips reddened with blood. Then Kidan had pounded on the locked door, shouting as the shadowy man gathered her sister and took off.

"You were supposed to be at the seminar," June whispered with such deep regret Kidan almost believed it. "After that, I hoped you'd move on, or think I was dead. I couldn't look back. If I did, I would have come running back. I couldn't say no to you. Never could."

Acid rioted in Kidan's gut. She didn't want to hear any more, but she hung on every word, waiting, praying, for a reason for all this. An explanation.

"Then you showed up at Uxlay, accusing Susenyos Sagad of kidnapping me." June

bit her lip. *"When I found out, I wanted to come to you right away, but Samson...*
he had another plan. He wanted you to get rid of Susenyos Sagad first. We all wanted
that." Her voice pinched a little. Kidan couldn't tell why. *"Adane House should*
be inherited by one of us, not Susenyos. So we used the 13th to frame him, link my
disappearance with Ramyn Ajtaf's death. I know it sounds cruel, but Susenyos has
done awful things, hurt many people. We...I never expected you'd end up helping him
instead." Her brows drew together as if that was the oddest thing out of all this.
"It doesn't matter now. You should help Samson. Give him the Sun artifact. He has great
plans that'll help us all." Her eyes lowered, a sad smile present, some fragment of
the old June peeking through this unrecognizable version. *"How is Mama Anoet?*
I hope you've forgiven her. I have. Now that you know everything, maybe I can come
visit you."

She was asking about Mama Anoet?

June didn't know.

Kidan shook her head. No, this wasn't her sister. It was the house again,
playing on her fear. A concoction of her guilt and anxiety.

June hesitated as if she wanted to say more. Kidan leaned in, breath tight.
June blinked away, and Kidan's frozen frame reflected on the black screen.

No.

Kidan scrambled to start the video again. Listened more carefully. Searched
for any sign of coercion or threat. June couldn't be saying all this on her own.
Air emptied from Kidan's lungs. She played the video again and stared, at times
hearing June, at times studying her mouth, her tucked fingers, nails clean and
unbroken, her long, curling braids. She looked beautiful, healthier than ever.
Kidan played it again and again and again.

"Kidan," a voice called. She must have fallen asleep on the couch, because Susenyos was hovering over her. "You need to get up. Eat food, get cleaned up. There's
still blood all over you."

She didn't think she could ever get up. Every bone weighed more, each
movement a harrowing task. When she ignored him, he sighed and left.

The hours bled into one another until her stomach cramped and seized. Hunger. She liked the sharp pain whenever she turned on the couch. It anchored her to this place, where she would remain trapped until her body decayed and rotted. Her eyes hurt from continuous screen strain.

The video switched off.

"Enough," Susenyos said. "You can play it once you bathe and eat."

He wanted her to be clean so badly, when all she wanted was to sink deeper into her filth. She got up, and her leg fell asleep. Susenyos caught her, but she pushed him off, trying to walk toward the screen and switch it on. His fingers dug into her shoulders, rooting her in place.

"Food. Bath. Then I'll leave you alone."

Kidan walked to the bathroom, mainly because she had to pee. Her reflection stopped her. Dried blood stuck to her mouth, chin, braids. She was disgusting. And no amount of water would ever wash this away.

The hallways flickered, leading her down the path to the glowing room—or perhaps warning her. The observatory burned her tears away and pulled at her heart like a tide. Kidan slid down on the cold floor.

The room feasted on her pain, stretching it around her like an impenetrable bubble. She glanced at her wrist, her bracelet gone. Had she imagined it all? She'd gotten better, hadn't she?

But June hadn't been taken. She had chosen to leave. And she'd plunged Kidan into the darkest period of her life. Kidan's mind searched for a reason. A hidden reason for why June would be so cruel—but nothing came to mind.

Kidan's head rested back against the wall. She'd once vowed to destroy such malice, the type festering inside herself and at Uxlay. But evil was everywhere.

"Kidan?" Susenyos opened the door.

His eyes raked over her with mild concern.

"She doesn't know," Kidan whispered in a haunted voice. "She doesn't know what I've done to find her. Mama Anoet..." Her lip trembled. "June left me behind and didn't look back. She doesn't know what I've done, how many times I've died trying to find her."

Susenyos crouched, voice tight with anger. "I know."

"I'm tired." A tear slipped free. "I'm so tired."

His eyes echoed her pain, appeared to feel it just as potently. "Let me lend you my strength."

He extended a hand and waited. It asked of her what she wanted to ask of herself: *Can you continue for something other than June?* It took her a very long time to reach toward him, desperate to know. His fingers curled around hers, large and warm.

70.

LATE THAT NIGHT, THEY ENTERED THE BATH OF AROWA. THEY STOOD before a stone bath accessed by climbing a set of small stairs. The smooth empty surface was etched with turquoise and gold drawings of Black gods modestly covered.

Susenyos went to the side of the wall and pressed on a protruding slot. A panel slid open, revealing towels, soap, and hair treatments. Robes and dresses in different shades of the sunset hung on the next panel.

Hot, gushing water filled the basin. Kidan knew she had to get undressed, yet her arms remained by her side, too drained. Susenyos removed her clothes for her, kneeling low to slip off her shoes, loosen her tie, and unbutton her shirt. She braced herself, heart coiled at first, but gradually, with each article of clothing, his intentions became clear. He wanted to help her.

How had they ended up here? In all her dreams and nightmares, this was never what he became. Someone she could almost lean on.

His gentleness always alarmed and disarmed her.

He turned away so she could undress completely and wade into the rippling water. The heat was scalding, but she clamped down on her hissing response. She would adjust soon, and just for a little while, she wanted her skin to burn.

Kidan breathed in and out, the rose oil and eucalyptus engulfing her senses. She moved lower, submerging her head. The tips of her ears burned, and her eyes did too, but when she resurfaced, they felt clear. Ripples of red appeared around her, dried blood loosening from her body and hair.

She curled in on herself in the middle and found him watching her with guarded eyes.

"We usually have it at this time, so you shouldn't be disturbed. I'll be outside regardless." His voice echoed in the cavernous room.

He walked to the engraved doors.

"I know I'm all out of asks...." Kidan spoke into her knee, hearing him pause. "But...don't leave."

The gurgling of water raised steam around her. A minute ticked by. Kidan couldn't bear to look and find him gone. In truth, she wouldn't blame him. After all the things she'd done to him, he shouldn't have helped her during their capture. How could he still stand being around her?

A splash pulled her attention to the opposite end of the basin. He'd dipped his legs in, pants rolled up, and settled on the edge. His coat was removed, so only his loose shirt remained. Her eyes creased, a ball forming in her throat.

"Come here." He rolled up his sleeves.

She went to him without question.

He turned her at the shoulders so her back rested on the curved edge of the bath and between his legs.

Susenyos lifted one of her braids and gently untangled it. She waited for the stubborn pain that came with doing her hair, but it never arrived. Only the pleasurable release at her roots made her know he was even touching her. Expertly he unwound each braid, removed the added hair, and let her natural curls fall against her cheek and neck. She snuck a glance at him between strips of black strands.

"Why aren't you angry with me?" she asked softly. "You know what I've done."

"Samson's weakness is his need to hurt me." Susenyos's tone was measured. "He would only listen to your proposal of companionship if he thought you were betraying me. That's why I gave you the clue from *The Mad Lovers*. You solved it brilliantly."

"But if I graduate, he'll come into Uxlay. He'll be my...companion."

A shudder went through her. When his fingers, long and slender, sank into her sore head, massaging it, she became liquid itself.

"Then you and I do what we do best."

She tried not to shut her eyes. "What?"

"Kill, yené Roana. We remove his heart from his chest and bury it beneath our house."

The way he regarded her, with care and lightness, absorbed into her skin along with the mist and heady essences. She spun, taking his large hand and tracing the veins along it, leading to his taut arm. She kissed the bottom of his wrist, just like he had done once, and tasted rose water.

The warmth from before ignited into a blaze, rushing through every fiber of her. She reached out and brought his neck down, her mouth close to his ear.

"I want you to do it here," she whispered. "Drink from my neck. Not at the companionship ceremony. Not with him. I want it here, alone."

She pulled him into the water, and he went willingly. They stood in the middle of the bath, half submerged, lost in the clouds of steam again. She traced his stuck shirt, rich brown skin peeking through. *Beautiful.*

He gathered her loose curls, and cold air licked her neck and ears. He kissed at the juncture of her neck and shoulder. She tilted her head to give him a wider access. His teeth scraped against the sensitive line of her throat, and she hissed in anticipation.

"Are you certain?" he murmured.

The vibrations of his voice made her body constrict and tremble. She needed to see his desire. Needed to feel.

Her eyes fluttered shut. "Yes. Drink, Yos."

His bite was splitting, sudden, and full of want. He crushed her toward his body as if every part of them touching wasn't enough, and he drank, deeply. Her vision traveled to the ceiling, merging with the illustrations there and swirling in color, and delved into his deepest longing. She saw them—Susenyos and her, side by side, restoring the ruins of Adane House. She saw Susenyos acquiring all the Last Sage artifacts, powerful beyond belief as master of the house, Uxlay impenetrable. She saw him reunited with his court, laughing by a large fire, thousands of people who held pieces of him coming together. Kidan drowned in his clear vision of what he wanted, his dreams, his hopes. Gradually, the desire faded, and she returned to her body, empty again.

She was aware of blood running down her neck, along her chest.

Lips stained, voice wet, he asked, "What did you see?"

She blinked up at him. "You want...everything."

His eyes and hair burned a fierce red-gold. "Yes."

"And what did you see?" she whispered, desperate to know. What had been her desire?

He pressed his forehead against hers. "Not enough. You don't want enough."

She gave a sad smile. Just as she expected. "There's really no hope for me, then."

His face grew shadows. "No. You've lost what you were fighting for, but you'll find a new purpose. You'll wake that terrifying love and loyalty I'm jealous of and use it well." His lips stretched when her eyes creased. "And God help us all if we're considered unworthy when you do."

71.

UXLAY'S INFIRMARY WAS EMPTY SAVE FOR THE THREE OF THEM. YUSEF lay in bed, his bandaged right hand close to his chest. The healthy bronze on his cheeks was still gone. Three of his finger bones had suffered permanent damage, and he couldn't close his fist or hold a pencil. Kidan's chest tightened whenever he winced in pain.

Professor Andreyas arrived at precisely five o'clock, waiting to hear the answer to their final assignment.

He addressed them with his hands in his long coat, four crisp cornrows braided down his scalp. "You three remain the last of this year's cohort. If it wasn't for the dean's insistence that I allow you a chance, you would have all been dismissed."

Kidan swallowed roughly. Everyone else had failed?

The professor peered out the pentagonal window where golden fire lit the torches of the Arat Towers. "So, what did Demasus ask in return? For this new world of peace and coexistence the Last Sage imagined but that appears to limit only dranaics—bound to some human families, weakened beyond belief, unable to sire without sacrificing themselves. Is there even a price the Last Sage could pay?"

They were all quiet, brows furrowed. They had spent hours here, trapped and launching idea after idea before settling on one. In the Dranacti text they'd translated, the Last Sage had given Demasus the price—a silver mirror to be passed down through each generation of the Eighty Acti Families. They'd figured out the metaphor for it, but still their answer appeared weak. Kidan had the horrible sense they had missed something. They couldn't fail now. There was too much at stake. Samson was at the gates, waiting.

"My right hand." Yusef stared at the ceiling with milky eyes.

"My father." Slen pinned her flat gaze on the professor.

"My sister," Kidan finished. "A personal price from each of us."

Professor Andreyas continued to watch the campus grounds.

They waited. One heartbeat, then two, then a dozen among them.

He loosened a sigh. "Another disappointing year."

"What?" Yusef trembled.

"Better luck next year." Professor Andreyas walked to the door, leaving them frozen, caught between shock and fury.

Kidan jumped to her feet. "We gave everything to this course!"

Professor Andreyas stopped under the white lights. "Apparently not everything."

Slen released a breath of exasperation and placed her head in her hands. She'd been utterly calm in the lair of the rogues but was on the verge of breaking down now.

The professor took another step.

"Wait!" Kidan shouted. The others whirled around to her.

Professor Andreyas turned slowly, his dark brows rising. "Careful."

She bunched her fists, shaking. How had they gotten it wrong? The answer had to be in the gifted silver mirror. It had to symbolize that each acti that stood before it would pay Demasus a different price. But if that wasn't the case . . . the only other option was that the mirror had faced Demasus. Was the price to be Demasus himself?

Her ears pulsed with the staggered rhythm of her words. "Demasus wanted us to know what uncontrollable desire is, to know what mind-bending thirst is, to know what a wretched existence is. Only when we did could we truly keep him company. He wanted everything we told you but . . . more. He wanted his price paid by each generation, so anyone who dares keep a dranaic company would first live and be punished as he was. The Last Sage asked Demasus to live as a human, with the Three Binds. Demasus asked for humans . . . to live as he did."

Yusef and Slen drew in a collective breath.

Why had Samson's vampires been able to feed on Slen suddenly? Her blood had been poison earlier in the year, so what changed? Most importantly, why had Susenyos been able to feed from Kidan all these months?

Kidan glanced at Slen, who had killed Ramyn. At Yusef, who had murdered his rival. At herself, who had burned her foster mother alive. She thought of June. None of the Nefrasi had fed on her. Not because they didn't want to, but because they couldn't.

Uxlay's muted reaction to death. The cemeteries crowded with young student corpses. Year after year.

Slen and Yusef must have sensed her direction of thought because they shook their heads, locking her in with wide, petrified eyes.

But the cost of peace was this. They were all Demasus. They'd become him the moment they'd . . .

"Killed."

Slen's eyes bulged, and Yusef let out a sharp gasp.

Her heart raced as she met Professor Andreyas's unblinking, ancient eyes. "Kill. That's what Demasus asked of the Last Sage. Take a human life and know what it felt like."

If Kidan was wrong, she'd just damned them all to hell.

The professor waited, making them doubt, sweat. "From the dead eyes you all share, I see there's some truth to what you speak."

"I'm not sure what you're talking about, sir," Yusef stammered in a hurry. "This is all purely theoretical."

Professor Andreyas did something very odd then. His hard mouth arched into a smile. "Congratulations. You've all passed."

"We have?" Slen blurted.

"You did miss one thing. Yes, Demasus asked for humans to kill, but not just that. Kill with free will. They must want to, they must act of their own volition; otherwise their blood wouldn't be drinkable. They'd be unable to keep a dranaic company."

Their eyes found one another in wonder, remembering their own murders.

Professor Andreyas's shoulders shone with the sunset, an angel of death hovering before them. "I look forward to our class next year. I always favor Mastering a House Law to Dranacti. Much more exciting."

Once he left, Yusef sagged back on his pillow. "Exciting? If next year's exciting, just let me go live as Demasus, the demon himself."

"So, they wanted us to kill. All this time," Slen whispered, tracing the floor with her eyes. "The first lesson was to betray your human self, the second to relate to dranaics' purgatory, and the last to...become them."

They sat there with their discovery, speechless.

Yusef gave a staggered laugh, winced, and grabbed his injured arm. "They're all sick. Is it too late to drop out?"

And in their frail state, ghosts of a smile touched their lips.

Susenyos had told Yusef about the 13th on purpose, goading him to kill. Made sure he graduated. Her lips stretched farther. Was there no end to his plotting?

"Uxlay might kill us for bringing rogues into this place," Slen said, calculating gaze already present. "We have to play it very smart."

"It's quite simple, then, isn't it?" Kidan said, finally clearheaded and brushing away some lint from Yusef's clothes. "We'll have to kill our rogue companions before then."

72.

IT WAS THE LAST WEEK OF THE SEMESTER, AND EVERY MATRIARCH AND patriarch of the great acti houses gathered in the Grand Andromeda Hall. The companionship ceremony was an event not to be missed.

The Ajtaf Family entered first, taking their place at the forefront. Slen walked in third, her mother and brother by her side. The absence of the head of House Qaros didn't diminish the house's excitement in congratulating its new possible heiress. Only her brother formed his lips into a line. Slen wore a traditional embroidered coat instead of her black jacket, and South African sterling silver for her graduation jewelry. The bronze pins were no longer. This silver glinted on her sleeve, the cup of musical instruments sigil emblazoned in the middle.

Yusef appeared from the eleventh row with his great-aunt, his right hand wrapped in a sling. He kissed her cheek and climbed the stairs to the dais, grinning at the light applause. He'd chosen a Somali silver-filled pin imprinted with the burning logs and woman made of blue flame.

Kidan went last. She had no relative, no people to fill the last rows of the grand room and cheer her success. She understood now what had taken them from this life. A plot to shatter a thousand-year-old curse by collecting powerful treasures. It was just rotten luck her family had become its guardians. And here she was, at her graduation, inviting those who had hunted for them to her house. Disappointment crowded her shoulders as she crossed the exquisite marble. So much sacrifice and blood. Would she ever make it amount to something?

Her house sigil shone on an Ethiopian-made silver plate. The pin settled on her sleeve, above where her bracelet had been, kissing her wrist gently and humming with its own frequency. Twin dark and light mountains intersected each other. It harbored its own heaviness, but she willed herself to carry it.

Professor Andreyas gathered the crowd's attention. "It is my pleasure to announce our new graduates from Introduction to Dranacti. I've tested them all, and these three have understood the teachings that built the foundation of all we enjoy today. Houses, applaud your potential heirs and wish them luck as they continue their induction into Uxlay society."

The applause vibrated under the soles of Kidan's feet. Her eyes were fixed on the closed doors. Any moment now, the Nefrasi would be dragged forward by Sicions for trespassing.

"Now, dranaics who wish to change their companions or are currently uncoupled, please stand."

Two dozen rose at once, freed their pins, and placed them in the wide cups provided, one for each of the twelve houses. Sleeves empty, they lined up in rows before the stage. As new initiates, they could only choose two companions but could collect more after they inherited their houses. Susenyos stood strong in the second row with Taj, black eyes trained on Kidan.

He gave a slight nod and her shoulders straightened.

Slen stepped forward. "May I say a few words before we start?"

Professor Andreyas arched a brow but allowed it.

Slen's voice transformed whenever she addressed something aloud. Like the Ojiran poem she once read, it had the tendency to spellbind. "In our studies, we came across a group of rogue dranaics that have caused Uxlay continuous harm. As such, in honor of Demasus and the Last Sage, we have chosen to take companions of those that have strayed from the normal path, those asking for a second chance."

Murmurs danced through the crowd.

Dean Faris, seated in the front, furrowed her brow. "Are you saying rogue dranaics have renounced their ways and pledged to our cause?"

"They will if you give them a chance."

On cue, the doors swung open and three Nefrasi came in, restrained by the Sicions. Immediately, they were pushed to their knees. Gasps floated around the room.

Kidan followed Samson's light eyes to where Susenyos stood. It could strike the devil dead, the malevolent force of that gaze. Samson's lips quirked cruelly. Oh, he was pleased. Susenyos appeared bored, but his jaw moved. A habit Kidan now knew meant he was aware and alert and touching the tucked-away nail.

Dean Faris ascended the stairs to quiet the crowd.

The head of Ajtaf House stood, indignant. "This is ridiculous. We can't have our children bond with these rogues."

"This is clearly a plot to bypass our defenses!" another shouted, from House Makary.

The dean focused on the three. "Where did you find them?"

Slen continued calmly, "In pursuit of one of our assignments, we ventured to the edge of town and engaged in innocent curiosity—"

"Curiosity! They're admitting to breaking the law!" House Makary again— Rufeal's father.

Kidan's blood boiled.

"Allowing rogues to enter the land is breaking the law." One of the Sicions spoke, voice as expressionless as their face. "These Nefrasi allowed us to find them. They did not hide from us."

Dean Faris searched Kidan's face. "Are they threatening you? If they are, speak now and we'll cut them down. I promise no harm will come to you."

Kidan burned with the desire to tell her the truth. To have Dean Faris read her mind. For GK, she bit her tongue.

Slen didn't rush to speak either, and Dean Faris noticed this hesitation.

Yusef spoke instead. "Isn't this why you teach us Dranacti? To create peace with immortals and live alongside them? Many vampires in this room were once rogue, until they chose Uxlay."

Another wave of furious whispers traveled, but they couldn't refute this fact.

After a long moment, Dean Faris faced her companion. "Very well. You know what to do."

Professor Andreyas smoothed out the slight furrow to his face and stormed to the kneeling Nefrasi, voice steely with authority.

"If you choose to join Uxlay, you must bow to all its laws. Any deviation from its Unbreakable Laws will result in your death or life exchange. You will attend personal sessions with me so I will vet your intention, and if I find one flaw, one error, you will suffer the consequences. Do you understand?"

Arin didn't hide her distaste well, her beautiful mouth curling. Samson forced a nod.

"Raise your hand and repeat after me."

They raised their hands and repeated the fealty of Uxlay's coexistence with the families. Samson sneered at the recounting of the seventh law—to obey and protect the acti.

Professor Andreyas returned to the center. "Slen Qaros. Who will be your companion?"

"I will take two companions tonight. I pledge to treat them as my equals, ask no more of them than I would my own blood." Slen kept her chin aligned with the floor. "Taj Zuri and...Warde."

Warde, the mountain of a dranaic who had overpowered Iniko and carried GK on his shoulders, bore a face that could frighten the devil. His steps shook the chandelier's crystals overhead. Even Kidan wanted to avoid his terror-filled eyes.

Taj appeared half his usual size next to the Nefrasi brute as they retrieved the House Qaros pins, put them on, and bowed. Although Warde's bow couldn't quite be called that—it was more of a slight tip of the head. They swore Slen the Uxlay oath, and then, with Warde at her wrist and Taj at her neck, drank from her.

The ceremony continued. Yusef shivered, unconsciously touching his injured hand. "I will take one companion tonight."

He chose the deadly vampire who had burned him. Arin smiled like a mischievous cat, sliding a withering glance at Susenyos, who regarded her with a guarded expression. Swiping a House Umil pin, she climbed the stairs in those high boots and drank from Yusef's other hand. Kidan locked her spine to keep her rage at bay.

Then it was her turn. "I will take two companions tonight and onward. I pledge to treat them as my equals, ask no more of them than I would my own blood."

Kidan had practiced these words in her room, and they still sounded wrong.

"Susenyos Sagad and Samson Sagad."

The two peeled away from the crowd and met in the middle, walking together. Their lips moved in silent conversation, although their eyes were on her. Samson reached for a House Adane pin and flicked it high into the air.

The mountains spun in a golden arc, drawing gasps from everyone. Samson frowned, distracted by the crowd. Susenyos caught the pin inches from the floor and secured it to his clothes. A visible sigh came from the crowd.

"Lesson one, rogues," Professor Andreyas barked, commanding all attention. "Your house pin represents house loyalty but also, more importantly, allegiance to Uxlay. Even with your dying breath, it should never touch the ground."

It was the first time Kidan had glimpsed the professor's stony exterior slip, and the vehemence of his words made her spine weaken a little.

The Sicions had all stepped forward, reaching for their weapons. Samson's mouth twisted, but he retrieved another pin, carefully this time. The Sicions resumed their post.

Kidan's companions climbed the stairs and bowed in perfect unison before her.

Susenyos moved close and tilted her neck to the ceiling. She shivered when he trailed a line down her collarbone and flinched when Samson's cold hand enclosed her wrist.

"Ignore him," Susenyos breathed into her ear, soft and warm. The feeling shot through her spine in delicious waves. "Imagine us there, in Arowa, alone."

And imagine she did. The room disappeared around them.

His words lulled her into calm waters, so she'd forget how painful the act of it was. Searing and binding. When the second bite arrived at her wrist, she was already floating high.

It was a collision of two worlds, two minds. Samson was there, young, human, no silver hand yet. Susenyos was awash in bronze, handsome, princely. They sat in a field, a castle behind them. A girl with soft fawn skin passed by, and Samson pulled out grass, avoiding her eyes. Susenyos shook with laughter, teasing. They were sixteen, maybe seventeen.

"If you keep looking at my betrothed, I'll tear out your eyes," Susenyos said, mischief dancing in his own.

The image faded too soon. Kidan returned to earth and studied Susenyos's red irises and brilliant hair, Samson a flickering shadow behind him. Their story appeared woven into the constellation of time, stitched with fierce friendship and betrayal.

After the ceremony ended, the attendees moved to the celebration hall. Light music played; food and drinks were passed around. Kidan snacked on the treats, smiling at Yusef, who was attacked with kisses from his great-aunt.

Samson approached, champagne in his gloved metal hand. It reminded Kidan of the armor displayed in the artifact room. The silver was gone. The rings and chains were gone as well, since Uxlay's laws did not allow silver body decoration.

Kidan's appetite died. Susenyos held her gaze across the room. Ready to come to her side if necessary. Slen lifted her chin. Yusef gave a tight smile. They were alert as well.

Samson lowered his voice, resting his drink on the tall table. "You give me the artifact, and you and your friends can walk away."

"You know, I came here wanting to burn this place down," Kidan confessed, brow tight. "I couldn't stand it."

"That could be arranged," Samson mused. "Once you give me the artifact, we can set this place on fire. The hardest part was getting past those boundary laws."

Yes. Uxlay was a beautiful fortress.

Then he said something that made her still as death. "June is in town and wants to see you. You can reunite with her tonight if you wish."

Just like that. Yet the thought only soured her mouth.

How is Mama Anoet?

June chose to leave and never looked back.

"I'm not going." Kidan stared at her amber drink. A smile threatened on her lips at the lack of guilt. The blissful quiet inside her mind after making the choice. A choice she made for herself, for once.

A storm gathered in his tone. "Your sister is waiting for you."

Her lip curved humorlessly. "Well, tell her to go to hell for me then, will you?"

Kidan turned away. He seized her arm with his metal hand, causing her pain, bone deep, pulling her against his hard chest. She bit down on a cry. Susenyos started toward them, but she gave a firm shake of her head. He stilled.

"If you don't care about your sister, I still have your devout friend—"

"Exactly." Kidan's nostrils flared. "And unless he's freed and returned, you and I have nothing to discuss."

"That wasn't our agreement. You hand over the artifact first," he forced through clenched teeth.

She gave him a cruel smile. "Welcome to Uxlay. Now let me go, or I'll scream."

His vicious fangs slipped free, launching her heart to her throat. A few Rojit students passed, and he let go but didn't step back.

His scarred neck brushed her cheek like crushed glass, dark words pouring into her ear. "I'll enjoy teaching you proper servitude, heiress. I'll savor breaking you."

Kidan glowered, shivers shooting down her spine. She turned her back to him and headed for the exit. Susenyos fell into step by her side.

"Well?" His voice was barely restrained.

"We're killing him," she returned. "I have a plan."

Susenyos tucked his hands into his pockets, lips curving. "There's that mind I love."

73.

SUSENYOS AND KIDAN SHARED ONE WEEK. ONE PEACEFUL WEEK where they didn't want to kill each other. He read her pieces of literature by his arched window, sun drenching their skin. They fed on ripe fruit, sweet nectar splashing on their tongues, and enjoyed discussing how to get rid of the Nefrasi.

Kidan no longer attacked Susenyos inside the pale blue observatory. That voice telling her to hurt them both had vanished. They should have been able to stay in there longer now, but instead it was Susenyos who couldn't manage it. He would encourage her to keep going, then walk unsteadily upstairs, making her brow furrow.

"Where is he?" she asked on the seventh afternoon, twisting a metal loop into what could be a jewelry box or a flat-shelled turtle. Kidan had started metalworking again, to keep busy and enjoy the stretching hours of the break. She would gather discarded antique pieces and mold one object to another. Creation gave her a blissful sense of control.

"You must have pissed him off at the ceremony." Susenyos spoke from his own station, restoring the broken artifacts with care. Artifacts that belonged to the Nefrasi. The sight always made her chest ache. He'd said such cruel things to them over the phone, and it was clear Susenyos wanted them to hate him. Perhaps he was still punishing himself. Kidan knew all about that.

"I thought he'd have moved in by now," she said.

Their plan of killing Samson couldn't really take effect without him, and she grew antsy with the wait.

Susenyos stopped working, lost in thought again, and stared at the goddess illustration. He did this every twenty minutes, fingers playing with the silver nail usually lodged in the roof of his mouth. She wanted to ask him what was wrong, but she already knew.

Samson was coming here to kill him. It was bound to weigh on his mind.

He pushed his chair away and went to stand in front of the goddess portrait. "You once asked me about this."

Kidan left her station and went to him. Susenyos shifted aside, giving her space she didn't need. As if he didn't want to brush her shoulder.

Kidan frowned at his reaction.

"What do you notice?" he asked.

The image always struck her, a familiar wrath stirring in her, aged and hungry. The cracked wooden mask captured the goddess's intense eyes, weapons strapped to her back glimmered violent silver, and her fisted hand wore a flaming red ring—

Kidan's eyes widened. "The Three Binds...the artifacts. She's wearing them. I never noticed. But I thought the Last Sage was a man?"

Susenyos's smile was faint. "Sages don't have a gender. But the one who created Dranacti was a man, yes."

"So there are others?" Kidan whispered.

"There were others. Many, once. There are none now." Loss swam and tightened his voice.

Kidan traced the mask. What had cracked it? Her skin thrummed.

"Do you think we can get this house to show us where the Sun artifact is?"

His tone edged on frustration. "I've tried for years, and you've seen how successful I've been."

She shot him a sympathetic glance. "There's one in this house and one with the Nefrasi. Where's the last one?"

"We don't know. We found the Water artifact—the blades—two hundred years ago. The Sun artifact, which is the mask, we found fourteen years ago. Then your parents concealed it in this house. Who knows how long it'll take to find the Death artifact."

He sounded wistful that even as an immortal, he might never see those three artifacts together.

They moved to the kitchen, and Susenyos peeled fruit, adding it to the platter. Grapefruit was his favorite. She studied his long and slender fingers, recalling how they unwound her braids and massaged her scalp. Their kindness.

Again she frowned.

Other than at the companionship ceremony, he hadn't touched her since the Bath of Arowa. Not a brush against her shoulders, not accidental contact of the fingers, and certainly not anything more. He kept a distinct amount of space from her, just like when they couldn't stand each other.

She was alarmed by how her body craved his touches. Perhaps he was no longer interested in her that way. Her gut tightened at the thought, but she shoved it aside.

He was discussing some artifact that resembled the Last Sage's ring when he nicked his thumb and blood spread over the spot. He pressed it to his lips and sucked to quell the pain. A very human instinct.

Kidan stilled on her chair.

Their eyes met.

And there, in those black eyes, that *something* she couldn't quite figure out, a piece that she knew had been missing for the past week, clicked into place.

"This is the kitchen." Her voice was strained. "You should be healing."

He gave a tight smile, grabbing a towel to wrap around the cut.

"I was wondering how long it'd take you to notice."

Ice washed down her back, her eyes darting from his thumb to his face. "You're . . . human in more rooms. How many?"

He hesitated, drawing in a long breath. "All."

"*All of them?*" She shot to her feet. "Since when?"

When he remained quiet, her mind raced to solve the puzzle, but she couldn't.

"Yos." She forced him to look at her. "When?"

He set down the fruit. "The night you went to save GK."

She blinked. "But you didn't leave the house. The house would only steal your immortality if you endangered the Sun artifact."

His eyes simmered with defeat. "I did endanger it."

Her brows pinched. "No, all you did that night was talk on the phone. You gave me the clue—" She gasped. "Is that it? You endangered the house when you gave me the *Mad Lovers* clue?"

Susenyos gave a strained nod.

"That can't count!" she shouted—and the kitchen stove caught fire.

Susenyos put it out with the towel, although the fire wasn't real. "Unfortunately, the house disagrees with you. I thought the clue wouldn't set it off, but I was wrong. This house is linked to my mind. It sensed my intention, and my intention was to save you by bringing a threat into this house."

His voice remained concealed, working hard not to rise.

He grabbed the platter and moved past her. "Let's eat."

Kidan was stunned. But then she said to herself, "It's only in this house."

She rushed to follow him. "If you leave, you'll still have your immortality, right?"

"Yes." He returned to the kitchen to grab plates.

She followed him, close on his heels. "Samson is coming here to kill you. Uxlay isn't safe anymore. You need to leave."

He paused, then offered her a lazy smile that didn't reach his eyes. "Why? Don't tell me you've started to care about my well-being now."

She didn't snap back, didn't smile, but merely held his gaze. She *was* starting to care and . . . it terrified her. When had her feelings for him shifted? Like the rooms of this house, her feelings had changed without her volition and without noise. Her mind tightened with the ruined image of their future. He'd be weakened, and the cruelty of Samson would break him. Dread crawled all over her skin. This changed everything.

His eyes grew dark in the quiet, and his voice rang carefully. "Keep your guard up, little bird. Don't waver now."

A line twitched along her jaw. "I'm not wavering."

"You are. Nothing I told you should change your plans." He almost sounded disturbed by her worry.

She pressed on her lips. "It doesn't."

"Good."

"*Perfect*," she snapped. "And when he kills you because you cut your finger and can't heal? What then?"

His lip quirked. Almost genuine this time. "Well, from the looks of it, you might avenge me."

She shook her head, fisting her hands. "This isn't a joke."

His intense gaze flickered, reaching deep into her soul. "Why would you send me away?"

She crossed her arms to add distance between them, to shield her fragile heart, which had just started beating again. "I needed you to help my friends. To save GK. I needed you to be strong, but now..."

Deep silence fell, adding weight to her words and turning them more vicious than she'd intended. But she didn't break it, couldn't. She let them settle into the selfish truth.

"You don't need me?" Something dreadful crystallized in his dark gaze. "Don't worry. You'll still have my strength."

His tone burned like pure ice, removed.

Kidan traced the floor with her eyes, feeling the rift between them grow. "But I don't get it. Why are you not shouting? Why aren't you angry? You're human—"

"Don't. Don't say that word." His jaw tightened, eyes flashing.

She bit her lip, frustrated.

"Why am I not angry?" The plates in his hands clattered to the table. "Of course I am. I will always be. Don't you remember the state of this room?"

She studied the lounge, recalling that confusing night. The fire eating at the space, swords punctured into walls, furniture broken, and so, so much *rage*. But June had been on the screen, and nothing else had mattered. Now she remembered. Understood that his anger had been because the house stole everything from him.

"So, you are angry," she said slowly. "Of course you're angry. Then why didn't you tell me?"

"I went to yell at you. I had every intention of doing so at the infirmary." She remembered him bursting through the doors like an angel of death, shouting her name. It was all so clear now.

His eyes were cast low, golden at this angle, wrought with two conflicting emotions. "You ran into my arms. You were hurt, and you came to me. Why did you have to do that? Took the fight right out of my words."

Kidan's heart twisted.

"I don't blame you, Kidan. I gambled, and it cost me. I made a mistake."

Her vision tightened. A mistake.

"This is the crux of my nightmare," he continued in a haunted voice. "I'm robbed of my strength. I can't stand the feel of my own skin, the dullness of my own heartbeat, and while every bone in my body is telling me to flee before death comes, I must stay. I *will* acquire all of the Last Sage's artifacts and keep Samson from such power." His fierce words shook the entire house. "There is nothing more important than that goal, and nothing will keep me from it."

He held her gaze with unwavering determination until she nodded. He inhaled deeply and released the breath. "Good. And as for why I didn't punish you, well, you did that all by yourself, didn't you? I watched you drown in your sadness after June's video. The house grew suffocating with your loss, until I couldn't breathe. Your pain..." His expression changed, dark and disturbed. "What scar could I add to the ones you already carry? Even I have my limits."

A fist seized her heart. He hadn't yelled at her because of June. For nearly two weeks, he'd pretended everything had worked out. Had carried this loss with him without sound. Had let her begin to have hope again.

"Thank you," she said softly, surprising them both.

Susenyos blinked as if he'd heard her wrong.

"Thank you for waiting, for giving me time." She squared her shoulders and leveled what she hoped was a strong, unwavering gaze at him. "I can handle it now. Don't hold anything back. You can yell at me for everything I've done. Everything I've ruined."

He regarded her beneath heavy lids until the clouds covered the sun entirely.

"I don't want to yell at you," he said quietly. "Enough with the self-loathing and punishment. Leave them behind. I'm only interested in what I can become. What you will become."

He walked to her slowly, and her body tensed, every nerve alert, eyes tracking his rising fingers, already feeling their warmth. She knew this stance of his. He was going to grab her chin, as he did whenever he was serious. But he let his fingers fall inches from her face, a frustrated line tightening his jaw. Kidan tried to clear the disappointment from her eyes.

His words grew steel, sharp with resolve. "You are Kidan Adane, heiress of House Adane, able to master this house until your will breaks all wills."

She blinked in surprise. But he wasn't finished. "Because if I fail—though I'll fight like *hell* not to—you will be ready. You will change the current law and craft one that'll return far greater than what I lost."

She stared into his unflinching face, that unbending resolve that made him stay in this house for decades. He was ablaze with this desire of his, and it would burn them both to ash.

"Is that an ask or an order?" Her eyes searched his, her voice equally hard. She needed to know what they were, how to move forward from this point.

His features tightened at the question, pupils swirling, before they settled into a concealed emotion. "We'll only know if you fail. Don't fail."

When he stepped back, her eyes dropped to his cut finger.

Human.

A word he couldn't even bear to hear. She could see the silent request in his expression. He needed her to treat him no differently even though every single thing had changed.

She gave him his wish, crossing her arms. "So, it's a race. To see who between us can master the house first."

Surprise arched his brows. "I suppose."

"Well, don't slow me down."

His face carried shadows, but his lips stretched a little. "Wouldn't dream of it."

The lights dimmed around them, the walls moving closer, pushing them together. Kidan wondered if he felt it too. Was he straightening his spine as well? What were they, exactly? Too many things to one another, maybe not enough of one thing to be whole.

The doorbell rang. It thrummed in the family portrait and the antique clock and the very core of the house.

Susenyos's mouth hardened. Frost spread down her veins. The hallway's lamps popped and shattered, darkness swallowing the path. The carpet moved and shifted like a current of ocean. It hadn't been like this in a while.

"You see that too?" she whispered.

He nodded. "Fear lurks in the hallway. That doesn't mean we don't cross it."

With each step, the carpet gripped the soles of their shoes, determined to drown them. They were suddenly fragile. On the brink of something new, and they had to flee together to protect whatever sliver of peace they'd found. One week was not enough. It would never be enough.

A shadowy figure stood behind the distorted glass. Terror stole into her chest. She had seen this shadow when it came to take her sister. And now here it was on her doorstep.

Susenyos nodded at her.

Kidan took a deep breath and opened the door. A rush of light irritated her eyes. The sun was bright, yet the house mirrored the middle of the night.

Samson Sagad adjusted his gleaming glove. "Sorry for the delay. I had something to collect." His gaze focused on Susenyos, hard as marble, and melted into a sick smile when it reached Kidan. "Although I feel you two didn't miss me."

"Always jealous, wendem. After all these years, I'd think you'd find a new flaw." Susenyos's eyes glittered as he crossed his arms and leaned against the wall.

Kidan was always impressed with how easily he masked himself.

Samson's jaw twitched, then smoothed into a dangerous smile. He turned to the side.

"Come here," he ordered.

Kidan's brow furrowed. A young girl stepped into view, the scent of wild-flowers and honey carried in by a gust of wind. Kidan's vision blurred, then focused. The girl wore a pale blue sundress, her brown skin aglow, curling braids grazing past her shoulders. A single butterfly bracelet with a three-pointed sun dangled from her wrist.

Kidan's lip quivered. She couldn't utter the name that could break her apart again. Her feet were already sinking in this hallway, and she'd drown. She willed her spine to straighten, pleaded with the deepest part of her soul.

Please, please. Give me strength.

The floor rumbled under her, and the shards of the light bulbs picked themselves up and webbed themselves whole. The ruined lamps roared to life as light flooded the hallway.

She turned to Susenyos in surprise, but he was already watching her intently, brows raised. The carpet lost its water and fear retreated, depositing itself in another room. Locked away tight.

Something else pushed against her feet. Sudden and jolting. The ground of her ancestors stirred like an ancient beast and opened its jaws. Earth enveloped her, unbroken and mighty, and dressed her in armor—starting at her feet, climbing along her legs, and cloaking her shoulders. Power coursed through her veins with a giddying rush. Kidan's hold on the doorknob *dented* it. She stared in awe at the damaged metal.

For the first time, Kidan commanded the house. It obeyed.

Slowly, she met her sister's gaze. One mirrored the lonely moon, one burst with the burning sun.

"June."

ACKNOWLEDGMENTS

Wow. This book. I've carried this dream with me since I was a teen. Back then, I was the only Black girl in my class and found refuge in books about vampires and all sorts of creatures. That's the power of stories—I believe they make us a little fearless. To be able to reimagine vampires with African origins, dark skin, and beautiful braids is my highest dream achieved. But like all dreams, it took time and a lot of people's support along the way.

To my agent, Paige Terlip, I want to extend my gratitude. Thank you for seeing something special in *Immortal Dark*.

To Ruqayyah Daud and Nazima Abdillahi, you don't know what a joy it is to publish a book like this supported by two Black editors. I feel safe and understood and guided. Thank you.

I'm appreciative of all the different teams who continue to collaborate to make this book a success. Thank you to the team at Little, Brown Books for Young Readers: Megan Tingley, Alvina Ling, Lily Choi, Alexandra Hightower, Deirdre Jones, Nina Montoya, Esther Reisberg, Jenny Kimura, Savannah Kennelly, Bill Grace, Andie Divelbiss, Emilie Polster, Cheryl Lew, Hannah Klein, Hannah Koerner, Janelle DeLuise, Jackie Engel, Shawn Foster, Danielle Cantarella, Christie Michel, Victoria Stapleton. Thanks also to copy editor Richard Slovak and proofreaders Lara Stelmaszyk and Brandy Colbert.

A special thanks to Tyiana Combs, who saw this book's pitch online and connected me to my editor. I was hoping it would reach the right audience, and it *absolutely* did.

I'm incredibly lucky to have my closest friend, and alpha reader, Hanna Bechiche. When I messaged her the idea for this book, she responded in all caps with a resounding *"YES."* Her boundless enthusiasm has carried me through countless rejections and every part of the writing process. Love you forever.

I have met so many wonderful writers on this journey who have offered me wise counsel and amazing positivity: Sarah Mughal Rana, Emily Varga, Esmie Jikiemi-Pearson, Fallon DeMornay, Kamilah Cole, Jen Carnelian, Tanvi Berwah, Maeeda Khan, M. K. Lobb, Grace D. Li, Yasmine Jibril, Mel Howard, and Alechia Dow. I can't wait to collect and cherish all of your books. To Birukti Tsige, my fellow habesha writer, thank you for making this space less lonely.

When I casually mentioned I'd be a published author to my friends over drinks, I was incredibly nervous. They were rightfully shocked, but I'd never felt more encouraged. Anasimone, Martina, Sally, Rebecca, Chichak, and Rukia—I adore you all.

To Loza and Salem, my lovely cousins, thanks for always making me laugh and for being the sisters I never had.

Mostly, I'm grateful for my family. In one night, complete with a Power-Point crash course on publishing and my book deal, they learned about my seven-year writing journey. They embraced it all and became my absolute rock while I edited this book. To my younger brother, Abenezer, who found me spiraling during a difficult plot point and gave me a Post-it note saying "stay hard"—okay, bro, will do. To my older brother, Micky, who breathes joy and reminds me not to take things too seriously—sure thing, will try not to. To my parents, who sacrificed everything to raise my brothers and me with a wealth of opportunities—I hope I made you proud. ሁላችሁንም ከልቤ አመሰግናለሁ. አወዳችኋለሁ.

Finally, to you, reader. Thank you for returning to the world of vampires with me.